A Lie of Omission

M. A. PURCELL

POOLBEG
CRIMS☀N

Published 2023 by Crimson
an imprint of Poolbeg Press Ltd.
123 Grange Hill, Baldoyle,
Dublin 13, Ireland
Email: poolbeg@poolbeg.com

The moral right of the author has been asserted.
A catalogue record for this book is available from the British Library.

ISBN 978-1-78199 -690-4

www.poolbeg.com

About the Author

Marnan Purcell is a Clare woman to her core, born in the townland of Caher in East Clare and living near the village of Feakle, well known for its trad music heritage. She has enjoyed success as a short-story writer but has long held an ambition to write a crime novel. During lock-down she took the plunge and put on paper one of the many stories bubbling in her brain.

Marnan is a qualified respiratory scientist. She has always loved hill walking and was actively involved in setting up the East Clare Way which wends its way through the wildest part of the region. She also makes aromatherapy oils and tinctures, and loves to imbue the spirit of a person into a signature scent.

She lives on the family farm where working-dog Tully, a collie cross, is the inspiration for this book's memorable Maestro.

For my mother,
Who taught us the most important things in life are love,
loyalty and reading.

Acknowledgements

Writing, like life, is a journey, and enroute I have been privileged to meet many wonderful people. Too many to name. That said, I would like to thank my initial readers: Isabel, Margaret, Majella, Fionnuala and Rose. Your feedback from the first draft helped me believe I had a story others would enjoy.

The courses facilitated by Writing.ie have been invaluable and a big thank-you goes out to the writers who generously tutor others in the art. A special thank-you to Tanya Farrelly, herself a wonderful author, who led myself and her merry band of scribblers safely through lockdown.

A heartfelt thank-you to Paula Campbell and Gaye Shortland of Poolbeg Press who are making a long-held dream of mine come true.

Last but definitely not least, my amazing family. Your support is greatly appreciated.

Chapter 1

"Tegan." Trout was upright, phone answered before he was even half awake.

"*Marty, Marty, you bastard, where are you?*" a voice squawked in his ear. A panting, fear-laced voice.

"Who's this?"

The sharpness of his query made no impact on the caller.

The quick *zing, zing, zing* of flying bullets.

"*Jesus!*" Scrabbling. Almost sobbing. "*Rasher's brought the lads … it's a trap!*" The voice was juddering, as if running. "*I'm heading for the dump!*"

Dressing one-handed as he listened, Trout, recently retired Detective Inspector Thomas Tegan, was collating what he was hearing. Was there something familiar about the voice? What the hell was happening? Why …?

Short, gasping breaths. "*You've … set me up … you bastard … I'm going to … tear your liver … out with my tee … eeeth …*"

Trout's straining ears heard the dull thwack of a body taking a hit, a scream cut off. A thud as something hit the ground.

1

Then, clearly, harshly, *"Find the fucking phone!"*

Thrashing about, gradually receding until there was nothing.

The ex-DI of the Special Investigations Unit was reaching for his badge when he woke up enough to realize that it wasn't his problem. He automatically checked the number – not one he recognised. That raised the questions who was the call from and why ring him? "Christ!" He ran a hand over his face and hit the keypad. His old station was still number one. The night officer answered promptly.

Trout identified himself. He could feel the young garda straightening. "Who's on tonight?"

"Sergeant McMillian, sir."

"Put me through to him, there's a good lad."

"Yes, sir."

"Yeah?" a voice mumbled tiredly.

"Mac? That you? Thomas Tegan here."

"Trout? Missing us already? I knew you –"

"I've just had a strange phone call."

"Only one. Lucky you. I've had three in the last ten minutes and –"

"Just listen and tell me what you think …" Trout proceeded to give a tightly worded account of the events of the past few minutes.

"Gunfire? Any idea where?"

Trout sighed. "No. That's why I'm on to you. You might run the number, see if we get a hit." He navigated to "calls" as he was speaking. "Here it is." He called out the mobile number.

A beat of silence. "No record here. Not that I can find. Probably a burner." Mac exhaled loudly. "We'll need a warrant to check the location. I can set that in motion but you know yourself, twenty-four hours if we're lucky … You mixed up in some sort of shite, Trout?"

"Not that I'm aware of." Trout thought for a minute. "*Damnation!* Nothing we can do until we have an idea of where it all went down."

"You reckon a handgun?" Mac sounded thoughtful. "You sure it's not out your way? Strange things can happen in them there hills."

"I don't know." Trout ran his fingers through his hair, feeling the unaccustomed length since he abandoned the regulation haircut. At least I have hair, he thought inconsequentially, and it's mostly black ... "There were no city sounds. Not that I could hear but there wouldn't be many at three o'clock in the morning anyway." He thought for a moment. "I'll think about it some more and when I get a clearer feel for it, we –"

"*We?* You're retired, Trout. Go back to bed. I'll deal with it." Mac's easy Cork accent, still unchanged after more than thirty years in Dublin, had sharpened considerably.

"If it turns out to be local?"

"I'll sort it. Sure, aren't we all one big happy family?"

"Yeah. Right. And, Mac ... you'll let me know the outcome, won't you? Curiosity and all that ..."

"Sure will, boy." Mac gave a big booming laugh. "You can retire a detective but you can't stop him thinking!"

"Thanks, Mac. We'll have a night soon."

As always with those middle-of-the-night calls, Trout was now wide awake. His retirement, a mere six weeks before, hadn't yet dulled his automatic reflexes. Hell, he joined the force the day after his twentieth birthday and worked his butt off since. What did he expect? To switch off nearly thirty-five years of his life like you'd flick a switch?

He padded downstairs and into the kitchen, his long, lean frame

3

taking the steps with easy familiarity. His childhood home, in the small village of Knocknaclogga in County Clare, was now once again his home. Serendipity, perhaps, that his parents wanted to move to the city just as he had decided to leave it. The swap between them, his apartment for the family home, was fortuitous. Although he suspected his mother might have had an ulterior motive. No doubt she wanted to experience city life while she could enjoy it but her muttered "You've a better chance of meeting a nice girl out in the country" told another story. Especially as it was followed by a conciliatory hug and a whispered "You aren't that old … yet."

A large, complicated-looking coffee-machine dominated the room. His retirement presentation after he refused point-blank to accept a clock. Coffee and wine were his pleasures and his hobby. He had plans to turn at least one of them into a little business. He had set up and managed the wine cellar in the Village Inn, the small hotel owned by his sister Lucy and her husband Mars for many years. He enjoyed sourcing the wines and found it a satisfying hobby that was lucrative enough to tempt him to take it further. Especially now, when the feelers he had put out suggested that small hotels and restaurants locally and in the wider area would be delighted to have good, affordable wines supplied by someone who knew what was what.

He ground beans, a mix a barista friend specially blended for him and, soothed by the ritual, allowed his mind to ponder on the call. Technically, he reminded himself, his duty was done. But, his mind argued, you can't ignore your instincts. What harm would it do to look at the pieces of the puzzle for a few minutes? Indeed, his old national schoolteacher claimed that he was always a nosy boy and that was what made him a good detective.

He filled a large mug with coffee, settled himself by the Aga and thought about what he had heard. He recalled the way his ears sharpened as he listened and now he set himself to glean what he could from the tone and background. He leaned back. High, narrow shelves were tucked into the alcove beside the Aga. They were filled higgledy-piggledy with books and papers. He reached out, rooted around and found a notebook, pencil tucked neatly into the spine. His mind replayed the call, word for word, each sound amplified in his memory as he probed for something, anything that would identify the caller. He made pithy observations, in what looked like hieroglyphics. Could he have missed something?

Male, accent Dublin with a hint of country, Limerick maybe or Clare, English his first language. Was there something familiar about the voice? The panting had distorted it. What about the running itself? There was no pounding, not like you'd get on a road or a pavement – more like countryside, possibly through bushes or heath. Maybe Mac was right and the whole thing was played out in the hills. Somewhere. The gunfire was unmistakable … and that cry … Trout shook his head. Wherever it was, death was the outcome he was sure. And the phone was important. He wondered if the harsh voice had found it. Felt a niggle … was there something familiar there?

He recorded everything he remembered, his thoughts and questions, Mac's information or rather lack of it. Then sat back to let his mind percolate and see what came up. Idly he doodled Lauren, wondered what she'd make of it. He'd run it by her later. They had agreed to hike Slí Buí this morning, weather permitting.

Lauren O'Loughlin was Lucy's best friend. Forever. He remembered her as a fiery kid with bright-red hair and a stubborn attitude. He hadn't paid much attention to her when they were growing up and had lost contact over the years. An occasional snippet from his sister, something about a guy treating her badly. His loss, Trout reckoned, now that he had become reacquainted with her. Mrs Dillon, their old schoolteacher, had coerced Trout into looking into a spate of poison-pen letters that beset the village recently. She had foisted Lauren on him, thinking he needed someone with knowledge of the locals and their doings. They had become friends. Lauren had good instincts and noticed little things. He dismissed the subliminal kick of pleasure that thinking of her gave him. That was for another day.

Chapter 2

It was a perfect hiking weather. Light cloud, gentle breezes and the whole day before them. A rough road brought them to the foothills, barely three kilometres from Knocknaclogga. They had walked, agreeing that a warm-up would prepare them for the climb.

Lauren raised her face to the wind, sniffed the air and laughed. "Slí Buí is living up its name: the yellow way. Look at that yellow furze! And doesn't it smell divine?"

"Amazing," Trout agreed, although anyone watching would have noticed that he was looking at the woman rather than the glories of the furze.

"Shall we head up the Hump, cross the ridge and come back down along –"

"The *Hump*?" He frowned and raised his eyes to stare at the hillside.

"Don't tell me you've forgotten the Hump?" Lauren turned to look at him. Her laughter died when she saw his face. "What is it?"

"I thought the voice said '*dump*' but suppose he said '*hump*'?" Deep in thought, he was absentmindedly rubbing his nose. His sergeant used to joke that Trout's nose was more accurate than radar when it came to detecting trouble. "Could it be that he was heading for the Hump?"

"He'd need to have known the area." Lauren didn't dismiss the idea. Trout had told her about his middle-of-the-night call. Now she picked up on his unease and turned to scan the slope. "There's a run of shallow caves at the back of the Hump," she said slowly.

"I'd forgotten them. Lauren … I've a bad feeling about this. I want you to go back and wait."

Lauren swung around and looked at him, her sparkling hazel eyes challenging his worried blue ones. "Get over yourself, Trout!" She settled her daysack more comfortably and set off up the track, the curly, red ponytail she'd carelessly pulled through the back of her baseball cap swishing defiantly at him.

Trout watched the slight, trim figure stomping away from him. Still stubborn, he thought, and loped after her.

They hiked in silence, a sense of urgency hurrying their steps at a faster pace than Trout had planned. The panting voice from last night's call nagged in his head. Could he have misheard? Was the "dump" in his memory really the hump of Slí Buí? He had seen enough random coincidences in his time to take nothing for granted.

The track was mostly a well-trodden trail through the heather and furze. As they climbed, the countryside opened behind them and the elevation rose in front of them like terraces in a paddy field. After the first push they stood, hot and winded, and viewed all around them.

"What would bring a gangland feud to Knocknaclogga?" Lauren studied the lie of the land. The village spread below them, the almost deserted countryside around them.

"Someone who knew a hiding place in the area and thought it

would be a safe bet." Trout turned to scan the rough terrain and the barely discernible path to the top. His eyes narrowed. "Is there much stock on the hills?"

"Stock? Like cattle?"

"Yeah. Or sheep?"

"Some. Usually later in the year, more into the summer. Why?"

"Looks like ravens circling. Over to the right, halfway up from here. Must be a carcass ..."

"Oh." Lauren turned, followed his gaze. "Deer live on the hills," she said doubtfully.

"You stay here while I –"

"Don't even think about it, Trout. I'm coming!"

"It won't be pleasant if it's what I fear."

"You know, Trout," Lauren was watching the birds wheel and dive, "I've felt more alive since you've been home than I've been for years. I'll chance it."

A straight-talking woman. Trout smiled a slow, easy smile that crinkled his eyes and softened the craggy lines of his face. He could live with that.

They made a beeline for the birds, zig-zagging diagonally upwards and across the face of the hill. The scrub gave a mostly solid foothold with an occasional boggy patch. The hollow-sounding *kronk-kronk* of the ravens became louder and added a sinister feel to the air.

They emerged slightly above the spot marked by the birds.

Trout shot out a hand and stopped Lauren. "Something rolled down this hill recently."

She looked where he indicated and nodded, too breathless to talk. Their eyes tracked the broken bushes, trampled heath, disturbed heather and followed the destruction to a dense thicket some twenty metres below them. A flicker of blue shone through the undergrowth, like a rag someone had carelessly abandoned. Only the muddy, red runner attached to the end of it proclaimed otherwise.

"Stay here."

This time Lauren made no objection.

Carefully, making a wide arc, Trout picked his way down towards a shallow indent closely covered with heather and ringed by a soft, fresh growth of furze.

He stopped level with the shoe. He looked for a long moment. The body was lying, almost hidden by the scrub, arms out-flung, face sinking into some boggy moss.

Trout turned slowly, surveyed all around him. His eyes panned to Lauren.

Poor sod, he thought. At least he's face down. The ravens haven't done too much damage yet.

He pulled out his phone and dialled a number.

Call complete, he opened the phone's camera and took a series of pictures from every angle without approaching too near the body. On the periphery of his vision, he saw Lauren pick her way down to join him. He was aware of how careful she was to place her feet where he had stepped.

He turned. "You OK?"

She nodded, shivered. "We can't really see anything."

"We can see enough. The lads will come as fast as they can. I said we'd wait, keep the birds off." He hesitated. "You don't have to if you don't want to." He lowered his gaze to study the pictures he had taken.

"It's OK, Trout. I'm a big girl. I can take a bit of waiting."

He felt her eyes on him as he stared at the body.

"You look like a dog pointing out fallen game," she said. "Do you know him?"

"I won't know for sure until he's turned over but he has the shape of a guy I know … Freddy … liked to call himself Freddy the Fly."

Lauren looked at the prone figure. "Freddy the Fly?"

Trout twisted his lips in the grim parody of a smile. "He fancied himself a fly on the wall of certain establishments."

"Oh."

"We'll know when … *Christ!* I wonder did they find the phone?"

"You could try ringing it."

"Except we don't know if it was found and, if it was, who might have it now."

"I suppose. Would it be worth the chance? Of course, it might be on silent …"

"Might be." He thought about it. "Right. I'll make sure my number's blocked, just in case." He fiddled with his phone.

Faintly, from underneath the body a heavy beat and *"Bla bla bla bla bla bla!"* rang out.

Trout smiled at Lauren. "Well called." He frowned. "I know that tune but for the life of me can't put a name on it."

"It's 'Safaera' by Bad Bunny. All the teens are singing it at the moment. He must be young."

"Too young! It's odd though, it seems to be under him. I wonder why they didn't find it?"

"Perhaps something disturbed them and they had to leave in a hurry."

"I suppose it's possible. Yeah, you're probably right. Your instincts so far have been spot on."

His compliment seemed to fluster her. "Well …" She shrugged, wouldn't meet his eyes. "I suppose we can try making ourselves comfortable. Will it cause problems if we sit? At least we're in the lee of the hill so we shouldn't get too cold."

In other circumstances Trout would have been amused to see her babbling, but now he reminded himself that she was showing remarkable grace under pressure. "Good idea. We're back far enough not to contaminate the scene." He looked around. "Near enough to shoo away the ravens." He hoisted the backpack and took out two stainless-steel travel mugs. "Coffee?"

"Yes, please."

He handed her both mugs, balanced a lunch box on a clump of heather and shook out a plastic-backed rug.

The ravens had circled back, making short, shrill calls. Trout flapped the rug in the air, shouting "*Off, off, off.*" They rose high into the sky and, still calling, withdrew some distance. He looked at Lauren. "Sorry. I can't offer you this seat. We'll need it to keep the birds away."

"No problem. I have a rain-cape we can use." Lauren placed the mugs carefully on the ground, extracted a bright-red square from a side pocket of her daysack and shook it into a large circle.

"Hey, swap!" Trout held the rug towards her. "The red will be a better deterrent to the ravens."

"And the rug will be more comfortable to sit on." She spread it across the heather, gracefully sank into a cross-legged position and retrieved the mugs in one fluid movement.

Trout joined her, taking one of the cups as he sat. "Not what we'd planned but …" He shrugged, pried open the lunch box and offered it to her.

12

Lauren chose a nut bar. She took a sip of coffee. "This is good."

"My coffee's always good." He looked at her and smiled wolfishly.

She met his gaze, the hazel of her eyes glowing greener as she noted his tone.

Trout cleared his throat, took a slug from his cup. "The lads shouldn't be too long. I was talking to the divisional sergeant and he said he'd alert Forensics and get the crew out here as fast as he can."

"Will they have some sort of land vehicles? It's a fair trek from the top of the road."

"I suggested they bring a couple of quad bikes if they have them handy." Trout looked around him. "They'll have to try and get the van on-site but ..." He shook his head.

They were on a flattish piece of ground, surrounded by heather and scrub with no discernible tracks. The caves Lauren had mentioned were off to his left, a tract of forestry looking dark and forbidding further in the distance.

"Do you miss it? The job?" Lauren's voice broke into his thoughts.

Trout smiled. "I haven't had time to," he said as he surged upright to once again shoo away the ravens.

"They say ravens are remarkably intelligent birds," Lauren observed.

"They're a bloody nuisance. They'll keep coming back. They'd destroy him in no time."

"Lucky we're here so."

Trout looked at the woman sitting quietly on a bleak hillside, sipping coffee as if there wasn't a corpse anywhere in the vicinity. "You're a revelation, Lauren O'Loughlin. How come someone with any scrap of intelligence hasn't snaffled you?"

Lauren gave him a long cool look as if debating on how to answer. Then said, matter-of-factly, "I thought I was engaged once but when Mam had her first stroke and I came home to care for her, he married someone else. I stayed in Knocknaclogga. Time passed and here I am." She turned her head one side. "What about yourself? You have the look of a good catch. And where did you get that ridiculous nickname?"

No punches pulled, Trout thought, and waved the cape at the ravens while he considered his answer. To his surprise, he found himself saying, "I've never met anyone who interested me enough to make it permanent." He laughed. "As for the nickname, Matt Gardiner gave it to me when I was six. I jumped into the stream after his dog and he had to use his fishing rod to haul me out. I remember him holding me in the air, saying 'Aren't you a proper little trout?' and the rest, as they say, is history." He sat down beside her.

Lauren threw back her head and laughed. Trout saw the white column of her throat, the flutter where her laughter pulsed and wondered what would happen if he placed his lips just there. He saw her eyes widen. She swayed towards him, her face alive with amusement. He watched her lips, anticipating a kiss.

"We've got an audience," she breathed. "Rocky outcrop. About ten after twelve."

Trout swore softly then, more loudly, "*Blasted crows!*" He jumped up, waving the red plastic, and rotated, shaking it at the birds.

"Ravens," Lauren corrected him, keeping her voice light.

He glanced towards the rocks. A glint betrayed the spot where someone was using, most likely, binoculars to watch them. He pivoted with the withdrawing birds while his eyes swivelled, raking the rocks, the rough terrain and the expanse of boggy heath that separated them from it.

"We're sitting ducks," he said sotto voce, without turning.

"He'd probably have picked us off by now if that was his intention," Lauren answered gaily, her actual words too quiet to carry.

He turned, feeling an itch between his shoulder blades, and dropped back beside her. "Did someone come back to see what was happening or were they waiting for a chance to look some more for the phone ... or something else?"

"And we blundered into it before they could?"

"Something like that." He pulled out his mobile phone and, keeping it shaded with his body, dashed off a text message. "Just telling the boys we have company and could they please get a move on."

Lauren smiled. "Surely adding a couple of more bodies would serve the watcher up there no useful purpose? Quite the reverse."

"Depends on how valuable whatever they're looking for is." He leaned towards her. "Still there?"

She nodded, dipping her head closer. "Are we in much danger?"

"Only if he has a rifle. A handgun wouldn't have the range." He saw the blood drain from her face, put a hand on her arm. "Sorry. I spoke without thinking. It's unlikely whoever did the shooting would still be hanging around." Mentally he cursed himself. It was a long time since he was so comfortable with anyone, let alone a woman, that he talked without measuring his words. "It was definitely something small calibre that I heard. Of course, they might have sent someone just to keep an eye on what's happening."

He glanced at Lauren. Her eyes looked huge but were calm and watchful. She nodded, but made no comment.

The ravens soared high and glided towards them, rallying each other with high-pitched croaks. Trout went back to his shouting and flapping, exaggerating his efforts, hoping that the watcher wasn't aware that they had spotted him.

"An unkindness of ravens," Lauren said.

"What?"

"That's what a flock is known as – an 'unkindness'. Now I can see why. They don't give up, do they?"

"How do you know so much useless information?"

"It's the job of a copyeditor to know things," she said primly. "Anyway, it's not useless. See, I'm able to pass it on to you."

"Thanks. I think." He looked at her and laughed. "It's a pleasure to be in an awkward situation with you, Lauren O'Loughlin."

"Thank you, kind sir," she mocked, then surged to her feet. "They're here! Look!" She pointed down the hill. A convoy of vehicles, looking like matchbox toys, were coming to a stop far below them.

Trout studied the hill over her shoulder. The glint was gone.

Chapter 3

They watched as ant-like people disembarked and unloaded various items too small to identify from where they were. Two of the ant-people boarded what looked like a miniature quad bike and headed towards them, following a zig-zag path through the heather. The ravens still hovered, throwing the occasional taunt, but seemed to be awaiting developments.

"Will it be the local gardaí, do you think?" Lauren was watching the progress of the quad which looked like it was moving in slow motion.

"They'll have a presence with back-up from Dublin." He studied her. "There's no need to be nervous. I'll tell them what happened and you'll be asked to give your version and after that they'll probably send us away."

Lauren looked at him. "You'd like to stay, though, and be part of it?"

He made a wry face. "Well, I am part of it." He stopped, conscious that she was waiting for more. "I'm pretty sure it's Freddy there. He was my man and, even if the phone call to me last night was accidental, he reached out to me. I guess I feel I owe it to him. Freddy wasn't really a nark but he thought he owed me a favour. He certainly didn't deserve to die like this."

"Surely they'll keep you in the loop? After all, you were a colleague up to recently."

"Protocol. An active case is the property of whoever is working on it." Trout watched the approaching bike. "I wonder who'll get the investigation. A lot might depend on that." He was half talking to himself. He turned to look at Lauren and grinned. "Obviously I'm not as far into retirement as would dull the old investigating instincts."

"Blame Mrs Dillon," she said lightly. "If she hadn't roped you into the poison-pen thing, you'd have a better run at dulling them." She became thoughtful, ventured quietly, "If you did want to do some private investigating, I could help you."

Trout's head whipped around. He stared at her. "You would too, wouldn't you?" His eyes narrowed. "A lot will depend on who gets the case," he repeated, almost to himself. His eyes tracked the bike as it gradually drew closer but was not yet near enough to identify the riders. "Time will tell." He grinned. "But if I do get involved, you'll be the first to know." Even to himself it sounded like a promise.

The quad slalomed to a stop below them and two men hopped off. The smaller of the two squinted towards them, muttered something to the driver and settled his cap more firmly on his head.

"*Shit!*" Trout swore. "I didn't think he'd stir himself to come out." He narrowed his eyes and studied the men before saying quietly, without turning his head, "Jim Cooper is a misogynist with a chip on his shoulder the size of Rathlin Island. Try not to let him get to you."

From the corner of his eye, he saw Lauren nod and wondered if he sounded as judgemental to her as he did to himself. He studied the older of the approaching gardaí, trying to see him as Lauren would. Just about regulation height, from this angle he looked squat, his head low on his shoulders, his body disproportionally broad. He carried himself stiffly like someone who was out of the habit of walking. The other taller, slimmer, more youthful man tucked himself in to one side, obviously shortening his stride not to outpace his senior colleague. Trout sighed and felt the clinch in his gut that suggested this wasn't going to end well.

The pair headed towards where Trout and Lauren waited, twisting and turning through the clumps of heather and rough grass. They stopped level with the body.

"Jim, Tony." Trout sounded civil.

"Inspector Cooper and Garda Sergeant Driscoll," the shorter man growled at the same time as the young garda grinned and said, "Afternoon, chief."

The Inspector glared at him. Sergeant Driscoll reddened to the tips of his ears but remained silent.

"Check the body, Sergeant Driscoll, and –"

"I can assure you he's dead," Trout cut across him. "I know you need to confirm it officially but I think it might be important not to disturb the scene too much. I've reason to believe the area around the body would benefit from technical examination."

Sergeant Driscoll hesitated while the two other men stared at each other, bristling like hounds over a piece of meat.

"You *think*? You no longer have authority to think in this situation." Inspector Cooper narrowed his eyes. "Have you contaminated a potential crime scene, Mr Tegan?"

Trout sighed. "You know me better than that, Cooper. No. I haven't. But if you just tell the team to come on, I'll explain."

"Explain, will you? I might remind you you're no longer a member of the Force and, as a civilian, all we require of you is a factual statement of the events leading to your call to the station."

Before Trout could answer, the Inspector swivelled his gaze and raked Lauren with his eyes. "Who are you?"

"Lauren O'Loughlin."

"What are you doing here?"

"Waiting, Garda …?"

"Inspector Cooper!" he barked. "How did you get here?"

Lauren opened her eyes wide. "I walked, Inspector."

Trout coughed to cover his splutter of laughter as Cooper turned puce. "I have some information that may be relevant to the investigation outside of what we have here," he said hurriedly.

Cooper glared at him.

Trout shrugged but said no more.

Without turning, Cooper ground out, "Mobilize the team, Sergeant Driscoll, and secure the area."

The young garda turned his face and muttered some words into his radio. He hurried to the quad, retrieved a roll of police tape and attached it to the scrub, leaving a wide space around the body.

Inspector Cooper watched Trout like he expected him to evaporate any minute. Eventually he said, "Are you two together?"

"Yes." Trout made no elaboration on his answer.

"I'll need statements from you both. In the meantime, give me a rundown of what you know." Cooper's professional ability had overcome his antagonism. He looked from one to the other and settled on Trout.

Sergeant Driscoll's circle had brought him back to the group and he began to take notes on his mobile phone as Trout talked.

Trout gave a succinct recap of their morning, added an account of his phone call during the night and speculated that the body could be that of a young man his acquaintance, one Freddy Loftus. Cooper listened without comment. He pursed his lips and stared at the body.

Trout added, "The phone or at least a phone is there – the ringtone seemed to come from underneath the body."

"How do you know that?"

"I rang the number that called me last night."

"You rang the number." Cooper had a strange note in his voice. He pointedly looked at the bleak landscape around them before adding, "I wonder what made you think it was the same phone?"

Trout felt the sting of the implied accusation. He held the gaze of his ex-colleague, "Someone rang me in the middle of the night," he said coldly. "I heard the shot I was pretty sure killed him and now there's a body. Why wouldn't I assume there was a connection?"

Cooper made no reply.

"Team's on their way, sir."

An uneasy silence settled on the group. A white van had detached itself from the toy-like vehicles and was cautiously making its way up the hill. They watched its manoeuvrings as if their salvation depended on it, Sergeant Driscoll standing to attention beside the crime tape and staring at the approaching van as if he could somehow add speed to its progress.

"So, you think this guy is Freddy Loftus?" Cooper was looking at the body, distaste curling his lips. "A small-time crook." He turned his head and glared at Trout. "What was he doing all the way out here? Have you something going on we should know about?"

"I have no idea what brought Freddy here. I'm surprised he even knew where it was. To the best of my knowledge, he's …" Trout cleared his throat, "was town born and bred. Never gave the impression that he knew anyone outside the city."

The uneasy silence prevailed. Trout glanced at Cooper's scowling face and moved nearer to Lauren. He indicated they should sit, which they did. Cooper looked at them sourly but said nothing.

Lauren drew her knees up, wrapped her arms around them and rested her chin on top. She looked completely relaxed. Keeping her face towards Trout, she said softly, "My granny had a friend called Winnie Loftus. She lived over the other side of Slí Buí."

Trout considered the information. He stretched back on his elbows and spoke so only Lauren could hear. "Might be coincidence." He watched the stocky, flabby Inspector with his antagonism bristling like a force field and his dismissal of Freddy – Trout's gut was sure it was him, a boy he knew and liked – as if he wasn't worth a second of his time. "I don't really believe in coincidence. Still, we'll keep it to ourselves for the moment."

Soon the van was disgorging white-suited people who looked like aliens against the rough backdrop of the mountain. All the newcomers saluted Trout with some of them greeting him by name. He stood up but, after a glance at the Inspector, stayed where he was.

An extremely tall individual with the build of a basketball player, big shoulders, long arms, small waist, sauntered towards them. He was carrying an impressive camera and had two more slung across his body. He moved with a lightness that belied his size and snapped off a few long-range pictures as he approached.

"Trout, good to see you, man! Retirement suiting you?" His accent was straight out of the Mississippi Delta.

"Grand, Jax. How're things in your neck of the woods?"

"Pulling the devil by the tail." He rolled his eyes towards the Inspector. "But no use complaining." He beamed an expansive smile and turned to Lauren. "Who is this lovely creature? Have you been holding out on us, Trout?"

Trout smiled. "A friend of mine, Jax. Meet Lauren O'Loughlin. Lauren, this here reprobate is one Jaxon Alexander. Best police photographer in Ireland but, as he says that himself, it's open to interpretation."

"Enchanted to meet you, Miz Lauren." He bowed his head towards her as she stood to greet him. "My apologies that I cannot offer you the hand of friendship but my hands being full make it impossible."

He rolled his eyes theatrically as Inspector Cooper bellowed "*Alexander! Get your sorry ass over here! You're holding us all up!*"

"My apologies, ma'am. You can see what we're up against. Call in for a glass of vino or two, Trout? I have a bottle I'd like your opinion on. Bring your lovely lady. A good wine is always enhanced by a beautiful woman." He sighed, tipped an imaginary hat towards Lauren, and turned back to where the forensic team were waiting.

"Sure, Jax. I'll be on to you in a day or two."

Trout smiled to see Lauren looking totally bemused by the exchange.

Jax was taking photos as he moved, using different cameras as he framed different shots, getting nearer and nearer to the body.

Lauren suddenly shivered and wrapped her arms around herself.

Trout moved towards her. "You OK?"

She nodded. "A bit chilled from sitting. Do you think we can go soon?"

"Don't see why not. I'll talk to Cooper. He has no reason to keep us any longer."

Sergeant Driscoll approached, his smile diffident, holding his phone in front of him like a shield. "I have to take your address and phone number," he said apologetically.

"No problem." Lauren beamed at him. She rattled off the details. "Will we see you when we go to give our statements?"

"I–I'm not sure. Possibly. It will depend on Inspector Cooper."

Trout was amused to see a slight blush stain the young man's cheeks. "We hope to go as soon as I can clear it with the Inspector," he said and moved towards Cooper.

Their exchange was terse and Trout turned quickly away. As he did Inspector Cooper raised his voice. "I'll expect you both at the station tomorrow to give your official statements."

Trout muttered something. He gathered the rug and coffee mugs, stuffed them into his pack and held out a hand to Lauren. "Ready?"

She nodded, swung her bag on her shoulder and placed her hand in his. Together they started down the hill, without looking back.

Trout set as fast a pace as the terrain allowed. His face was grim as if he wanted to put as much distance between himself and his ex-colleague as possible.

Once they were far enough away that their voices wouldn't carry, Lauren said, "No love lost there."

Trout sighed. "We were friends, once. When I was young and innocent, before I discovered our friendship depended on Cooper being top dog. And finding out he didn't care how he achieved it." His voice told a story of betrayal and sadness with an under-layer of anger that showed he was more deeply affected than he cared to admit.

Lauren glanced at him. "I know what it's like to be betrayed by someone you trusted," she said quietly. "If you'd like to offload, I'm here. Shorten the road and all that."

"Shorten the road. A great old Irish tradition." He thought about his chequered history with Jim Cooper. "I've probably built it up in my head into something more than it is," he said at last.

"All the more reason to purge the memory, keep it from becoming a prison of your own making." Lauren smiled. "At least that's what your sister told me once upon a time – and we both know that Lucy is very wise."

"So she is."

He slowed his pace. "Here I am trying to make a good impression on you and you expect me to share the gory details of my youth."

Lauren said nothing. A comfortable silence threaded between them.

At last, he said, "We started in Templemore the same day. Me a culchie who wanted save the world and Coop a townie who choose the force instead of a gang. In a lot of ways, we were as mismatched a pair as you could find but the powers that be thought we'd work well together and we did." He slowed further. "I'd have trusted Coop with my life and on a couple of occasions did." He paused. "On the streets he had the instincts of a hoodlum while I was as green as the grass down there in Paddy Murphy's meadow." He indicated the lush green expanse rolling up to meet the hills. "I learned more about how to read a street from Jim Cooper than any textbook ever written. We became buddies, then friends. We more or less matched each other through the ranks. Coop had street smarts and I had book learning and between us we got through anything they threw at us." He took a deep breath. "When I made inspector and he didn't, it all sort of blew up between us."

"Was he jealous?"

Trout shrugged. "Maybe. He knew I was ambitious. Coop hated the bookwork. We had this system – I'd study the stuff, make a synopsis of it and he'd learn it off. It worked great." He laughed. "Coop thought the scenarios the college threw at us had no concept of the reality we might find ourselves in. So, we'd have these really hot debates. Basically, it meant I learnt about the streets and Coop was able to answer the book questions. We flew through the exams." His look turned inwards as he thought back over the years. "I started taking extra classes almost from the beginning. He used to give me right stick over them but I was fascinated – law, forensics, psychology – the more I learned the more I wanted to know. Coop couldn't hack the books and was royally pissed off when he discovered that he needed a degree to go for inspector. And …" He hesitated, wondering fleetingly if he should tell her the whole story. Maybe an edited version … "He was already inclined to take short-cuts. If he thought he knew the culprit, his thing was to wade in and deal with it. Street style." He made a grimace. "The powers that be saw that he got results but … he made a lot of enemies, on both sides of the law. It got worse when the rumours started and he was accused of taking backhanders from old gangland pals. He managed to exonerate himself but it left him very bitter."

Trout was silent until he heard Lauren draw in a breath to make a comment. Before she could say anything, he continued, his voice strangely harsh.

"By then I was in the Special Investigations Unit. It came to a head when he started making up lies about me." Trout's voice flattened. "He started rumours … tried to claim I was using drugs and coercing women into sexual favours. He even went so far as to hint that I did certain people specific services that helped to fast-track my career."

"Nasty."

"More than nasty. Any one of those is a sackable offence. Lucky my Super didn't agree and managed to nip it in the bud but I was damn near suspended and that would have ended my career in the CSB."

"CSB?"

"Crime and Security Branch – they call us C3 – we're responsible for the really serious stuff – national security, counter-terrorism, serious crime investigation, that sort of thing."

"Wow! You never told me you were such a heavyweight!"

"Yeah, well, I worked bloody hard for it and to think that little shit nearly caused me to lose it …" He forced himself to take a deep breath. "As it happened, he ended up stepping on some very powerful toes which resulted in him being transferred up north. He made out he hated it but I've sometimes wondered if that was only show." He sighed, continued grimly, "He blamed me whatever way he was playing it and I guess his career sort of stagnated after that."

"But he's an inspector?"

"He made it eventually, looked for the extension that would get him a bigger pension. I didn't enquire too closely how he did it. He claims only for me it would have happened years ago."

"Would it?"

"I doubt it. I helped him out of enough scrapes and still he doesn't get that our job is to gather evidence that will put an offender securely out of the public domain." He decided to err on the side of caution and held his own counsel on the nature of the scrapes he rescued his erstwhile friend from. He was suddenly aware of his use of the present tense and paused.

"He's the person heading up this investigation," Lauren said doubtfully. "Can't say it's inspiring confidence in me."

"Me neither." He sighed. "I just can't sit back and let him mess it up."

"In reality, can you do anything about it?"

"Possibly. It may tie in with something …" His voice trailed off. "I'm going to find out – asap."

Lauren grinned. "Call me as soon as you know."

Chapter 4

Trout brewed an indulgent cappuccino. He took no heed of the so-called experts who claimed one shouldn't drink coffee in the evening. They were probably drinking the piss that passed for coffee in most institutions. The Italians now, they knew the value of the right brew at the right time. A cappuccino was the perfect blend of nourishment and stimulation.

He took down his notebook, gulped a mouthful of coffee and thought about the events of the day.

And of Knocknaclogga.

Knocknaclogga was home. The place of his childhood, his youth. It was small, sleepy even, and he'd swear everybody knew everybody else's business, and that for the most part it was populated with honest, hardworking people. Of course, strangers moved in, that was a given, but the ones that hadn't fully integrated and become more local than the locals generally kept to themselves. Could it be an outpost of organized crime?

Trout wasn't naïve and, sitting on the hillside, a train of thought had inserted itself into his mind that demanded to be heard. What if there was a connection between the events of the past twenty-four hours and the meeting he had with his friend and mentor, Terence Henderson, in the ruined hunting lodge known as the Hellfire Club, over two months ago?

He was still Detective Inspector Thomas Tegan of the Garda Special Investigation Unit then. Now he cast his mind back, remembering the way Terence had materialized through the encroaching dusk, that misty March evening.

"That you, Trout?" The cultured voice held no doubt. "Miserable evening. Still, all the better for us. I appreciate you coming."

Tegan noted the use of his childhood nickname and understood that, whatever his long-time mentor wanted, he intended to avail of their friendship to get it.

"Let's get out of this infernal mist," Terence said.

They ducked into that empty, rubble-strewn space, as grey as outside but dry, where the quiet voice told him such an incredulous story that he wondered was the eminent judge losing a little of his legendary acumen. He listened with growing incredulity, wondering how such an authority and its brief had remained unknown in a small, inward-looking community. Until …

"You want me to *what*?" Tegan had given up the battle to keep his features neutral and stared at the man opposite him.

"I'm not asking you to go rogue or anything like that, although if you thought it would get results, we could consider it."

"We?"

"The few of us taxed with the ultimate integrity of the law. We have noted the direction certain individuals are heading and want it stopped before too much damage is done."

Tegan leaned forward. "I've worked bloody hard to get where I am and you're asking me to jeopardize my retirement – to – to go and work for some shady organization that isn't even supposed to exist!"

"Technically, you could have retired any time in the last five years." Terence's dry tones held an undercurrent of a smile. "Soon enough you won't have any choice in the matter. You're already an anomaly, staying on so long after your thirty years. Not but they're lucky to have you. Too many of the best get out." He held Tegan's gaze. "Now's the time to change tack. Come and work for me. Investigating is your lifeblood and, without the constraints the Garda are bound by, you could really serve the course of justice."

"We're not bound by that many constraints."

"Too many for the people we're dealing with." He held up a hand as Tegan went to speak. "The evidence has to be absolute and undeniable and we won't get that by ordinary means."

"Admissibility?"

"I'll deal with that when the time comes." The lean, ascetic face was grave. "My hands are tied. You have the skills and the knowledge to bring me what I need. What's more, I believe you're capable of finding it, although I'm aware – let's be honest here – perhaps not as legally as you would like." He watched Tegan with unwavering eyes. "And, Trout," again the use of his childhood nickname wasn't lost on Tegan, "most importantly, I trust you." He sighed. "There are so few at the moment that I can reliably say that about."

Trout sighed. He drank his coffee, started to write and filled one page, then another with his customary hieroglyphics, determined to apply an objective eye to his home place.

Knocknaclogga and Slí Buí ... as a boy he'd known every crack in the pavement, every tussock on the hill, but that was a long time ago and, if the place hadn't changed, he had. He could see the possibilities that made the area an attractive proposition for someone who knew what was what. It was relatively accessible, less than two hours from most of the big centres of population, three hours max if you wanted to go to the very north, with miles of coastline practically on its doorstep.

He tilted the chair and balanced it on two legs as he imagined the area around him. The countryside was deceptively quiet with large tracts of uninhabited land. In reality, it was the sort of place where the unusual stood out. If something was happening, somebody would see it. They might keep their own counsel but it would be noted and remembered. That said, it was hiking country and hikers were tolerated with a polite amusement that would render them almost invisible. They might be noticed but they wouldn't be interfered with. The locals liked to chat but generally took people at face value and left it at that. A live-and-let-live attitude prevailed unless something threatened the fabric of the community itself. Then the likes of Martha Dillon, retired schoolmistress and matriarch of the parish, stepped in and set about restoring order as they saw fit. Trout made a note to talk to Mrs Dillon as soon as possible.

He tapped his lips with the pencil. He wasn't aware of the area being tagged as a place of interest during his time with the serious crime squad but that would only enhance its value to gangs looking for a bolt hole. He'd talk to Mac. See if anything had popped up since he'd left. Something with a connection to Knocknaclogga, even a tenuous one.

He added a squiggle and a star and gazed out through the large window that made up most of the back wall of the kitchen. From where he sat, the back garden looked like a hodge-podge of trees and bushes, the results of his parents' rewilding efforts. A patio and paved area extended from the house to the greenery, below the level of the window and out of his sightline. He would have sworn Freddy was a lad for pavements rather than hills, which raised the question: what brought him to Slí Buí?

Mac, his old sergeant, considered Freddy something of a protégé of Trout's. He wasn't sure that was the right word. He had found Freddy huddled in a doorway, following a stand-off with some drug dealers. He was little more than a child, semi-comatose from whatever his pals had given him to celebrate his fourteenth birthday, shaking with fear and guilt. The indignity of having his stomach pumped was a salutary lesson and with his sister Nikki on his case and Trout's interest in his survival he had managed to break away from his so-called friends. Something about the youth roused Trout's protective instincts and he had kept in contact.

When he discovered Freddy's talent in using wood, he had encouraged the lad to stick with it. Even at that stage, using salvaged wood and the most basic tools, Freddy had created some beautiful pieces, including a storage box with a false bottom, so cleverly inserted that it was nearly impossible to detect. Trout bought two of his pieces immediately he saw them: an inlaid coffee table which was in his apartment and the delicately carved book-holder currently keeping his mother's cookbooks tidy. Trout glanced at it, frowning. He had managed to persuade Freddy to take advantage of a local youth scheme and, through it, Freddy had secured a place in the College of Design and Technology. When his passion for wood was fostered,

Freddy had blossomed. By the time he reached his final year he was considered one of the star students. He was working part-time with a master craftsman and three nights a week in a cocktail bar. Woodwork and the tools involved were expensive and, as Freddy explained to Trout, to do a good job you needed good tools.

Early on in his time in the cocktail bar, Freddy had told Trout that he was like a fly on the wall – he was there but no-one took any notice of him. When he started bringing him snippets of information, Trout realized what a valuable asset he could be but was reluctant to get him too involved. The gardaí already suspected the bar of being a front for gangland crime. He feared Freddy would be vulnerable, but the information was valuable and Freddy was anxious to pay back the debt he felt he owned Trout. Their collaboration was very much under the radar and Trout was sure nobody knew about it. Except now Freddy was dead and Trout felt a heavy sense of responsibility … He sighed.

After his retirement Freddy had contacted him and told him he had information that would be of interest to him. He was mysterious about it, said it was safely stored and he'd be back to him in a couple of weeks when he had the final piece in his possession.

Now Trout made an inarticulate noise and tightened his fingers until the knuckles glowed white. He had reminded Freddy that he was retired, only to have the young man tell him that the word on the street had him making a sideways move. One that would free him to work without interference from Garda regulations. No amount of questioning had elicited where Freddy got his information. In the end Trout had to content himself with warning him to be careful but Freddy had laughed and said, "I'm a fly on the wall, man – no one sees me, I'm that quiet."

Now he was dead.

Trout added a series of questions to his notes:

Why was Freddy in Knocknaclogga?

Why was he killed?

Where did last night's phone call fit in?

Trout's pencil stilled. He thought deeply for a long moment, his face grim, then added:

Why did Jim Cooper personally take the case?

Could that be the connection Terence was looking for?

A long shot? Perhaps? But ... there were already too many coincidences. Could he use it to his advantage? Get on board the investigation and use it as cover for ... another thought slammed into him ... was Lauren in danger from being on the scene and more importantly with him?

He drummed his fingers on the table, frowned over the notebook. Terence had given him carte-blanche ... well, within reason, but he needed a bona-fide 'in' to the investigation. He thought a bit longer and slowly a plan formed.

He reached for his phone, a small smile tugging the corners of his lips. He knew exactly where he'd start.

Chapter 5

The phone came to life in his hand and Trout noted the time. In spite of all the happenings it wasn't yet six o'clock, still time to make the call that would set the first phase of his plan in motion. Danny Mortimer owned and ran the biggest private detective agency in Ireland. He did little of the work these days but ran a stable of experienced people who worked everything: from digging the dirt for a divorce, to locating missing whoever, whether the person wanted to be found or not. He had often tried to recruit Trout, so much so that it was a long-running joke between them. Trout located the number he wanted. Now he would offer himself on a plate. But carefully. Danny was no fool. He ran a tight ship and rarely left the office before six. He was infamous for the number of associates he surrounded himself with. He would suit Trout's plan to perfection. He highlighted the name and pressed call.

"Well, well, if it isn't Special Investigator Tegan himself." The voice, redolent of a fifty-a-day smoking habit, grated on his ear.

"Ex, Danny, ex," Trout said mildly. "How's business?"

"Lucrative, very lucrative. My people can't keep up with the work." A New York twang overlaid the inner-city accent on some of the words. "Suits me, suits us all. Yeah, I took the talk of your retirement as being greatly exaggerated."

Trout heard the deep drag of a cigarette. "No exaggeration, Danny. I had enough of it. Took the money and called it a day."

Danny's laugh morphed into a hacking cough. Finally, he got his breath back. "Got tired of the red tape? Told you that you would one day."

"Maybe." Trout made his voice cautious.

A pause. "Job offer's still open if you're tired of the civvies already. Your skill set would make you a perfect associate of mine. Thought I'd wait a few weeks before I got on to you but, as you're calling me, I'll take it as a sign."

Trout heard a creak of leather. He imagined Danny Mortimer leaning back in his big black chair, his gut straining over his pants, the triumphant smile he wasn't even aware of when things were going his way splitting his face.

"I'm thinking about it." Trout knew he would get further playing hard to get than by acquiescing too easily. He heard a thump as Danny righted the chair.

"You're shitting me, Tegan."

"When did I ever shit you, Danny?" Trout infused his voice with hurt.

"Maybe, maybe not, You play your cards close most of the time." The silence stretched. "If you're serious I'll see you here tomorrow. Two o'clock. We'll work something out. And, Tegan, don't be late."

The triumphant edge to Danny's voice might have considerably lessened if he could have seen Trout's satisfied grin.

The next phone call was more difficult. Trout looked at the

number a long time before he made it. Nikki Gill née Loftus was Freddy's sister. More than a sister – she reared him when their mother couldn't or wouldn't. To the best of Trout's knowledge, she was the only constant in Freddy's life outside himself. If he could call himself one of Freddy's constants. Nikki had done her best and, if there was anywhere Freddy could call home, it was with her. She never gave up on him, bawled him out when necessary, encouraged him to follow his dream of being a master-craftsman and was pathetically grateful to Trout for looking out for her lad, as she called Freddy.

"*Tommy, oh Tommy! Is it true?*" The wail echoed down the line.

"I'm afraid so, Nikki. I'm sorry." Trout felt the inadequacy of his words sear him.

Harsh sobs rattled the line. Trout pictured Nikki's narrow face scrunched into grotesque sorrow. He stayed silent, allowing her grief the space to spend itself.

The sobs slowed to hiccupping gulps. "*The stupid git!*" She drew a deep shuddering breath. "He told me you warned him that – that he was playing with fire and that he should stop. But would he listen? Not at all. He thought he was invisible ..." Her voice trailed to a whisper, hardened. "He promised me he'd finish with that bar place, a few more days he said and he'd have everything he needed." She wailed. "*What was he up to, Tommy?* He was simmering, excited like, the last time he was here. He wouldn't tell me what it was but he said he owed you too much to stop and once ye were all square he'd be able to move on ..." A strangled sob broke through.

"Did he give you any inkling of what he was doing?"

Nikki sniffed. "Not a dickybird but he was mighty pleased with himself."

"When was he with you?"

"Two, no, three days ago. Said he'd be back for Jenny's birthday at the weekend and by then he'd have all you needed to put ..." she lowered her voice and whispered, "to ... to put Marty Lambert away forever."

"He definitely said –" Trout paused, "that name?"

"Yeah. He was sort of excited, you know, pumped up."

"Pumped up? Was he using?"

"No! He's been clean this five years. What am I saying, it's nearer seven now, it is. Not even a fag the last year, since Jenny was born. He took that pact you made with him very serious. He had plans, big ones, his own workshop even. Seems some nobs saw his work at the college and offered big money for his project. He said it wouldn't have happened if you hadn't talked to the fella over at the college. Gave him a chance at life, you did, and he had to live up to your expectations, like."

Trout wondered if Nikki's vision of Freddy was a bit too rose-tinted.

"He was a good lad, Tommy, and he, we both, appreciated that you saw it and gave him a chance."

"I know he was a good lad, Nikki. And it grieves me to think I might be responsible for his death."

"Never! Only for you he'd be dead a long time ago."

"Somebody did for him, Nikki, and it doesn't sit well with me." Trout felt his voice grow hoarse and cleared his throat. "Freddy rang my number briefly that night – by accident – he didn't know he was talking to me and I didn't recognize his voice. I intend to know what happened to him."

"You'll find them, Tommy, and make them pay." She sniffed. "You could say he was my baby. Our mam put him into my arms the day she brought him back from the hospital. I was ten years old and he was mine from that day on. I minded him and schooled him and no matter how heart-scalded he made me he always came home to me." Her voice cracked. "Until now. Find them, Tommy, and make them pay."

"I'll do my best, Nikki – you know I will." Trout hesitated, plunged on, "Will you do something for me?"

"Anything I can. Just ask."

"As next of kin you'll have to identify him."

"Oh no!" Nikki moaned. "How can I do that? My heart's broken."

"Think of him as sleeping," Trout said gently. "Get that done in the morning. Then, as near to two o'clock as you can make it, go to Danny Mortimer on Thomas Street and hire him to look into Freddy's death."

"Hire a flatfoot? Me?"

"Yes. Agree to whatever his terms are. I'll cover them. And, Nikki, if you see me there you don't know me, you've never seen me before."

"See you ... know you? Oh ..." Nikki was silent for a few moments. "Sure, how would I know a highfalutin' detective like yourself? I'll do what you ask, never you fear ... Only mind yourself, Tommy. The people you're after are not nice. Not nice at all."

"Don't worry about me, Nikki. Talk soon."

Trout cut the call and sat back. His coffee was long gone. He went back to his hieroglyphics, thinking about the phone calls he had made, and smiled grimly. One more to go and he reckoned he would have everything in place for ... well, time would tell.

He dialled a number only he and one other person knew existed.

He listened to the series of clicks that denoted multiple rerouting and encryption.

A precise, cultured voice spoke in his ear. "Trout."

"Terence."

"What news?"

In a few terse sentences Trout outlined the day's events. In the middle he broke off. "*Shit!*" He ran a hand through his hair. "I forgot to mention the watcher in my report. *Damn!* I need to do that asap. They'll have to get the techs up there, to the caves, see if they can pick up any forensics around the area."

"Perhaps." Silence hung on the line. "Is your girl reliable?"

Trout felt his gut clinch. *His girl.* Yes. Already he was thinking of Lauren as his girl. "Absolutely."

"Good. We have to be careful here. If there is any chance Slí Buí is associated with our … shall we say, situation … it's need to know and, unfortunately, we can't be sure where Inspector Cooper fits in." There was a pause. "I suggest a limited version of the truth for your friend and ask her to forget about the watcher. And don't mention it to anyone at the station yet. You'll have to check that out yourself and decide the best course of action."

"Except I sent the station a text message to tell them move their butts as we had company."

A big sigh carried down the line. "I'll see what I can do. We may be able to intercept it. I suppose there's no chance it didn't go?"

"It went. I checked."

"What plan are you considering yourself?"

Trout smiled. "I'm going to become a PI and get myself hired to investigate the killing."

"Nice one. You get to tread on toes with a bona-fide excuse."

Terence chuckled. "I like the way you think, Trout. I'll get back to you on that other." A pause. "Be careful, Trout. These people take no prisoners. Good luck."

The line went dead.

Two warnings in little over two hours. Lucky he had no more calls for the moment. He smiled, a grim twitch of his lips. If he got a third one, he'd be inclined to be worried.

Chapter 6

Trout's Lexus purred to a stop outside Lauren's gate at nine o'clock the following morning. She was ready and waiting. He stood out, debating with himself how best to present his request to withhold some of their information, looked up and saw her. He took a deep breath and a moment to appreciate the slim, vibrant woman coming towards him. Her red curls were tamed into a classy chignon and still some tendrils escaped to frame her face and emphasize her smile. She had opted for a classic look: a jade-green suit with the skirt just tipping her knees, set off by a cream silk shirt, open at the neck to show apple-jade beads. Nude court shoes brought her head level with his shoulder and for a moment he imagined how it would feel nestling there.

Her smile faltered at Trout's appraisal. "Will I do? I've never been interviewed by the police before."

"You look amazing." He cleared his throat. "There won't be a man at the station able to keep his eyes off you."

"Oh, come on, Trout!" Then she realized he was serious and said, "Thank you. All compliments gratefully received and accepted."

He strode around the car and opened the door, watched as she sank gracefully into the seat and forced his mind to ignore the shapely legs revealed by her skirt. He crouched down to bring his eyes level with hers.

"There's something I need to tell you before we get to the station."

She met his gaze, her eyes made greener by the reflection of the jade studs in her ears. "I thought you might."

Distracted, he said, "Why?"

"Why?"

"Why did you think I might have something to tell you?"

Lauren shrugged, a delicate twist of her shoulders. "I'm not sure really."

Trout was watching her closely. "I need to know what made you think there was more to the story?"

She half laughed. "You make it sound like a matter of life or death."

"It could be."

"Oh." Lauren looked down, twisted the gold band she wore on the middle finger of her left hand. "I'm a reader as well as an editor ..."

Trout made to say something. She held up her hand.

"A professional reader. I check stories for flow and things that might jar in the telling. When I was thinking over all that happened yesterday, it felt as if something was missing and ..." She paused. "We never told them about the watcher on the hill."

"I actually forgot until I was writing it down last night ... and it turns out we may have to leave it forgotten."

"But didn't you text someone?"

"It's most likely that text won't see the light of day, for the moment anyway." Trout shook his head. "I'll say it again. Your

instincts are spot on. Maybe even too much so for your own good."
He rose, closed her door and went round to the driver's side. He
got in but didn't immediately start the car. "Lauren, there are things
I can't tell you about this investigation. Please trust me when I say
it suffices for you to know you are in less danger by not knowing
them. Even at that, I have to ask you a favour." He drummed his
fingers lightly on the steering, turned to look at her. "The only way
to ask you is straight out. Lauren, when you give your statement,
will you please leave out any reference to the watcher on the hill
and …" he hesitated, "if anyone asks you about me be as
circumspect as you can."

Lauren frowned. "I'm not sure what you mean," she said, her
words trickling out slowly. "OK … I can forget to mention the
watcher. I presume … you have a good reason for asking."

Trout nodded. "I need you to trust me on it."

"As for the rest," she shrugged, "all I know is you're retired, you've
moved back to Knocknaclogga, we're friends since childhood. How
much more circumspect can I be?"

He could see she was miffed, felt the sting of her dismissal.
"*Ouch!* I put that badly but some people are going to be very
interested in what you can tell them about what I'm doing and I'd
prefer to keep them guessing …"

Lauren stayed silent and Trout felt like kicking himself. It was
rare for him to feel himself making a hash of things. But he'd started
now, so in for a penny, in for a pound. "There's one other thing."
He smiled at her. "How would you like to be a PI's assistant?"

Lauren laughed, a clear involuntary peal. "A Private Investigator?
What are you up to?"

"I'm planning on investigating Freddy's murder so I'm interviewing for a PI post this afternoon and I want you as part of the deal. You up for it?"

"Are you thinking of Sherlock's Dr Watson now or Poirot's faithful Hastings?"

"Only you're far too young, you could Miss Marple, the wise head in the story."

"You're a Christie fan. She's one of my favorites of the classic detective authors."

Any dissention was forgotten and the journey passed pleasantly as they compared notes on their preferred fiction from all eras.

The station was a large glass-and-steel building that looked more like a modern office block than a police station. The desk sergeant greeted Trout by name and made no attempt to disguise her curiosity about Lauren. She was a tall, pleasant thirty-something with the build of a long-distant runner.

"Lauren, this is Sergeant Moira Baker – Moira, Lauren O'Loughlin. We're here to give our statements on finding the body on Knocknaclogga yesterday."

"Himself said ye'd be coming in." Moira's voice was carefully neutral. "Sign the book, please." She turned a large diary-like ledger and indicated where Lauren could put her name, address and telephone number.

Trout scribbled his details on the next line and Moira pressed a buzzer that gave them access to the main building. A fresh-faced young man came forward to meet them, almost saluted when he saw Trout then stood irresolute with his hand half raised.

"Garda Doherty will escort you to the interview rooms." Moira flashed an apologetic smile at Trout. "Regulations, sir, *em, er,* Mr Tegan."

"No problem, sergeant. I still remember the rules." Trout flashed her a brilliant smile and nodded. "Lead on, Garda Doherty. We'll follow you."

The young garda cleared his throat. "Inspector Cooper said to bring Miss O'Loughlin to his office and to tell you, sir, that Sergeant Driscoll would meet you in Interview Room One."

"Did he now?" Trout smiled at Lauren. "That OK with you, Lauren?"

She nodded. "Fine."

"I'll meet you at the front desk when we're finished."

Trout continued down the corridor while Garda Doherty pressed the button on the lift that would take Lauren and him to the third floor.

Trout knocked briefly on the door and sauntered into the interview room.

"Morning, Tony."

Sergeant Tony Driscoll jumped to his feet, a faint pink tinging his cheeks.

"Good morning, sir, Mr Tegan, *em* ...."

"Tom will do, Tony, until we come to the formalities." He pulled out one of the two plastic chairs on the far side of the table. "Long day yesterday?"

"Yes, sir ... *er*, Tom."

"I well remember the formalities. T's crossed and I's dotted, tedious but necessary. I presume the identification was confirmed as Freddy Loftus."

"Yes, his sister is coming in later to officially identify him but his prints are on the system. Surprisingly," Tony frowned, "he doesn't have that much of a record in the great scheme of things. A stint in juvey, a fine for possession with no evidence of intent to sell, and a couple of cautions." He plonked onto his chair, shuffled some papers. "I was just having a look at his file. Nothing at all for the last five years. He was working the bar at Club Diablo at night and was taking classes in woodwork of all things. He seems to have kept his nose squeaky clean." Tony frowned. "Nearly too much so if you get my drift from what happened yesterday."

"Interesting." Trout watched the younger man, kept his voice casual. "Anything from the phone?"

"A burner. Some numbers. The tech guys are working on it at the moment." Tony raised his head. "But you knew that, sir. You called it in last night. I've a copy of Sergeant McMillan's report here."

"That's right." Trout half smiled. "It took me a few minutes to realize that it wasn't my problem but I'd already asked Mac the usual questions."

"Why would Freddy Loftus be ringing you in the middle of the night?" A hint of suspicion laced the question.

"I'd like to know why myself. He was obviously in trouble."

Tony frowned. "And he rang you?"

"That's right. Only I didn't know it was him at the time."

"I have a transcript of your conversation with Sergeant McMillan – will you read it, please, and confirm if it's an accurate reflection of the call?" He handed Trout a typewritten sheet.

Trout read it over. "Sounds about right." He went to hand it back. "I guess I'd better initialize it?"

"Yes, please . . . And you had no idea who was calling you?"

"No. I didn't recognize the caller, possibly because he was running and panting, both of which tend to distort a person's voice. It wasn't until we found the body – face down – and heard the phone ring under it, that I put two and two together and thought it could have been Freddy."

"Why did you ring the phone?"

"Lauren – Miss O'Loughlin – suggested we try ringing it when I wondered aloud if it had been found. I had the number and, hey presto, the phone rang."

"Just like that."

"Just like that, Tony."

"Inspector Cooper thinks you know more than you're telling us," Tony blurted out.

"He would." Trout drummed his fingers lightly on the table. "That thing on?" He pointed to the recorder.

Tony looked startled. "No. I ... I forgot."

"Good. Off the record, Tony. For the moment," he added, seeing the young sergeant's uncomfortable look. "Freddy occasionally supplied me with information that I needed with regard to certain illegal activities in the city."

"He was an informer?"

"Not exactly ... More like an acquirer of information."

Tony looked at him. "What's the difference?"

"Freddy was straight, working where people are inclined to talk without seeing any danger. He was in a position to overhear certain conversations that were of interest to me. Now and again he willingly answered some questions I might have."

The young sergeant looked sceptical.

"All above board. No money exchanged hands. The arrangement was based on mutual trust. He knew my number, I knew his. Neither of us had it written down. I'll bet they won't find my number anywhere in that phone except when he rang me. He had to key it in – the number. I reckon he rang mine by mistake. He did so because he knew it so well and possibly got it mixed it up with whatever number he was trying to ring."

"The phone was a burner, only three incoming calls from a withheld number and one out going to you." Tony sounded glum. "But what was he doing on the mountain? He was a townie fair and square."

"I'm wondering the same thing myself. From the call last night, he was expecting to meet someone called Marty and he blamed him for bringing Rasher and the gang. I doubt that ye've rounded up Rasher Madigan since I retired?"

Tony shook his head.

"So, I'd go with him until we find out different. Marty?" He shrugged, "Who knows? But there's a Martin Lambert, goes by Marty with his friends – you'll be familiar with him?" At the sergeant's nod he continued. "We reckoned he's a possible link between the gangs and … shall we say certain business interests. He's always on the fringe of things and he was a friend of an ambitious low-life who made good. You've probably heard of Bowser Corrigan?" Again, he waited for the nod of confirmation. "True-blue gang leader, born and bred. He cleaned up his act around twenty years ago and morphed into a businessman named Robert Carrig."

Tony whistled. "You think that's the way the wind is blowing?"

Trout drummed his fingers on the table. Tony was busy writing.

Trout said, "Try the Lion's Head on Middle Street. It used to be one of their hang-outs and, Tony …" He stopped, waited for the young man to look at him. "It might be best if you figured all that out for yourself while you were studying the printouts and asked yourself a couple of pertinent questions." He tapped his nose. "You know, teasing it out, connecting the names and all that."

Tony gave him a long considering look. "Oh. I see." He thought about it for a long minute, nodded, reached for the recorder button and intoned solemnly, the date, time, his name and badge number, asked Trout to confirm his name, date of birth and state the events that led him to finding a body on Slí Buí. Trout complied, gave a brief and largely accurate account of his involvement, and answered appropriately any questions Tony asked him. As Tony made no reference to a text message or the sighting of a watcher on the hill, neither did Trout.

By the time all the necessary paperwork was finished and his statement signed, more than two hours had passed. Trout was getting angsty about Lauren. He declined Tony Driscoll's offer to escort him out, tapped his nose significantly once again when the young sergeant went to thank him and hurried to the front reception area. It was empty.

Moira Baker was typing quickly and confidently on a laptop. She looked up briefly as Trout came through the door. "Your friend said to tell you she was going to find a coffee shop. I recommended the Hook and Ladder on the corner."

"Thanks, Moira."

Trout hesitated but before he could say anything else she added, "I'd say her interview with Inspector Cooper didn't go well. And, judging by the way the Inspector is spitting nails in every direction, I'd say he doesn't think so either."

Chapter 7

Trout found Lauren sitting at a table for two, her back to the door, an empty coffee cup before her. The set of her shoulders suggested she was tense and unhappy.

"Lauren?" He slid into the chair opposite. "Are you OK?"

She looked at him. "Your ex-mate is a sleaze bag to the nth degree." She picked up her mug, found it empty and placed it with deliberate precision back onto the table. "He had the gall to suggest that I ... I would be a useful asset to you. He said, not suggested, mind – said I was with you to pimp your contacts. That my many charms would be perfect to elicit information from anyone, including himself." She made a good hand of mimicking the Inspector's voice.

"What?" Trout rocked back in his chair. "*The bollix!*" He began to rise. "I'm going find him and give him a good kick in the arse!"

"Too late. I already did."

"You what?" He dropped back onto the seat. "I don't know whether to be impressed or worried." He narrowed his eyes at her. "What exactly did you do, Lauren?"

"Well ..."

"Wait! I need coffee to hear this. What's that you're having?"

"An Americano."

"Won't do. To tell all, you need at least a latte." He signalled to the waiter.

"A whole milk latte and I think I need a macchiato."

He gave Lauren a long searching look. "Start at the beginning," he said.

Lauren rubbed her hands over her eyes. "He is one nasty bit of goods, Trout, and, boy, does he have it in for you!" She took a deep breath. "The beginning. Sounds like the Bible."

Trout gave her a look.

"OK, OK. The beginning. Well, you saw that pleasant young garda bear me aloft to the Inspector's office ..."

"Lauren."

"Well, he was nice and words are my business ..." She made a face at him, sobered, said primly, "It became apparent very quickly that Inspector Cooper had no interest in my statement. None whatsoever. I was very put out, especially when he invited me to lunch where, in his words, we could have a more in-depth chat and get to know each other better."

Trout held himself very still, aware of the slow burn of anger low in his belly. His ex-colleague and one-time friend had not only made a pass at Lauren but his behaviour was totally unprofessional.

"When I politely refused, he pushed harder, pointing out the mutual benefits of us getting to know each other better."

Trout stirred.

Lauren held up a hand. "And, no, you don't want to know what he had in mind."

"Bastard," he muttered.

"When I left him in no doubt that I wasn't interested, he started asking me about you. What you were doing in Knocknaclogga? How long did we know each other? Were people from the Force visiting you? I was staring at him, thinking he was totally out of line and trying to decide what to do . . ." She paused and smiled her thanks as the server placed a tall, caramel-coloured coffee before her. She stirred it with deep concentration and took a sip of the creamy brew. "*Mmmm* ... lovely." She looked up at Trout and grinned. "That's when I remembered. I edited a book one time that had a girl being interviewed in a police station. She was all excited about helping with police enquires and seeing the inside of a real interview room."

Trout was wondering if she'd lost her marbles. Where was she going with this?

She smiled at him. "The girl was an avid reader of detective novels and was disappointed at the ordinariness of the place. I decided to channel her and see what happened. So, I leant towards him, like this ..." Lauren arched her body towards Trout and opened her eyes very wide. "*Is that a mirror?*" she whispered.

Trout stared at her.

She straightened. "That big thing that looks like a window,' I said, pointing. 'It *is* a window,' he said. 'Oh,' I said, disappointed. 'I thought it might be one of those two-way mirrors'." She grinned. "Then I made a big play of looking around his office. '*Is it hidden?* I whispered. He looked confused. 'Is what hidden?' '*The tape-recorder?*' 'We don't have a tape-recorder.' 'But how are you going to take my statement if you don't have something to record it? DCI Hilary Green always makes sure the tape is running even when she –' He cut across me, quite rudely." Lauren pouted, put on her Cooper accent: '*This isn't a book, Miss O'Loughlin.*'"

Trout was smiling, he could feel the laughter burbling in his belly. He was imagining Cooper's frustration at having his plans thwarted.

"Well, naturally, I was put out by that. I told him the detectives in books are reasonably polite and always professional. They don't sit around inviting witnesses to lunch. I could see he was going a bit purple around the gills so I worked myself up into a royal snit and flounced out of his office in such a way that everyone working at the desks in that outer place looked up and, boy, could you see the speculation spreading!"

Trout threw back his head and laughed. "You are priceless. That was better than any kick in the arse! Coop is very aware of how things look and having the bullpen speculating as to what he said to you won't suit him at all. The only thing is, Lauren, he's a bad enemy and he doesn't forget."

Lauren shrugged. "He was unprofessional, Trout. I wouldn't give him the satisfaction of playing his game."

Trout caught sight of the clock. "*Shit*. It's twenty to two. We have to be in Thomas Street by two. Come on, we'll just make it."

He put the money on the table, gave a thumbs-up to the server and hustled Lauren out the door.

Chapter 8

31B Thomas Street was a narrow, red-brick building sandwiched between a tanning studio and a discount store. The peeling grey paint and dull brass knocker looked more like an exhortation to abandon hope than an inspiration to confidence. An acrylic sign, misted as if it had absorbed water, proclaimed: *Daniel James Mortimer & Associates, Private Investigations, 2nd Floor.*

"Don't be fooled," Trout said. "Danny Mortimer is as sly as a weasel and just about as dangerous. I'll do the talking but we'll have to wing a lot of it."

He raised the knocker and let it bang sharply. A disembodied voice seemed to come from the middle of it. "State your business."

"Thomas Tegan. Two o'clock."

There was a whirring noise, a loud click and the door creaked open. Inside everything was dark. Dark-blue walls funnelled a person to a grey iron staircase. The open treads looked dirty and the balustrade felt sticky. Trout handed Lauren a handkerchief when he saw her react to the handrail. She smiled her thanks.

"Stick to the middle. I'll steady you."

They clattered up the two flights.

"Best warning system ever invented," Trout said in Lauren's ear. "Nobody can go quietly on an iron staircase."

A glass door at the top opened into a waiting-area-cum-office. A once pearl-grey couch sagged by one wall, flanked by two dirty-looking bentwood chairs. A utilitarian desk with a telephone, an old-model computer and a top-of-the-range intercom faced the door.

A nondescript elderly lady raised her head and beamed at Trout.

"Special Investigator Tegan. How lovely to see you again!" she twittered. "Danny is expecting you. He said to show you straight in. And you've brought a friend. Oh my, my! She is quite lovely."

"Hello, Maisie." Trout leaned forward and kissed the papery cheek, catching Lauren's surprised look out of the corner of his eye. "Still keeping the show on the road?"

"I do the best I can, as always." Maisie fluffed her hair as two bright spots of colour pinged on her face.

Trout held out a hand and drew Lauren forward. "This is my friend, Lauren O'Loughlin. Lauren, Maisie McCann. Don't be taken in by the little old lady act. Our Masie is a mathematical genius who can smell a fraud a mile away." He smiled as the two women acknowledged each other.

"Go on with you, you old charmer!" Maisie swatted Trout's arm while her eyes assessed Lauren. The shrewd, penetrating look seemed to miss nothing but the smile that softened her thin lips suggested that Lauren had passed some sort of an unspoken test and would remain unchallenged. For the moment anyway.

Maisie manipulated a button on the intercom and a door one side of the desk noiselessly opened. "Go on through," she said, waving her hand towards it.

Trout and Lauren entered into a twilight zone of half-drawn blinds and a single desk lamp. A pall of cigarette smoke, old and new, hung in the air. The desk, an antique mahogany monstrosity, its patina defying the scars of everyday use, commanded the room. The desk was big, the man bigger. A large, flat face, features sagging as if melted and reformed awry was dominated by a pair of silver eyes that sparkled through the folds of flesh. He rose like a Great White surging out of the water and held out a hand.

"Special Investigator Tegan. Welcome."

He was as tall as Trout but twice the width, his belly straining to escape the confines of a brown leather belt, his accent back-street Dublin, tinged with a nasal New York drawl.

"Ex, Danny. Ex." Trout felt his hand sink into warm, doughy softness and made the handshake brief.

"Not for long, eh?" He grinned. His teeth were very white and even. "Once an investigator always an investigator." His eyes swivelled towards Lauren. "You've brought company, I see."

"My friend Ms O'Loughlin. Lauren, meet Daniel J Mortimer, the best PI in the country."

"Pleased to meet you." Lauren's eyes were wide, whether in an attempt to penetrate the gloom or at the sight of the mountain of a man Trout wasn't sure.

"Lauren." Danny held on to her hand and licked his lips, looking at her as if she were a tasty morsel he was about to devour.

"Lauren and myself are thinking of setting up an investigating business." Trout kept his voice neutral. "I told her we needed a stint with one of the best to get a feel for the business."

"Of course." Danny sighed and reluctantly dropped Lauren's hand. "A good name is everything. All my associates are the best –

I only contract top-class investigators." He waved them into a couple of chairs, lay back on his own and frowned at Trout. "You're already an investigator. Why would you need me?"

Trout spread his hands. "I no longer have access to the Garda resources and, as you well know, I would be acting with different authority. It helps to have the backing of a successful operative like yourself when setting out." He leaned forward. "I think it would be of mutual benefit if we were working together."

"Special Investigator –"

"*Ex.* Come on, Danny! You don't need to be so formal."

"Tegan … you would be a welcome addition to my associates." He pursed his lips, drew his fingertips together. "But I get the feeling there's more to this gig than I can see."

Trout shrugged.

Danny sat still as a Buddha, the silvery glitter of his eyes boring into Trout. Finally, he nodded. "It's worth the chance." He straightened, became brisk and businesslike. "When can you start?"

"Now." Trout shrugged again. "Whenever. The sooner we get going, the sooner we can get Lauren a licence and get ourselves up and running."

"You'll come on board as associates. That will allow you to work while you're organizing the licence. I'll have Maisie draw up a contract." He pulled a spiral notebook from a drawer. "Name?"

"Name?"

Danny cocked an eye at Trout. "You're setting up in the business, right?"

Trout nodded.

"You need a business name to work as a contractor, take out insurance …"

"TLC Investigations." Lauren made it sound as if it was already a given.

Trout gave her a mental thumbs-up.

"TLCI. A play on your names with a comforting connotation. I like it." He went back to his notebook. "Lauren?" He looked at her. "It isn't recommended that first names are used in a business identity …"

Lauren shook her head. "Not Lauren, Loughlin."

"You're dropping the O?"

"It works better." She shrugged. "After all, Loughlin is the surname, with or without the O, and I know my tribe."

Danny's gaze was locked on to Lauren as if he needed to lip-read to understand her words. He licked his lips, cleared his throat and went back to his writing.

Trout hid a smile.

Danny frowned. "C?"

"Consultant."

He looked at her.

"If the problem doesn't fit our skill-set we can pass it on after the consult," she said smoothly.

"Clever." Danny nodded. "Savvy." He wrote a few more lines. "The usual rates, fees and expenses will apply. I'll have Maisie type this into an associates' contract and –"

The intercom buzzed discreetly. He leaned towards it.

"There's a Mrs Nikki Gill here. She insists she needs to see you urgently." Maisie's voice was clear and tinged with aggravation. "I've tried to explain that you're too busy –"

"It's all right, Maisie. Bring the lady in. We have a new associate on board." His eyes rested on Trout as he cut off the intercom.

"Well, well. Might be your lucky day, Tegan. Let's see what the cat's dragged in."

The woman Maisie ushered into the room was stick-insect thin. The messy top-knot on her head elongated her frame, making her seem taller than she was. She wore skinny jeans and a zipped denim jacket that seemed to contain her limbs rather make a fashion statement. Her face was puffy, her eyes red-rimmed, but her lips were set as if she was done with crying and now wanted some answers. Her two hands clutched at the strap of a canvas cross-body bag. A faded motto on it *"Stay Positive and Good Things Will Happen"* seemed to mock the angry despair that piloted her towards the desk. She started to talk before she was halfway across the room.

"You have to help me, Mr Mortimer. My Eddie says you're the best. I'll pay whatever you want. I have some savings. They're all my own. I was keeping them for when Jenny got a bit older but this is more important." She reached the desk, swayed against it. "You have to help me."

Danny pushed his chair away from the desk. "Now ... Mrs ..."

"Gill," Maisie said from the door.

"Mrs Gill. Calm yourself." He heaved himself upright, held out a hand as if warding her off.

Trout rose and pushed his chair behind the woman as she wobbled alarmingly. She sank into it without seeming to register him. "I've just come from the morgue and it's not right, so it's not. You have to find out who done it."

"OK. Take it easy. We need to start at the beginning." Danny tore the page from the notebook and handed it to Maisie. "Type that up, will you, and perhaps a cup of tea for our . . . for this lady."

Mrs Gill made to talk, but again he held up his hand, this time in a classic stop sign. "First things first," he said.

Authority radiated from him and the woman sagged as if punctured.

Danny plopped down, pulled his chair back in to the desk and picked up his pen. "Tell me your full name and address."

"Nikki Gill." The practicalities seemed to settle the woman and she rattled off her address and a telephone number.

"What exactly is the problem, Mrs. Gill? May I call you Nikki?"

"Yes. Of course. I … I …" Nikki took a deep breath, closed her eyes and said, "My brother Freddy was found dead yesterday." She opened her eyes and stared straight at Danny Mortimer. "He was shot in the back and left to die on a mountain. He was twenty-two years old. Our mother left him into my arms when I was ten and he's been my baby since." The tears were running down her cheeks now, dripping off her chin unheeded. "He was a bit wild at times but he didn't deserve to die like that. Nobody does. I want you to find who killed him and bring them to justice."

Trout slipped a wad of tissue into her hand. Her gaze never faltered. Even as she mopped her face, blew her nose, shredded the tissue onto her lap, her eyes locked unblinking on Danny's face.

Maisie quietly placed a steaming mug in front of her and said, "Let me take that, dear." She gathered the tattered tissues, placed a full box beside Nikki and pressed the mug into her hand. "Drink up. It'll do you good."

Nikki automatically lifted the mug to drink. The hot liquid jolted her out of her trance. She blinked. "Will you help me?"

"Would your brother be Freddy Loftus?" Danny asked with a bare shift of his eyes towards Trout.

"Yes, yes. Do you know him?"

"Not personally. I've heard the name." Danny scribbled something on his notebook.

Nikki waited, sipped her tea almost unconsciously. Her face held a heartbreaking mixture of hope and resignation.

Danny said, "We charge two hundred a day plus expenses."

She lifted her chin. "I told you. I have savings." She balanced the mug on the edge of the desk, pulled the canvas bag onto her lap, scrabbled inside and produced a bundle of notes, tightly folded and tied with an elastic band. "You want something up front. I have five hundred here." She waved the money in the air. "That's two days and a bit. 'Twill get you started." She placed the money in front of him. "Count it. 'Tis all there."

"I believe you." Danny drummed his fingers on the desk. "OK, Nikki. This is what I'll do. This here is Mr. Tegan, an associate of mine ..."

Nikki twisted around in her chair and looked at Trout. "I beg your pardon for ignoring you. I'm so upset."

"No problem," Trout said with a smile.

"And his associate, Ms O'Loughlin."

Lauren nodded.

"Hello," said Nikki.

Danny bared his teeth at Trout. "I'll set them on your case immediately."

"No problem," Trout said again. "Indeed, if Mrs. Gill was agreeable, Lauren and myself were about to go for lunch." He turned to the woman. "Perhaps you'd have time to join us and we could get the full details for ourselves."

"You'll do it? You'll really do it?" Nikki crumpled in on herself, made a desperate effort to straighten. "Thank you." She closed her eyes, took a shuddering breath. "I don't know what else I can tell you but I'll do my best."

Trout stood up quickly and, seeing Nikki was on the verge of tears again, said briskly, "We'll be off so. If you lead the way, Mrs Gill … Lauren, go with her … I'll be with you now."

He turned to Danny as the women left. "Does Maisie have the contract ready?"

"You can sign it the next day you're in and …" he watched Trout through hooded eyes, "give me a full report on all developments."

"Of course." Trout turned and left.

He felt Danny's speculative gaze boring into his spine and could almost hear the thoughts that went with it: *Let Tegan play his own game. For now.* He'd owe him and Danny knew a favour owed in the right place was worth his weight in gold.

Chapter 9

Trout waved at Maisie as he passed and hurried down to join the women on the footpath. The sunlight dazzled his eyes like a spotlight, after the gloom in Danny's office. He blinked a couple of times and placed a comforting hand on Nikki's shoulder.

"Nikki, this is my friend Lauren," he said quietly. "She's going to help me investigate Freddy's death."

Lauren shook the work-roughened hand held out to her. "Pleased to meet you."

Nikki scrutinised her. "Likewise. I'm glad Tommy has a friend." She turned back to Trout and, lowering her voice, said, "Did I do all right, Tommy?"

He tapped his lips lightly and said out loud, "So, Mrs Gill, are you able to join us for lunch so we can go over the case with you?"

"Well, I could but I don't know if there's anything more I can tell you."

"Just need to clarify a few things. Mama Cass's place is around the corner. We'll go there." Trout was herding the women towards the café as he spoke. "One of Danny's goons is taking a lot of interest in us," he murmured.

The café was bright with bare wooden tables, sturdy chairs and a delicious smell of roasting meat and coffee. Trout choose a table at the far end near the window and sat where he could survey the room or the street with a casual turn of his head.

"We'll order food and then we can talk," he said.

"A cup of tea will be fine, Tommy." Nikki clutched her bag like a lifeline.

"You'll have a proper lunch, Nikki, and eat every bit of it." Trout was kind but firm. "You need to keep your strength up for Jenny and Eddie, and to help us get to the bottom of this."

"I suppose." She leaned towards him. "So, did I do OK?"

"Perfect, Nikki." He turned to Lauren. "Nikki and myself are old friends. I told her to hire Danny but not to let him know we're friends and," he smiled, "she played a blinder. Well done, Nikki!" He patted her hand and returned thoughtful eyes to Lauren. "As for you … words fail me, I'm so impressed. TLCI – brilliant. Good work all around."

Nikki beamed a watery smile at Lauren. "It isn't often that words fail Tommy. You must be something special."

Lauren returned the smile but Trout was aware he would have a lot of questions to answer when she got him on his own.

They ordered soup and sandwiches all around and when the waiter left Trout palmed a neat fold of money into Nikki's hand. "That's your money, Nikki. Slip it into your bag now in case I forget it after we've talked."

She looked startled. "I don't know, Tommy. I don't feel right taking it."

"Of course you'll take it. I told you last night I'd cover the fee."

Softening his voice, he added, "You're doing me the favour, Nikki, giving me an 'in' to the case."

She hesitated a moment longer then dropped it into her bag under the guise of finding a tissue. "Thank you."

In no time the waiter, a teen with pink hair and a nose ring, returned with three steaming bowls of thick vegetable soup and the selection of sandwiches they had ordered.

Silence reigned as they applied themselves to their food. Tegan was pleased to see that Nikki ate hungrily. He decided to leave any discussion until later.

Eventually the waiter returned to remove the bowls and the now empty plate.

"Dessert?" he asked.

Trout glanced enquiringly at his companions.

Both the women shook their heads.

"I couldn't eat another bite," said Nikki. "But a cup of tea would be nice."

Tegan turned to the waiter. "OK. Two Americanos and a pot of tea for one. And three slices of Mama's apple pie with cream." He looked from Lauren to Nikki with an easy smile. "Just wait till you taste it before you say a word."

Lauren laughed. "You haven't guided us wrong so far."

Trout smiled at her and felt she understood that all of them enjoying a dessert together would make it easier for Nikki to talk.

With the dexterity of a well-trained server, the waiter offloaded a pot of tea, two large mugs of coffee and the desserts.

The apple pie more than lived up to expectations. After the first bite, they all dug in enthusiastically.

Trout waited for the onslaught to ease, then asked, "Has there been any developments since I was talking to you last night, Nikki?"

She shook her head and swallowed a morsel of pie. "Not really. I went to the morgue and identified Freddy." Her lips trembled. "The guy there said they would be doing a post mortem this evening … I … I tried to imagine he was sleeping like you said but that terrible colour he was nearly made me sick. The attendant was very nice, brought me out to sit down and got me a glass of water." She paused. "That other fellow though," she stabbed at a piece of pie as if she was stabbing the memory, "that Detective Cooper, he's a nasty piece of goods if ever there was one. He tried to make me say that Freddie was dealing but I was having none of it. Told him I'd have him up for bullying, the way he was going on. He changed tack then, wanted to know if you'd been in contact with me, Tommy. Of course, I told him no – what would you be wanting me for? I think he was satisfied but he said it was my duty to tell him if you contacted me and that he'd have me up for obstruction of police work if I didn't." She raised watery eyes to Trout. "He's a bad 'un, Tommy, and he has it in for you. I saw the queer look he got in his eyes when he said your name."

Trout had let Nikki talk uninterrupted – now he reached out and patted her arm. "It's OK, Nikki. You did good." He thought for a minute. "Did he say anything about wanting to see Freddy's room?"

"Yeah, said he'd be over around five and not to touch anything before he came."

"Five." Trout looked at his watch. "It's quarter to four now. Do you think, if we hurry, we might be able to have a look before he comes?"

"Course you will. It won't take us ten minutes to get home. We'll go in the back and hopefully nobody will ever know you're there."

"And we'll need a recent photo." He looked at Lauren who was licking the last morsel of pie off her fork. "Will you come?"

"Try and stop me."

"We'll make tracks so. We need to be there and gone before officialdom turns up. Nikki, if it's OK with you we'll let you go out first. That way it will look as if we've parted company and we'll have a better chance of spotting if anyone is following us."

All three stood. To the casual observer they were taking leave of each other. Nikki left and Trout settled the bill.

He and Lauren lingered outside the door while he had a good look around. He gestured to the street. "Do you know the Liberties?"

Lauren shook her head. "No. It always seemed to be one of those places you stayed out of."

Trout looked at her, mock-serious. "It's one of the oldest parts of Dublin, history in every brick and stone in the place." They started to walk, Trout pointing out landmarks. "It looks as if we're OK," he said sotto voce, as he continued giving her the historical spiel while simultaneously taking her by the shortest route to Nikki's home, in a cul-de-sac off Gray Street.

"Nice street."

"It is now. All this area was part of the old Dublin slums. It was rebuilt in the early 1800's but remained working-class poor until more recent times. Now it's a mixture of the original families and upmarket newcomers. It can be difficult for families to hold on to a place as the houses have become so valuable. Nikki inherited her grandmother's house."

As he talked Trout guided Lauren through a lane that was cast in gloom by houses, guarded by high brick walls on either side.

"The houses stand directly on the street with a small garden to the back." He stopped for a moment and listened intently. Muted traffic was the only sound. "The gardens are accessed from this lane. It's a throwback to the days when people actually had vegetable gardens with their houses. Most of the people here have kept their little bit of green."

Nikki was peering out of a doorway halfway down and she beckoned to them to hurry. "My sister is hanging on to Jenny for another while so I'll keep an eye on the front while you have a look upstairs." She hurried them through a spotlessly clean kitchen and out into a small hallway, tiled in the original terracotta worn smooth by the years. A polished wooden stair curved up to the second floor. "Top of the stairs, back room, second on the left. Oh, and here's a photo. It's from Jenny's christening." She sounded unbearably sad.

"I'll copy it and get it back to you," Trout promised. He fished a couple of pairs of plastic gloves out of his pocket and handed a pair to Lauren. "And here ..." He produced plastic overshoes from another pocket. "Like walking in the hills. Leave no trace."

Freddy's room was small and chock-full of the detritus of a young life. An old-fashioned dressing table was just inside the door, its spotted mirror blocked by a silver stereo system and two freestanding speakers. A double bed took up most of the space with a shelf over it that contained childhood mementoes, a small silver cup black from lack of polish, a deck of cards, a scale model of a Yamaha Red-Wing motorbike, a broken Swiss army knife and a jam-jar full of mixed coins. The corner beside the window was occupied by a plain, hand-dowelled, shelf-unit that looked like a school woodwork project. It held a variety of books, some from childhood, the majority crime fiction, from Edgar Allen Poe to Jonathan Kellerman, Ruth Rendell, Ian Rankin and many more, a stack of wood-working manuals, a very old much sellotaped book on the work of Thomas Chippendale and a folder of photocopied pages labelled *Designs of Sheraton*. All obviously read and reread. The bottom shelf was crammed full of tattered boxes of games – Monopoly, Cluedo, Scrabble, Battleship, Snakes and Ladders, Buckaroo, all stuffed any way they fit into the space. On the other side a wardrobe hulked between the window and the door.

"We haven't much time, so try and figure out where a young fellow would put something he didn't want found. I'll take the wardrobe." Trout was pulling open the door as he spoke. He began to swiftly, efficiently and neatly check pockets, shirts, and between folded T-shirts and jumpers.

Lauren stood still and looked all around the room. "Where would make a good hiding place?" she muttered half to herself.

Out of the corner of his eye, Trout saw her move towards the corner with the books. He glanced around, noticed her reach for a book only to change her mind and stoop to examine the shelf full of games. He moved to examine the stereo. When he looked again, Lauren had pulled the Cluedo box from the shelf and was riffling through the detective pad, frowning at scribbled words, turning it backwards, upside-down and sideways.

"*Tommy! They're here!*" Nikki's anxious voice floated up the stairs.

"*Shit. We need to get out. Fast.*" Trout gestured to her. "*Come on!*" Lauren hastily jammed the lid back on the Cluedo box and followed Trout out and down the stairs.

Nikki shooed them back through the kitchen and out the back door as the front doorbell rang. "*Quickly. Out to the back lane. They won't see you there.*" She locked the door behind them and they heard her shout, "*I'm coming! No need to get your knickers in a twist!*", her voice receding as she moved towards the front of the house.

Trout hurried Lauren across the small garden. He eased open the door in the wall, glanced left and right then drew her through and closed it quietly. He stared when he saw the game she still carried. "What …?" He checked himself, pulled off the gloves and overshoes, indicating that she do the same. He grabbed hers, rolled them all into a ball and stuffed them into his pocket. "We'll dump them later." He caught her arm and propelled her down the alley in the opposite direction from which they had entered. It exited onto a bigger street and Trout guided her, quickly and silently, in a roundabout way until they emerged at the Guinness Storehouse.

He scowled at the imposing, grey façade. "Have you been?"

Lauren, clutching the box to her chest, shook her head.

"Some of your education is sadly lacking." He sounded as if he was aiming for light-hearted but then growled under his breath, "They have a gift shop where we can get a bag for that bloody game."

Lauren shivered. "Don't we need a ticket?"

"Not to go to the shop. This time, that's all we'll do." He glanced around. The crowd on the pavement was increasing as workers emerged from buildings in the vicinity. He slipped an arm through hers and, in case anyone was taking an interest in them, said, "But I promise I'll bring you back someday soon and show you the sights, all the way up to the Gravity bar."

The store was enormous. Merchandise of every type imaginable, mostly Guinness-themed, was displayed throughout the space.

"We need a fairly big bag so we'd better buy a few things." He held up a sweatshirt. "His and Hers?"

Lauren attempted a laugh. "Don't be daft. Get something small – we'll just ask for a big bag."

Trout was already hurrying to the till, carrying two sweatshirts. "We can use them as the TLCI uniform, put them on the expense account." He grabbed a canvas bag with wooden handles in passing. "Just the thing. I did say the name is brilliant, didn't I?"

He felt Lauren's startled glance. "Yes, you did." She was hurrying to keep up and sounded a little breathless.

"Well, I'll say it again. It was a stroke of genius. Only ..." Suddenly his tone became reserved.

Lauren looked at him. "What?"

"We need to get back to the car." He paid for the purchases, pleased to see the shop assistant pack them into a large carrier with a prominent Guinness logo. Before heading for door Trout stopped near a display and reached for the Cluedo box. "I'll just put this out of sight."

He wrapped the box in one of the sweatshirts, put the other on top, stuffed them all back in the carrier and the whole lot into the canvas bag.

Outside the evening rush hour was in full swing. "Are you OK to walk back? It's a good twenty minutes to the car park." He eyed the height of her heels. "You've done a lot of going already in those shoes."

"My shoes are fine. I choose them particularly because I can walk in them."

Lauren was picking up on his uneasiness but Trout felt the explanation would have to wait until they were well out of Jim Cooper's district. "At this hour we'll probably be faster walking anyway. The traffic is fairly backed up."

She was watching his face, gnawing at her lower lip. "Is something the matter?"

"We'll talk when we get back to the car. Come on." He took her hand and they cut across Bellevue, around by a park Lauren didn't know existed and eventually reached the car park.

They got in and sat in silence for a minute. Trout drummed his fingers on the steering.

"We'll head off, stop somewhere and have a debrief."

"A debrief? Don't you mean discuss our progress so far?"

Trout started the car. "We need to assess what we've got in the bag and, yes, you could say discuss progress."

"What are you not saying, Trout? You've been on edge since we left Nikki's place and I get the feeling I'm the cause of it."

"Lauren …" Trout negotiated the car into traffic and glanced at her, "it's complicated. I'll explain when I can stop and talk properly." And, he added to himself, when he had figured out how to tell her she had removed potential evidence from a crime scene and thus rendered it unusable.

Chapter 10

Trout drove in silence until they reached the junction for Kildare Village. He swung the car off the motorway and turned into the anonymity of the outlet car park.

"I'll get us coffee, unless you'd like something else?"

"Trout, I need to know what's happening here." Lauren grabbed his arm as he made to exit the car.

"Look, I'll get the coffee and –"

"*Just fucking tell me what's going on!*" Lauren looked as shocked as Trout felt at her outburst.

"OK." He turned towards her and said quietly, "If there's evidence in the Cluedo box we won't be able to use it."

"Why not?"

"Without a properly documented 'find trail' we can't prove where we got it. Heck, we can't even say where we got it because we shouldn't have been there in the first place."

"Why did you go so?" she demanded. "Anyway, you saw me pick it up."

"I didn't realize you had taken it until we were outside. The thing is, we've tampered with evidence? Nobody will look at evidence if there's any chance it's contaminated."

"*Damn and blast and …*" Lauren took a deep breath, let it out slowly. "We don't know yet if it's anything," she said miserably. "I just followed a hunch and picked up the Cluedo. I hadn't finished examining it and I hung on to it when we rushed away. This is ridiculous, Trout. I don't know anything about being a detective. How can I help your investigations if what I do renders the evidence unusable?"

"Well, as you say, we don't know if we have anything or not but your instincts are such that I reckon we do." He took her hand, threaded his fingers through hers. "Look, if there's anything there it will help us, regardless of what role it might play in a case." Trout shook his shoulders, shedding his annoyance like a dog shaking water from a wet coat. "I'm new to this private-investigating lark myself so I guess we need to cut ourselves a little slack." He sounded more like his usual level self.

"That's not the point. If we're going to have a detective agency, you need to know you can rely on me."

"That will come. You have to start somewhere and I think we have the making of a very good team. Not to mention that Nikki is depending on us."

"Nikki!" Lauren sighed. "Maybe you should tell me about Nikki and Freddy and where you fit into it all."

"That's a long story for another day. Suffice it to know that Freddy was one of my boys. And he was clean, had never been in prison and, whatever Jim Cooper might say to the contrary, he didn't do drugs." Trout paused, then added grimly, "And I intend to prove it."

"Then I guess we'd better have coffee," Lauren gave a wry smile, "and see what's this evidence we won't be able to use. If we have it."

"OK. Here's a pair of gloves. Dig out the Cluedo and we'll have a look at it when I come back."

When Trout returned with two take-out coffees and a selection of chocolate and bars, Lauren had the Cluedo box on her knees. She was staring at it, her face a study of trepidation.

He took one look at her. "Coffee," he said. "And chocolate." He riffled through the bars and thrust a dark chocolate with salted caramel into her hands.

She looked up, startled. "How did you know?"

Trout tapped his nose. "Eat." He handed her a coffee. "Drink." He took the box from her knees. "We'll deal with the rest afterwards."

The Cluedo set was old, much used but apparently complete. Trout pulled on a pair of gloves, and opened the box, revealing the game-board, cards, tokens and a battered paper envelope file. He lifted out the file. It was held together with sellotape and grubby from much handling. It contained the Cluedo detective pad, old notes, pages from previous games and photocopied pages of what looked like accounts, memos and letters. He extracted the notepad, replaced the file in the box, closed the lid and balanced it between them, on the handbrake.

"Why did you pick the Cluedo?" he asked.

"I don't know. There were all those detective/crime type books and the Cluedo seemed to go with them." Lauren hesitated, then said slowly, "If Freddy was interested in detective fiction, then Cluedo could have been a favourite game and, when something is good, it feels like a safe space and maybe also a safe hiding-place."

"Good instincts." Trout turned the notebook over in his hands then flicked it open. He turned a page, then another and another, his face becoming more incredulous with each turn. "What the hell was Freddy up to?" He looked at Lauren. "This is in a code we made up one time when we were looking at how to get messages to each other." He studied the letters, numbers, symbols. "There's names, I definitely recognize one of them, and dates but I'd need a bit of time to decipher it properly."

He handed her the notebook and she opened it at random. "Looks intricate," she said. "What sort of code is it?"

"Actually, simple enough. I'll show you when we get home." He removed the file and riffled through the remaining papers. "We might use it for our ... *Jesus!*" He raised dazed eyes to Lauren. "Tell me again why you picked the Cluedo?"

"What is it? What's wrong?"

"Wrong. Nothing's wrong. Only, some of these pages are photocopies of classified information, memos from a government department," he flicked a couple of more, "shipping invoices, a haulage contract for a company suspected of belonging to one of the biggest crime cartels in Ireland. How did Freddy get these? He must have been gathering evidence but ..."

Lauren clapped her hand over her mouth. "Oh my God! And I've made all it unusable?"

"No." Trout shook his head. "On the contrary. It probably means that you've preserved the evidence even if we have no idea how we can use it. Not at the moment, anyway."

"What do you mean 'preserved'?"

Trout looked grim. "This is a dangerous game, Lauren. Now is the time to get out before you know too much."

"Get out? Now? No friggin' way! Just tell me."

"The name," Trout hesitated, stared at the innocent-looking file, "is that of a prominent government official who happens to be a friend of Jim Cooper's."

"Oh."

"Freddie was most likely murdered for the contents of this file." He slipped the notebook into it, replaced the file in the box and slid it under his seat. "And," his voice was laced with anger, "if what I suspect is true, some of my ex-colleagues are in it up to their necks."

Chapter 11

Trout's eyes popped open. He stared at the dull white light edging where the curtains weren't fully pulled together and asked himself if he was awake. He had a heavy dullness in his head that suggested more sleep but his mind was instantly engaged in berating himself for his short-sightedness. What possessed him to get Lauren involved in this caper? Sure, he saw how having her as part of his would-be detective agency would give it credibility. Not to mention her quick mind and the intuitive leaps that had resulted in yesterday's discovery. *And? Be honest with yourself, Trout.* He enjoyed her company and wanted to get to know her better. But ... the reality was he had walked her into who knows what danger and he had done it without once considering what it could mean in terms of keeping her safe. Now she was in and determined to stay the course and, he groaned, she thought the agency was for real. When the voice in his head slyly whispered *'You could make it real'*, he threw back the bedclothes and headed for the shower. The water wasn't yet warm enough but it sloughed away the heaviness and allowed him a bit more clarity than the fantasy his half-asleep mind proposed.

After dropping Lauren off the evening before, he had spent a couple of hours deciphering Freddy's code, reviewing the photocopied documents and growing more and more disturbed by what he was seeing. The code was childish in its simplicity yet that very factor made it relatively effective. It needed to be. He had studied his scribbled notes and found the contents damning for some very prominent people, if they could be validated. The photocopied papers were worthless on their own but dynamite for anyone who had access to insider information in a certain government department. Trout felt the heaviness in the pit of his stomach that told him more clearly than words that anyone outside the keep who knew of the contents was in serious danger. He weighed the cost of keeping the transcript against having to do it again and decided to err on the side of caution. He burned his notes. He lingered longest over a sentence that, if he was reading it correctly, suggested that Freddy had recorded or copied some information onto some type of device and stashed it someplace he called "Paddy's Locker". Whatever that was!

Trout remained pensive as he brewed and drank his coffee. He rinsed out his cup and turned it upside-down on the drainer. Lauren had invited him for breakfast. It would give them a chance to review their find and plan their next move. Before they left the car park they had agreed to give the case a rest until Trout had looked at the notebook. That gave Lauren scope to talk about any plans Trout might have going forward for TLCI. She was full of enthusiasm for their agency and wanted him to fill her in on what he envisaged their scope of practice would be. The mere thought of trying to explain that it was mostly a cover story made him feel such a heel that he let her prattle on. Her analysis of the experience they both had to offer that would make for a successful collaboration had him almost thinking they could make it real. If only it was that simple. Now he debated how much to tell her, only too aware that he had involved her in the mess. He decided to play it by ear. It was still early so he decided to walk to her place. It would give him time to think.

Lauren's home was once an old two-up, two-down gate-lodge. Her family had lived in it for generations as gate-keepers for the big house, when there was one. Finally, they had managed to buy it outright in the early 1920s when the big house burned down and the land was sold off. The various additions over the years had given it a quaint lopsided look. Lauren herself had added a conservatory and here Trout found her.

She was sitting at her work-table, busily typing on a neat laptop. She looked up as he rounded the corner and beamed a welcome.

"Nicely timed. I was just thinking a bite of breakfast was needed."

"Good morning. This place is a real suntrap. You look like you've had a productive morning so far."

"I have." She turned the laptop towards him. "I've opened a file on Freddy's case and put in all I know. I can add your info after breakfast."

She stretched and Trout's eyes followed the sinuous movement. He had to bite his tongue to keep from offering to massage out the kinks.

"It's all ready," she said as she rotated her neck. "We can talk while we eat." She hurried through to the kitchen.

The other end of the table was set for two. Trout pulled out one of the chairs and sat. He drew the laptop towards him and began to look over what she had done.

Lauren returned with two plates of food. The tantalizing smell of rashers and sausages made his stomach rumble and he set the laptop aside. She fetched freshly baked brown bread and a pot of coffee.

He raised an eyebrow.

"I like to cook when I'm thinking," she said.

"I'm definitely not complaining." Trout buttered a slice of the warm, springy bread and tucked in.

He ate with relish for a few minutes and was pleased to see Lauren was enjoying her food as much as he was.

"You've made very comprehensive notes." He swallowed a chunk of sausage. "And your To Do list is spot on. I thought we might have a look at those caves this morning."

Lauren nodded. "It seemed the place to start, especially as the watcher was on the hill near them. Any luck with the notebook?"

"It's probably the reason Freddy was killed." He looked at her. "Someone must have twigged that he was being too curious. Lauren –"

"Don't even say it. I'm in and I want to see it through."

"It's not a game, Lauren. Well, maybe it is, but it's a dangerous one. Anyone who gets involved will be at risk, to some extent."

"I'm willing to take the chance." She hesitated. "I edit books but I know the difference between real life and fiction." She frowned, became thoughtful. "I've lived my life vicariously for too long. Now I'm getting a chance to do something, maybe actually make a difference in someone's life. I'm not backing out and we make a good team." She scooped up a forkful of mushrooms, chewed and swallowed. "Two heads and all that." She looked at him, those mesmerizing eyes daring him to contradict her.

"There is that." He mopped up the last of his egg, his sigh a mixture of contentment and resignation. "The notebook has lists of times when people were places they said they weren't, at meetings they claim to know nothing about and a couple of references to money changing hands that shouldn't have happened. I made a transcript but thought better of it and burned it." He saw Lauren's frown. "Believe me, it was the safest option in the long run. The papers are copies of memoranda that should never have left a government office. We'll make our own copies, maybe scan them, back them up to the Cloud – I'm trying to figure out the options." Suddenly he bunched a fist and growled, "*The bloody young fool!* I told him time and again not to take chances that would get him into trouble."

Lauren reached over and gave his fist a squeeze. "You can't put an old head on young shoulders. He probably thought he was James Bond and Mike Hammer all rolled into one."

"Probably." Trout attempted a grin. "He was a good kid, Lauren. He didn't have a great start but with Nikki's help he was turning things around. He had given in his notice at the club, he was doing well at the college. Hell, he was doing better than well, he was brilliant. Some of his stuff was pure art. He'd come to the notice of some people who thought he had the flair to go far. I reckon he thought he'd one last chance to dig some dirt for me, maybe get a bit of insurance for himself ... *Damn it!* If only I'd realized!"

"There's no point in blaming yourself. It won't change anything." Lauren pushed her plate aside and pulled the laptop towards her. "I'll make a quick synopsis of where we're at." Her fingers danced across the keyboard. "Our job now is to vindicate Freddy."

"Right. I'll tidy up and we'll be ready to roll."

She paused for a moment, glanced at him deftly stacking the plates. "I don't have a dishwasher."

"No problem. Mum made sure we learned the basics of washing-up." He carried the used crockery through to the kitchen, calling over his shoulder, "We'll leave for Slí Buí when we're done here."

Chapter 12

Lauren drove a silver, 2015 Vitara and handled it with relaxed confidence. They decided to approach the hill from the far side as it brought them nearer to the path that led directly to the caves. The day was dull but dry and they made good time. The caves were situated in a rocky outcrop that stuck up out of the bog like some giant hand had pitched it from space to land where it might. There were six indents, four so shallow they barely offered shelter and two fairly substantial structures. One of those burrowed into the rock for a couple of hundred metres and was the only one that could truly be called a cave.

"I haven't been near these since I was a boy." Trout watched the maw of the caves coming nearer. "Back then we thought at the very least we'd end up in Narnia. That said, I can't recall ever being disappointed by a visit to them."

"The Archeological Society wanted to develop them as some sort of a tourist attraction a couple of years ago so I was up here a few times. Not recently though."

"Knocknaclogga has an Archeological Society?" Trout's tone was so incredulous that Lauren burst out laughing. "Come on, who around has an interest in archeology?"

"Don't let Mrs Dillon hear you say that. She's the secretary and takes it very seriously. Tom Bow is the chair and the rest of us turn up when we're summoned. Apparently these rocks are a geological phenomenon of some sort."

Trout surveyed the desolate scene. They had climbed to the top of a rough hill. The bog spread out around them with the cave cliff to their right, brooding over the landscape. "It does look a bit out of place all right. Still hard to see what they could do with it."

"Not much in the end. The whole area is relatively inaccessible unless you're a committed hiker – it was decided to leave it alone." Lauren stopped and looked around. "Any development would have cost a lot of money which we didn't have and the whole place is a special area of conservation. The regulations around any development were totally off-putting." She pointed. "That's the Mass Rock over there, remember it? And the view from the top of the crag itself is tremendous. You really can see for miles in every direction. History records suggest that the big cave was a hiding place for priests during the penal times." Lauren laughed self-consciously. "Listen to me going on. Sure you know all that . . ."

They approached the caves. The nearest one was merely a shallow indent in the rock but they could see the recesses getting deeper as the crag curved.

"This first couple would barely shelter you from the wind."

They walked on.

Lauren pointed at the third cave. "This one's better but still nowhere to hide."

The area around the next one was trampled, bits of broken

heather sharply white against the dark growth.

Trout turned to look around. "We're almost directly above where we found Freddy. Far enough away that we wouldn't notice someone against the stone but near enough to chance a potshot if someone was desperate."

"Looks like someone was here lately as well." She stopped at the mouth of the next and deeper cave. "Footprints."

"Some superimposed on the others. We won't go in – anyway, we can see the back wall from here. The next one is the biggest if I remember correctly."

"Yes. People have been known to camp in it. It's fairly dry and deep enough to offer good shelter."

An attempt had been made to camouflage the entrance with furze bushes. The flowers were beginning to wilt but the needles were still green.

"Fairly recent addition," Trout commented "There's just enough room left to edge into the opening without disturbing them. Someone knew what he was doing."

"Do you think he's still there?" Lauren's voice betrayed the first sign of apprehension Trout had seen in her.

"I doubt it. Too much activity around the last couple of days. You stay here and I'll take a look."

"No flippin' way. I'm coming with you."

Trout opened his mouth, looked at her, shrugged and said, "We'll keep to the side and try not to disturb the footprints."

He produced a large torch from his pack and followed the powerful beam into the cave, Lauren on his heels. The light showed a narrow passage that curved to the right. The walls were of coarse grey sandstone striated with darker material. It was surprisingly dry.

The soft mossy entrance gave way to a solid rock floor that snaked into the darkness, and led them curve by curve, until they found themselves in the cave itself. It was a medium-size cavern, high enough for Trout to stand comfortably. A narrow ledge at waist height widened into a broad shelf on the back wall. The torch lit up an array of boxes, ends facing out, lying flush with the outer edge of the shelf. A large gas can with a ring burner stood by the wall and two aluminum deckchairs were stacked neatly beside it. Hanging from the edge of the shelf, hooks held various accoutrements: an old-fashioned billycan, a small saucepan and an oven glovet. Two mugs sat on the shelf, one with a robust camping tool sticking out of it.

"Someone has good housekeeping habits," Lauren couldn't resist saying.

Trout pulled some gloves from his pocket and handed a pair to Lauren. "Don't touch anything without the gloves and then only minimally."

Lauren nodded and they moved together to the shelf. Up close the boxes tapered from a large wooden crate, to a deep aero-board box that once held broccoli, to an orange crate and finally a biscuit tin, the USA logo almost faded away. Trout lifted the lid of the crate to reveal a quantity of dry goods, mostly rice and noodles – there were also tins of beans, ham and hot dogs, a bottle of ketchup and a jar of pickles. A see-through plastic lunchbox held an assortment of chocolate and bars.

"Whoever's here won't starve anyway."

He opened the aero-board box: two Patagonia sleeping bags, neatly rolled, curled into two yoga mats. A laundry bag held clothes: jeans, shirts, hoodies, underwear and socks. Tucked into the middle of them was a well-used pair of Steiner binoculars. "Looks like we've found our watcher."

Trout moved on to the orange crate. A dozen litre bottles of water, two bottles of beer and a bottle of red wine. He tilted the wine and looked at the label. "Campo Viejo Rioja. Nice one. Pity to drink it from a cup." He pushed the crate back into place. "A proper little home from home." He looked back along the shelf. "The ledge is getting deeper the further around we come. I'd forgotten there was so much space here."

Lauren stifled a nervous laugh. "This doesn't look like a makeshift camp."

"Doesn't feel like one either." Trout pried the lid off the biscuit tin and turned it towards her: a box of tea-bags, a tin of instant coffee, small individual tubs of creamer. "He certainly likes his comforts."

Lauren looked around. "Horrible place to be though. So dark." The air had an oppressive tang, like the lair of some wild animal.

"Yes. You wouldn't want to be claustrophobic."

"I'm feeling a bit like that, to be honest." She walked back to the passage leading out of the cave and stared along it into the darkness. As her eyes adjusted, she could see a faint lightness filtering in from outside. Suddenly what little light there was went black. She stopped, her senses on full alert.

She looked back over her shoulder. "*Trout!*" she whispered urgently. "*I think there's someone coming.*" His torch instantly went out.

She instinctively flattened herself against the rock, hoping to blend in with the darker shadows of the wall. She held her breath. An almost invisible shape glided past her and a torch flared into light, picking out Trout in its beam.

"Who are you and what the hell are you doing, pawing through my stuff?"

The voice was harsh, flat, possibly a midlands accent.

Trout's torch suddenly came on and, as the lights clashed, Lauren could see the form of a man, medium height, round head rising from a camouflage jacket that was barely discernible in the dark.

She bit her lip to stifle a gasp – the hand not holding the torch held a gun that was pointed directly at Trout.

"Not Dr Livingstone, I presume," Trout said lightly. "Nice set-up you've got here."

"It suits me." The newcomer didn't sound any more friendly. "Drop the light and answer my question."

"Which one?"

"Cut the crap. In case you haven't noticed this here is a gun I'm holding."

"I've noticed and I'm glad to see your hand is quite steady. I always feel safer when the person holding a gun on me seems to know what he's doing."

"I know what I'm doing – *so drop the fucking light before I'm forced to give you a demonstration.*"

Trout let the torch fall to the ground, "Your light will shine for both of us," he quipped.

"You're a barrel of laughs, aren't you?" The gunman scrutinized him. "You can't be a cop even though you have the look of one."

"Very astute observation."

"Hikers generally stay well away from here. Too soft nowadays to rough it. So, you must be the snoop Marty warned me about. Well, well, isn't that handy? Half our problems removed in one swoop."

"The blood will mess up your nice clean floor," Trout said mildly

"That's my problem. Not yours. Although bleeding out will make it yours in a way." He swung the torch higher to dazzle Trout.

Trout looked down at the floor. "I can see your dilemma though – you've blabbed so much you really need to eliminate me."

The gunman gave a harsh laugh. "At least you know the score." He raised the gun. "Who knows you're here?"

Trout put up a hand to shade his eyes. "Well, my friend Lauren does for one." He lowered his voice confidingly. "As a matter of fact, she's just there behind you."

"You won't get me with that old chestnut." He steadied his aim. "I asked you …"

Lauren, silent as a ghost, launched herself at him and drove him into the solid wall. His head made a resounding crack as it connected with the rock while a bullet zinged off the roof, causing a chunk of stone to hurtle wildly through the air.

The gunman slid silently to the ground.

Lauren stumbled back. "Oh my God, have I killed him?"

"I doubt it." Trout checked his pulse. "Steady and regular." He pulled out his phone. "No cover in here. Go outside and call 999. Ask for the gardaí and an ambulance." The stricken man stirred and groaned. Trout looked at him. "A first responder might be enough." He reached towards his back pocket and swore. "We could do with a pair of handcuffs," he muttered. "Needs must."

He handed Lauren the phone, unzipped the assailant's jacket, turned it back over his shoulders and proceeded to zip it up again. Once the gunman's arms were secured behind him, Trout shuffled him into sitting position and tied his boots together. By this time the man was awake and watching him balefully, a trickle of blood running down his face from the gash on his head.

"Sometimes the old chestnut is true," Trout said as he extracted a wallet. "*Sam Maguire*," he read off the driver's licence. He studied the picture in the light of the torch. "Pretty good likeness. No doubt your prints will confirm your identity."

Lauren came back in. "They're on their way. Ambulance control say they'll send the car up first because of the access difficulty." She handed Trout his phone.

Sam Maguire stared at her with venomous eyes. "*Bitch!*" he hissed. "*You're a dead woman walking.*"

Chapter 13

It was well into the afternoon before Trout and Lauren were free to leave the mountain. The gardaí came and, after the paramedics had deemed Maguire fit, removed him from the scene. They proceeded to secure the area for forensic examination and all the time they asked questions. *Why? How? What?*

Lauren was drooping with fatigue. Trout knew that the post-adrenalin rush would play havoc with her body but doubted that telling her would help. Instead, he found reasons to keep her moving so that she wouldn't crash completely. He gently and persistently insisted she drank some water and one of the travel mugs of coffee they had brought with them. She refused the protein bar saying she wouldn't be able to swallow it.

At last they were given the nod to go. Trout set a moderate pace and they both concentrated on keeping their footing. This section of the path was now much trampled and had become slippery.

When they reached firmer ground and could walk more freely, he said, "Any thoughts where Sam Maguire might fit into things?"

She gave him a startled look, shook her head. "How would I

know. I'm a complete novice here." Then asked in a desultory tone, "Did you know him?"

"No. At least not by that name." He looked thoughtful. "I've a feeling I've seen him before but for the life of me can't place where." He frowned. "It'll come to me eventually. I'm trying to fit him into the picture but, so far, I'm not having any luck. Pity he clammed up completely after that rather morbid threat."

Lauren shivered. "It was horrible. His voice as much as the words. I've never heard anyone so menacing in my life."

"His stock in trade. Intimidation. He's a bully boy, most likely sent around to menace and frighten people. And, if that isn't enough, he has the ground prepared to make more serious threats."

"He certainly intimidated me. Will they be able to hold him?"

"Pointing a gun at people is frowned upon by the law and, if he doesn't have a licence for it, which is likely – very few people are permitted to carry handguns – it should be enough to hold him while checking other things out."

"Like what?"

"Whether the gun's associated with a known crime, if there's a record of it being stolen – sometimes even the type of gun can raise questions. I'd say they'll have plenty to hold him. The big question is, will they?"

"Why wouldn't they?"

"Who knows?" Trout looked grim. He growled, "What in tarnation did Freddy stumble into and why didn't he just tell me instead of going off half-cocked?"

They walked in silence for a couple of minutes. Then Lauren stopped abruptly. Trout turned to look at her, one eyebrow raised in question.

She stared at him, took a long breath. "There were two sleeping bags, really two of everything," she said slowly. "Someone else was living … or hiding out in the cave."

"I was thinking the same thing. Only Maguire turned up. What's the bet the most expendable person was sent in to reconnoitre?"

"It must be important to whatever's going on if they automatically check out such a remote hiding-place. Do you think the other person was around, watching what was happening?"

"Maybe – but would have scarpered as soon as things began to look dodgy … Lauren, you realize that second person might have seen you emerge and make the phone call. Damn it to hell, this is getting too dangerous. You'll have to pull out. Have you a friend you can go stay with until all this blows over?"

Lauren, her equilibrium suddenly and firmly back in place, laughed. "If I've been seen I'll be in danger anywhere I go. Our best way forward is to clear this up as fast as we can, so we'll both be safe."

The drive back to Knocknaclogga was made in relative silence. Both were engrossed in their own thoughts. When Lauren made to drop Trout off at his own place he would have none of it. He insisted she come in, saying that after the excitement of the day they both needed something to eat and possibly a stiff drink to go with it.

"I'm driving."

"One glass of wine won't do you any harm."

He brought her straight through to the kitchen, ensconced her in the armchair beside the Aga and produced a bottle of Borosso Ink. He poured two glasses. "Just the wine to warm us while I whip us up a nice, satisfying omelette. I like mine loaded, how about you?"

"Loaded sounds good."

He poured oil on a cast-iron skillet and put it on to heat, then began to chop mushrooms, peppers and spring onions at speed.

She took a sip of wine and felt the rich fruity warmth embrace her tongue and relax her stomach. "I guess now that I don't have to cook something for myself, I feel hungry."

"I'm always ravenous after an adrenalin rush. I suppose the body uses so much energy coping in the moment, it needs something to replenish it. I've learned that something substantial but not too heavy calms the system and removes the last bit of jangly nerves." He added the vegetables to the pan.

"'Jangly nerves' is a good description. You're on edge but have no real reason for it any longer nor any way of fully discharging the feeling." Lauren sounded as if she was unravelling a puzzle. "That's why you kept after me on the mountain to move and drink and not go into myself. Gosh! Thank you. I thought you were just being annoying … Oh … Sorry, I shouldn't have said that."

Trout laughed. "Why not? It's the truth and I was annoying you. Only it was in a good cause." He deemed a change of conversation the best option. "I had a quick word with Jax – the photographer – and he's invited us to dinner, tomorrow evening, seven-ish. Will that work for you?" He concentrated on whipping eggs. He felt rather than saw her sharp glance.

"I suppose. Do you really want me to come?" Uncertainty came off her in waves.

"Of course I do. Anyway, he specifically told me to bring you." Trout's tone had a disgruntled edge.

Lauren sipped her wine and let her body sink into the chair. She allowed herself to smile. "He seems like an interesting character."

"He is. A real down-south Louisiana boy. He was a well-known photographer in the States until he tired of the celebrity circus and wanted something more … satisfying, I suppose. He studied forensics out of curiosity and got interested in forensic photography." Trout poured the eggs over the sizzling contents of the pan.

"I didn't even know there was such a thing."

"There is. The Americans have forensics down to a fine art. Their facility in Quantico is state of the art. Amazing place. I met him there, way back, maybe '05, '06. It was a great boost to us when he decided to relocate to Ireland."

Lauren was looking at him, her mouth half open, glass poised mid-air. "You were in Quantico?"

"Yeah. It was brilliant." He slid the pan under the grill. "I nearly stayed in America that time." His eyes took on a faraway look. After a few moments, he quickly and efficiently began to set the table.

"Jax is brilliant – what he doesn't know about photography and photos isn't worth knowing. He has an uncanny eye for detail. It's thanks to his shots we were able to get …" He stopped. "Sorry, shop talk."

He put a granary loaf on the table and fetched a tub of coleslaw from the fridge.

"I'm fascinated." She studied him thoughtfully. "I can easily see you in storybook US. You'd be perfect as a good cop in the likes of a Nora Roberts novel or maybe a mate of Cormoran Strike, only he's English."

"I'm trying to decide if that's a compliment. I'm familiar with the Robert Galbraith character but all I know about Nora Roberts is that she's my mum's favourite author and I'm not so sure my ego could take being a pin-up for Mum's pals."

Lauren laughed outright. "You're probably that already."

He grinned and checked the omelette. "Food's ready. Sit over and we'll eat."

Chapter 14

Jax Alexander lived in a corner apartment on the top floor of a luxury development in the heart of the Dublin Docklands. The high ceilings gave him space to move freely and the floor-to-ceiling windows gave him access to a wraparound terrace and a bird's-eye view of the city. Trout and himself greeted each other like the old friends they were. They fell into easy conversation as Jax conducted Lauren to admire the view from the terrace, then ensconced her in a comfortable armchair, one of two large solid affairs that were placed one either end of a matching L-shaped couch. The arrangement was grouped around a flickering gas fire and allowed one to gaze either at the windows or at an enormous flat-screen TV that occupied the corner.

Jax produced a heavy dark bottle with the flourish of a magician executing a favourite trick and served them with curvy glasses of chilled manzanilla sherry – the perfect aperitif apparently to prepare the palate for the traditional gumbo Jax had prepared for dinner.

"D'you have to drive home tonight?"

"No. I'm taking up your invite put me up, old pal, and Lauren is going to stay with friends in the city. We'll pour her into a taxi later."

Jax raised an eyebrow but made no comment. He twirled the last of his sherry and watched the play of light on the pale aromatic liquid.

"Good. I have a very fine Chenin Blanc from Savennières I'd like your opinion on." His tongue rolled the French words with the ease of a native. "It would be a pity not get the full feel of it by having to rush our evening."

"Savennières." Trout smiled. "Did you take the Loire Valley tour after all?"

"I sure did. It was all you promised and more …"

A passionate discussion on the merits of French wines and the benefits of searching out small single-estate vineyards followed. Lauren confessed that her knowledge of wine extended only as far as enjoying drinking it. The two men took great pleasure in furthering her knowledge until she was totally confused and Jax announced dinner was ready.

The gumbo was delicious, rich and spicy, the wine complemented it perfectly and the conversation flowed over many topics. By tacit consent no mention was made of the investigation until they had returned to the comfortable armchairs and Jax served a post-prandial Calvados and rich dark coffee.

"I guess the social part of the evening is over for now." Jax flipped a file onto the glass-topped table in front of Trout. "A full set of pictures from the hill and a preliminary copy of the autopsy report." He settled himself back onto the couch. "We're under specific orders not to share anything with ex-Detective Tegan, hence I made sure to get copies of everything I could get my hands on."

Trout glanced at Lauren. "Cooper and Jax rarely see eye to eye on things." He laughed "Although given the height difference it's easy to see why."

He turned his attention to the pictures, fanned them across the table top. They started with a long-range view of the area, the rise of the hill and the rocky outcrop where their watcher had lurked, and moved progressively closer until the body was revealed in close-up. A series of images from every angle was followed by the same sequence reversed when the body was turned over. Lauren gasped. The pasty, bloated face barely resembled the good-looking, smiling young man in the picture Nikki had given them. A further series of pictures documented the wounds, taken both onsite clothed and unclothed on the post-mortem trolly. The bullet-holes, three in total, were surprisingly small, mere black-rimmed holes in the jacket, black also on the flesh but here the holes showed a puckered rim surrounded by a spreading area of redness.

"No exit wound," Jax said grimly. "The bullets played bloody hell with his innards. He didn't stand a chance, the poor *couillon*."

"Nine-millimeter?" Trout was studying the photos intently.

"Semi-automatic. Two of the cases were recovered at the scene. Ballistics are running the marks to see if anything shows on the system."

Trout nodded. Handled another run of pictures, hesitated, looked across at Lauren. She was pale, composed but holding herself very still.

"These are the actual autopsy photos," he said. "Perhaps you'd prefer not to look."

She nodded, put her glass carefully on the table. "I'll use your bathroom if I may," she said quietly to Jax.

"Of course. Second door on the left."

"Thank you."

Trout swore softly. "I forgot Lauren isn't used to the more graphic details of our work."

"You're comfortable with her, *mon ami*," Jax said shrewdly. "Only for that I'd make a play for her myself. An interesting woman like Ms Lauren is sure hard to find."

Trout frowned at him.

Jax grinned. "I said *would*, man, not *will*. Least I can do is give you first chance to win her." He leaned closer. "But if you don't succeed, then I guess all's fair and dandy."

Trout stood as Lauren emerged from the bathroom and drew her back into the circle. "We'll leave Freddy for the moment – there's nothing new and Jax has some information on our friend from the caves."

"Sam Maguire has closed up tighter than a clam but an interesting print was lifted from the goods in the cave. Gent by the name of Martin Lambert." Jax frowned. "There was mention of some pal of his, someone who's made it big in the world, but dang if I can recall it."

"Bowser Corrigan aka Robert Carrig?" Trout suggested.

"Maybe, couldn't swear to it." Jax nodded to himself, added, "Rumour at the big house has it that this Lambert and Jim Cooper were buddies once upon a time, maybe still are."

"They grew up on the same estate, the three of them did. Ran together in the same gang before Coop chose …" Trout stopped. "It's not possible …"

"You think?" Jax said quietly.

"We started in Templemore together – surely I'd have known

if …" Trout was looking into himself. "How would I know? I was an innocent, fired up on saving the world. I thought Coop was the same but …"

Lauren was looking between the two friends. "What are you saying?" she demanded. "That Inspector Cooper is an insider for a criminal gang?" Her voice rang with disbelief.

"Well, Ms Lauren," the smooth southern accent washed over her like honey over porridge, "it's a possibility we need to keep in mind. For your sake and to keep this here pal of mine alive and kicking for the foreseeable."

Chapter 15

Trout collected Lauren shortly after eight the following morning. He had dark circles under his eyes that told of a late-night session with Jax but he brightened perceptibly when he saw her.

"We'll have breakfast and a recap in Avoca," he said, guiding the Lexus through the straggle of the morning rush hour. "I trust you slept well."

"I did. Very well, thank you. Better than you by the look of things."

"That bad, eh? We had a lot to catch up on and Jax talked me through the photos. He had some good insights on how Freddy was shot." Trout indicated and smoothly changed lanes. "What did you think of him?"

"Jax? Interesting man. Handsome." Lauren smiled. "I'm surprised he's not married."

"Divorced. His ex and a kid, a daughter, live in New Orleans." Trout paused. "Although Annabelle's not a kid anymore. She must be ... oh ... twenty-two or thereabouts. Jax thought Marcie might come to Ireland with him, change of pace, maybe have a shot at saving the marriage. She refused. He came anyway."

"Ye're good friends."

"Yeah, we are. We clicked the first day we met and it grew from there. We've a lot in common. He's a wine buff and a passionate fisherman. He thought my Irish accent was cute and that I needed a minder in the big bad world of American Forensics." Trout laughed. "He may have been right but with Jax on my case I didn't get a chance to find out – he steered me right when I was most likely to make a fool of myself."

"Of course, you returned the compliment when he came to Ireland."

"For sure. He showed me a part of America you'd never get to see if you weren't in with a native. The Louisiana swamplands are amazing. Jax has a boat and a camp on the bayou."

"Isn't a bayou camp a sort of shack in the woods?"

"More or less. Although Jax's is a proper structure. It's a fairly decent log cabin even though it's as basic as the caves, a tad more comfortable maybe. It's got a couple of beds and a stove as well as a gas cooker. He'd give me a nudge, say fill the cooler, and we'd head off for a couple of days' fishing. Eat what we caught, drink the wine ..."

"Wine? Surely it should be beer?"

"It started as a joke – OK, so maybe I was showing off. See, the first time he brought me I went all out and really got a selection of wines that I thought would complement fish. Jax laughed so much when he opened the cooler to get a beer that we just had to keep it going." Trout sighed. "It was some experience. The whole bayou thing was like nothing I'd ever seen before. We've nothing here you could compare with it."

"We don't have alligators either and I've read that they make the swamplands dangerous places to fish."

"Only if you fall in. They don't recommend that and if you do happen to fall in you'd want to be a mighty fast swimmer." The amusement in his voice told how much he enjoyed his trips there. He added, his tone full of smiles, "The first time he visited me here I brought him salmon-fishing in the river above Knocknaclogga and he was completely hooked." He laughed outright. "Pun intended. Jax found our salmon every bit as challenging as the bayou catfish. He came over a couple of times every year before he finally moved for good." Trout took the turn-off for Avoca. "I don't know about you but all this talk about fish has whetted my appetite. I'm well ready for breakfast whether it be fish or sausages."

While they ate, Trout filled Lauren in on the late-night talks between the two men. The death and autopsy results were straightforward enough. Jax would let them know if a match with the bullet showed in the system. Marty Lambert's print at the caves added a layer of question marks to whatever Freddy was doing. Trout was considering the possibility that Freddy was meeting Marty on the mountain and reckoned that it would go some way to explain the mixed-up phone-call. He also wondered if there was a connection with Bowser Corrigan aka Robert Carrig and through them both to the gangland crime scene. So far that picture remained blurred.

Lauren was trying to get her head around the relevance of the two names. "What's the story with the whole Bowser Corrigan-Robert Carrig thing?" she asked. "I'm sure I've read about Robert Carrig in the *Times* financial page. How could he be the same person as a gangland thug wanted by the gardaí?"

"No doubt you did read about him. In some circles he's a big-shot business man with assets in manufacturing, real estate and technology. But the reality is he started life as a gurrier named Robert Corrigan, nicknamed Bowser because of his reputation for being able to deliver anything, no matter how volatile, to anywhere you wanted it."

"You mean like the aviation fuel transporter?" Lauren sounded incredulous.

"You are good. Not many people know what a bowser is." Trout held up a hand. "Don't tell me you edited a book about an aviation fuel tankard."

"It was a good book too and, see, I learned something from it. It still doesn't explain the change of surname."

"Jonathan Carrig was the founder and owner of Carrig Enterprises. He could buy and sell an Arab oil sheik but none of it made up for the fact that he had no son."

Lauren snorted but said nothing.

Trout grinned. "He had four daughters but in his mind that didn't count. He put all sorts of trusts and red tape around his millions until daughter number two, Isolde, a headstrong twenty-something at the time, turned up with the bold Robert. Obviously, he was from the wrong side of the tracks but for some reason himself and the old man hit it off. He made a big play about it needing only the right environment for someone like himself to turn his life around and become a pillar of society. Eventually Carrig gave his consent to their marriage on the condition that Bowser gave up his unlawful ways, at least in public, and took Isolde's surname. Bowser jumped at the chance to become legit. He was always a businessman of sorts and he was good at it even when it was illegal. What Papa Carrig didn't know, he's dead a couple of years now, is that while

Bowser apparently distanced himself from his old associates, he actually set about consolidating his businesses under the cover of the Carrig name. He appointed his pal Marty Lambert as his man on the ground and proceeded to use Carrig Enterprises as a front for the largest organized crime syndicate in Ireland."

"It sounds like something from a novel." Lauren hesitated. "If the gardaí know all this why can't they do something about him?"

"Therein lies the crux. He's been giving us the runaround for years." Trout ran frustrated fingers through his hair. "Hell, even the Revenue can't touch him. You said it yourself – you read about him in the paper. He's a public figure, bad guy made good by the love of a beautiful woman. He plays it up to the hilt and Isolde supports him at every turn. They've been together nearly twenty-five years, have three more or less grown-up kids, endow college departments and support high profile charitable organizations He has politicians coming out of his back pocket. We're afraid –"

The *burr-burr* of his phone cut across the words. He frowned at the screen. "Hi, Nikki."

"*Tommy,*" Nikki's voice whispered in his ear. "*Someone's in Freddy's room.*"

"*What?*" Trout was on his feet. "Where are you?"

"*At home,*" she whispered. "*I took Jenny to the crèche and came back to get ready for work. The minute I opened the front door I knew something was wrong. I can hear him now, moving around and thumps and thuds and –*"

"Nikki," Trout interrupted, "I want you get out now, quietly, out the front door. Ring the Guards when you're outside. We're in Avoca – we'll be with you in twenty minutes or so."

"*But, Tommy –*"

"No buts, Nikki. This person could be dangerous, *get out of there, now*." Trout was almost at the car, Lauren running to keep up with him.

A half-scream, followed by a grunt, echoed from the phone.

"*Nikki! Nikki! Are you OK?*"

Silence.

Trout tossed Lauren the phone. "Call nine-nine-nine, one-one-two, whatever the hell it is nowadays – give them Nikki's address." He rattled it off, had the car already moving. "Tell them send the gardaí and an ambulance."

Trout and Lauren reached Nikki's house first. The street looked quiet, the cul-de-sac devoid of people. Nikki's front door was wide open. Trout moved cautiously towards it, gesturing for Lauren to stay behind him.

Nikki was sprawled at the foot of the stairs, her skinny legs looking like twigs in flowery leggings, blood pumping from a gash on her head.

Trout bent over her while Lauren hurried into the kitchen and returned with a clean tea towel and a bag of frozen fish. She folded the towel into a pad and placed it gently on the wound. "First thing I found," she muttered, placing the bag of fish on top.

Nikki groaned and stirred. She opened dazed eyes and frowned. "Tommy? What happened? My head hurts." She tried to sit up.

Trout slipped an arm under her shoulders. "Take it easy, Nikki, you're hurt."

"Bastard hit me." She started to cry, big silent tears streaking blood down her face.

Lauren kept the makeshift ice-pack in place while she used a wad of tissues to mop the blood and tears from Nikki's cheeks. "It's all right, Nikki, we're here."

Nikki struggled into a sitting position. When it became clear that trying to keep her lying down was only agitating her, Trout and Lauren propped her upright, one either side.

"I heard someone in Freddy's room." Her voice was faint. "I had dropped Jenny to the crèche, came back to get ready for work." She wavered, her head lolled onto Trout's shoulder.

"Don't try to talk, Nikki. You can tell me about it later."

"He was in Freddy's room, must have been looking for something ... I heard ..."

An advance paramedic jogged in, carrying her emergency bag, and squatted in front of them. She half smiled at Lauren's effort to stop the bleeding and indicated to her to remove the thawing bag.

"Let's have a look, see the damage." She carefully lifted off the tea towel. An ugly jagged gash ran across Nikki's hairline, blood coagulating at the edges. "Nasty." She grabbed a sterile pad and covered it. "That's going to need a couple of stitches." She tilted Nikki's head and withdrew a pen-torch from her pocket. "I'm just going to check your eyes." She moved the light back and forth across both eyes. "Eyes equal and reacting. Any headache?"

"A bit," Nikki mumbled.

"OK, I hear the ambulance outside – we'll get you to the hospital and give you a proper check-over."

"I can't go to the hospital, have to go to work, collect Jenny." Nikki was getting agitated again.

Lauren leaned in. "I can organize that for you, Nikki," she said quietly. "I'll get on to your husband – he'll sort it out."

"Yes, Eddie will sort it." She subsided, mumbled weakly, "Number on the fridge ..."

Lauren squeezed her hand lightly. "I'll find it." She stood up and carried the sodden towel and fish into the kitchen.

"We need to get her to hospital – she needs a CT brain asap." The paramedic was signalling to her colleagues to hurry.

The two ambulance paramedics skillfully maneuvered a stretcher into the hallway, collapsed it level with Nikki and carefully loaded her onto it.

They were wheeling her into the ambulance when an unmarked squad car screeched to a halt beside it.

Inspector Cooper levered himself out of the front seat. "*What's going on here?*" he demanded.

Trout inserted himself deftly between the trolley and the irate detective. "Someone was searching Freddy Loftus's room and attacked Mrs Gill when she returned from leaving her child to crèche."

"What are you doing here, Tegan? You're no longer a member of the Garda Siochána. You have no authority to be here whatsoever."

"Mrs Gill has retained me to look into her brother Freddy's death," Trout said mildly.

"Retained you? Load of bull. How can she retain you? You're nothing more than a private citizen!"

"I'm an associate of Danny Mortimer's and as such can be retained as a private investigator."

"You're a *what?*"

"An associate."

"I won't have it." Inspector Cooper poked a finger in Trout's chest. "I won't have you interfering in my case, trampling all over my crime scene, removing evidence ..."

"You have no say in the matter. I'm employed by Mrs Gill. As for your crime scene, getting my injured client tended to was a lot more important than investigating the scene. I haven't been any further than the hallway and," Trout lowered his voice warningly, "as you well know, Cooper, I don't tamper with evidence …"

The Inspector clenched his jaw, went to say something, thought better of it and swung round to Sergeant Driscoll who was standing beside their vehicle. "Call Forensics, get a team out here straight away. Then follow me into the house."

He marched through the open door without a backward glance.

The ambulance pulled away.

Trout took a deep breath and went to join Lauren in the kitchen.

Tony Driscoll joined them in the kitchen, dutifully transcribed their statements onto his phone and, with a careful look over his shoulder, accepted the cup of coffee Lauren had made him. He looked in another couple of times. Once to say softly, "No fingerprints. He must have worn gloves."

Eddie Gill had come rushing home from work, quickly changed into clean clothes and with barely a word to anyone had hurried to the hospital.

Later Tony looked in again to announce that the gardaí were finished and anyone who wanted to was now free to enter the bedroom. His wink as he said it left no doubt who his official tone was aimed at.

Trout and Lauren waited until the squad car was out of sight, then climbed the stairs. The door to Freddy's room stood open. Trout swore. Lauren clapped a hand over her mouth to smother a cry. The room was thrashed. Books were thrown on the floor, games scattered, the bed was upended. The drawers of the dressing-table were pulled out and the contents emptied, the stereo and speaker looked to have been taken apart. Even the wonky shelf was torn from the wall, its small treasures added to the wreckage on the floor. They stared at the carnage for a long silent moment.

"We can nearly guess what they were looking for."

"Does that ..." Lauren cleared her throat, asked on a shaky breath, "Does that mean they know the Guards didn't find anything significant when they searched the room that day they were here?"

"Yes," Trout said heavily. "It probably does."

They were back in the kitchen when Eddie Gill made a brief stop-over. He had little to add to their conjectures. He had gone to work as usual at six am and knew nothing more until Lauren had phoned him. He was back to collect night wear and toiletries for Nikki. The CT had shown no internal bleeding but the hospital was keeping her for twenty-four hours to monitor her in case of concussion. He had collected Jenny and delivered her to her aunt, two streets over, where she was having great fun being spoiled by her older cousins. He was nearly incoherent in his efforts to express his gratitude to Trout and Lauren, for coming so promptly to the rescue and for staying on in the house so he could be with Nikki. He left as soon as he had the bits and pieces gathered into a small duffel bag, still thanking them and reiterating that only for them being on hand Nikki could have been seriously injured.

Chapter 16

A subdued Trout and Lauren sat either side of the kitchen table, nursing mugs of coffee. The contrast between Nikki's neat, tidy kitchen and the destruction in Freddy's room was stark.

"Sitting here isn't getting us anywhere." Trout swallowed a mouthful of the cut-price brew with a grimace. "Would you be comfortable staying here on your own for a short while?"

Lauren was startled out of some deep contemplation. "I think so. Anyway," she hurried on, "I'm thinking that we can't let Nikki come home to find the room in that state."

"What can we do? You can't possibly clean it up yourself and I'm in no frame of mind to be gentle with the chaos in it."

"You think I couldn't?" She gave him a look but continued before he could say more. "I was wondering about our budget. You know that specialty cleaning service with the eye-catching vans? Home Magic, I think it's called. I read somewhere that they usually keep a crew on hand for emergencies. I could ring and see if they'd come and clean up for us."

Trout was staring at her. "That's a brilliant idea. It never even occurred to me. Do you think they might have a crew available this afternoon?"

"I'll call and ask. I can give them a hand, keep an eye on what's picked up. Whoever thrashed the room was so vindictive he might have overlooked something." She looked at him curiously but refrained from asking the question uppermost in her mind.

Trout anticipated her. "I'm going to see Danny Mortimer, make sure the associate thing is up and running. Knowing Coop, he'll check it. He's not the sort to take it as given, no matter how well he knows a person."

She nodded. "I'll ring Home Magic and see what they have available." She reached for her phone. "That reminds me, my laptop is in my bag in your car. I'll get it before you go and I can update our file while I'm waiting."

"No problem – I'll get it for you."

Lauren was busy accessing Home Magic's webpage to find their phone number and so missed Trout's admiring glance. He shook his head, briefly wondered what it would take to faze Lauren O'Loughlin, tribal O or not, and went to retrieve her laptop from the car.

She was smiling at her phone when he returned. She looked up. "There's a crew free. They'll be here in less than an hour. Looking at their online profile they sound amazing. I wish I knew about them when we were at college."

He placed the laptop in front of her. "Why?"

"Because," she grinned, "that's what we did when we were students and broke to the ropes. Cleaning. It was something we could fit in around classes. We were mega. Lucy and myself and another friend Anna did it between us. It was a bit boring mostly whereas this crowd specialize in cleaning crime scenes. How cool is that?"

"Sounds a bit gruesome if you ask me."

"Lucky I'm not asking you so." She turned back to her phone. "They really sound like the bee's knees. Super-professional. It says here they started out as a family-run cleaning agency until the daughter spotted a gap in the market for speciality cleaning. She was studying chemistry and decided to direct her studies towards cleaning crime scenes. Apparently, she's transformed it into a hugely successful business."

"That's where I heard the name before. They're the clean-up experts. Another great call."

"Flattery will get you everywhere." She laughed. "Go on with you! Tell Maisie I said hello."

"And you know whose good side to keep on." He was smiling as he pulled the door closed behind him.

Trout was exchanging banter with Maisie while she produced the associate form for his signature when Danny appeared in the connecting doorway, trailing a cloud of cigarette smoke.

"Special Investigator Tegan."

"Ex, Danny."

Danny sucked deeply on his cigarette and slowly added the resulting carbon monoxide to the air. "Two days on the job and you've apprehended a wanted criminal, got a house thrashed, landed your client in hospital and pissed off the most powerful man in Ireland's criminal underworld." He squinted through the haze. "I don't know whether to be impressed or apprehensive."

Trout signed the last page with a flourish. "What can I say, Danny? It just happened that way."

The big man sighed and turned away. "Come through and we'll have a chat."

He lodged himself behind the faded dignity of his desk and waited while Trout selected a chair. He took out a fresh cigarette, looked at it longingly and carefully replaced it. "I've promised the wife to cut back," he said sadly. "Currently I'm down to thirty a day, almost … days like today when a certain Marty Lambert is whispering sweet threats in my ear about one of my associates, it's touch and go."

"Marty was on to you?" Trout's gaze sharpened. He leaned forward. "Did he mention me by name?"

"I regret to say, yes."

"And he knew I was an associate of yours. Who did you tell I was coming on board?"

"That's the thing." Danny played idly with the cigarette packet. "Neither Maisie nor myself mentioned it to anybody. Who did you tell?"

"Nobody before today." Trout considered the implications. "What time did you get the call?"

"An hour, maybe an hour and a half ago." He flicked open the cigarette box, started to draw one out, pushed it back in and flicked the box behind the intercom. "What the hell's going on, Tegan? I've managed to run a business in this town for nearly forty years without a call from …" he hesitated, "anyone. I take you on and in two days I have a gangland fixer who thinks he's starring in the *Sopranos* telling me what I can and can't do."

"Did you record him?" Trout asked mildly.

"What do you think I am? I run a business here. If my clients thought I was recording their calls I'd have to close the door."

"He wasn't a client but I get the gist."

Danny banged the flat of his hand on the desk. "You get the gist? This is my business and I don't know what in tarnation is going on. So, Special Investigator Tegan, *I am asking you what's going on?*"

"Sometimes, Danny," Trout said very quietly, "you're better off not knowing. Plausible deniability and all that."

"Fuck it. I thought you might say something like that." He scrabbled behind the intercom, grabbed the pack of cigarettes and had devoured half of one before the flare of the lighter died.

Chapter 17

A thoughtful Trout clattered down the stairs and paused before releasing the door. He pulled out his phone, tapped it on his fingers, frowned and finally dialled a number from memory.

"How's things, Trout? Any more highfalutin' calls?"

"Maybe, maybe not. You out and about, Mac? It's probably too early for a pint but you tell me that place on Thomas Street makes real Barry's tea?"

"Barry's it is, boy, all the way from Cork. See you in fifteen. If you're there first, order a pot and a big slice of porter cake with it."

Trout smiled at the phone. If there was a more honest-to-goodness person in the world than Con McMillan he had yet to meet him. He wondered briefly was it right to involve him in the upcoming shit-fest but told himself that he was one of the few he knew for sure he could trust. Mac believed in law and order and showed no ambition other than being a true upholder of said law and order. Trout met him his first day on the beat. He started out as his mentor and ended up a solid friend. The two of them were a regular team for years and they shared a mutual respect. Once Mac made sergeant, he was content to do his work and so far had refused all offers of promotion. He was well over the minimum retirement age and proclaimed to all and sundry that he had no intention of leaving until the State kicked him out. Trout would and had trusted him with his life

The Teahouse was about halfway along Thomas Street. It prided itself on the quality and diversity of its tea and made no apology that the only other beverage it served was water. Trout was there in no time. He settled himself at a corner table and suddenly realized that he was hungry. He ordered a pot of tea for two, a ploughman sandwich and two slices of porter cake. A tray piled with mugs, a large brown teapot and two plates of food was being off-loaded as Mac marched through the door.

The burly sergeant was greeted like a regular and when he aimed for Trout's table the server deftly removed the spindly chair opposite and replaced it with a stout wooden one.

Mac grinned. "How's she cuttin', boy?"

"Good to see you, Mac. Thanks for coming." He reached for a wedge of sandwich. "You want one of these?"

"Nope. Got everything I need here." And he busied himself pouring out tea, slathering butter on the cake and cutting it into neat squares. Once everything was arranged to his satisfaction he took a sip of tea, savoured it for a moment and said, "I hear you're becoming a private dick instead of a public one."

Trout nearly choked on his sandwich and had to gulp a scalding mouthful of tea to help him swallow. "Jesus, Mac, you could have started a bit gentler on my ego."

"Ego, my eye! You're up to something. I didn't indoctrinate you in the ways of the Force without me learning something about you. Spit it out, boy!"

"It's bad, Mac. I'm not even sure I should be talking to you ..."

Mac snorted. Popped a square of cake in his mouth and chewed with the serene concentration of a cow chewing the cud.

Trout sighed. "*Something is rotten in the state of Denmark*," he quoted and started on another chunk of sandwich.

Mac nodded and waited.

"It looks like Freddie Loftus stumbled onto something that is making a lot of people nervous and he was killed before it was located. Someone bungled the job. His room at his sister's place was thrashed today and I mean thrashed but I doubt they found anything." He paused then said carefully, "Inspector Cooper himself turned up to assess the damage."

Mac raised a bushy eyebrow.

"He wasn't impressed to find me there and even less impressed when he found I was looking into the case for Nikki. Actually," he grinned, "he was downright steaming – maybe a bit more than the case merits ... and Danny Mortimer has had a communication from Marty Lambert that has him smoking like a chimney."

"He's always smoked like a chimney."

"But he was cutting down and now he claims the stress has scuppered his plans."

"Yeah, right," Mac refilled their cups. "Interesting thing, the lads scraped up a hit-and-run out near the Strand Road last night. A smalltime crook with big ambitions by the name of Leo Kelly. We pulled him in a couple of times but he's been quiet for a while. Rumour had it he was working for Marty Lambert."

"Harsh voice. I thought I recognized it the other night but couldn't put a name on it."

"We can nearly hypothesize he made the mistake of taking out

Freddy. We might be wrong, mind you but, between ourselves we might be right too."

"Marty Lambert keeps turning up. He's not usually so obvious. Why would he bother himself with small fry like Freddy?"

"You're forgetting the phone call – according to yourself, Freddy was supposedly calling Marty." He leaned forward, lowered his voice. "His prints were found in the cave ye routed the other day."

"Not his usual type of billet, probably a bolt hole where he could buy a bit of time in a crisis. Or maybe he was visiting somebody." Trout drummed restless fingers on the table. "The phone must be important. Was there anything on it?"

"Nothing back yet. I doubt there was anything on it. Only a bloody burner when all is said and done."

"Which raises the question, did Freddy get it himself or did someone give it to him?"

"Who knows?" Mac shrugged. "Freddy has had a fairly consistent work record for a long time now. Nothing raised a red flag that I could see ... He was tending bar at the club three nights a week, taking classes on two days at the Institute of Design and Technology and working with Miko Downes the rest of the time. Apparently, Miko's an uncle, a carpenter and a master craftsman. The word was Freddy was damn near as good as him. One of the top students in the college. They say his design and woodwork was beyond brilliant. And that's only what's legit. Who knows where he was doing nixers? You'd never know who or what he might have come across."

Trout looked thoughtful. "I knew Freddy's work was good but hadn't realized he was that good. He kept that one quiet. I don't know where it might fit in but, you know yourself, we won't know what's important until we know."

Mac cleared his throat. "Yourself and your retirement have stirred up a right hornet's nest, Trout. Are you sure retirement was your wisest course of action?"

"It was the only one." He levelled a look at Mac. "I won't ask you to keep this meeting to yourself because I know you will but, Mac, be careful. We don't know who's watching who and I'm afraid this could go all the way to the top."

"Back at you, boy. I'll let you know if I hear anything. Thanks for the tea." He looked around. "This here little spot isn't much frequented by the boys. It's a good place to meet and you're guaranteed a good cuppa." He nodded once, got to his feet and marched away.

Trout made one other stop on his way back to Nikki's house. The Institute of Design and Technology was housed in an old building that was holding on to its dignity by a thread. A new premises was under construction but in the interim this relic of old decency nurtured a diverse and eclectic bunch of students.

Trout was lucky enough to find the secretary of the wood technology department in his office. When he explained what he was looking for the rather morose individual produced a syllabus and a timetable that he said would show the times and classes that Freddy Loftus was signed up for.

Trout thanked him and went on his way wondering what, if anything, Freddy's timetable could tell him. But the biggest part of an investigator's job was gathering information. He always believed that it was easier to put information together when you had a diversity of facts. Something could jump out at you and spark an idea. He was mulling over the options when he turned off Gray

Street and found a large pink-and-purple van taking up most of the space in the cul-de-sac. A rainbow arching on both sides bore the legend, *Home Magic*. It wasn't discreet in any shape or form and he realized the he had often seen such vans zipping around the city or parked in various places. He pulled in behind it.

Lauren opened the door on his ring. "Nice timing. We're having pizza. Peter thought it would leave less of a smell than Chinese."

"Peter?"

"Yes. Peter and Sophia came to do the clean-up. Turns out Sophia is the daughter who started it all and Peter is her partner. We're all firm friends by now."

She led the way back to the kitchen. Two large take-away pizza boxes were open on the table. A guy of medium height with fading red hair and intense blue eyes was cutting one of them into triangles. He looked up and allowed his lips twitch into a smile.

"Ah, Lauren's friend. Good. Come. Have food." His accent was continental tinged with Dublin and even after years in Ireland his delivery betrayed that English wasn't his first language. He held out a hand. "Piotr, you Irish say Peter and that is fine. Lauren, she calls you like the fish, Trout – is OK?"

"Yep, it's OK. That's what my friends call me."

They shook hands. Peter's handshake was firm and Trout liked the direct way he spoke.

A whirlwind of dark hair and crackling energy erupted into the room from the back garden. "There, I've checked the garden. It's fine. Peter darling, is that the food? Goody. I'm starving." She was reaching for a slice when she spotted Trout. "*Ohoo, dishy!*" Her eyes laughed at him. She delicately licked tomato sauce from the side of the slice and added, "Lucky I'm taken or you wouldn't stand a chance."

"Stop teasing him, Sophia, and sit down." Lauren selected a slice of pizza. "We're not using plates – we'd only have to wash them again. So, dig in and we'll tell you about the clean-up."

"Yes. The clean-up." Sophia flopped onto a chair. "That was a vindictive thrashing if ever I saw one." The teasing tone was gone and she frowned, remembering the state of Freddy's room. "We've cleaned it up and Peter put the bed back together, replaced the shelf and repaired the dresser. It only needed a bit of glue and a couple of screws. We've put everything back as best we could and put the broken stuff into a box so that ..." she glanced at Lauren, "Nikki?" continuing on Lauren's nod, "can decide what to repair and what to dump. We did the best we could with the games and the books and Lauren personally picked up every coin, button and ..." She paused dramatically and threw a hand towards Lauren. "*Ta-da! The floor is yours!*"

"She's exaggerating, don't mind her. But, Trout," Lauren couldn't keep the note of excitement from her voice, "look what I found." She held out her hand. On the palm lay a small brass-coloured disk with a hole in the middle. "There were two of them. I put the other back in the jar."

Trout picked it off her palm and examined it. Engraved around the hole were the words, *Paddy's Locker*. He stared at it for a long while, turning it over and over. Three pairs of expectant eyes watched him.

In the end Sophia chirped, "Go on, I know you're dying to say it – we're bloody marvelous."

He smiled. "Well, as you've said it for me there're no need to repeat it. I guess I'm stunned really. I thought Paddy's Locker was most likely a code for, I don't know, some thing, some place."

"What do you think it is? It looks like a token of some sort." Lauren could contain herself no longer. "Remember the old slot machines in Rathmines? They used to use something like that."

"I think there might have been a game called Paddy's Locker," Sophia said. "Something about hidden treasure, maybe a shipwreck. Those old slot-machines were ancient when we knew them. Unless ... I wonder if there's a vintage gaming place around?"

"Vintage is popular." Lauren was thoughtful. "There's all sort of clubs built around it, even people who like to live as if they're from another era." They were all looking at her. "What? You know, those people who like to dress and live as characters from fiction or comic books – what's that they're called?" She stared into the distance. "I know – I edited a book about it not that long ago. Definitely in the last couple of years. What are they called?" She shook herself. "I'll think of it – and, if not, it will be in my records. Leave it with me."

Chapter 18

Trout stood and stared out the window. The events of yesterday lay heavy on his mind. His sleep had been fitful and the sense of something forgotten was a lead weight on his system. He brooded on the scene in front of him.

His house was the last, or the first depending where you thought the village began, of a straggling line of mismatched dwellings. They were for the most part cheerful, colourful and welcoming and in a surprising way were a fairly accurate reflection of their inhabitants. The Tegan home, a substantial two-storey from the 1920s, stood at an angle on the rise up from the street. It commanded a clear view of the first third of the village. It had been renovated in the early fifties when his father, the local schoolmaster, married Mary Bourke, the only daughter of a substantial farmer from a little way outside the village. The house was a wedding present from her father and they had used her dowry to renovate it into a comfortable home including, wonder of wonders at the time, putting in a bathroom.

This early in the morning peace and quiet reigned, not even Big Jack's mongrel stirred and he was the bane of the village with his barking. Trout allowed his thoughts to meander where they would, while tracking the street with his eyes. He followed the broad grey ribbon of road until it curved out of sight at *Madigan's Select Bar & Grocery, Purveyors of Fine Goods since 1899*. Trout considered the bend in the road. The case was a bit like that, some parts plainly visible until a turn obscured the way forward. He made a mental note to ring and see how Nikki was this morning.

The rising sun glinting off the gold lettering on Madigan's window drew his eye. They had always kept the place well and the next generation was carrying on the tradition. No need to mention that it was burned down in 1920s and the current, much more substantial slated building erected to replace the thatched two-up two-down. The success of the business was down to the people who ran it, and how it got there was of no consequence after all these years.

Trout felt the gut punch. "*Shit.*"

He closed his eyes, reviewed the last few days. How did he miss it? Why had nobody asked such an obvious question? Or if someone had, why wasn't the answer in circulation? No, he was more inclined to think that it had got lost in the happenings of the past few days. The big question of … How did Freddy get to Slí Buí?

Trout examined what he knew about Freddy, his history and his inclinations. Freddy was never one for joy-riding, and Trout could never remember him having a car. That didn't mean diddly-squat. He could have a car ten times over and Trout would have no reason to know about it. Any time they met it was in town and Freddy had taken a bus or the Luas.

And now another link: Miko Downes. Mac said he was an uncle and a carpenter. They would probably need to find him, see where he was based. Although what difference it might make to things

Trout wasn't sure. He glanced at his watch: nearly half-six. Mac would still be on duty. With a bit of luck he'd be free. He dithered for a moment and finally dialled Mac's private number.

"Morning." Mac saw no point in using two words when one would do.

"Are you busy?"

A grunt. Trout interpreted it as no.

"Mac, did anyone ever check if Freddy had a car?"

"Damned if I know." Mac lowered his voice. "Want me to check?"

Trout thought for a minute. "Not at the moment. If you do it could be flagged and I'd prefer to find out quietly if possible."

"Can't do anything quiet round here, boy, that's for sure."

"I'll try Nikki later and get back to you if need be. Any developments?"

"Not so you'd notice – just a memo warning that anyone found to be involved in assisting ex-officer Tegan in any way would be subject to getting their knuckles rapped."

"Right."

"Nothing new there, boy. Word on the vine says Inspector Cooper looked for a meeting with the Super and the two of them were closeted for most of an hour. Apparently Coop left it looking grim."

"Lovely picture you paint, Mac, you have a way with words."

"A word in your ear, boy, watch your step." Mac disconnected.

Trout stared at the phone until it went black. So, Coop and the Super had compared notes. Interesting. They didn't usually seek out each other's company. He wondered what conclusion they might have reached. He had once asked Mac about the antipathy between them. Mac had tapped his nose and said, "Too bloody alike the two of them." Trout had deemed it wiser not to ask for an elaboration.

Himself and Superintendent Glasson had locked horns on more than one occasion. Mainly when Trout thought Glasson was interfering in one of his special investigations. The Super was politically ambitious and as such often went out of his way to court publicity. On more than one occasion Trout had taken issue with him when he pushed his oar in at a particularly crucial point and potentially jeopardized the results. Most of the time Trout and his team were able to regroup but it left a bad taste and Trout had difficulty trusting the man.

The street had started to come to life but it was still early. He debated calling Nikki but thought he'd give her a chance to be up and about. Hospitals started early but there was no point in waking her if there was a possibility she was still asleep.

Eddie had been tired out by the time he'd arrived home the previous night. He'd left Jenny to stay with her aunt. He had told Trout he was hoping to pick up Nikki from the hospital around ten. Trout reckoned he would talk with her before then. He felt restless and dissatisfied. He wanted to thrash out what they had with Lauren but was wary of his need to do so. He thought of the gym he'd set up in the spare room – a couple of rounds pumping iron might settle the gnawing apprehension in is gut. The uneasy feeling that he had missed something more than Freddy's possible car was ping-ponging between his head and his belly.

The exercise and a good breakfast somewhat restored Trout's humour and he was borderline philosophical by the time he rang Nikki.

She sounded cheerful. Said she was up and dressed and waiting for Eddie to take her home. She was effusive in her thanks for his coming to her rescue, talking almost non-stop and bouncing from one thing to another. "And Eddie tells me your lovely lady and her friends cleaned up all the mess. She's a keeper, Tommy, I hope you know that," before going on to the details of her stay in hospital, what the doctors said, how nice the nurses were.

He let her talk, knowing that a lot of healing comes from being able to express your feelings in a given situation. Eventually she wound down and Trout slipped in his question, "Any idea, Nikki, how Freddy got to Slí Buí?"

"In his car, of course."

"I didn't realize he had a car."

"Oh yes. Eddie helped him out with it. A mate of his had an old banger going cheap, only don't get me wrong, it had passed the NCT and all that, so even though it was old it was perfectly roadworthy. We made sure he got his tax and insurance so it was all above board." She paused. "I suppose the gardaí took it from wherever he parked it."

"Maybe," said Trout. "But I heard no mention of it."

"Oh. So maybe he didn't take it there."

"But if he didn't take it there," he pressed, "where would he have left it?"

"At Miko's. Where else?"

"The carpenter, right?"

"Yes. Miko Downes. Our uncle … grand-uncle really. He's Granny Lofty's youngest brother. He was a bit of an afterthought, only a couple of years older than our dad. He came to live with Granny when his mam died. He never got married and stayed on when Granny Lofty passed. He'd tell Freddy the place would be his when it was his turn to go." She faltered, took a steadying breath.

"Miko's a bit strange but himself and Freddy got on well. That's where he went to get clean when you gave him that ultimatum. I was hoping he'd stay there but he was always a city boy at heart."

"I never knew." Trout blew out a breath. "Nikki, why would Freddy leave the car at Miko's? Surely he'd need it to get to Slí Buí?"

"Not at all. All he had to do was cross the road and take the path through the forestry. It would bring him directly onto the mountain and he'd know the car was safe. He was very attached to that car."

"Look, can you –"

"*Oh no!*" Nikki cut across him with a wail. "Nobody's told Miko! He can't hear it on the news, it would kill him. Tommy, Tommy, what'll I do?"

"Look, give me Miko's address and I'll go and see him, tell him what's happened and check for the car at the same time."

"Thanks, Tommy." Nikki sounded calmer. "I don't know what I'd do without you."

Trout disconnected, muttering, "What else don't I know about you, Freddy the Fly?"

Chapter 19

A google search of the address Nikki had given him turned up an Eircode for Miko Downes. After a quick call to ascertain that Lauren wanted to go with him, he keyed the code into the SatNav, collected her and was off. Killanee was the other side of Slí Buí and Miko's house turned out to be less than half a kilometre from where they had accessed the path that led across the hill to the caves.

"I'm annoyed with myself for not thinking of the car sooner."

"You have now," Lauren pointed out, "and it looks like nobody else thought of it at all."

"That's the thing. Why didn't they?" Trout gathered his thoughts. "The incident room will have a big map of the area with all that's occurred in relation to the case pinned around it. How come nobody wondered how he got from Dublin to Slí Buí? Or, if they did, why wasn't it followed up?"

"Lack of manpower perhaps." Lauren thought about it. "Maybe they didn't think it the most pressing problem."

"Maybe." Trout sounded doubtful. "Or maybe someone didn't want the car found too soon for some reason."

Lauren gave Trout a startled look. "Are you suggesting that … what exactly are you suggesting?"

"Hell, I don't know. Something doesn't sit right in this investigation …"

"Could it be you're frustrated that you don't have access to what's going on in the way you were used to?" Lauren asked quietly.

Trout was silent, a worried crease between his eyes. "Perhaps." But he wasn't convinced.

The Sat-Nav guided them onto a local road and off that up a narrow boreen that curved between old stone pillars and landed them in a stone flagged yard at the back of a small house. It was a grey, dismal building that sat sad and neglected on one side with a row of rough outhouses facing it on the other. The yard held two cars, a 96 maroon Mazda, dusty but seemingly in good condition, and an equally old jeep, battered and mud-spattered.

A dog created a hullabaloo from somewhere and Trout said, "Stay in the car until we see what sort of a reception we get."

A round-faced individual with a straggly comb-over appeared from one of the cabins with the barking dog prancing at his side. He held the dog's collar tightly with one hand and viewed them from under shaggy white brows with barely concealed hostility.

"State your business or I'll let the dog loose."

"Miko Downes?"

"Who's asking?"

"My name is Thomas Tegan. I was a friend of your nephew Freddy …"

"Was? Why wouldn't you still be?"

"Mr Downes, if you could just quieten the dog for a minute, I have some information for you. Nikki Gill gave me your address."

"Nikki?" Miko frowned. "Nikki sent you, must be serious then." He heaved the dog into the shed and slammed the door. "*Stay there, Maestro, and shut up!*" The last was shouted and the dog went quiet.

"Perhaps we should go in?"

"You'll tell me here or not at all." Miko straightened himself and folded his arms.

"Your call, Mr Downs, but the news I have is not good."

"Spit it out, man. I haven't got all day."

"Your nephew, Freddy Loftus, is dead."

"*Dead?*" The man looked bewildered.

"Yes. He was murdered on Slí Buí three days ago."

"Freddy? Freddy murdered?" The old man slumped against the door.

"I'm sorry but you insisted." Trout made a move towards the man. "Are you OK?"

Miko waved him away. "Just give me a minute," he muttered. "I was wondering what became him. I reckoned it must be serious when he left the car. *Murdered!*" He looked at Trout. "Was he the fellow they talked about on the news? They never said a name."

"Yes."

"Why didn't Nikki let me know before this?" Miko was getting belligerent again.

"She couldn't. She had to identify Freddy and then she was attacked at home and is in hospital herself."

That seemed to flatten Miko. "Nikki in hospital. Attacked at home. Is the babby all right?"

"Jenny's fine and Nikki should be home today but, Mr Downes, I really need to talk to you about Freddy."

"*Talk, talk, what's there to talk about? Freddy's dead.*" His knees seemed to buckle and Trout barely made it across the space to catch him.

"You need to sit down. Where can we go?"

Lauren was out of the car in a flash and beside the two men. "I'm Lauren O'Loughlin, Mr Downes – let me make you a cup of tea of something."

The old man's glazed eyes sharpened. "Loughlin? O'Loughlin? Any relation of Maggie O'Loughlin's over Knocknaclogga way?"

"She was my grandmother."

"Maggie was a great friend of Winnie's," the old man muttered. He seemed to have revived somewhat although Trout was still supporting him. "I suppose ye'd better come in," he said with a sigh.

He straightened himself and led the way, staggering only a little. The unlocked door opened directly into the kitchen. It was reasonably clean although very untidy. Piles of books and papers covered every surface except a wooden armchair that filled the space between the end of the table and an ancient range. Miko scooped up a couple of piles and cleared two chairs. He indicated they should sit as he dumped the papers onto another overflowing chair. The once cream range gave off a comforting heat and when Miko pushed the rather grubby kettle over the hot plate, the sound of its singing made the place feel homely.

"We'll have tea. The talk can wait till I get my breath back." He slowly busied himself with the paraphernalia for preparing tea. "I heard your mama passed on a while back," he said to Lauren. "I was sorry to hear it. My sympathy to you."

"Thank you. It was for the best in the end. The final stroke paralyzed her."

They talked back and forth in the way of finding common

ground until Miko said, "Sit in to the table, the tea's ready." He had moved the papers from the top half of the table and set out cups, a beautiful rose-pattern china one with a saucer for Lauren and a mug proclaiming it came from Trinity College for Trout. His own vessel was surely as big as a pint. He noticed Lauren looking at it. "Saves having to get up for a refill." He shrugged. He cut thick slices of home-made soda bread, buttered them, added marmalade and put one on a plate in front of each of them.

Lauren hid a smile at the look on Trout's face, cut her slice in half and took a bite. "This is really good! Did you make it yourself?"

Miko looked at her suspiciously, saw she was serious, and said, "Winnie taught me and she was the best baker in three parishes."

"She taught you well. This is the best bread I've tasted in a long while." Her eyes challenged Trout.

Reluctantly he broke off a bite and chewed carefully. He had to admit she was right and understanding that the acceptance of Miko's hospitality would make his questions more palatable, he proceeded to eat it all.

When they had finished. Miko rooted around on the window sill and produced a pipe and a pouch of tobacco. He pointed the stem at Trout. "'Tis coming to me now who you are. You're the gent who persuaded Freddy to clean up his act. Nikki, the silly chit, calls you Tommy."

Trout nodded.

"I was mighty thankful to you for that." He busied himself with preparing the pipe. "Tell me what happened now."

Trout told him all he knew including the phone call in the middle of the night, the ransacking of Freddy's room and the attack on Nikki. Miko puffed on his pipe and listened, his face guarded.

Trout finished, "The idea of a car only occurred to me this morning, Nikki gave me your address and here we are."

"You're an ex-cop. Where do you come into it?"

"Lauren and myself were discussing setting up a private investigation service and when Nikki asked me to look into Freddy's death, we decided to give it a go." Trout saw no reason to add Danny Mortimer into the mix.

"What can I tell you?"

"When did you last see Freddy and what sort of form was he in?"

"Let me see. Today is Friday, Freddy appeared Sunday evening. He was all excited about something but wouldn't say what. Said he was meeting a pal of his at the caves and he'd leave the car here. He expected to be back in a couple of hours and promised he'd fill me in in the morning."

"And that's all he said?"

"More or less. But," Miko closed his eyes, concentrated, "He had one of those mobile phone things, kept looking at it. He said something like 'This here baby is going to pay all my debts in the one go'."

"All his debts," Trout repeated. "And he didn't say what he meant by debts?"

"No. Just he'd fill me in, in the morning."

"Do the words *Paddy's Locker* mean anything to you?"

"Can't say they do." He puffed a bit. "Wasn't there an old slot-machine game called something like that? I've a feeling I played it in Ballybunion or some such place, oh years ago."

"Yes, possibly." Trout waited to see if Miko would ask why he was enquiring about Paddy's Locker. When he didn't, he asked,

"Would you mind if we have a look at Freddy's car?"

"No. He left the keys with me in case I needed to move it. What'll become of it now?"

"The gardaí will have to be told it's here." Trout hesitated. "Freddy's name is due to be released today, probably the media already have it," he said slowly. "Would you mind waiting until you hear the announcement on the news and then ringing it in?"

"I'm trusting you have a good reason for that request."

"I don't know," Trout said honestly. "Let's have a look in the car. It might have something in it that will help us."

Chapter 20

Miko led the way out to the yard. Trout stood a moment to study the row of outbuildings opposite. They looked old but were all intact, whitewashed and well maintained with tightly fitting stout wooden doors. He noted two at least had chains and padlocks to further secure them. Tools, he thought, and perhaps work pieces that would be made and assembled in a workshop and brought on site as needed. The doors and buildings looked as if they would be difficult to breach. So Miko was aware of security.

His wonderings were cut short when Miko stopped at the car and looked at him expectantly. "This is it."

Freddy's car was old but obviously much loved. No dent marred its exterior and underneath its coating of dust the maroon paintwork was well cared for. The inside looked clean and tidy. Miko fished a bunch of keys out of his pocket and Trout, after donning a pair of gloves retrieved from his car, took them. There were five keys hanging from a silver ring, attached by a chain to a small Swiss army knife. The car key was readily identifiable, as were the two door keys. Miko agreed one was his and the other was most likely Nikki's. Of the remaining two, one was an obvious padlock key but the fifth was an unusual one, flat irregularly grooved with random dots as if someone had written on it in braille.

Trout turned it over and over, examining it carefully. "Strange, I've never seen anything like this before."

Miko cleared his throat. "Yes. Well. It's the key of my toolbox and you'll find the other one fits the padlock on the workshop door."

Trout looked at him enquiringly.

Miko continued, "I'm a carpenter and toolmaker by trade but, in reality, I can turn my hand to almost anything." His voice held no boast. He simply made a matter-of-fact statement. "I've had a good little business going here many a long year." He looked into the distance, carried on heavily, "Freddy was shaping up to be a right good craftsman. He could put his hand to any tool. He had precision and a good eye." Miko's eyes blurred. He put a shaky hand on the car. "He favored woodwork and was a brilliant cabinetmaker but he was going to come and work with me and eventually take over the business ..." He broke off, turned abruptly away, blundered across the yard and disappeared through a small gate. They watched him go.

"Poor man, he's heartbroken." Lauren had tears in her eyes.

"That's a part of the fallout of these things that's usually forgotten, the ones left to grieve, knowing the senselessness of it all." Trout sounded sad then flashed with anger. "If only the little fool had come to me with whatever he had instead of going on a solo run!" He gave the nearest tyre a vicious kick. "*Bloody stupid git, wanted to be a hero!*"

A short intense silence ensued.

Trout shook himself, "Better get on with it." He opened the car and carefully leaned in to examine it.

The dog howled. Miko reappeared and hurried to open the shed door. Maestro jumped at him, barking and frisking around him. Miko quietened him and the two of them came and stood near the car.

Lauren stood to one side, watching and waiting.

The inside of the car was as clean as it looked outside. The pocket on the driver's door held a set of Allen keys and a novel by Jane Harper, bought second-hand in a bookshop near the Halfpenny Bridge. A litre bottle of water rolled in the footwell at the passenger side, a five-euro note and an assortment of change lay in the middle console. A pair of polaroid sunglasses sat on the dash. There was nothing under the driver's seat and no sign that anyone had ever used the back seats. Trout leaned over, unlocked the passenger door and moved around to that side. The glovebox held a substantial user's manual and a mobile phone.

"That's where he left it," Miko said. "He told me he was leaving his mobile behind in case anyone was able to track him with it but it wasn't in the house." He stopped.

Trout had flicked open the phone. It was password-protected but the icons showed that calls, messages and WhatsApps awaited. The battery was signalling low.

Miko continued, "I asked him why anyone would want to track him in the mountain, and he sort of laughed and said the fuckers he was dealing with could do anything." His voice trailed away, then hardened. "He knew that and still he went."

Trout sighed. "He thought he could get evidence for me that would put some very dangerous and elusive criminals behind bars. He had no idea what he was dealing with … Not really. And he trusted the wrong person." He replaced the phone and moved around to open the boot. The spare tyre, jack and wheel-brace were neatly fitted into their slots, a blue rucksack lay on its side, a paper bag with two vintage crime novels from the same second-hand book shop beside it. Trout pulled the books out to show Lauren. They were brown with age. "Freeman Wills Croft and Raymond Chandler," she said, smiling. "He certainly had an eclectic taste in crime."

A careful riffle through the rucksack yielded only a change of clothes and a washbag containing the usual accoutrements. Trout weighed the toothpaste tube in his hand, squeezed a blob onto his finger and smelled it. "Toothpaste." Likewise, on examination, the shaving foam appeared to be just that. He replaced everything as he found it. He studied the spare tyre before lifting it out of its well.

His eyes narrowed and he stared.

Lauren and Miko moved closer until they could see what he was looking at. Four small plastic bags of white powder were taped to the bottom of the well.

"*What? No way was he a druggie!*" said Miko.

"What does it mean?" said Lauren.

"OK." Trout dropped the wheel back in place. "We know Freddy hadn't taken drugs for years and I know that even when he was taking them he never sold. Somebody set him up before he ever he went on the mountain."

"By trying make out he did drugs?" Lauren sounded doubtful. "Wouldn't a blood test prove that wrong?"

"By making out he was a dealer. All they needed was to destroy his credibility." Trout's tone was grim. "And provide a decoy from whatever was actually going on." He looked at Miko, "Would you mind showing us your workshop?"

"No, I don't mind. I'll show ye but I'm telling you here and now

I'm taking those keys off the bunch before I hand them over to anyone else." His stance challenged Trout.

"You do whatever you have to do," Trout said quietly.

The workshop was a revelation. It was the length of at least two of the outhouses. The roof to the back was mostly made up of Perspex skylights and so the interior was flooded with natural light. Two workbenches, one steel, one wooden, were set into the floor at one end, an appropriate lathe attached to each, with a circular saw, winch bench and compressor lined up one side of them. Some larger tools and implements hung from hooks along the wall and lengths of timber and steel were stacked underneath them. Shelves held smaller items and some works in progress. The end wall was half-covered with floor-to-ceiling shelving holding an array of workmanlike items – the other half was taken up with a large steel structure, a leather tool-bag gaping open on top of it.

Between the workbenches stood a smaller mobile bench complete with a hydraulic platform and on it the most beautiful doll's house Lauren had ever seen.

She moved towards it. "Oh my God, what a beautiful piece of work!"

Miko moved to join her. "Freddy made it. It's a scale replica of some nob's house, out past the city somewhere."

"It's exquisite." She gently maneuvered the knob on the miniature Georgian door and the whole front swung open on well-oiled hinges. She gaped at the inside. The house was laid out with a dining room on the left, a sitting room on the right, both curling back to a kitchen area with a tiny utility room off it. In the middle a beautifully polished stairs curved upwards through the two stories to open into an empty attic space. Two bedrooms and a bathroom made up the second floor with the third divided into a library, an office and a games room. Each room was partially furnished as if Freddy had made the furniture when a suitable piece of timber or steel presented itself.

"I could play with this myself." Lauren picked up a beautifully carved dining table. "Look at the workmanship! "She placed the table back and picked up a mahogany desk from the top floor. "Remind you of anything?" She showed it to Trout.

He took it from her and laughed. "As I live and breathe, it could be Danny Mortimer's desk!"

"Yes." Her smile broadened only to sober on a thought. "He had such talent," She replaced the desk and closed the door. "What a waste!" she said sadly.

Trout looked at Miko. "I'd like to open your toolbox, if I may?"

"You've got the key," Miko said gruffly, pointing to the large steel structure. "Work away."

All three of them moved to the other end of the workshop. Miko hefted the tool-bag out of the way. The so-called toolbox, was unlike anything Trout had ever seen before. It was a steel structure nearly as tall as himself and looked as if it would survive a bomb blast. He inserted the fancy key into the slot Miko indicated. Silently and smoothly the whole box split in two. Each side was laden with equipment and swayed outwards from each other, the top rose upwards to display compartmentalized drawers of nails, screws, washers, rawl-plugs and a myriad other bits and pieces.

Trout whistled appreciatively. "Nice."

"Well, I've built up a good stock of tools over the years. In this business, if you're serious you buy the best. Freddy thought my security was crap and he sourced this here baby for the two of us."

Miko laid a reverent hand on the toolbox although "box" was far from the correct description. "It's got recessed wheels that you can activate when it's closed by pressing this here button. Freddy was charmed with it. He was big into design and functionality … *bastards!*" He looked at Trout. "You have to find the devils who did him in. Make them pay."

"Did Freddy ever leave anything here for safe keeping?" Trout asked gently.

"Like what? His design books are all here, if that's what you mean. He insisted on locking them away." Miko pressed another button and a drawer at the bottom slid into view. He half-smiled. "Young pup said he was going to write a book like that dead fellow who made all the designs." He thought for a moment. "Sheraton. That's him. Thomas Sheraton."

A couple of artist's sketch pads, a graph book and some notebooks took up most of the space, while a separate compartment held a slide-rule, calipers and a compass set like Trout himself had in school a long time ago. Various types of pencils filled the spaces in between.

Trout reached down and picked up the sketch pad. He flicked through it, stopped at a page and studied it intently. He lay the book on top of the box open at a page depicting a large house and reached for the graph pad. A quick flick through that and again the intent study of a page. "*Jesus!*" He looked at the two, baffled comprehension in his eyes.

Lauren was studying the drawing. "Isn't that a drawing of the doll's house?"

"Yes," Trout said. "It's also a drawing of Robert Carrig's house in County Dublin and this," he held up the graph pad, "is the scale replica of that house and the actual design for the doll's house."

"Oh my God!" Lauren clapped her hand over her mouth.

Miko looked between the two of them. "Is that the nob's name? Freddy never said but he visited the place a few times to make drawings and check out furniture and the like."

"He made drawings, took measurements, moved around the house freely, probably was there at times when Carrig himself wasn't," Trout muttered. He turned to Miko, "May I take these? I promise I'll keep them safe and return them when this is over."

"You can if you think they'll be a help."

Trout had a quick flick through the notebooks and removed one of those as well. He gathered them up and watched as Miko closed the toolbox and locked it.

"Miko," he said, choosing his words carefully, "you can't under any circumstance let anyone – *anyone at all* – know we've been here and taken away these books."

Miko gave him a long shrewd look. "'Tis like that, is it?" He nodded. "I'll remember."

"If they want to see the workshop just show them – you don't know who the house was for and as far as you're aware all that's in the toolbox is what was always in it."

"Freddy had a locker in that school place, maybe he left stuff there."

"The Guards have been to the College. I don't know if they looked for a locker. You can mention it if they get sticky, ask you where Freddy might have left things."

Together they moved towards the door.

"Make sure your workshop is well locked up," Trout said.

"Always do and Maestro takes care of the rest." Miko fondled the dog who was waiting patiently, lying across the threshold. "He's a good guard dog."

Trout took a plastic bag from the boot of his car, dropped the books into it and stowed it back in the boot. He peeled off his gloves and pitched then in as well. "What news do you usually listen to?"

"The one o'clock, when I'm eating my dinner." He pulled a big old hunter pocket watch from inside his coat. "In about ten minutes' time."

"That'll do perfect. When you've heard the news, ring the number they give out and report the car." Trout thought for a minute. "They'll want to know why you weren't bothered about him before this."

"He's done it before, hasn't he? Left the car and gone off for a few days. Just because it hasn't happened in a long time doesn't make it any less true."

"Right. We'd better make tracks and let you listen to the news."

"Aye, and wash away the signs of visitors."

"God yes. I hadn't thought of that." As Trout made to sit into the car, he held out his hand. "I'm truly sorry about Freddy. Thanks for all your help."

Miko shook it vigorously. "Just get the bastards, that'll be thanks enough."

Chapter 21

"I hear lunch calling, preferably in the opposite direction to wherever authority is likely to come from." Trout paused at the bottom of Miko's boreen. He studied the SatNav. "Looks like the main road is to the left so we'll go right. Any ideas?"

Lauren thought for a moment. "There's Malachy's. It's a pub-restaurant about equal distance from here and Knocknaclogga if you go the wrong way round. I mean, it's … never mind, just turn left at the end of this road and go right when we come to the four crossroads. We'll be taking what you might call the scenic route, all the small local roads, but you might as well be getting to know the by-ways as well as the highways."

Trout laughed. "Sounds just what we need. How far?"

"Twenty minutes give or take."

"That should do. We'll be well out of the way if anyone goes looking for us. Hold on to your hat!"

He followed Lauren's directions and in spite of the nature of the roads, floored the accelerator. They made it in fifteen. Lauren expressed heartfelt thanks that they were the only ones using that particular route at the time.

"Holy cow, Trout, what sort of speed does this thing do?"

"Enough to get us here and at a table being served when the inevitable phone call comes."

"What phone call?"

"Let's get settled. I won't pre-empt anything – we'll await developments."

Malachy's was an old road-side Inn that had survived all attempts to modernize it. A low off-kilter doorway dropped three steps into a dimly lit room and ensured that all but the shortest people needed to duck their head to enter. Only a sharp warning from Lauren saved Trout from decapitation. He had turned to point the key and check the car was locked as he approached the door and failed to notice the step down into the bar.

"Thanks," he said wryly. "I'd forgotten the death-trap for the unwary. It's years since I was in this place." He looked around. "It doesn't seem to have changed much."

The room was small with a bar on the left that occupied most of it. The polished wooden counter curved around out of sight and supported the elbows of half a dozen patrons who seemed totally engrossed in the food in front of them. The backdrop of carved oak was darkened by time and smoke and was suitably in keeping with the ancient feel of the place. The shelves were thick and solid, well stocked with all types of liquor and gleaming mirrors reflected what little light came from the mullioned windows. Three small, scrubbed tables awaited customers and further narrowed the passage to the back room and the main bar area. Blackened beams crisscrossed the ceiling, giving Trout the impression that he'd bang his head if he stood up straight. He knew it was an illusion; there was plenty of height but the misconception was disconcerting. He followed Lauren as she continued forward. Small interconnected rooms radiated from the bar area like spokes on a wheel. There was a good scattering of clientele at the tables. Mostly workmen on their lunch break. A good sign for the food, Trout thought.

A rotund man of indeterminable age came forward to greet them. "Afternoon, folks! What can I do for you?"

"Hi, Mal," said Lauren. "Lunch, please. For two. Is the patio open today?"

"Lauren! Good to see you – and your friend." He beamed at her, turned twinkling eyes on Trout. "Indeed, the patio is open. Not much call for it today so if you're looking for privacy it will be perfect." Again he gave Trout an assessing glance.

"Thomas Tegan, Trout to his friends," she said. "Trout, meet Malachy Hennessy, proprietor extraordinaire of this establishment."

"Now, now, Lauren, you know it's Damien's cooking that brings people here and of course your book." He turned shrewd eyes and studied Trout more openly. Whatever he saw seemed to please him. "You are most welcome, Thomas Tegan. I find your sobriquet … interesting. I look forward to the day we may use it here with impunity. Come," he beckoned expansively, "this way."

He plucked two menus from the bar as he passed and led them to where a wooden veranda perched drunkenly against the outside wall. A raised floor allowed for a somewhat level seating area overlooking and with access, via some rough wooden steps, to a well-tended garden. Four tables were dotted randomly around, well distanced from each other, set and ready for diners, but the place was currently empty. Mal showed them to a generous-sized, solid wood table and left them to decide on their meal. They opted to sit side by side, with the intention of discussing their visit to Miko.

"A book and first-name terms with the proprietor?" Trout raised a quizzical brow.

"You're out of the habits of a small locality, Trout. As for the book, that was Damien's. I only edited it. It was a cookbook he did to raise funds for the hospice. It was actually great fun. Mal took the pictures."

"Cookbook? Was it by any chance called *Damien Roche's Year in Recipes*? I've seen in my mother's collection."

"That's it. It did really well but, besides that, the food is fabulous here. They use local produce, some from their own garden and it's all cooked fresh. Mal is a dote and Damien can take the plainest fare and deliver a Michelin-worthy feast. It takes a bit more time but is well worth it. Mal will only serve what he'll eat himself so the daily menu is a bit limited variety-wise but wait till you taste the offerings. It's beyond excellent."

"He certainly looks well fed –" Trout held the rest of his comment as the man returned with a carafe of water, two glasses and cutlery wrapped in tissue.

"Are you folk ready to order?"

"Well, I am," said Lauren. "I'll have your special fish and chips and –"

"A large salad on the side," said Malachy.

"Well called. Yes, thank you." Lauren was pleased that he remembered.

"I didn't think you were that predictable." Trout smiled to take any sting from the comment.

"You haven't tasted their fish and chips!" Lauren shot back

"Yourself? The same perhaps?"

"I'm looking at the steak – how do you cook it?"

"Whatever way you want."

"Rare, not blue?"

"Absolutely. Our sirloin is perfect for rare. All the trimmings?"

"Yes – sauce separate though."

"A man after my own heart. Anything to drink?"

"Water is fine for me. I'm driving. Lauren?"

"I'll have a glass of your house chardonnay, please."

"There will be a little delay – everything is prepared fresh. I'll bring you a little something to nibble while you wait and your wine, of course." Mal nodded to himself and lumbered away.

"You've made a good impression." Lauren leaned forward. "Only the approved ones get 'a little something' at lunchtime …"

The burr of Trout's phone interrupted her. He held up a warning finger and half smiled as he answered. "Hi, Tony. What's up?"

Garda Driscoll stuttered over greetings and plunged into an account of Miko's phone call and the possibility that Freddy Loftus had a car. He seemed particularly aggrieved by that as he himself had checked with Vehicle Registration and found no record of a car in Freddy's name. Apparently, the registration cert had been stuck in someone's in-box …

Lauren's phone jangled.

Out of the corner of his eye Trout saw her root in her bag and take out her phone. She frowned at the screen, swiped it open and said a cautious "Hello?" With Tony Driscoll burbling away in one ear, he cocked the other to hear Lauren's conversation.

"Inspector Cooper?" Her frown deepened. "Where am I? I don't see why that is any of your business."

Malachy returned with a plate of nibbles: olives, tiny crackers with smoked salmon, pâté, cheese and sun-dried tomato, curls of melba toast arranged around a ramekin of sauce and a generously filled glass of wine for Lauren. He looked disapproving to see them both on phones.

With Tony still recounting his tale of woe, Trout mouthed thanks, smiled and gave Malachy a thumbs-up. He shrugged and left them to it.

Lauren was listening to her phone, her face flushed, her eyes wide and incredulous.

"Cooper thinks you were there," Tony said. "There's no reasoning with him. I hope you're not anywhere near the place?"

"I'm in Malachy's having lunch. Not sure where that is in relation to your site." He reached for a cracker and popped it in his mouth.

"Probably not far enough away to satisfy him." Tony launched into an account of the aggravation the investigation was causing him.

Across the table, Lauren said, "As it happens, Inspector, Trout is here with me. We are having our lunch in Malachy's." The iciness of her tone would frost glass. She listened then drew in a sharp breath. "Excuse me – I've been working all morning. Am I a suspect in something, Inspector Cooper? Because if not you have just gone way over the line. It would waste a lot less time if you actually investigated the case instead of harassing innocent by-standers." She paused, listened. "I'm not accusing you of anything, Inspector, but if the cap fits, wear it!"

Lauren disengaged and for good measure turned off her phone. She lobbed it into her bag, made a grab for her wine, thought better of it, picked it up gently and took a sip "What a horrible man!" She glanced at Trout, saw he was still on the phone, took another sip of wine and selected a nibble with trembling fingers.

Tony Driscoll said in Trout's ear, "Did you know Freddy Loftus had a car?"

"No. He never struck me as the type to own a car, but then I never met with him except in town."

"The old duffer who rang ..."

"His uncle, you said, Tony." Trout's voice held a rebuke.

"Grand-uncle actually. He said Freddy had come to visit him by car once or twice and even left a car there before so he didn't worry about it until he heard his name on the news. Oh, and sir," Tony lowered his voice, "that Rasher Madigan, he's on the wind – neither his wife nor his girlfriend have seen him for a week. *Ahem* ... yes, Inspector ..." He continued in an officious tone, "So if you come across any relevant information –"

"*Tegan!*" came Cooper's voice. "If I find you anywhere, and I mean *anywhere*, near my investigation, I'll have you arrested for obstruction of justice." The phone went dead.

Trout looked across at Lauren . "Well, that was interesting."

She scowled at him. "Inspector Cooper is an obnoxious git," she enunciated clearly. "What is his problem?"

"He doesn't like me anymore and you've got caught in the crossfire. Also, he's out of his depth, and he's probably realized that the someone pulling his strings would have no problem eliminating him ... if he thought Coop was unable to make the investigation go away or at the very least point it in a direction that wouldn't implicate a certain, shall we say, organization."

"Oh! OK, when you put it like that ..."

Their food arrived and the aroma that wafted from the plates was enough to drive everything else from their minds. For the moment anyway.

By unspoken agreement neither mentioned the case until both were replete. They lingered over coffee.

Trout leaned back and said, "So you were working all morning, *hmmm?*"

"I was. FYI, I had four hours work completed on my latest manuscript when you called and I've spent the last couple of hours on our TLCI case. All work."

"I like the sound of TLCI." Trout's eyes were half closed. He had the relaxed alertness of a lion contemplating an approaching wildebeest. "Every time we pull a thread it unravels in a different direction. There has to be a hub somewhere. Something that links them all."

"Robert Carrig keeps cropping up. Could Freddy really have found something lying around the house? Presuming he had a free run of the place?"

"Anything's possible. It could even be something innocent enough that if it was combined with something else could turn into dynamite. He had those papers. Where did he get them?" Trout pursed his lips. "I'll have to go through them again, bearing in mind that Freddy had access to Carrig's mansion."

"Does anyone know –" Lauren started.

Trout laid a warning finger to his lips. His eyes flickered sideways. A couple of men had climbed the steps and come silently onto the patio. The smaller one grabbed a chair and quietly rammed it under the door handle in such a way as to make it impossible to open from the inside. In unison they jerked two empty chairs around and straddled them, effectively blocking Trout and Lauren inside the table. The bigger of the two bared his teeth in a parody of a smile, the smaller one just looked mean.

"Well, howdy doody, if it isn't my old sparring partner – Special Investigator Tegan. How're you keeping, Tom?"

"Good, good. And yourself, Rasher? A little bird told me you were gone AWOL." If possible, Trout looked even more indolent as if any minute he would slide into a puddle of satiated slumber.

"*Tut, tut*, Thomas. Do I detect a little finger on the pulse of what you should be keeping your nose out of?"

"Gossip, Rasher, it's a terrible thing the way people talk. Am I acquainted with your little friend?"

Meany snarled. Rasher put out a hand and stilled him. "I don't think you've had that pleasure. Yet. But the day is young. We could organize something if you're interested."

"I'm retired, Rasher. I'm not interested in anything you have to offer." Trout sounded bored.

"No offer. I'm looking for something you have that a mate of mine wants and, Thomas, I intend to get it."

"What would that be, Rasher?"

Rasher narrowed his eyes at him. "The fuck you don't know."

"I don't know but if you can enlighten me as to what it is I could be even more sure that I don't have it."

"The data-stick Freddy the stupid noob was foolish enough to steal."

"So that's what all the fuss is about." Trout smiled wolfishly. "I was wondering at the over-reaction on all sides. Sorry, Rasher, I don't know anything about it so I can't help you."

"Let me loose on him, Rash, he'll soon change his tune." Meany leaned forward, his lips curled into a cruel grin.

Again, Rasher put out a hand and stilled him. He tried to make his tone reasonable. "Thomas, old pal, at this stage you're the only one who could know." He rocked forward. "It did occur to me that you might be a bit reluctant to part with the information but then I said to myself a little encouragement will jog the Special Investigator's memory. *Voilà*." He jerked his thumb towards where Meany was resting a small-caliber gun on the back of the chair. Its barrel was elongated with a silencer. He had it aimed directly at Lauren's heart.

"French, Rasher? I'm impressed." Trout didn't stir, simply continued in his conversational tone. "Language is interesting, isn't it? Take Lauren there, words are her business. She understands the sounds ... and the meaning ..." He huffed an explosive "*Kyup!*" and upended the table onto the two thugs. Lauren threw herself backwards, holding onto the chair as it flipped over and landing with a thud on the wooden flooring. The gun made a popping sound and a bullet embedded itself in the wooden railing, Rasher raised his head to glare, Trout caught him with a left hook to the chin and sent him spiralling on top of Meany, upending them both into a tangle of arms and legs. He grabbed the gun and stood over them.

Lauren picked herself up,

"You OK?" He kept his eyes on the two.

"Yes, thank you. Well called." She righted her chair and dropped onto it as her legs gave way.

A rattling at the door attracted Trout's attention. The commotion had brought people running only to find the door barred. Trout circled the two on the ground, keeping the gun steady on them, and kicked the chair from under the door handle. It surged open to reveal a tall muscular individual brandishing a carving knife. Malachy was beside him, waving a frying pan, shouting, "What's going on?"

A diverse group of their clientele, mostly by the look of them workers from a nearby building site on their lunch break, crowded in after them.

"We had a bit of excitement with these boys." Trout never took his eyes off the two. "They tried to hold us up – demanding money. I managed to get the gun from the weedy one but we need to secure them. Anyone got zip-ties? Sorry about the this, Malachy. It never occurred to me that we would be bringing trouble to your door. Could someone call the Guards?"

A red-headed young fellow hurried off and came back carrying a handful of ties. "They're cables ties, will they do?"

"We'll find out. Yourself and your pal there, one of you pull the arms and hands together at the back, the other fasten the ties. Same with the legs and, for God's sake, don't get in the way of the gun."

Trout stood over them until both men were trussed and lying like beached whales.

"The Guards are on the way!" someone called.

"Who are these people?" Malachy was wringing his hands as best he could while holding the heavy pan. "What are they doing on my premises? Trying to intimidate my customers!"

"Lauren!" Damien was beside her in half a stride. He hauled her into a bear hug. "Are you all right?" Holding her one-armed, he swished the carving knife through the air. It made a sibilant hissing sound. He glared at Trout. "Anyone who hurts my friends deals with me."

"Again, I can't apologise enough for drawing these two bucks on you. They're trouble wherever they go." Trout kept his tone even, transferred the gun and held out a hand. "Damien, I presume. That steak was the best I've ever had."

"Lauren's friend." Damien pumped his hand enthusiastically. "Mal told me she had someone interesting with her." He scowled at Rasher. "And these scumbags interrupted your lunch!"

"The gardaí will be glad to put cuffs on them." Trout retrieved his hand. "Luckily, we had just finished eating." He turned to Malachy. "I'm afraid there's some damage – when you have time to assess it, I'll settle whatever's owing." He shook his head. "If I had any inkling this would happen, we –"

"You didn't do anything," Malachy interrupted. "These, these," he shook the pan at the trussed pair, "dared to disrupt your lunch!"

Trout was anxious to get going. "Would you have some sort of clean plastic bag?"

The bag was produced. Trout dropped the gun into it. "Can you manage from here? Tell the Guards that Thomas Tegan disarmed them and his prints will be on the gun."

Rasher glared at Trout with the one eye that was visible. "*You'll pay for this, Tegan!*"

"Sure, Rasher, sure, but right now I've somewhere to be, can't stop and chat." He held out a hand to Lauren and pulled her into a quick tight hug.

Mal pressed a card into his hand. "Come back soon. We'll introduce ourselves properly – you'll both have a meal with us."

"Thanks. We will."

He bundled Lauren out before him.

Back in the car, he drove off before she had her seat-belt tied.

"Should we not wait for the guards?"

"I don't think so," he said quietly. "As far as I'm aware only Cooper and Driscoll knew where we were. I'm not waiting around to see who else turns up."

Chapter 22

They drove in silence, engrossed in their own thoughts. Trout wondered where the pattern was and why Freddy's car was ignored when it had already been seeded.

"Do you think Miko Downs is on the level?" he asked abruptly.

"Miko?" Lauren surfaced from her own thoughts and gave the question due consideration. "My gut says yes."

"So does mine. It's just seems strange that he didn't try even to contact Nikki when the car was there for more than a day or two."

"I bet Freddy told him he might have to leave it there for a while and not to make a fuss about it."

"That's possible, I suppose. Wouldn't you be curious?"

"I don't know. Miko knew Freddy's history, he saw him as his successor so obviously in spite of everything he trusted him. I'd say he took it all at face value. But … I wonder if he knows more about Freddy's intentions than he's told us."

"What makes you think that?"

"We're presuming that everything we've come across is linked, right?"

"I've discovered during my years of connecting dots in investigations," Trout's tone was dry, "that all the associated incidents of a main event are somehow part of it."

Lauren smiled. "Ergo, Miko knows something."

Trout took his eyes off the road to look quizzically at her.

She counted off on her fingers. "One, he didn't do anything about the car. Two, he knew Freddy had more or less free access to some nob's house even if he claimed not to know the name. Three, he'd heard about Paddy's Locker, didn't even have to think about it. I know he gave us that vague sort of memory of having played a game called that years ago but, oddly, he didn't ask us any questions about why we were asking."

Trout nodded thoughtfully. "We'll need to talk to him again … First, we need to sit down and review what we have … and revisit the stuff in the Cluedo."

"And I need to go through my files and find the information about the people who are into the vintage scene. It was like they were living in a parallel universe but right here in the real world." She stared out at the passing countryside. "It's niggling at me as if it might be important," she half-laughed, "or maybe I'm just annoyed that I can't remember what it's called."

"Right. I'll collect the stuff from my place, we have the notebooks in the boot and we'll have a regroup and strategy session when we get to yours."

They settled into Lauren's conservatory. The table was big enough for both of them to work comfortably and had an under-shelf where they piled the papers for easy access.

"We'll go through each one individually, make notes on anything that pops and we'll compare what we've got afterwards. Are you happy to leave the vintage angle until later?"

"Sounds like a plan. My files can wait. The ones I want are in the attic. I can get then whenever."

They worked in silence, reading, sifting, noting.

After a while Trout stirred, stretched and asked, "Any chance of coffee?"

Lauren barely brought her attention to him, saying vaguely, "Top cupboard, water's in the kettle. I'd love a cup."

Trout was pleased to see a decent array of coffees and a four-cup French press and he had a pot prepared in no time. He added a dash of milk to Lauren's mug, filled it with coffee and left it on the window ledge beside her. He smiled to himself at her absentminded thanks and went back to his reading.

Eventually they both surfaced and looked at each other.

Lauren blew out a breath, "*Phew!* What now?"

"Now we collate what we have, put it –"

"Hang on," Lauren held up a hand. "We need more coffee and possibly something to eat."

"Sounds good."

"Two minutes and I'll rustle up something."

In no time, she returned with a tray bearing coffee, a plate of ham, cheese, olives and grapes, crackers and cutlery.

Trout had taken a page from the largest sketchpad and attached it to the middle of a large rectangle of cardboard he'd retrieved from where she had left it, a flattened-out box ready for recycling. He had written Freddy's name in the middle of the page and propped the board against one of the windows.

"It's makeshift but it will serve as our evidence board so we can see all the bits and pieces together."

Lauren nudged the papers to one side and set down the tray. "Good idea."

"We'll start with names – see how they connect and with whom."

Trout loaded a cracker, popped it into his mouth and chewing contentedly started adding names to the board with a black marker. *Robert Carrig aka Bowser Corrigan, Marty Lambert, Rasher Madigan, Sam Maguire* and *Leo Kelly* with a question mark, all went neatly across the top. He added *Nikki, Eddie, Miko* on the left and *Inspector Cooper, Sergeant Driscoll* and a row of question marks on the right.

He reached for his mug of coffee.

"We'll connect what we're sure of in red and leave the lower end of the page for random information."

Lauren was frowning. "Who is Leo Kelly?"

"Mac mentioned him – he was the fatality of a hit-and-run the other day and we wondered if he was the one who topped Freddy."

"Because he was the victim a hit and run?"

"No. But he was known to work with Marty Lambert's gang so hypothetically he was a hit-and-run victim because he failed to retrieve whatever Freddy had and killed him in the process. It's speculation – we'll put him in with a question mark."

Trout proceeded to draw red lines. By the time he was finished the whole page was crisscrossed with lines. "It looks like Freddy was personally involved with all the main players."

"Looks like Freddy got his hands on a USB of Carrig's and was negotiating with Marty to return it, then rang you, but by mistake, when he found he had walked into a trap on the mountain."

"I don't know about giving it back. I'd have thought that would defeat the purpose of taking it in the first place but he did ring me and it would appear he did so from memory. It's possible the number he thought he was ringing was only a digit or two different from mine. And, let's face it, if he hadn't rung nobody would have associated him with any of them. Hell! We wouldn't have ourselves if we had simply found his body."

"But why Slí Buí in the first place? All these lads were townies – surely they would have been more comfortable in their own environment?"

"That's a good question. Maybe Freddy suggested it thinking he'd have an advantage on them, not realizing that the caves were already being used as a hide or a meeting place. But for what? That's what we need to know."

He took another page and made a rough sketch of the mountain, the caves, the position of Knocknaclogga and Killanee in relation to them. He added the roads around the area and their accessibility to the motorway. He pinned it beside the names page.

Lauren was studying the board. "The caves were in regular use judging by the supplies we saw. It must have been more than a temporary arrangement." She nibbled thoughtfully on a cracker and cheese. "Could they be some sort of a holding place? By your map the motorway is much nearer to Slí Buí than I would have thought it was."

"I see that too." Trout considered the map. "It might work as a holding or transfer site. It would need to be something small or at least light enough to carry easily. There's still a good distance to trek from either direction. We saw no sign of tracks that would indicate the use of quads or bikes."

"They'd draw too much attention. The farmers and the

164

Archeological Society ran a campaign a couple of years ago to have all vehicles banned from using the tracks. They were messing up the surface and damaging the environment. It was largely successful. A spate of young fellows chance it, every now and then, but not enough to cover regular activity."

"There's still a lot of small things that might need temporary concealment and could be carried easily in a rucksack."

"Like what? Drugs?"

"Drugs, money, jewelry, phones even, anything really that's portable and not too cumbersome."

"Did they find anything more than we did in the caves?" Lauren finished her coffee, took a sheet of paper and wrote *To Do* on the top.

"We haven't heard about anything from the caves except what Jax and Mac told us about Marty's fingerprints. I'll follow up on that. If there was drugs residue it would link back to the seeding of the car." He leaned forward and made a note on Lauren's *To Do* page.

"Is that possible that drugs residue would show up on the rocks?"

"On the rocks, in the boxes, on the clothes. You'd be surprised at what can be detected by Forensics. If there's any hint, especially of drugs, they can usually tell."

"Amazing really what's possible."

"Well, if science fails, the dogs will sniff them out."

"Remind me never to take up a life of crime."

"Unfortunately, the more sophisticated forensics gets the more creative the criminals get." Trout started to fill the bottom of their evidence page with incidental information: *doll's house, Paddy's Locker.* "I did wonder if Paddy's Locker could be a bog version of 'Davy's Locker' but somehow it doesn't work."

"We'd nearly have heard of it." Lauren made a note. "I'll get up into the attic and search out my old notes. The doll's house is fabulous. According to his notes, Freddy was making it for his final year project as well as having the commission from the Carrigs. Is there any chance he hid something in it?"

"Like a clue? You examined it more than I did. What do you think?"

"Well, some of the furniture is quite sturdy and the doors on the built-in presses all open and close." She thought deeply. "I wasn't looking for anything in particular so I can't say. Might be worth another look. If we're going to see Miko anyway I can examine it while you're talking to him." She added it to the To Do list. "Trout," she hesitated, then rushed on, "did you notice the detail Freddy went into in his sketches and comments? Are you sure he didn't have some … ulterior motive?"

"Like he was casing the place?" Trout said slowly.

Lauren nodded.

"No. I don't believe it. Freddy had his own, strict code of honour. When he gave his word to whoever, right or wrong, he meant it and he kept it. The doll's house is a scale model. The detailed drawings are just Freddy's way of making sure he has it right."

"I'll take your word for it. You knew him, I didn't, but there's something about those drawings … They're nearly too detailed … something doesn't feel right."

The crunch of tyres on the gravel drew their attention outside. A bicycle swerved to a stop in a swirl of dust. A lanky teen waved at them, propped his bike against the wall and started towards the conservatory door.

Chapter 23

Trout pulled their board face-down as the young man gave a perfunctory knock and entered. His eyes shining, he blurted, "Is that your crime board?"

"Hello to you too, Brendan," Lauren said tartly.

"Hi, Lauren." He grinned at her. "I've come with information."

"What sort of information?"

"About the murder. Mrs Dillon was in the shop and she said anyone who knew anything, no matter how insignificant should come and talk to you."

"I see." She turned and indicated Trout. "Brendan, this is my friend Tr … ah, Thomas Tegan – he's a detective."

"Hi, Thomas."

Trout said very seriously, "Did you tell anyone you were coming?"

The young man became defensive. "No. I didn't tell anyone. I watch telly so I know if you tell anyone the bad guys find out and, *poof*, next thing you know you've met with an 'accident'." His fingers described punctuation in the air.

"That's a good call. What do you think we should know?"

Suddenly the boy deflated. "Well, it's just … I don't know … but when Mrs Dillon said … I thought … It's probably not important …"

"Let us judge whether it's important or not. Sometimes the smallest thing can be the key that unlocks a case. Why don't you sit down and tell us?"

"OK." Brendan folded himself onto to one of the chairs.

"Would you like a drink of water? You look as if you cycled hard to get here."

"Yes, please."

Lauren fetched a jug of water and three glasses from the kitchen. She handed one to Brendan and filled the other two for herself and Trout. They each took a cool mouthful.

Brendan cleared his throat. "Mrs Dillon was in the shop this evening." He turned towards Trout. "You know, Sallins', on the lower road?"

"The one with the petrol pumps?"

"Yeah. That's the family business and we all have to work in it whether we like it or not." He considered his grievance for a second then said fairly, "At least Dad pays us proper wages when we get old enough and Mam says we learn responsibility." He looked up. "I'm going to be a detective – well, a Guard first when I'm finished school." He looked shyly at Trout.

"Good for you. If there's anything I can advise you on feel free to ask."

"Wow, thanks! Anyway, sometimes, you know, I'd be practising observing things, like the number of a strange car, or the type of card a person pays with, that sort of thing, and I noticed this guy that's turned up maybe three times – it could be more but I've dealt with him three times." He stopped.

"And?" Trout prompted.

"Well," Brendan shifted uncomfortably, "I'm almost sure he was the same guy but, you see, he looked sort of different every time, like his hair was black one time and fairish another time. And he had glasses then he hadn't. And," his voice speeded up, "the car was the same make but had a different number each time and the name on the card was different too."

"What made you think it was the same person, when there were so many differences?" Trout kept his voice neutral.

"His hands," Brendan answered promptly, then blushed. "I mean, most people don't notice a person's hands but they're really individual and sometimes I challenge myself to recognize a person just by looking at their hands. It's easy enough with the locals but the people who only come now and again are really interesting … " He trailed off.

"Tell me about this man's hands."

"They were, you know, sort-of groomed, like he'd had a manicure. The nails were shaped properly, even the cuticles were pushed back, and … the third finger of his right hand had a silverly scar across the top." Brendan was indicating his fingers. "The nail came over it but you could see it plain when he held out his hand to take something and," he hesitated, then finished in a rush, "he always put in his pin with his middle finger."

"I'm sure it's not that unusual to use the middle finger?" said Trout.

Brendan shook his head, "Most people tap it in with their first finger, this guy always used his middle. I noticed it particularly, especially as it was easier to see the scar when he did it."

"Well observed. Was there anything else you picked up on?"

169

"The car," he said promptly. "When we were kids my mates and myself used to study cars." He grinned. "To see what type we'd get when we were grown up – course we were always changing our minds but there was this one car we were all mad about, a BMW M3, six-cylinder turbo engine." He looked at Trout, cleared his throat." Anyway, that's the car, it's metallic grey with maroon seats and cool sport wheels, only one of the nuts must have been lost on the back passenger wheel and someone put a different one on and forgot to change it. It's not that much different but it is noticeable …"

"Nicely spotted, and that's the car with different plates," Trout smiled at him, "Did the driver stop for anything in particular?"

Brendan thought for a minute. "He got a fill of petrol every time, like maybe he'd come a long journey and still had a way to go."

"Was there any particular time he came?"

"When I was there it was in the evening, after school and study so maybe seven o'clock or a bit later. We close at eight."

"Did he come from the same direction every time?"

Brendan frowned, concentrating. "Yeah, he pulled in to the pumps from the left, same side as his tank – he never had to turn the car to fill her."

"When was the last time you remember seeing him?"

"The day before the Guards came. No, not that day, the day before that. He was grey-haired that day with thick black-framed glasses. He was in bad humour, very snarly. I've got the numbers of the car." He produced a small dog-eared notebook, opened it and handed it to Trout. He looked at him, his eyes hopeful. "Do you think any of it is helpful?"

Trout was copying the numbers onto the *To Do* sheet. He looked up. "It's very helpful," he said gravely. "And I must impress on you the importance of not breathing a word of this to anyone."

"I won't. I promise I won't say a word but," he wriggled his thin shoulders, leaned forward, "will you tell me what happened? Afterwards. Please?"

"Yes. We will. Lauren will give you a call, you can have tea with us and we'll tell you everything."

"Cool."

"But, Brendan," Trout waited until he had the young man's full attention, "it all depends on you keeping shtum."

Brendan made an exaggerated cross-my-heart gesture. "I will."

They watched Brendan mount his bike and ride away with a spurt of gravel.

"Trust Mrs Dillon," Lauren said wryly. "What do you think?"

"There goes a clever young man. The Garda will be lucky to get him. He's hit the jackpot there."

Lauren raised an interrogative eyebrow.

"Marty Lambert has a crooked top to the third finger of his right hand. He sliced it off while playing with one of his dad's knives when he was a child. Apparently, the surgeon in the emergency department did a right good job, saved the top of the finger except for a slight scar and a barely noticeable curve."

Chapter 24

"Christ, it's been a long day." Trout rubbed a hand over his face. He glanced at his watch, "And it isn't even seven o'clock yet."

"There isn't much more we can do here and we're both tired. I vote we call it a day." Lauren was shuffling papers, separating them according to their content. "Hang on, I'll get a box." She disappeared in the direction of the utility room and returned carrying a long, low cardboard box with colourful artwork that proclaimed it once held lemons from Assam. She layered the papers across the box in such a way that they could be identified at a glance. Trout folded their evidence board and placed it on top.

"I'll take them," he said. "I need to figure how best to keep them safe and I have no intention of inviting any more trouble than necessary to your door."

"Thanks. I'll give a quick look in the attic when you're gone and we'll be ready to resume tomorrow. What's on the agenda?"

"We'll review the To Do list in the morning and decide where to go from there." He looked at it ruefully. "We didn't get that much on it in the end. I'll talk to Mac at some stage tonight or in the morning, see what I can find out. He'll run the car numbers if I ask him but I'll probably leave it. I don't want to bring too much attention to what we're doing." He noticed Lauren frown. "Mac's as straight as a die, except maybe if Cork were playing in an all-Ireland final."

Lauren laughed. "Well, if that's his only weak spot I'll accept him as a worthy participant in our cause."

She walked Trout to his car.

"Would you like to come for breakfast?"

"Yes, I'd love to."

"Half eight be too early?"

"Nope, perfect. See you then."

Trout lugged the box into the sitting room. It was the least cluttered room in the house and he had set it up as his office. He dumped the whole lot onto the table that served as his desk and looked about for a good spot to hang the evidence board. He finally propped it on the mantelpiece. It sat above a small stove that fitted into what was once an open fireplace. He stood back. Yes. It was at a good height for contemplating. He turned his attention to the box of papers on the table and flicked through them. They were mostly Freddy's and to his knowledge no other copies existed. That made them vulnerable. First of he needed to make copies and to this end he gathered them into a bundle and carried them into the kitchen. His mother had a printer tucked into a corner of the kitchen worktop. He made two copies of everything and carried the lot back to the sitting-room-office. Now he needed to secure them. He looked around – the stove, cushions, bookshelves, all way too obvious. His eye fell on the supply of pre-paid postal bags his mother kept for sending impromptu presents and an idea presented itself.

He chose the largest of the padded bags and made short work of filling it with a complete set of the copies he had just made. He sealed it and addressed it to himself at the apartment in Dublin. He knew neither his mother or father would open it and there it would remain safe until he needed it. He left one set in the box along with Jax's folder in case himself or Lauren wanted to check on anything, folded the To Do list and carefully slipped it into his pocket. He gathered the originals and the sketchpad and considered his options. He wandered back into the kitchen and pushed the sketchpad casually into the jumble of the books on the shelf beside the Aga. Then smiled, his mother's folder of recipes cut from magazines and papers was lying across the top shelf. He distributed the pages between her cut-outs.

When he was satisfied that he had done all he could, he rooted in the freezer, found a dish of his mother's emergency lasagna, debated with himself and popped it in the oven. His mother had no time for the microwave and prepared her dishes to be cooked appropriately. He set the timer, shrugged into his jacket and hurried to the postbox in the middle of the village. As the package slipped into the box, he noted with an unexpected sense of relief that he was on time for the late evening post.

Trout enjoyed his lasagna with a couple of glasses of Chianti Classico. The wine, from a family winery in the hills of Siena, bore the black cock logo and was one of the wines Trout had his eye on. He intended to promote it once he had his business up and running. It was a wine with the clear ruby colour and the floral notes of the much more expensive Selezione and Trout felt it would be perfect for a family restaurant that served good food without too many embellishments. He was pleased to have discovered it on one of his meandering tours around that part of Italy.

He leaned back on the chair, savouring a mouthful of wine. He felt replete, almost content. He should have asked Lauren to join him, he thought drowsily. A small grating noise impinged. He frowned, rubbed his nose, strained his ears and pinpointed the whereabouts of the sound. Someone was trying to open the back door without the benefit of a key. Silently he let the chair back on its four legs. He slipped out of his shoes, padded to the front hall and paused briefly to retrieve his gun from the console drawer. He had a licence to carry as a private citizen, he reminded himself grimly, as he eased open the front door and slithered along the side of the house with the stealth of a stalking lion.

He flattened himself against the corner and peered around. A person all in black, a hoodie covering his head, was crouched by the back door, carefully manipulating a tool in the deadbolt knob. As Trout watched he heard the hiss of satisfaction and watched while the intruder stood to dismantle the Yale lock on top.

Trout raised the gun and stepped away from the wall.

"*Thomas! Thomas Tegan! I know you're there in the garden,*" a woman's voice carried clearly on the evening air. "*I can see the front door is open!*"

Trout saw a flash of a balaclava-covered face and startled eyes as the intruder swivelled, saw him and clocked the gun. He set off at a dead run before Trout could react, skirted the shrubbery and vaulted the wall into the field at the back of the house. He had sprinted out of sight in seconds. Trout swore. An engine fired up in the distance and the sound of a car taking off with speed echoed on the still air.

"There you are!" An elderly lady, bespectacled and determined, trotted along the garden path. Her momentum would have her at the corner in seconds. He swore again under his breath and turned to meet her, hastily stuffing the gun into the waistband at his back. He hoped his top was sufficient to cover it effectively.

"Good evening, Mrs Dillon." Trout hoped he sounded more civil than he felt.

"Good evening, Thomas. I was passing and I thought I'd call in to see what progress you've made with the trouble on Slí Buí."

"It's not for me to make progress, Mrs Dillon, it's a Garda matter."

"Nonsense! The Garda are very efficient, I'm sure, but they don't have local knowledge." She sniffed disdainfully. "It's up to us to clear the mess before it contaminates the whole community." She peered up at him, bird-like eyes darting behind her glasses. "I'll come in and sit for a minute and you can tell me all about it."

"There's really is nothing to tell but you are welcome to come in."

She snorted and preceded him into the house.

Trout surreptitiously returned the gun to the drawer and closed it in passing. "May I offer you a glass of wine?"

Mrs Dillon planted herself on a chair by the kitchen table. "You may and if it's anything like the stuff you recommended for Lucy to serve in the hotel, I'll enjoy it immensely."

Under cover of getting a glass, Trout checked the back door, removed the slim high-tensile pick stuck in the knob and relocked the door. He slipped the lock-pick into his pocket.

He returned with a stemmed crystal glass into which he poured a generous serving of wine.

Mrs Dillon sniffed delicately and sampled a mouthful.

"Delicious," she pronounced and sat back to enjoy her drink. "Now, what progress have yourself and Lauren made on the case?"

Trout was immediately transported back into the last century and the local school. He felt like a small boy summoned to explain his latest high-jinks to the teacher.

"Well ..." he said cautiously.

"None of your hedging, mind. I want the truth."

Trout refilled his own glass. "*Sláinte!*" he toasted, sifting through the information in his head to decide what to tell her.

"*Salute!* It *is* Italian, isn't it?"

"Yes. A Chianti Classico from the hills above Siena. I think it's rather good."

"Perfect. Now, no more waffling – information, please."

He gave in on a sigh. "You realize everything I tell you is classified and cannot be repeated to anyone."

"Teach your granny to suck eggs, would you, young man? Get on with it."

"The murder victim was identified as Freddy Loftus ..."

"Loftus, Loftus, there was a Winnie Loftus over Killanee way, would he be anything to her?"

"She was his grandmother."

"She had a brother, Mick, Mike, something like that. A right good tradesman if I recall."

"Miko. He's living in her place and was training Freddy to take over the business."

"Was he any good?"

"Who?"

"The grandson, Freddy."

"He was an exceptional craftsman, was studying wood technology and design in the Institute. What I've seen of his work is first class."

"That sort of skill is handed down in the genes. What a waste of talent to get murdered! Why was he killed?"

"He pissed off some seriously dangerous people and to make it worse he did it because he thought he was helping me."

"Was he?"

Trout looked at her.

"Was he helping you?"

"Yes," he said shortly.

"I see."

Suddenly Trout realized she really did see. Mrs Dillon had no illusions about people yet she championed what was good and did her best to keep what was bad to a minimum. He made the decision there and then to tell her the full story. It was a chance to put it in order in his head and perhaps get feedback from someone uninvolved but familiar with the nature of people. He divided the remainder of the wine between them and told her the story to date.

She listened without comment, sipping her wine, her eyes occasionally flickering alarmingly. When he finished, she said, "I don't like it, Thomas. There are undercurrents that I don't fully understand. You tell me these people have been using our mountain for their evil purposes. No wonder there's been disquiet around."

"What exactly do you mean by disquiet?"

Mrs Dillon thought for a minute. "I've noticed a restlessness in the young people that I hadn't seen before. Something was stirring them up but it wasn't anything I could put my finger on."

"Could it be drugs? Are they much of a problem around the area?"

She sighed. "I'm not so naïve as to think we don't have a drug problem but it's been pretty well contained. Our young people are still involved in sports and music and such things and while it won't stop the problem it does tend to postpone the age of experimentation until children are older and less under the parental thumb. That can be a great help in giving young people a chance to decide what's worth taking a risk on."

"You have a point there. I certainly haven't noticed any signs of what you might call drug culture around nor have I seen any vandalism in the village. Is that something people complain about?"

"There are always people who complain but by and large it's not a problem. There was a bit of a fuss last year when some kids spray-painted the sport field wall but, to be quite honest with you, I thought it improved the look of it and it resulted in the local committee plastering and painting the wall properly. So I'd hardly count that as vandalism."

"Has anyone been unexpectedly flashing cash? Maybe someone that wouldn't be expected to has shown signs of extra money recently?"

"Interesting you should ask that. I've heard talk ..." she hesitated, "gossip really and I don't usually hold with gossip but for what's worth ... apparently Pa Jones has been flush recently, in a way that doesn't correspond to the amount of work he does."

"Jones." Trout frowned. "Do I know him?"

"He'd be a good few years ahead of you at school, you may not remember him. He could be sly and wasn't above pilfering if he thought he'd get away with it."

Trout smiled. "You classified all of us, didn't you?"

"It's been my observation, young man, borne out by all my years teaching, that the boy is the father of the man," Mrs Dillon said tartly. "I can only think of two instances where it didn't follow through and I was of the opinion that one of them was acting out of character in the first place."

"And the other?" Trout was curious.

"Time will tell but I'm pretty sure there are things hidden that will eventually come to light."

Trout hid a smile at her ominous tone. "Pa Jones. OK. Anything else? Even little things can sometimes offer illumination."

"Speaking of which," Mrs Dillon perked up, "did young Brendan Sallins contact you?"

"He did."

"There's an exceptionally bright young man. Reminds me a bit of yourself. Not as nosy as you were but very observant. I thought to myself that if anyone was likely to notice anything he would. So, I just dropped a general hint when I was in the shop this evening. Was it any help?"

"If that's your version of a hunch, it paid dividends. I've warned him to keep what he said to himself. For his own safety, I didn't mince my words but I didn't want to frighten him too much either."

"Brendan has a good head on his shoulders. He'll keep his own council. Always did, he ... *glory be to God!* Is that half twelve! I should be at home in bed." She shot out of the chair and fussed around finding her coat and umbrella.

Trout insisted on walking her home. Her house was at the other end of the village and, while she protested, he could see she was pleased to have his company. The street was quiet, families and their dwellings were, for the most part, dark and peaceful. They walked unhurried but with intent and conversed softly. Mrs Dillon had a pithy comment to make on nearly all of the households.

At one stage she stopped and looked up at him. "Now, Thomas, tell me why exactly you were out in the garden when I arrived?"

"You don't miss a trick, do you?"

"I could see that I interrupted something but it did occur to me it was for the best. Especially as it looked suspiciously like a gun you tucked into your waistband."

"Jesus!"

"There is no need to take the Lord's name in vain, young man."

"You really do have X-ray eyes. I was beginning to doubt it, now that I've been out of school for a few years."

She laughed. "Flattery won't save you. I still expect you to tell me."

"I had an uninvited visitor trying to get in my back door, but your arrival effectively routed him."

"I see. Dangerous and definitely not a game." She thought for a moment. "You'll get to the bottom of it. It's your way. I always know my children's abilities."

Trout appreciated once again that Mrs Dillon knew the nature of people, knew and still had faith in them. He thought of how aware she was of the politics, for the good or the bad, of the village. She knew the foibles, eccentricities and strengths of the community; both from her years teaching and her years living in it. She was a respected figure and people trusted her, knowing instinctively that their secrets were safe. Secrets that would only be divulged in a matter of life or death and then only if it would truly, in her opinion, make a difference.

All these things passed through Trout's mind as he bid her goodnight and waited until he heard her door lock click into place. He walked home quickly, his eyes and ears alert. His mind was fizzing. His nose was itching. He recognized the portents.

The strands were converging, tangled and knotted as they were. He knew one pull in the right direction and all would unravel.

Chapter 25

"Be the japers, Trout, are you intending to round up all the wide-boys we've had our eyes on these past few years, all by your lonesome?" Mac answered his phone in full flow.

"What can I say, Mac, they keep turning up. Wherever I am, there they come. At least the last two did." Trout's tone went from lighthearted to grave on the turn of the sentence.

"That so, boy? Had you advertised your location? That location thingy on the phone is a terrible nuisance."

"The location app on my phone is disabled. Although I'll have to admit I never even thought of it. I had rather laid the arrival of our callers firmly at the feet of your colleagues."

"It may be so but I've often warned you about preconceived notions. Didn't I drum it into you that anything preconceived can blind you to what's under your nose?"

"First day on the job, Mac." Trout felt suitably contrite. "And the advice has stood us both in good stead all these years."

"Righto, boy. This here situation is a shade too delicate not to have your I's dotted and your T's crossed. So, what can I do for you besides give you advice?"

"A couple of questions. Does the name Pa, I presume Patrick, Jones ring any bells? And I was wondering if anything turned up in the cave that might point towards what it's been used for?"

"Offhand I can't say I know the name. Let's have look-see. This here magic machine spits out answers if you happen to know the question you want to ask it." Mac's breathing filled the airways.

Trout imagined him laboriously printing the name, one-fingered, focused on getting each letter right.

The breathing stuttered into speech. "Patrick Somerset Jones, Knocknaclogga, that your boy?"

An image of Mac, squinting at the computer, his lips moving as he read the report filled Trout's mind. He smiled. "Somerset sounds a bit out there but the address is right. What's the story?"

"Nothing much on him – he was pulled in a couple of times, drunk and disorderly, failure to pay a television licence, driving with no tax, usual sort of thing. Fines paid. None of it shouts major criminal to me. What's the interest?"

"Not sure. His name came up. Seems he's been flashing cash lately that has the locals wondering if he's come into a legacy. I'm wondering if he fits in somewhere in our picture. He'd know the area and could move fairly freely around. He's probably too unreliable to be a mule if drugs are in the equation but …"

"No drugs. Not in the caves anyway. We brought up the dog but he had no interest except to go for a run in the heather – but we found something as good …" Mac lowered his voice. "As nice a little bundle of notes as you could ask for in a month of Sundays. Beautiful they were, clean and crisp and ready to spend. Twenty grand no less. Only thing was, the central bank never issued them. Not a halfpenny of them were legit."

"Counterfeit?"

"Lovely job too. Passed the finger test no problem. Damn nearly good enough to be real. The fraud boys are ecstatic – they've been trying to get a handle on the problem this past six months. Mind you, Sammy boy has closed up tighter than a bad mussel in boiling water so they're getting no joy there. Still, if they can join a few more dots there's a chance they'll convince him it's in his own best interest to talk."

"What sort of notes?"

"Mostly small denominations. Nothing bigger than a fifty, lots of twenties, a few tens, slip one here and there, pay off a few small jobs and you've a nice spread-out circulation. Your lad might fit the bill there, a retainer to keep an eye on local activity, a mix of notes and Bob's your uncle."

"You reckon they're that good."

"They are. They haven't figured out the process of printing yet, but I'm telling you, boy, even the infra-red had difficulty spotting them."

Trout thought about it. "Lauren noticed how near the caves are to the motorway even though you'd never think it. Notes would fit the bill for something easily transportable. They're light, easy to carry and were stored in a fairly assessable location."

"Hardly enough there, though – the boyo had only five thousand on him. Unless they're a consignment buried somewhere in the bog. If that's the case they're there to stay. That loophole is closed now." Mac was silent for a beat. "I guess the big boys will lie low until the heat dies down … Your girl has a good head on her."

"I'll pass on your compliment, even though she'll hardly appreciate the honour it is to have Con McMillan praise you." Trout paused. "The next big question is: where does Freddy fit in? And what did he do to get himself shot?"

"Could he have noticed the dud notes? The club was an ideal clearing ground, especially later on in the night when people might not be as observant as earlier. Although I'm telling you, Trout, even the experts had difficulty telling them apart."

"Could he have discovered the scam or even come across the information somewhere? Rasher claimed they were looking for a data-stick and it looks like Freddy may have had fairly free access to the Carrig house. Bloody hell, Mac, why didn't he come to me with whatever he had instead of going off halfcocked on a solo run?"

"He was young and enthusiastic." Mac sighed. "No point in getting into a lather over it, boy. It's done now and you need to keep a cool head and see to it that he didn't die in vain."

Trout took a deep breath. "Right as always, Mac. The break will come. We just need to be ready for it."

Later that morning Trout let himself into Lauren's house by the conservatory door. He tutted to himself when he found it unlocked and made a mental note to remind her be more careful, especially while the investigation was ongoing. He sniffed appreciatively as the smell of freshly baked bread wafted towards him and drew him into the kitchen.

He stopped abruptly, captivated by the sight of Lauren shimmying around the kitchen, setting the table and singing along to the Eagles' 'Desperado'. She had a good voice, singing true and holding the notes like a professional. She took a breath to lower her voice into "*Desperado!*", swung round, saw him and stopped. "*Oh!*"

"Keep going, I was enjoying the show." He was leaning casually against the jamb, a smile playing around his lips. "You're a really good singer."

"Thank you." Lauren sketched an exaggerated bow and reached to turn off the music.

"Leave it on, I'm a fan." Then in a stunned voice, "It's a record player. You're actually playing vinyl?"

"Of course. It's the only way to listen to the Eagles."

He moved fully into the kitchen and picked up the record sleeve. "It's the original album cover."

"It's the original album," Lauren said dryly. "I bought it at a sale of work when I was about ten. It was pristine when I got it and I guarded it like gold-dust." She slanted him a glance, "And there's no need to remind me that it's from the last century."

"I wore mine out I played it so much." Trout's voice was tinged with nostalgia as he turned the cover to look at the tracks. "Anyway, I'm well back in the last century myself as it happens – I had a visit from Mrs Dillon last night." He laughed. "It's funny how you revert to your schooldays whenever she's about. I felt like I was being summoned to account for my actions in the playground."

"I know what you mean and she wasn't even a Tartar but she has a way of looking at you that says 'I know all about you'. Did she want to hear about the case?" She gently lifted the arm to the side and clicked off the player. "Breakfast's ready, you can tell me all while we eat."

Trout recounted the events of the evening. Lauren was a good listener. He told her about posting the papers to the apartment in Dublin, the routing of his unwelcome visitor and the subsequent observations of Mrs Dillon. All the time he was speaking a part of him marvelled, for the umpteenth time, at how comfortable he felt discussing the case with her.

"She's a prime old bird and, boy, does she have a grasp on what's going on in the area!" he said.

Lauren nodded. "She seems to have a finger in every pie going. Of course, she's taught at least two generations of the parish and is either friends with or keeps in contact with two more."

"That's a broad span – are you sure you're not exaggerating just a little?"

"Think about it, her age group are her contemporaries, she taught their children and grandchildren and she's involved in a living communities project that connects the elderly with the youth. I'd say she has an insight into every man, woman and child in the county."

"Point taken. She talked about a Pa Jones. Can't say I can place him but apparently, he has rather flexible morals."

"Pa. I know him. Always wanting to know everyone's business. More of a chancer than anything else, I'd say, but then how does one know? If a person is shady in one thing, chances are he's shady in a lot of things." Lauren looked into the distance. "Like, what would he do if the reward was greater?" She threw her hands wide and shrugged.

"As indeed it might be. I talked to Mac this morning." Again, Trout proceeded to fill her in.

"Counterfeit money! Jeepers!" Lauren sounded worried. "Are we all walking around with dud notes if that's the case?"

"It's a possibility but I doubt there would be that much around here."

Lauren threw him a sceptical glance.

"Pardon my English but no dog shits on its own doorstep if it can help it," he said. "We're thinking the caves were a holding centre so they'd want to keep attention away from them, therefore the immediate locality would be a no-go area. I reckon the distribution would take place well away from here. Anyway," he shrugged, "the notes would stand a better chance being circulated in a bigger population spread."

"That changes if Pa was involved," Lauren pointed out. "All he'd see was money for porter."

"There's been no talk of the banks questioning the money being lodged from the shops around here." Trout downed the last of his coffee and reached for a refill. "Mac said the forgeries were excellent but still the banks have quite sophisticated methods for checking their notes. They didn't find that much in the cave, only twenty thousand, mostly in twenty and fifty-euro notes."

Lauren choked on a mouthful of coffee. "*Only* twenty thousand!" she spluttered.

"Pocket money to these boys. Maguire had five thousand euro on him. That's about a day out at a small race meet."

Lauren was staring at him, a stunned expression replacing her normal calm.

"Money has a different value, Lauren, when you don't have to earn it." Trout was very serious. "The crime gangs deal in a cash economy, drugs, counterfeit of all kinds, that's why sometimes our only recourse is through Revenue. It can be difficult to hide cash flow without a noticeable income. Having access to legitimate businesses, high-end goods that sort of thing, is a huge plus."

"I wonder ..." Lauren frowned at the piece of bread she was buttering.

Trout watched her and waited.

She took a breath and looked at the window. Trout could almost see the cogs spinning as she assessed the thoughts inside her head.

"I found the file on the manuscript I talked about. It was five years ago ... it started off as a treatise on Cosplay that was turned into a book. It actually did well sales-wise." She turned towards him. "Do you know what Cosplay is?"

"No. I can't say I do."

"The eventual book was called *Cosplay – A Lifestyle, A Life-choice*. It was by a couple called DeeDee and Alain Hirst. I met them numerous times. They were very intense, very committed to their ideals and completely invested in their lifestyle which they called Cosplay. Basically, as I was saying that day, Cosplay is a lifestyle choice where people choose to dress up and live their lives as fictional characters or historical figures. It can be from a period of history, or an era like the 1920s. It can be a character from a work of fiction or a super-hero ..."

"These people actually live in fancy dress?"

Lauren smiled. "You could say that but to them they are choosing a way of life more in tune with their sensibilities. It can be an occasional thing, like weekends or evenings after work or like the Hirsts a lifestyle they adhere to. When they wrote the book, they were going through a nineteen-twenties period. DeeDee was channeling Eileen Gray and Alain fancied himself as Marcel Breuer. They had acquired some really fabulous furniture ..." She trailed away, added in a rush, "They came to mind when you talked of high-end goods."

"Are you seriously telling me these people pretend to be someone else and live the lives others have already lived?"

"Sort of. They generally only live the good bits."

Trout laughed. "And they wrote a book?"

"The Hirsts had a lot of experience in the field, as it were. They had already lived as a number of historic and literary figures – Lord Byron and Lady Caroline Lambe come to mind – but there were many others. They had less success with the comic books as they found the super-hero culture a bit limiting and had no time for the memes although, because the Japanese love them, they had experimented for business purposes." Lauren put an elbow on the table and propped her head on a palm. "It's a very expensive hobby and as a lifestyle the costs are exorbitant. The Hirsts are no fools. They run a company that supplies custom-made costumes, and money seems to be no issue for them." Her head flew up. "Oh my God, I've just realized their company is called The Clothes Locker! You don't think there's any chance it's connected to Paddy's Locker?"

Trout thought about it. "Maybe. Probably a long shot but these people sound as if they're nuts so anything's possible."

"Hang on." Lauren hopped up and was back in a couple of minutes with her laptop. "They used to have a website." She was half-muttering to herself. "Here it is. The Clothes Locker." She clicked into the site and quickly scanned the information. "Yes. Just as I thought – '*Clothes from all eras and civilizations, suitable for Cosplay, Film and Theatre productions or for people who enjoy experiencing the fashions of another generation or genre*' – each era is divided into lockers and labelled accordingly – *Catwoman, Daniel Boone, Emma Woodhouse, Little Bo Peep* …"

"Emma Woodhouse?"

"Honestly, Trout," she flicked him a disdainful glance, "haven't you read Jane Austin?" She went back to her perusal of the website. "It's got pretty tight security settings. It says here: '*To browse all our collections, sign up to our community newsletter and get a free consultation to determine your ideal Cos-world.*' Hmm. I wonder." She opened a new tab and brought up her email account.

"What are you doing? There's no need to get yourself involved in –"

"Not involved, research. The book I'm working on at the moment is a period piece and I intended to research the clothes of the era anyway. DeeDee really knew her stuff. I'm just sending her a request to pick her brains about the early twentieth-century clothes."

"Are you sure that's wise?"

"What's unwise about it? It's a bona-fide request. Worst-case scenario I'll get all the info I need without the hassle of going to a hundred-and-one sources." Lauren was typing, her fingers flying over the keyboard as she talked.

"I don't know," Trout said. "It's just that your hunches have a way of paying off and I don't want to expose you to danger."

"I appreciate your concern," Lauren smiled across at him, "but we can't cross a bridge until we come to it." She tapped send. "There! We'll deal with whatever comes out of it when we have to. So, what's on today's agenda?"

"Another visit to Miko. I want –"

Lauren's phone jangled. She picked it up, "It's a message from Brendan." She swiped the screen, opened it.

"You have Brendan Sallins' number on your phone?" Trout tried not to sound surprised.

"Of course. I've lots of young people's numbers. I give grinds – it's the easiest way to keep contact," Lauren answered, distracted. She frowned over the message, then said urgently, "Brendan says the car is there, different plates and a driver he hasn't seen before – he'll try and stall him if we want to get to the shop fast."

"Jesus!" Trout was on his feet. "We'll take your jeep, my car is already on their radar. Have you ever tailed anybody?"

"No." Lauren grabbed her bag and keys, followed him out and quickly locked the patio door.

"Trust me to drive it?"

She silently tossed him the keys and hurried round to the passenger side. In minutes they were swinging out her driveway and heading for the lower road and Sallins' Shop.

Chapter 26

As the Vitara approached the junction to the lower road, a grey car peeled away from the petrol pumps to their left and accelerated past. Tout indicated and turned after it. Lauren caught a glimpse of Brendan hovering at the edge of the shop courtyard. She gave him a quick wave and was relieved to see him give a thumbs-up in reply.

The BMW was travelling well above the speed limit but as the turns on the road became sharper it slowed to a more reasonable, although still fast, speed. An older Vitara wouldn't be expected to either catch up or pass it so Trout tucked their vehicle well back but still within seeing-distance of the big car.

The car went right at the crossroads and left at the next junction. It was still travelling fast but was hampered by the narrow twisting road and soon enough by a mud-splattered tractor that lumbered about its business oblivious to the frustration of the cars and drivers behind it. No amount of horn-blowing could widen the road and the BMW was forced to slow right down. Trout took the chance to draw nearer but maintained enough distance to dispel any suspicion.

"Is he headed for the airport, do you think?" Lauren was

reviewing the possible destinations accessed from the road on which they were travelling.

"Could be. This is one of the backways that gives access to the motorway … hang on, he's turning off … we'll see where he goes from here."

On the motorway the BMW increased speed until it was a speck in the distance. Luckily the traffic was light and, in spite of lacking the same turn of speed, the Vitara was able to stay within squinting distance of the bigger car.

"He's indicating," Lauren said tersely. "Junction after next. Definitely the airport."

The Vitara did its best and within minutes was taking the off-ramp for Shannon airport. The traffic was heavier here but at the roundabout they were in time to see the BMW continuing on the airport road. Trout moved through the traffic until four cars remained between then and as the speed limit decreased maintained that distance.

The approach to the airport was getting busier.

"Watch where he goes," said Trout. "I'll have to concentrate on the traffic for a few minutes."

Lauren strained forward, her eyes glued on the grey car. "He's turning for the long-stay car park. It's the first left and a sharp right."

Trout maneuvered the Vitara expertly, following her instructions easily.

Lauren raised herself higher. "He's heading for the back corner. It's pretty full. Yeah, he's got a space. I'd say we'd be as well to park, we're only a couple of rows away. I've marked the spot – it's between a blue people-carrier and a red, looks like a Fiesta, one of those small-type cars anyway."

Trout spotted a space two rows back and to the left of the BMW. He drove in as Lauren continued, "He's out, looking all around as if checking to see if anyone is watching. What's he doing?" She kept her eyes fixed on the man who had exited the car, noted aloud for Trout's benefit, "Medium height, broad shoulders, not heavy but not light either, dark hair." She halted her catalogue to say, "That's strange – he's putting the keys on top of the back wheel, driver's side. At least that's what it looks like he's doing. Wow, that was fast – only I was watching so closely I'd have missed it."

"OK, I've spotted him." Trout turned off the engine. "He's on the move."

"He's not gone far, only to the white van over in the corner."

"*Shit!* One of the most anonymous vehicles in the country. Keep your eyes on him, I'm going to see if I can get the number."

Trout slipped out, leaving the key in the ignition. "In case it's someone that knows me and you need to scoop me up in a hurry," he said with a grin and circled the back of the Vitara, intending to look as if he was coming from the opposite direction. He scanned the carpark, looking exasperated, a typical 'where the hell did I put it?' expression on his face, as if he was returning from somewhere with no recollection of where exactly he'd left the car. He jogged to the top of the row and peered all around, went to cross to the next row as the van pulled out and drove up. He pulled back to let it pass, carefully avoiding looking directly at the driver and noted 12 LK 2122. As the van passed, he darted across, held up a key and pointing it towards the row of cars pressed the button repeatedly. In the periphery of his eye, he saw the van drive on as decorously as one driven by an elderly gent out for a Sunday drive.

Pulling his phone from his pocket Trout frowned at it, as if he was getting a message that annoyed him. Under the guise of typing an answer he recorded the number of the van. He hurried down the next row and cut across to emerge in front of the Vitara.

"What now?" Lauren hopped down to meet him. "Do we follow?"

"No point. I'll let the boys know the car's here and that our man's on the move." He brought up the number and pressed call. "Thomas Tegan here, put me through to Tony Driscoll there's a good man." He turned the phone away and said to Lauren. "Keep your eyes on the BMW just in case. Tony? Tegan here. A bit of information for you. We followed a BMW we believe is involved in the Freddy Loftus case to the airport. The driver was unknown to me but he's parked the car at the back of the long-term carpark and has now left driving a white VW van, 12 LK 2122. My information was that a BMW matching the one we followed was seen in Knocknaclogga on at least three occasions around the time Freddy was murdered. I don't know why you didn't hear about it. A BOLO on the white van asap and an officer to take charge of the BMW." He threw his eyes to Heaven. "We'll wait but there isn't anything else I can tell you." He snapped the phone shut. "How much icing do they want on it?" He muttered, caught Lauren's eye and shrugged ruefully. "You heard most of that. I said we'd wait but I want to have a quick recce. Are you OK to keep look-out?"

"What am I looking out for?"

"Who knows? But if anyone or anything strikes you as off, ring me fast."

"OK. Be careful."

Lauren climbed back into the Vitara. She settled herself at an angle and allowed her eyes to roam all the corners of the car park.

Trout walked nonchalantly, following a zig-zag path until he reached the BMW. His first check was the back passenger wheel where four matching nuts were joined by a squarer, slightly longer fifth. He straightened and walked slowly around the car. There was nothing visible inside. He could feel his fingers itching to check the glove compartment and door pockets. For once he had no gloves on him so had to content himself with eyeballing the interior. The reg was a 161 D, different again to the ones Brendan had already given him.

Trout was considering his next move when clear as a bell Lauren's voice sang out, "*Look right!*" He swivelled round to see a heavy-set man barreling towards him, his gait made unsteady by the hand scrabbling for something in the pocket of his jacket. Trout swore, scooped a handful of gravel and dust and tossed it towards his would-be assailant and ducked behind the car. He segued into a crouching run and circled it. The newcomer spluttered a curse and flapping at his eyes with one hand, pulled a gun free with the other. Temporarily blinded, he was waving the gun alarmingly in all directions.

Lauren started to scream in a high-pitched continuous screech.

The man furiously about-turned and aimed the gun in her direction. "*Shut the fuck up!*" he bellowed.

She dropped out of sight as he let off a volley of shots which ended abruptly when Trout tackled him from behind and he landed face down with an audible *oomph.*

Two security guards arrived panting, "What's going on?"

"This gent rocked up with a gun and started shooting." Trout was sitting firmly on the middle of the guy's back. "The gun is under him and I'm afraid someone will get hurt if I let him up." The man was spluttering curses and spitting gravel but, after the initial heaving failed to dislodge Trout, he lay still.

The security men watched the play with doubtful looks. The older one unhooked his radio, called for back-up and requested that the Gardaí be called asap. The younger man tried to move the gathering crowd back from the two men on the ground.

Lauren crept around to the front of the line of cars. "Are you OK, Trout?"

"I am," he grinned at her, "thanks to you." He caught his prone attacker by the hair and lifted his head. "Meet Ringo Star. Ringo is considered something of an artist with a gun. Never misses a target. Isn't that so, Ringo?"

Ringo let out a string of curses that made the air vibrate.

Trout gently replaced his face back on the gravel. "Enough of that, there are ladies present."

Tony Driscoll and Moira Baker pushed their way through the crowd. Trout hailed them. "Just as well I agreed to stay on, Tony, Ringo here came to call while we were waiting."

Sergeant Driscoll looked between them, opened his mouth and closed it again. Moira smiled.

Trout said, "Any chance of a pair of cuffs? I'm getting a pain in my backside from his bony spine."

Moira pulled a pair from her belt and yanked the nearest arm from under him. "Ringo Starr, you are under arrest for attempted assault."

"He lying on his gun, possibly still clutching it," Trout said warningly.

"And possession of a firearm with intent to endanger life," Moira continued calmly and nodded at Trout.

In one smooth movement he rose, pulled Ringo onto his knees while she hauled his other arm back and cuffed his two wrists together.

A blue metallic snub-nosed gun glinted in the gravel. Ringo scowled at it. Tony Driscoll pulled on a pair of gloves and carefully picked it up, engaged the safety catch and dropped it into an evidence bag.

A collective sigh rippled through the crowd and finally the security guard, flapping his arms as if herding cows through a gap, got the people to move, repeating like a record stuck in a groove, "*OK, folk, shows over, move along!*"

Trout was eyeing the BMW. He looked from it to Ringo, from Ringo to Tony Driscoll. "I wonder what exactly is in the car. Ringo doesn't usually come out to move the machinery," he said thoughtfully.

Ringo snarled and made a lunge at him. Moira jerked him back. "The keys are on top of the back wheel, driver's side. You've the gloves on, Tony – want to have a look?"

As Tony moved towards the car, his phone rang. He swiped to answer it and listened intently, staring at Trout. "OK, go ahead and book him. Sergeant Baker and myself are dealing with an incident at the airport." He flicked the phone shut and said tersely, "A white VW van was pulled near Portlaoise and the driver was arrested when he tried to make a run for it." He gave a tight smile. "His fingerprints identify him as Greg Halliman, wanted by INTERPOL for more crimes than I'd be able to enumerate without recourse to his file."

"*Holy Moly!*" Moira Baker turned twinkling eyes towards Trout, went to say something, thought better of it and bit her lip to hide a delighted grin.

A patrol car and a golf cart with the head of airport security arrived simultaneously from different directions. The older security guard went to talk to his boss and Moira handed over Ringo into the charge of the two gardaí.

"Lock him up good and tight until we have time to deal with him." She told them. "We'll be here a while longer." She looked at the car. "We'll probably need a transporter to move the car, what do you think, sarge?"

"We'll have a look and determine if it's OK to move it or if Forensics need to see it onsite." Tony had found the keys and was weighing them in his hand. "I'm not sure you should be here for this part of it," he said miserably to Trout. He juggled the keys some more. He gave a quick shake of his shoulders, drew back his lips. "Feck sake, you handed them to us on a platter. One little look at the goods isn't going to make that much difference one way or the other. Let's see what these buggers were hiding."

He clicked the key and the boot rose silently into the air.

Lauren moved closer to Trout as they all crowded in to have a look.

"Jesus Christ!" Tony's shocked expression was mirrored in those around him. "Call an ambulance. Are there paramedics in the airport?" He reached into the boot. "It's OK, we'll help you …"

A young woman, scantily dressed, curled into the foetal position and trussed like a chicken, lay there. She was staring at them with big, frightened eyes. Colourless duct tape stretched across her mouth and bound her hands and feet together.

"Are you hurt?" Tony asked.

Her eyes flickered and filled with tears.

"You're OK now. Here, someone give me a hand to get her out." Tony Driscoll made to reach into the boot.

"The First-Aid team are on the way – maybe we should wait and let them assess her injuries before moving her." The security man was back on his two-way. "They'll be here in minutes."

"We need to get the tape off her mouth, let her breathe properly." Tony touched the corner of it.

"It'll bring her skin with it if you yank it," Lauren protested. "Something to moisten it, that would loosen it ..."

"Help's here, move back!" Trout cleared a space around the car.

Another golf cart, this time with two people wearing arm-bands that read *First Aid* pulled up close to the back of the car. They briskly assessed the woman and, seemingly satisfied that no immediate danger was present, levered her upright and using their arms as a seat transferred her to the golf cart. She wobbled precariously on the seat and the woman medic gently steadied her while the man produced a flat-edged bandage scissors, a bottle of alcohol and a wad of cotton wool. He handed the alcohol and cotton wool to his colleague.

She turned and spoke directly to the young woman. "This is going to smell to high heaven but we'll be able to take the tape off your mouth without hurting you. Do you understand me?" She waited until she saw a small nod of comprehension and added, "Les is going to cut off the tape on your hands – he's using a special scissors. It won't hurt but prepare yourself for pins and needles."

She saturated the wool and carefully patted it onto the tape. The smell of rubbing alcohol filled the air but the tape quickly started to loosen. At the same time the scissors made short work of the binding on her hands and Les rubbed them lightly to help the circulation return. When he saw her hands reddening with blood flow he started on the tape around her ankles. The tape over her mouth finally slipped off as the young woman swooned against the medic's shoulder. Her face was stark white and a blue tinge was visible around her lips.

Les was rubbing her feet – he looked up at his colleague. "She's very cold."

Moira Baker shrugged out of her jacket and wrapped it around the young woman. In the distance the wail of an ambulance could be heard. Soon the flashing lights were at the edge of the car park and in seconds it pulled up behind the golf cart.

Les ran to them. "She needs oxygen."

One of the paramedics turned into the back of ambulance and reappeared carrying an oxygen cylinder and a mask. She placed it over the young woman's face while her colleagues checked the vital signs. "She's dehydrated. We'll need to put in a line."

Working with practised efficiency, the paramedics quickly had a drip set up and, with the oxygen helping her breathe, the young woman began to regain colour. She stirred and moaned.

"We'll get her on a trolley and to the hospital."

Moira retrieved her jacket as the paramedics wrapped the young woman in a thermal blanket and hoisted her into the ambulance.

"I'll come with you," she said. "For her protection," she added firmly, seeing that the second paramedic was about to protest. "She appears to be a kidnap victim and we've no way of knowing if the perpetuators will try to harm her to keep her from talking."

He blew out a breath. "OK. Strap in. We'll blue-light it to the hospital – she needs more than we can give her."

They took off in a cloud of dust.

A moment of silence descended on the group.

Then the head of security cleared his throat. He turned to Tony

Driscoll. "We'll leave you to it. But I'd appreciate an official report of the incident at your convenience."

Tony agreed and the security men left. He took out his phone and put in a request for a patrol car to secure the BMW and a transporter to take it to headquarters for examination. He then rang the forensic team and alerted them that a car which had held a possible kidnap victim was coming to them for inspection. When he finished, he looked between Trout and Lauren. "You'll need to make a statement – sometime in the next couple of days will do." He shook his head. "I don't know how you do it. I just don't know."

Chapter 27

"Did I ever tell you I used to have a boring life?" Lauren said.

She was in the driver's seat, Trout pensive beside her. He was tapping a message into a phone, hers as it happened. He sent a thumbs-up icon and an emoji of a face with its lips covered to Brendan. At least he hoped that was what it was, it might have been a diver or, he squinted at the tiny figure, a guerilla in combat gear. Either way he hoped Brendan got the message.

"What's this you're saying about a boring life?"

She slanted him a look. "Not boring anymore." She grinned. "Honestly, Trout, Ringo Starr?"

"Yep. All above board. Changed his name by deed poll when he was legally able to do it. Mind you, the moniker he was carrying around was a serious impediment to his chosen life of crime."

"I'm intrigued. Are you going to tell me?"

Trout chuckled. "Bosco St John Real. In all fairness, knowing his mother, he was called after St John Bosco, not the television puppet."

On a peal of laughter, Lauren spluttered, "I concede he may have had a point." She sobered and shivered. "What's going to become of that poor girl?"

"At least she's alive. That's a good start." Trout stared at the road unwinding in front of them. "We know the gangs have a finger in every illegal pie going but she raises the question as to what exactly is being trafficked besides money and drugs?"

"Girls."

"People. The sex-trade nowadays is many-faceted. She didn't say anything but she looked East European to me. The sad thing is these young people think they are coming to a better life."

"Oh my God! That makes it even more terrible." Lauren concentrated on driving then said, "I'm getting a look at the underbelly of life in a way that's far removed from reading about it."

"You can pull out, you know." Trout turned and studied her profile. From this angle her chin jutted out with stubborn determination. She drove easily, quietly confident, fully alert on the lesser-known backroads. "I can't tell you it's not dangerous, you've more than seen that it is."

"You do it."

"I'm trained for it, you're not. That said, you've handled yourself better than some I've seen that are trained and," he hesitated, "you're a great sidekick to have on board."

"And I'm currently the only other operative of TLC Investigations."

"That too," Trout said gravely. He frowned. "You do understand that TLC Investigations is the means to an end?"

"The end being solving the case. Right?"

"Yes." Trout was looking at her doubtfully. He opened his mouth to say more, thought better of it and lapsed into silence.

"OK then." Lauren indicated and pulled into a filling station with a café attached. "I see they're advertising Old Barrack coffee here, and even you can't object to that. I need coffee."

"Are you suggesting I'm a coffee snob?" Trout huffed.

"And possibly chocolate," she continued as if he hadn't spoken. "Maybe even chocolate cake."

They bickered good-naturedly as they chose their coffee. Lauren went for a smooth mid-roast Brazil while Trout ordered a dark, single-estate Guatemalan. Both more than lived up to their expectations. They settled in to check phones and plan the remainder of the day. Lauren smiled and turned her phone so Trout could see the three monkeys, not seeing, hearing or saying anything, that was Brendan's reply.

He was laughing as he answered his phone.

"Is that you, Thomas?"

"Hello, Mother." He had to resist the urge as always to enquire who she thought she'd rung.

"It's so nice to hear you laughing. Is Lauren with you? Martha visited last week and told me the two of you were thick as thieves. Lovely girl. I've always liked her. She's Lucy's best friend, you know. She can be a stubborn little thing but you'd have no time for anyone who let you walk all over her and –"

"Did you ring for anything in particular, Mother? I'm in the middle of something here."

"Can't a mother just ring to say hello?"

"Well, yes, but …"

"As it happens, I did ring for something, now what was it? Oh yes, I wanted to tell you a rather bulky package arrived for you in the post. I thought you'd want to know."

"Brilliant. I was expecting it. Put it somewhere very safe for me, please, and I'll get it the next time I'm up."

"Now that you know I'll let you get back to your something. Bye, darling, say hello to Lauren for me."

"Mother …" Trout stopped, he was talking to air. He gave the phone a disgusted look. "Mother said to tell you hello." Lauren raised an eyebrow. "Apparently Mrs Dillon visited and, to quote verbatim, told her we were thick as thieves."

"Poor Trout. Do I detect a hopeful mother in the background?" Lauren teased.

"Well, you are warned and I seem to have the matriarch of the county in my corner."

She leaned towards him, her eyes alight with laughter. "Are you sure she's not in mine?"

Trout caught his breath and wondered what she'd do if he kissed her. As fast as the thought he went to close the distance between them.

Then her phone jangled and she glanced at the screen. "It's a reply from DeeDee." She quickly swiped to open the message and read the email. "She's sent me a link to their private site and an invitation to the opening of their newly refurbished Clothes Locker Emporium." She opened the attachment and scrolled through the pictures. "They work out of the big old house that has been in DeeDee's family for generations. They seem to have done a complete renovation job on it. *Wow!* This is amazing."

Trout caught brief glimpses of rooms, resplendent with the trappings of other times and places, of wardrobes, cupboards and rails laden with the clothes that went with them. Of futuristic spaces that beckoned to those who fancied themselves as comic characters or memes. A run of photos recorded the actual revamp. Lauren gave a running commentary as she scrolled. "Looks like the stables and out-houses had been turned into a showcase of rooms decked out with everything a cosplayer's heart might desire." She read the blurb aloud – which stated that each room had been remodeled by a master-craftsman who was sympathetic to the ethos of Cosplay.

"Holy cow! Look who their master craftsman is." She handed the phone to Trout.

Smiling out at him in technicolor, holding a hammer in one hand and a delicate fleur-de-lis cornice in the other, was Miko Downes.

Chapter 28

As Lauren drove to Killanee, Trout filled his notebook with hieroglyphics.

He stared at it, frowning. "Does your gut still think Miko's on the level?"

"I think so." She considered the question some more, gearing down and idling to allow a herd of cattle cross the road. The farmer and his helper both saluted their thanks for her patience and she pulled away smiling. "He may not have told us the whole story, at least not the bits he wanted to keep quiet about." She accelerated smoothly. "We'll find out when we ask him."

Miko's yard was deserted. Not even the dog barked to greet them. They sat undecided, studying the yard, looked at each other and in unison clicked the seatbelts and climbed out. There was a stillness in the air and an emptiness in the yard that caused a thrill of unease, as if they were invading an alien space.

Trout closed the door with a resounding thump.

Lauren jumped, laughed and said shakily, "I feel as if we've landed in some other dimension."

"Just nerves. You get used to it eventually. Let's have a look around."

They wandered, looking into cabins, peering through dusty windows. The workshop was firmly padlocked as was the shed next to it.

Through a small square of cleaner glass Trout made out the shape of a van. "Looks like he has a work-vehicle as well as the jeep."

They completed the round of the yard and ended up back at the dwelling house. Lauren went to knock on the door. A clatter of wheels disturbed the silence and the jeep rattled into its customary space. Miko was slouched over the steering, driving with his whole body. Maestro was on the passenger seat with his head out the window.

Miko scowled. The dog barked. Miko hushed him with a placating hand. They both climbed out the driver side.

"I reckoned ye'd be back," Miko said.

He had shrunken into himself and become an old man since their original visit. He dragged himself to the door as if tired beyond endurance. His hand trembled as he reached up to the lintel and retrieved a large iron key. "Stay, Maestro." He shuffled through the doorway. "Ye'd better come in."

Lauren looked at Trout. He shrugged and stood aside to allow her precede him into the house.

Miko went to the range, rattled the firebox and threw a couple of bits of kindling on the embers. He watched while the smoke spiralled into a flame and added heavier timber until the box was full. He pulled the kettle over and leaned on the handle, staring unseeing at the top of the range.

Trout and Lauren waited.

"The cops took Freddy's car," he said. "They didn't seem to care too much about him but once they saw the drugs … that satisfied them." A wealth of bitterness laced his words.

Lauren laid a hand on his arm. "Why don't you sit down? You have a story to tell and we'd like to hear it. It need go no further than us three if that's what you want."

Trout went to say something but she shushed him, holding her hand in a classic say-nothing gesture.

"You're right, girlie, I have a story and 'twill explain a few things … maybe …"

He lapsed into silence. They waited.

"Ye wondered why I hadn't done something about the car sooner and the truth is Freddy and myself had a terrible row that day. I thought he was paying me back by not coming for the car, that he really meant it when he said he never wanted to see me again." He dropped onto his chair and stared at his hands, gnarled and work-scarred, "You see, Freddy wasn't my grand-nephew – he was my son."

Trout nodded. Lauren bit back a gasp. Miko continued to stare at his hands but the floodgates were open and he began to talk almost without drawing breath.

"Geraldine and Nicholas should never have got married. Nick was Winnie's eldest and she doted on him. She couldn't see that he was the spit of his father and as lazy a son of a bitch as his father ever was. Oh, he was good-looking and he could sweet-talk – but provide, no." Miko shook his head. "Geraldine fell for him hook, line and sinker. She thought he was the knight who would rescue her from a bad home situation and then found she had gone from the frying-pan into the fire itself. They used to come here, regular like, when Winnie was alive and just kept it up when she was gone. Sometimes when things were very bad Geraldine would gather up the kids and they'd all come here without his lordship. But all the useless fucker had to do was crook his little finger and she'd go running back." He turned his face towards the ceiling. "She had started to drink a bit herself by then but the kiddies would thrive when they were here and of course I'd make sure they were provided for and ..." he stopped, twisted his hands, "I was the willing shoulder she could cry on. To tell the truth, I loved having them. I'd pretend they were mine." He sighed. "I suppose it was inevitable. One-night things went too far ... one thing led to another ..." He stopped again, then continued softly. "It was the happiest six months of my life. Until it all fell asunder. Geraldine found she was pregnant, Nick came back from whatever skite he was on, she made sure there was a big reconciliation and Freddy was born early to all intents and purposes." He cleared his throat. "Feck it, I need something to help me finish."

He levered himself to his feet and went to the dresser. He produced a bottle of Paddy and three glasses. "Ye'll have a mouthful – 'twill finish easier with a bit of lubrication." He poured a generous measure of whiskey into the glasses, passed one each to Trout and Lauren, sat back down and gulped a large mouthful.

"She stopped coming after that – the drink was getting a more powerful hold on her. She'd send the kiddies on their own sometimes. I could see 'twas Nikki was doing what was needed and God help us Geraldine let her. For all that she was jealous as hell over the bond Nikki had with Freddy." He stared into the golden liquid as if seeking inspiration. "Now and again, she'd go on the jag and threaten all sorts of things but she never did anything until that last day." He drained his glass, splashed in another measure and sank back on his chair. "Whatever spat they had she went and told him I was his real father. Now don't get me wrong, Freddy and

211

myself have always been pals. What stuck in his craw was that we lied to him. Omission, he called it. Said it was the same as a lie." He turned the glass round and around, downed a slug and said bitterly, "A lie of omission."

Miko was silent so long Lauren went to say something. Trout shook his head.

Miko took another gulp of whiskey. "He was in a right tear when he got here. I said before he was excited but it was more than that, he was upset, agitated like, he wouldn't listen to anything I had to say. He kept waving that phone under my nose and shouting '*When I'm finished with this, I won't owe any of ye anything!*' I didn't know what he was on about. I could get no good out of him and, in the end, he stormed off as if his tail was on fire. I suppose it was, in a way. I thought to myself 'A good long walk will soften his cough and we'll be able to talk properly when he gets back'. I never thought I wouldn't see him again." Miko stopped, rubbed a weary hand over his face. "Now ye know it all."

A heavy silence settled over them. Finally, Trout said, "Does anyone else know you're his father?"

"No. Even Nick didn't suspect a thing. Whatever figary came over Geraldine is beyond me. She knew Freddy was coming here, that he worked with me. Maybe the old jealousy got her and she let fly ..."

"Talking about working with you, did Freddy work on the Clothes Locker renovation?"

"He did surely. Whenever he could. He was busy with the studying and he kept the job in the city when he was going to be there anyway. But he usually managed to fit in a day or two a week with me, sometimes more. They gave us a more or less free hand to fit out the place." Miko half smiled. "We did some powerful work there. Did ye see it?"

"Only on the website. I'm invited to the opening," Lauren chipped in. "DeeDee and myself worked together one time."

"They've strange notions but sure they're a harmless lot."

"We were wondering if Paddy's Locker was connected to them somehow. Aren't all the rooms called lockers?" Lauren kept her voice light.

Miko frowned. "I don't recall one of that name and I'm almost sure it's some sort of a game."

"Why?"

Miko looked blank.

"Why do you think it's a game?" Trout pressed him.

"I don't rightly know, I'm that mithered at the moment I hardly know my name but that's what's in my head when I hear you saying Paddy's Locker. They have a right fancy games rooms, kitted out with all sort of things you'd never see nowadays and modern things they got made in China. Freddy did most of the work on it – he was looking up old-fashioned slot machines and games of chance. Research, he called it. He even made a couple of them, did the cabinet work here and finished them on site if I remember correctly. He thought the whole thing was a great laugh."

"And you think Paddy's Locker was one of the games or at least you associate it with the games room?" Trout sounded thoughtful

"I sort of put them together in my mind if you understand and I recall saying to Freddy that I was almost sure I'd played a game like that somewhere when I was a boy."

"So, Freddy made games for the Clothes Locker?"

"He made a few. I remember a mahogany cabinet that was for a game and," he smiled "one of those oak thingy-me-bobs, like a coffin it was, for cutting people in two. I helped him with that one. We had great craic doing it."

"He was a busy lad."

"He was a great little worker – right proud I was to think he was mine. Didn't matter that nobody knew. I did and that's what counted. I'm heart-sore to think that when he found out 'twas a row we had – with no time after to make it right." Miko's face twisted into a grief-filled grimace.

"I'm so sorry," Lauren said helplessly.

"You can't do a thing, girlie. If there's nothing else, I'd be thankful if ye left. My grieving is best done without company."

"Thank you for telling us." Lauren took a deep breath. "May we come back another day? I'd like to look at the doll's house a bit more?"

Miko jerked his head. "You can surely. Now, if you want … but, if another day would do, I'd rather another day."

"Another day will be fine." Trout hesitated. "Have you a mobile phone, Miko?"

"I have."

"Call out the number and I'll ring it. That way you'll have mine and if you ever need me, call. Any time, day or night."

When Miko's phone rang, Trout took it and added his name to the contacts. "Any time. Even if it's only for a chat. We'll see ourselves out."

Trout and Lauren left. Maestro rose from the step when Trout opened the door. He sidled in past them and the last they saw was his head on Miko's knee and the big rough hand coming to fondle his ears.

Chapter 29

"I didn't see that one coming." Lauren closed her eyes, blew out a breath. "The poor man."

"Classic mistake really. We saw an old man but twenty odd years ago he was only in his mid-fifties."

"In his prime, you might say." Lauren slanted a glance at Trout and tried to lighten the mood.

He smiled, appreciating her effort. "You might indeed." He thought for a minute. "Now we know that Freddy was excited about his gangland knowledge, het-up over the news about Miko and possibly was mad as a cut cat with his mother. Not a good combination for a situation that needed a cool head."

Lauren started the Vitara. "It sounds like a recipe for disaster, if you ask me."

They made good time back to Knocknaclogga. The street light cast pale pools of shadow along the pavement. Lauren pointed to a small, grey tractor that looked like it should be in a museum. It was pulled up on the footpath near Madigan's.

"That's Pa Jones' vehicle of choice when he comes to town. If you fancy a pint, you'll probably find him in Madigan's. They do have small bottles of wine but I'd imagine you'd be much better off with a pint."

"You think?" Trout made a grimace but said no more.

She dropped him outside his house, refused his offer of food and drove away. Trout watched her until she turned out of sight. He felt a pang of disappointment that she had chosen to go home, even as he recognized her need for some space. He kicked at a stone on the path – he was going to have to look carefully at his feelings for Lauren O'Loughlin – soon if he knew himself as well as he thought he did. He went moodily towards the house.

"*Shit!*" His car was at Lauren's. He hadn't as much as given it a second thought. He felt himself become more cheerful – he'd collect the car tomorrow. Right now, he needed food. He glanced down at Madigan's – he'd be in a better position to consider a pint when he was refuelled.

The door opened directly into the pub. The grocery and hardware section were attached but at this hour of the night the communicating door was closed, although everyone knew that if you wanted some provision or other, it was a simple matter of popping into the shop to get it. The patrons lined up at the bar turned as one. Trout felt the eyes rake him and assess his potential. Nobody pretended to be indifferent to his entry. The scent of new blood always attracted attention. He nodded, said a general good evening and moved along until he reached a clear spot at the far end of the counter. The room opened up into a good-sized space with a scattering of tables and chairs. The glow of a fire lit up the far corner, almost hidden by the three old timers cozied around it.

At least one of them surreptitiously blew smoke from a blackened pipe up the chimney in blatant disregard of the smoking law.

Jeremiah Madigan, Jerry to all and sundry, welcomed Trout and enquired what he could do for him.

Before Trout could answer, a cackle from the fireside interrupted, "Well, if it isn't the little Trout himself. Come over here, lad, and tell us all the news. Jerry, a pint for my friend the Trout!"

Jesus, Matt Gardiner is still alive, he must be a hundred if he's a day, Trout thought. He nodded to Jerry and moved towards the men around the fire. The old fellow in pride of place on the hob uncurled himself, casually laid his pipe one side and held out a claw-like hand.

Trout took it in both of his and shook it gently, feeling the distortion and the fragility of the arthritic bones. "Still going strong, Matt, I'm glad to see."

"Hard to kill an old codger like me. Pull up a chair there and we'll have a chat. Make a bit of space, lads, for my old friend Trout. I christened him myself, full immersion like the Lord in the Jordan." The old fellow beamed in self-congratulation. "Pulled him out with my fishing rod."

There was a general shuffling around the fire. Trout plucked a chair from beside the nearest table and added it to the circle.

"Do you know these boys?" Matt was twinkling at him, "The one with the whiskers is Jamsie Dolan, the one with the nose is Pa Jones." Matt gave his cackling laugh when he saw Trout understand that no other description was necessary. The two men were examining Trout, Jamsie openly, Pa Jones from a sideways stare. "Thanks, Jerry." Matt nodded as two pints appeared beside them.

A small silence followed. Trout sampled his pint. It was satisfactory as pints go. He stifled a sigh. Porter was not his drink but needs must. He understood the ball was now in his court and asked, "How've you been keeping, Matt?"

"Pulling the devil by the tail but while he's paying me no attention, I've no complaints." Matt rattled his pipe and gave a sly glance at Trout. "Done much fishing since you've been back?"

"Haven't had a chance with one thing and another."

"I hear yourself and young Lauren found that fellow on the mountain. Did they put a name on him yet?"

Trout became aware of two things, that Matt well knew the answer but was testing him in some way and the fellow with the nose had gone completely still.

"I heard the name Loftus mentioned, a young lad," Trout said. "Freddy, I believe, was the name they called him."

"Someone told me all right that he was a relation of Miko Downes, over Killanee way. His sister was married to a Johnny Loftus. A useless hure if ever there was one. Winnie was the one who kept the place together. They're all dead now, God rest them. Weren't you a friend of the eldest lad, Pa? What's this they called him? Nick, was it?"

Pa Jones mumbled into his pint, "That was years ago, Matt, sure he went to Dublin and got married and all."

"He did too." Matt looked longingly at the pipe, left it carefully to one side and took a swig of his pint. "Was the young lad one of his? He was a long way from Dublin on Slí Buí."

"They all make out it was Knocknaclogga." Jamsie sounded like he was saying a mantra.

Matt gave his cackling laugh. "They do, they do. He was on the Knocknaclogga side of the hill, wasn't he?" This was addressed to Trout.

"He was, near enough to top, about halfway between it and the caves."

"I know the spot. It's in the middle of the commonage. You've a bit of it, Pa, haven't you? Was that the night you were out searching for the bullock? Didn't you say something about hearing shots and going to have a look-see if someone was lamping deer?"

Pa started. "Ah, I don't think 'twas that night, Matt."

"I'm nearly sure you told me about the animal going astray and 'twas the evening we heard about the body." Matt looked at him, his eyes sharp and knowing. "We were over at Keeley's Cross and you were telling me the trek you had when Frank stopped with the news. He was coming from work and was full of all the hoo-ha on the mountain."

"You might be right an' all. I hardly know the day of the week most of the time." Pa concentrated on his drink.

"You know when 'tis Friday though." Jamsie Dolan seemed oblivious to any undercurrent in the conversation. "Pension day. The extra few bob is a great. You got the fancy electric fence I see, Pa. Did you say 'twas solar powered? They're awful expensive yokes."

"They tell me they'll pay for themselves in a year," Pa muttered.

"Be japers, you must have a knack for making the pension stretch." Matt gave in and applied a match to his pipe. "Mine barely sees me out the week."

"I had a bit of luck on the horses last week, got enough for the fence and a bit left over to buy ye all a pint." Pa waved at Jerry and held up four fingers.

A small silence settled. Trout waited.

Matt puffed contemplatively, aiming the smoke up the chimney. "So your visitor's gone, Pa?"

"Visitor? What d'you mean gone?" Pa sounded flustered.

"Only you're here, aren't you? Didn't you say you couldn't come out while your cousin was visiting?"

"That's right, that's right. She went this morning."

"Powerful lot of cousins have turned up this summer." Matt nodded. "That's always the way when they discover a relation with a free bed. You should bring them to meet us, buy them a pint, show them a bit of culture."

"They never want to come out, always too tired after a day gallivanting." Pa was back to muttering.

"Tough on you. They sound like an ungrateful bunch. Did you say they were all Mary's family? How many did she have anyway?"

"I've lost count but some of them belonged to Charlie. Here's the pints, lads." The relief in Pa's voice was palpable but Matt wasn't finished.

"Did you tell me the last one came from Russia? I didn't know either of them was in Russia."

"You'd want to get new batteries for the hearing aids, Matt, sure Mary's in England and Charlie's in Boston. How could they be in Russia? Here, drink your pint and don't be raving."

"Thanks, Pa, that's right generous of you." Matt toasted the company. "*Sláinte!*" He took a long swallow and winked at Trout.

The conversation turned general after that. The affairs of the nation needed discussing. Pa Jones visibly relaxed, various people came and went. Trout bought his round and tried to remember when he last had four pints in a row. He reassured himself that the resulting sickness he would face in the morning was a small price for the information gleaned. It occurred to him that the holding place for the girl they had rescued this morning had been identified in the conversation. Now he needed to figure out what to do with it. A forensic team needed to access Pa Jones' house as soon as possible but it would never do for him to be associated with that event.

He eventually got home. Little things like closing time were apparently more fluid in Knocknaclogga than in the city.

Trout rang Mac.

"Who have you for us this time? It might be hard to beat an international hit-man though." Mac's matter-of-fact tone had a smile running through it.

"Mac." Trout's gut felt heavy and his head sluggish. He was trying to get what he wanted to say straight in his mind.

"Yes?" Mac's tone sharpened.

"Those bloody pints. I don't know how ye drink the stuff and survive. What am I trying to say?"

"You're muttering, Trout. Sober up and spit it out."

"Right." Trout straightened his shoulders. "Did ye get anything from the girl? I think I may have identified where she was held but it will require a bit of planning to pull off a search without alerting everyone and anyone."

"*Whoa!* You're losing me, boy – pull what off, did you say?"

"A look at the place she was kept while it's still fresh. Hang on, there's a coffee ready, that'll help me think."

"While you're thinking I'll be filling you in. The poor little girl is from Moldova and has barely any English. By the time we found Áine to translate for us, she was sedated and the docs told us wait till she wakes naturally. The creature was very traumatized and badly frightened by the whole thing. It sickens me to see what's done to those young ones."

Trout downed half the coffee in one go and winced to feel it fighting with the beer in his gut. He waited a moment to let things settle. "All the more reason to do this carefully." Trout felt the caffeine surge in his system and became marginally more alert. "I was sounding out the locals in the pub and that fellow I asked you to check up on ..."

"Pa Jones?"

"That's the one. Apparently, he's had a mysterious niece or cousin or some such staying for a few days. She left this morning and she's one of a number of relations that have discovered him in the past few months. They're never seen around and while they're visiting Pa stays at home to entertain them or so he tells the boys."

"Sounds promising. I've had a quick gander at this Halliman's statement. A cool customer, says he was delivering the car as a favour to a friend and knew nothing about what might be in the boot. Says it didn't occur to him to check. All he was to do was leave the car at the airport, pick up the van and use it for as long as he needed. The boys say he repeats the same thing like a poem he's learned by rote."

"Whatever the favour was, he was in Knocknaclogga this morning, either picking up the girl or the car with the girl in it. Any way we can get a look at Jones's house without arousing suspicion? I presume there was a house-to-house carried out initially?"

"I'm not rightly sure but I don't think so. There's only the two, maybe three houses in the vicinity and they were deemed too far away to be of consequence."

"Any chance of a coordinated check, three houses should be manageable and it wouldn't be Pa's in isolation that way?"

"I'll see how things are going down here and what might be possible. How do you want to play it?"

"I can't afford to be seen having any hand, act or part of it."

"An anonymous tip so is the best bet. I'll say the voice sounded disguised and I wouldn't be surprised if he was drunk but sure we can't afford to ignore such a prime piece of information." Mack's booming laugh lingered in the air after he'd rung off.

Chapter 30

Trout groaned and made a feeble effort to disentangle himself from the sweaty sheets. It sounded like all the church bells in the world were pealing, clashing, vibrating and vainly trying to escape the confines of his skull. His stomach roiled and rose, surfing on the swell of sound until he felt engulfed by the clamour, a clamour that was orchestrated by a thick jute rope that disappeared upwards into the blackness of a bell-tower. The heavy knot at the end swayed across his eyelids and dangled just out of reach. He made a wild jump, almost caught it and found himself tumbling head over heels into a dark cavernous space, the bells spilling around him in a cacophony of noise.

His eyes flew open. The phone on the bedside locker was jangling and vibrating with a persistent demand to be answered. Trout groped for it and with a flick silenced the damned bells. Now if only he could switch off the turmoil in his gut . . .

"Tegan," he said hoarsely.

"Trout?" Lauren's voice was tentative. "Are you OK?"

"Lauren! Jesus! Hang on." He swung his legs over the side of the bed and sat up. His stomach flipped but didn't take it any further. His mouth was dry and tasted like rotten eggs. His head felt heavy with residue sound of the clanging bells *dong, donging* in the background. He rubbed a hand over his face. "Jesus. How do those old fellows do it? I've been known to drink a couple bottles of wine and I never feel like this."

"Out on the razz, were you?" Lauren laughed softly. "You'd better get yourself a gallon of water and some coffee. Oh, and maybe a couple of painkillers."

"Yeah, yeah. What time is it anyway?"

"Nine o'clock or thereabouts."

"Nine o'clock – Jesus!" Trout felt sluggish, he made a valiant effort to concentrate his mind but talking seemed to be taking way too much energy. He made to crawl back under the duvet. "It must be important if you're ringing …" He groaned. "Don't tell me we were supposed to be somewhere …"

"No. Not until this evening. . . I thought you'd be interested to know Pa Jones has been brought in for questioning."

"*Whoa!* Back up. Pa Jones was arrested?"

"I don't think so. The word is he is helping the gardaí with their enquiries."

"How do you know?"

"Mrs Dillon rang. Don't ask me how she finds out these things but it seems the houses on the lower flank of Slí Buí were visited early this morning by the Guards and as a result Pa was taken away in a squad car."

Trout silently digested the news. He stared at the ceiling and tried to make his mind reason in a rational way but the cramping of his gut kept interfering. "Listen, I need to get that gallon of water you talked about and a shower among other things. I'll give you a ring when I'm fully functioning and we can see where we go from there."

"Do you think things are hotting up?"

"I'd say they're on fire. Talk later."

Trout stared into his coffee cup and remembered why he didn't drink beer. It made him as sick as a dog. Briefly he wondered how somebody came up with the idea that dogs typically got violently sick, but his own condition was taking all his available thoughts so he abandoned the speculation. His stomach roiled and rolled like the sea in a storm. His head *thumped-thumped-thumped* like metal music heard through a wall, distant but incessant and without mercy. A doctor once told him it was something to do with his metabolism or blood type or something and just stay from any and all types of beer or porter. Now he tried to tell himself that last night's indulgence was worth it, especially if the visit to Pa Jones' house yielded some information that put a spanner in the gangland works. OK, so it would take a few hours for things to settle and really convince himself that the end justifies the means. In the meantime, he was seriously considering going back to bed.

A distant *ding-dong* penetrated the fog in his mind. It took him a couple of minutes to distinguish the doorbell from the banging in his head. He thought not to answer but it was insistent and while whoever it was didn't keep their finger on the bell they kept ringing – ring-pause-ring-pause. Finally, the repetition convinced him they weren't going away so for peace's sake he staggered to the door.

The harsh words died on his lips when he saw Lauren holding a covered dish, steam gently pulsing from it, in one hand and a pint glass of strange-coloured liquid in the other. He squinted at her but, before he could form any words, she breezed past him. He closed the door very quietly, took a careful breath and followed her into the kitchen.

"Sit down. I've brought you a cure. Down the hatch." She handed him the pint glass.

He eyed it suspiciously. "What is it?"

"Granny O'Loughlin's special hangover cure."

"I don't know. It'll more likely make me spew my guts."

"You won't know until you drink it. Just swallow it. I've a first-class fry as a chaser. By then you'll be back to the whole of your health. Hopefully."

"Hopefully is not much of a guarantee."

"Guarantee or else, this fry won't keep warm forever. Drink it down."

Trout took a tentative sip. It wasn't exactly noxious, more unusual. He was still doubtful and the thought of a fry was totally turning his stomach.

"Sips are no good – you have to drink it down. Come on, Trout, don't be a wuss!"

He attempted to glare at Lauren but it took too much effort so with a mock toast towards her, "Suffer the consequences!" he tipped his head back and poured the liquid down his throat until the glass was empty. He looked at it with a grimace and waited for the inevitable results. To his surprise it stayed down. The storm at sea in his stomach abated, his head quietened.

"Now for the fry."

"Are you sure that's not tempting fate a bit too much?"

"Sit and eat. I'm making tea. It's a better option at times like this."

In the face of such steely determination Trout gave in.

Lauren had found a teapot somewhere and brought a pot of tea to the table. She sat to the side, poured two cups and sipped quietly while he ate. Which, surprisingly, he found himself able to do.

As he swallowed the last mouthful of sausage, she said, "What happened last night?"

Trout gave a wry smile. "I went to Madigan's and had a couple of pints with Matt Gardiner and his cronies."

"A couple of pints?"

"I'm not supposed to drink beer. It doesn't agree with me. Something to do with my metabolism."

"Oh. How come you've no problem with wine?" Lauren sounded interested.

"It's not the alcohol's the problem, it's the beer itself. Which is why I didn't expect your cure to work. So, what's your magic ingredient?"

"Can't tell you. It's a closely guarded family secret." Lauren smiled. "But it does seem to have helped. So did you find out much?"

"That Pa Jones has been having unknown cousins to stay recently for a couple of days to a week at the time – one of them reportedly 'Russian' – that nobody sees or meets them but they keep him away from the pub while they're around." Trout sighed. "Lauren, it's imperative that we're not seen to have any part of knowing this. I'm telling you because you've probably figured it out already but …"

"Don't worry so much. It's going to come out that you were so sick after a couple of pints you needed Granny O's cure so you couldn't possibly be responsible for early morning raids on anyone."

"How's that going to come out?"

"You want me to list the number of people that passed by and commented on your visit to the pub as I unloaded Granny's cure and a chaser of fry outside your gate?"

"Village life! I'd almost forgotten what it's like."

"If it's any consolation, once they have a reasonable explanation it will save them making up one of their own and possibly putting two and two together fairly accurately." She thought for a moment. "It would probably help if you offer to get Jerry a case or two of your favourite wine for when you do go in. It will give you credibility with the lads also that it's a real problem and not just a way of avoiding their company."

"How did you get to be so wise, Lauren O'Loughlin? The wine's a brilliant idea and will fit in perfectly with my plan for a business."

"You never really said what your plans were before you came out with this PI lark."

"Didn't I? I suppose it's been in my head so long I think people automatically know." He drained the teapot into his cup. "My idea is to supply smaller local establishments with good wine at a reasonable price and maybe coffee."

"That sounds great. The only place you can get a decent glass of wine around here is at the Village Inn and Lucy tells me you do all their wine selections as it is."

"Yeah. I enjoy it. Matching food with a wine is such a pleasure and Lucy and Mars were delighted when I set up the wine cellar for their hotel."

"How did you get interested? Not many lads from around take their wine seriously. Guinness, now that's a different story."

Trout made a wry face. "After enduring a few years of mornings like this morning I decided enough is enough. The Garda Medical Officer did some tests and told me I was borderline allergic to malted grains and that it would only get worse." He half laughed. "This is Ireland. It helps if you can take a drink, it doesn't really matter what it is as long as it's alcohol. I've never liked the taste of spirits, any type of beer could end with anaphylaxis so I tried wine, discovered I liked the taste, the ambience around it and later vineyards and wine tours and," he spread his hands, "the possibility for a business I would enjoy when I retired."

"Didn't someone once say '*In wine there is truth*'? Sounds like a plan." She paused, then added, suddenly self-conscious, "Any time you want help tasting or whatever I'll make myself available for you."

"Can't think of anyone I'd rather have with me," Trout said softly. He enjoyed a moment of anticipation, thinking of a secluded gite in the Loire valley he always felt would be all the better if he had someone to share it. He opened his mouth, hesitated, finally said, "Hey! I'm cured. Is it too juvenile to high-five you?"

"Since when were high-fives juvenile?"

They slapped each other's hands and laughed.

Chapter 31

"Now that you're back in action, is there anything we need to do this morning? The opening of the Closet Locker isn't on until five this evening?" Lauren spoke over her shoulder as Trout carried two steaming mugs of coffee into the sitting room.

"I've made us a real drink to help us concentrate. What are you up to?"

She had their evidence board balanced on top of the stove and was standing back studying it. A neat pencil line was drawn through the names Rasher Madigan, Sam Maguire and Leo Kelly. "Two in jail and one dead," she continued, turning back to stare at the board. "Two more, no three that came out of the woodwork are also in jail and still no explanation as to why Freddy was killed." She took a mug and looked directly at him. "What else is going on here, Trout? What are we missing? Or is it just me?"

Trout held her gaze and smiled but before he could say anything Lauren added, "Don't bullshit me, Trout. One of the things that makes me a good editor is that I can spot inconsistencies a mile away."

"Those instincts of yours. Too sharp for your own good." Trout frowned at the board, perched himself on the edge of the table-desk and took a slug of coffee. "If I say I can't tell you just yet, will you trust me?"

Lauren looked at him over the rim of her mug.

He looked back at her. "It's sensitive and it's dangerous. I'd prefer if you could deny any knowledge without having to lie. Truth has a different energy to lies. It takes an experienced liar to tell one like the truth and even then, there are tells that give one away."

Lauren smiled. "That sounds so American."

"Technically it is. The stuff they do in Quantico is amazing." Trout thought for a moment, "Although in some ways it's a reconnection with our most basic instincts as much as anything else. I remember my gran would know what anyone of us was doing with an uncanny accuracy – as for lying to her, not if you valued your ears. She'd have 'em boxed before you'd finished the sentence." He chuckled. "*Don't you lie to me, young fellow. I can see the blackness of it around your head.*" He sobered. "They showed us energy photos of people telling lies and there was a sort of dark aura around them, so maybe she was right."

"I've read some of that stuff. It sounds amazing but, as you say, our intuition is super-reliable if we just listened to it." She drained her coffee. "At the moment my intuition is telling me trust you and go with the flow."

"Thank you. I appreciate your trust and the minute I can I'll tell you the whole story."

"Me and Brendan?"

"You. Brendan will get the version best suited to him. In the meantime, has your intuition anything else to say?"

"Well ..."

"Spit it out."

"I think we should find out how the Carrigs came to order Freddy's doll's house."

"O-k-a-y. That's interesting. Why?"

"I'm not sure but it came to me last night that the doll's house is significant in some way."

"Right. That's today's task sorted."

"The Clothes Locker opening is at five," she reminded him.

"Bring a change of clothes, we can change at the apartment ..."

"You'll risk your mother's knowing looks?"

"Needs must," Trout grinned. "Not to mention it will make her day."

The Carrig residence was a testament to the privacy money can buy. It took centre stage in an exclusive cul-de-sac girdled and guarded by a circle of tall trees. The electric gates opened silently on Trout saying his name after a disembodied voice from the intercom demanded to know their business. He had taken the precaution of ringing in advance and asking for an appointment with Isolde Carrig. Her personal assistant was determined that he wouldn't get one. As she went to hang up on him, he suggested she tell Mrs Carrig that he wanted to talk to her about Freddy Loftus and the doll's house. At that her attitude did a dramatic about-turn. Suddenly there was a window in the Carrig schedule at two o'clock. It barely allowed them two hours to get there. They made it with three minutes to spare.

A short driveway curved to where the house stood in an oasis of lush lawns and colourful flower-beds. When they stepped from the car the swish of waves on a shore proclaimed that the sea was nearby although, from where they stood, it was out of sight.

Lauren gazed around. "This is a north-side I'm totally unfamiliar with …"

"It's real nonetheless. Didn't Freddy capture the house to perfection?"

They stood for a moment and admired the graceful façade, all curving lines and sparkling glass. Its silver-grey stonework provided a perfect backdrop for brilliant white window frames and a glossy green front door. As they approached the door opened and a tall severe-looking woman of uncertain age watched them with narrowed eyes and unsmiling face.

Trout's eyes crinkled. "Looks like we're expected even if we're not welcome," he said out of the corner of his mouth. "No stealing the spoons now, Lauren, we're on our best behavior."

Lauren stifled a laugh as he escorted her into the house.

Isolde Carrig was unexpected. The disapproving assistant led them to a book-lined room with an antique lady's desk and a modern ergo-dynamic office chair set into the curve of a bay window. A petite woman with short dark hair, a wispy fringe carefully tossed across her forehead, uncurled from the chair and rose to meet them. She assessed them with shrewd brown eyes, expertly made up and framed by spiked lashes to give the impression of wide-eyed ingenuity. Her black leather jeggings fitted like a second skin and were complemented by a red bat-wing top and black high-heeled ankle boots. Diamond studs sparkled with the full weight of their two-carat brilliance in each ear. She neither said hello nor offered her hand.

"Sit and tell me about my doll's house." She waved them to an arrangement of chairs one side of the unlit fireplace as the jewels on her fingers flashed and flared a testament to her wealth and importance. Her voice was carefully modulated, her command to be carried out without question.

"Good afternoon, Ms Carrig. I'm Thomas Tegan and this is my associate, Lauren O'Loughlin." Trout allowed a trickle of amusement to shade his words.

Isolde Carrig arched a carefully shaded eyebrow. "So, Giselle told me you were coming. You have information about my doll's house."

"We are looking for information about the doll's house."

"Then you're no use to me. I want to know where it is."

"Why did you commission Freddy to make the replica of this house?" Lauren interjected softly.

The sharp brown gaze raked her. "I wanted it and he could do it justice."

"Your children are surely too old to play with dolls?" Lauren infused the words with just enough disbelief to warrant an answer.

"It's not a toy, was never meant to be. It's to form the centrepiece of my collection."

"You collect doll's houses?"

"Rare and unusual ones or," Isolde almost smiled, "ones with a secret."

"So, Freddy's house has a secret?"

"Why do you say that?" Isolde asked sharply. She turned fully towards Lauren. "Have you seen it?"

"Yes. It's a magnificent piece of work." Lauren paused and added delicately, "If it's to be the centrepiece of your collection, the others must be truly amazing."

Isolde bit her lip, watching Lauren through the spiky lashes. Finally, she said, "Do you want to see them?"

"I'd love to."

"Come on. I'll show you." She looked at Trout. "You'd better come too. I can't leave you here on your own."

She led the way across the entrance hall and up a broad staircase that curved sharply to the right and opened into a half-landing that branched left and right. She turned left and opened a door halfway along the corridor. The room was square, elongated into a large bay window corresponding with the room below. It contained no furniture other than ten doll's houses, on the floor, on pedestals and on shelves. The middle space was occupied by a sturdy square table obviously awaiting a substantial addition to the collection.

"*Wow!*" Lauren breathed.

"Aren't they fabulous? But it's their stories that make them really special." Isolde touched a delicate clapboard house on a shelf at eye-level. It was high-gabled and turreted with fragile fretwork balconies. Both sides were open to allow access to the rooms. "This one is American, from the nineteen twenties. Have you heard of the Butterfly Murders?"

Lauren shook her head.

"This house is one of two that the murdered girls used for hiding their jewelry. Isn't that just delicious?" She darted to a large house standing waist-high in the corner near the window. "This is one of my favorites. The Borgia house. They say Isabel de Borja used dolls and this house to instruct her daughters in the way of winning favours from the most influential noblemen of the time."

The house was of dark wood, with small windows and a brooding façade. The whole front of it opened to show sumptuously decorated rooms from which malice and the smell of mothballs emanated in equal measure.

Lauren shuddered. "Are all the houses associated with murder and mayhem?"

Isolde looked around. "I suppose. I've never thought of them like that. This one …" she laid her hand on a medium-sized plain wooden house with an arched window at one end, a square tower at the other and a banded wooden door in the middle, "is early German." The window and door opened independently to show plainly furnished rooms and the tower looked squat and solid. "It was used to smuggle jewelry and bonds when the family were fleeing the Nazis. The tower has a cleverly concealed release mechanism that opens it." She fiddled with a tile on the roof and the whole tower opened to reveal a snug felt-lined cavity. "Clever, isn't it? Freddy was fascinated with my houses. He promised me he'd … never mind, you've seen enough."

"Did you have a contract with Freddy?" Lauren was looking around the room with carefully hidden distaste.

"Contract?" Isolde frowned. "Why would I need a contract? We had an agreement."

"How will you claim the house from his estate if you have no proof it's yours?" Trout asked quietly.

Isolde went white behind her make-up. "It's mine," she said tightly. "Freddy was making it for me. He put my …" She slanted a look at Trout. "If necessary, I will be able to prove it's mine."

"Well, then you've nothing to worry about," Trout said blandly.

She glared at him, made a dismissive *pfft* and without another word led them from the room. They traipsed down the stairs after her. She stood to one side at the bottom and watched with impassive eyes as Trout and Lauren bid her goodbye and saw themselves out.

Chapter 32

"She's nuts." Once they were safely in the car and heading for the gate Lauren felt free to talk. "Those creepy doll's houses!" She shuddered.

"You didn't find them creepy until you found out they have a misfortunate history," Trout pointed out. "They're just wooden toys that have been through some awful times." He negotiated his way out of the cul-de-sac and turned towards the seafront. "A breath of fresh air is called for, I'd say."

"Good idea."

He found a parking spot and they both got out. Lauren took a deep breath of the salt-laden air. "Have we time for a walk?"

Trout pulled out his phone. "We have. Oh – a missed call and a text from Mother," he muttered. "Had the phone on silent for the interview with her ladyship." He accessed the message and grinned. "She's devastated that herself and Dad are with friends trekking in the Wicklow mountains and will have to miss us. She says work away. I have my own key." He dashed off a quick reply. "We can afford a short walk. Come on, blow the Borgias out of your head!"

He grabbed her hand and set off along the promenade. "What do you think we learned from the lady of the manor?"

Lauren allowed herself be pulled along until she settled into her stride. "We need to examine Freddy's house more carefully," she said breathlessly.

The Clothes Locker was situated in a country house some forty minutes from the city in the midst of lush countryside. A short avenue of beech trees led to open lawns and a period house of two stories with an attractively windowed attic and a single-storey wing attached to each gable. Trout whistled when he saw it. A sign indicated that parking was in the stable yard to the left. The car park was almost full. A young man directed them to a space between an ancient mini and a new Mercedes. Trout thanked him and followed the indicated path to an arched exit that brought them to a gravelled area with a long conservatory and wide-open French doors. The conservatory sat at a right angle to the single-storey front wing and continued out of sight in a series of long, low buildings. Through the glass they saw people milling about in exotic costumes of every era imaginable. They were carrying champagne flutes and excited chatter floated on the air, like birds twittering in an aviary.

Trout and Lauren entered through the nearest open door. A Marie Antoinette character detached herself and glided towards them. "Lauren darling, you made it!" She snapped her fan shut and offered her cheek for a social kiss. "The nineteen-twenties suit you," she said, examining Lauren's dress. "Not quite authentic Schiaparelli but near enough to fool all but the most discerning eye."

"Thank you, DeeDee. It's good to see you. This is my friend Thomas."

Marie Antoinette extended a bejewelled hand and Trout obliged by formally raising it to his lips. She assessed him with sultry eyes then tapped him lightly with her fan. "Naughty boy. You're not taking us seriously or perhaps," her eyes narrowed, "you are sending us a message coming as Robin Hood."

"Neither, I'm afraid." Trout laughed. "It was the best I could cobble together from my parent's wardrobe. Forgive my lack of preparedness, Your Majesty."

"You'll do. Come along in and circulate. Champagne on the trays, and there's a bar in the games room if you'd prefer something stronger. Alain is around here somewhere, say hello when you see him. Go and have a look around. I'm thrilled with what we've achieved here. I'm sure our sponsors will see it as money well spent."

"You have sponsors?" Trout edged the doubt in his words with admiration.

"And why not? We cater to a very specific market: some organizations prefer their altruism to be specific." Her voice challenged him and, when he bowed his head in acquiesce, she nodded. "We'll chat later, Lauren." She drifted away and left them to their own devices.

"*Ouch!*" Trout said in Lauren's ear. He plucked two glasses of champagne from a tray and handed her one. "What do you think? Would she use a handbag or a stiletto for the duel?"

Lauren spluttered a laugh. "DeeDee takes her Cosplay very seriously. Come on. Let's explore while we can."

The conservatory was a large open space with random arrangements of tables and chairs, a couple of sofas and a chaise lounge – most of the seating was occupied. A Catwoman stretched sinuously on the back of the chaise lounge while Attila the Hun fed her champagne through a straw. A Southern Belle took up a whole sofa, her crinoline spread out around her like a visible forcefield. Young men in straw boaters, girls looking like extras from Downtown Abbey, Margaret Thatcher and Denis mingled and wandered, drank and chatted. Trout and Lauren watched the interplay of characters before turning their attention to the surroundings. From where they stood, they could see that the series of single-storey buildings continued all around to form a quadrangle with a paved courtyard and a central lawn. Four paths dissected the lawn and converged on a classic fountain where nymphs and cherubs cavorted under cascading water. All the buildings opened onto the courtyard.

Carrying their drinks, they meandered, discovering that each building was interconnected. They each had two or three rooms, designated as lockers and containing clothes and furniture congruent with the era they represented. Some of the rooms were basic, the Primitive Man consisted of furs and skins with rocks as seating and shared space with the Mighty Peasant, while others were decked out in full period décor and, like Courtesans Through the Ages, held rail after rail of sumptuous apparel with delicate furniture and a heavily scented atmosphere. Comic Book Heroes and Memes occupied a full building with futuristic furniture, flashing lights and scenes of super-powers playing on a loop over the walls. Facts from each era were strategically placed for anyone who was interested. Trout couldn't see the point but clearly saw that Lauren found it totally fascinating,

Characters swanned about in every direction. Nobody pretended to be a normal person and Trout was pleased that Lauren had insisted he came in costume. Eventually they reached the games room. It was one big space with a glass domed ceiling and small windows. On their left was a Wild West saloon complete with a well-stocked bar, tended by a shirt-sleeved, mustachioed proprietor. A bowler-hatted individual played honky-tonk on a tinny piano while cowboys and saloon girls ambled around and some miners downed whiskey like they were dying of thirst. A very tense-looking game of poker was being played in the corner.

Trout raised a querying eyebrow; Lauren shrugged her shoulders.

To the right a number of carefully constructed Casino set pieces segued from the elegance of Monte Carlo to a raucous Las Vegas. Trout briefly wondered about gaming licenses but decided it was none of his business. In the middle a pool table and a billiard table competed for attention while the gleam of polished wood caught the light in the far corner. Trout watched a spin of roulette, Lauren wandered on. He found her in an alcove, formed within the angle where the two walls met. It contained four beautifully constructed, old-fashioned game machines. A gaudy sign over the first one proclaimed "Sweets For My Sweet" and looked like an old Bush radio, set onto a large wooden funnel with the narrow end curving out to form a small plate. Lauren reached forward and twisted the knob – a cockcrow, loud and shrill, greeted her. "What the ...?" She turned it again. Rick's gravelly voice from *Casablanca* growled at her about gin-joints. She laughed, turned the knob once more – to hear Sugar from *Some Like It Hot* sadly complaining about fuzzy lolipops.

"My gran had one of those." Trout reached a hand to the knob. "It was nearly impossible to tune." He twirled the knob and "*Sweets for my sweet, sugar for my honey*" thrilled from the box while a small pouch of Jelly Babies dropped onto the plate. "Clever." He picked it up and with a flourish handed it to Lauren.

"Thank you." She laughed. "That is so cool. Quotes from the

movies and sweets." They moved on. "Look at this one."

The Derby Stakes was a re-purposed drinks cabinet. The glass and mirrored top held a painted racetrack, grey against a backdrop of trees and flowers and blue skies. Two horses and their jockeys awaited the punters' pleasure at one end of the course. Two paddles protruded from the front. Lauren tentatively pushed at one of them: one of the horses jerked. "The mechanism for moving the horses must be hidden in the cabinet." Lauren's eyes gleamed. "Bet I could win. Want to take me on? Yellow's my colour."

Trout grinned. "Yellow looks like an old nag. Red has a winning look. What's to play for?"

"My Jelly Babies." Lauren solemnly left them on the side of the cabinet.

They each took a paddle and on the count of three set about sending the horses around the track. Lauren worked her paddle furiously. Trout tipped his along quickly and efficiently. They were neck and neck coming up to the turn. The red edged ahead on the curve and looked well placed for a spectacular finish.

"*Come on, come on, Bashing Banana, you can do it*," Lauren yelled, jiggling the paddle.

Trout looked at her. "Bashing Banana? What sort of a name is that?"

She ignored him and in that moment of inattention the yellow jockey surged ahead to cross the finish line first. A cacophony of bells and whistles greeted the winner. Lauren pumped the air. "*Champions!*"

"You distracted me with that stupid name," Trout protested, laughing.

"Bashing Banana won fair and square. And I get to keep my Jelly

Babies." She picked them up, "Poor Trout, don't worry I'll share." She slipped her hand through his arm. "That was fun. Let's see what's next."

They moved along laughing, to stand in front of the next game. This one looked shiny and bright and new. It was crafted in oak, polished to a golden sheen and shaped like a small sideboard with two doors in front and a high back intricately carved and scrolled. Underneath the decorative work was a narrow shelf supported by two slender, turned and shaped pillars. A leprechaun perched on it, fishing rod aloft, dangling a line through a hole on the top of a large glass case. It looked like an enclosed aquarium depicting a shipwreck with a multitude of debris scattered all around. It was fitted securely under the shelf. A spinning prism cast a glitter of jewel-like colours among the wreckage and picked up here and there an answering sparkle from a hidden gem. A bright banner invited – *Help Paddy Fish for Jewels in Davy Jones' Locker!*

"Is it possible?" Lauren read the banner again. "He could have called it 'Paddy's Locker' for short."

"Anything's possible." Trout was examining the game. "What's he fishing for?"

"Jewels, of course. I wonder how it works?" Lauren studied the leprechaun. "I presume you have to get Paddy fishing."

"He's sitting on the pillar ..." Trout attempted to move the pillar but it didn't budge in any direction. "No sign of a switch or button that would activate him either."

Lauren was running her hand over the smooth surface of the cabinet. "It's beautiful wood ... Hang on, I felt something move." She wiggled the curved lip over the doors and a wooden tray inlaid with a console of directional arrows slid into view. A rubber joystick flipped upright from where it nested along the edge of the tray. "Wow! This is so clever."

"I see someone has discovered my favourite corner – you almost make me believe in luck." The measured words were spoken behind then.

Lauren spun round. "*Dr Spock*," she gasped. "Oh, I used to love *Star Trek*."

The Spock character quirked a slanted brow. "Men, my pardon," he looked straight at her "and women, sometimes see exactly what they wish to see."

"Why is this your favourite corner?" Trout was trying to recall what he knew about Dr Spock. Sure he had watched *Star Trek* but he was more a *Bonanza* fan.

"Because it's fascinating."

Lauren clapped her hands. "You used to drive Dr McCoy nuts when you said that."

"No offence but your mutual admiration society isn't getting us any nearer to figuring out how this game works." Trout sounded peeved.

"I fail to comprehend your indignation, sir."

"Trout. This is Dr Spock. He's half Vulcan – he works off pure logic." Lauren's eyes were dancing as she reprimanded him. She turned to Spock. "Did you design this?"

Spock sighed and said in a more normal tone, "I wish I could say yes, but I did program the game as envisioned by the young man who built it. And you're right, it is clever." He tipped the middle of the console and a diffused light filled the aquarium. Blue wavelets undulated around and within the wreck. Glimpses of sparkling jewels appeared and disappeared at random. "It's a mix of steady hand, eye co-ordination and skill. You use the arrows to position the line and the joystick to grab for a jewel. The fish-hook is magnetized so it's attracted to …" he shrugged, "hopefully whatever bauble you've set your eye on and it's up to you to secure it and get it out."

"Are they real?" Lauren gasped.

"No." Spock smiled. "If they were you wouldn't be able to catch them with a magnet. But if you manage to secure three pieces you can swap them for a real jewel of your choice."

"Oh!" Lauren was gazing at the tank like a child in a sweetshop. "I'm surprised there isn't a queue here."

"There's so much to see tonight it hasn't been discovered yet. I thought I'd have this corner to myself. I salute your good taste."

"It's a beautiful piece of cabinetmaking. Who did you say made it?" Trout was admiring the scroll-work decorating the unit.

"It is indeed beautiful and I didn't say but as you are interested, Robin Hood Prince of Thieves, it was a young man of great skill and ingenuity by the name of Freddy Loftus."

"I've heard that name somewhere recently …" Trout sounded thoughtful.

"Possibly on the news." Spock touched the cabinet and finished sadly, "He was murdered a week ago." Before either of them could say anything, he turned to Lauren. "My apologies. I've tinged your pleasure in the game with my sorrow. I liked Freddy and I admired his work. I find it difficult to comprehend that such talent was destroyed by a needless act of violence."

"What did you say? Needless violence?" Trout asked sharply.

"I am frequently appalled by the low regard you Earthmen have for life." Like the flick of a switch Spock returned to character. "I'll leave you both to the enjoyment of the evening." He glided away.

Lauren watched the retreating figure, looked at the console, turned to Trout. "I'm beginning to wonder if I've wandered into a dreamscape."

"You're a nineteen-twenties flapper, I'm Robin Hood and we've just had a conversation with Dr Spock of *Star Trek*. Of course it's not a dream."

They looked at each other and burst out laughing.

"Oh my God, this is so ridiculous." Lauren wiped her eyes. "Have we got anywhere, do you think?"

"We know Freddy built this game from scratch and that he very cleverly fitted the controls out of sight." He turned back to the unit. The lights had timed out and only the spinning prism attracted attention. "Let's see how this actually works." He pushed the joystick into its groove and, holding it in place, pushed the tray back into its space. It slipped in with an almost imperceptible click. "So, there is some sort of a mechanism." He examined the lip. It fitted snug, looking like part of the structure with no visible sign that it moved. He pulled on it gently, pushed it and eventually found when he pushed in and down at the same time the tray slid out. "Neat. I wonder if he has any other hidden spaces." He pushed it back into place and examined the doors. "Locked, but that's most likely to protect the works." He turned to Lauren. "Here," he said. "You play the game while I have a look at the rest of cabinet." He tipped the front and once again, the console slipped out and the joystick flipped upright.

Lauren kept half an eye on him as she set up the game. The middle key turned the lights on and the arrows allowed her position the fishing rod. The lights and wavelets provided distraction and she soon found she needed total concentration to manoeuvre the rod with any hope of catching a jewel.

Trout mooched around, appraising the cabinet as if completely taken with it. He touched the wood, ran his fingers over the decorative scrolls and whorls. That he pressed a little harder here and there was not noticeable. He moved to the other side.

Lauren used the tips of her fingers to control the joystick and position the rod. Carefully she edged the hook forward, barely allowing it to sway and, bingo, she snagged a red-stoned ring. Holding her breath, she began the delicate task of raising the line and getting the ring out. It was almost at the opening when …

"Got it," Trout's muttered and distracted her.

"*Sugar!*" The ring fell back into the wreck. "It had better be good. I just lost a ruby ring," she grumbled as she turned to see what Trout was doing.

"The scroll-work at the end on this side moves," he said quietly. "Can you cover me until I see if it opens?"

She moved as if she was going nearer to the joystick to begin the game again. This put her at a right angle to Trout and gave the impression that they were both absorbed in the game. Trout used the same principle as he used on the console, pushing in and down. The decorative knot that curled and curved into a vine, trailing over the edge, shifted and a section of the side slid out. Quick as thought Trout palmed the small black cylinder that sat in the hollow of the wood and pushed the whole lot together again.

"*Drat.* I've lost it again!" said Lauren.

"Third time lucky!" Trout said cheerfully. "I'll get your ruby for you." He hooked the red ring and swung it towards the opening only to see it fall back and out of sight. "I guess you'll have to make do with the Jelly Babies this time."

Lauren smiled her agreement and together they continued their tour of the Clothes Locker.

Chapter 33

Trout and Lauren continued to explore as nonchalantly as they could after their discovery. They wandered through the 1800s, the Wild West, and the Tudors. They found the 1920s in the middle building on the far side of the quadrangle. Vague young men in striped jackets and boater hats were tangoing with lithe women in flapper dresses and shiny headpieces. The music was blaring from a wind-up gramophone, the hiss of the needle on the record adding its own rhythm. Lauren moved to read the information on the era and spotted Marie Antoinette on the lawn.

She indicated the French doors and mouthed to Trout, "Need a quick word with DeeDee."

Trout followed her, discreetly. He felt she might learn more without him hovering at her side but was curious to hear what DeeDee might have to say.

Although not yet fully dark, strings of lights were gleaming through the trees and sparkling on the fountain. Scented torches and diffusing lamps cast a glow over the lawn. It looked like a magical kingdom from some whimsical Disney movie.

Lauren hurried across and Trout heard her say, "DeeDee!" She sounded a little breathless. "May I photograph the information in the nineteen-twenties room?"

DeeDee turned. "Whatever for?" She pursed her lips. "Didn't you sign up for our newsletter? You'll have full access to all the information. Much more convenient, darling."

"Cool." Lauren nodded. "This place is brilliant; you've done an amazing job on it."

"It pleases me." DeeDee cast a benign, albeit calculating, eye over the scene. "The book helped and the work you did on it ensured we reached a far greater audience than we could have ever anticipated. We tapped into a market that we could only hope existed. It grew from there."

"I'm glad."

"I suppose we were lucky too." DeeDee glanced at Lauren. "A rather well-known entrepreneur became interested in us. You may have heard of him – Robert Carrig?"

"Robert Carrig?"

"Yes. Why? You sound surprised."

Trout, in deep contemplation of a water nymph, tensed then smiled as Lauren softened her tone and added a touch of awe.

"I've read about him in the financial pages. I'd have thought he'd be way above a small operation like yours. Not that yours is small, if you know what I mean."

"A niche market, you mean?"

"Exactly."

"You're probably right but his daughter wanted to experience Cosplay and when I wouldn't sell him the company, he offered to invest a substantial amount in our little enterprise."

"DeeDee," Lauren hesitated, "I hope you didn't ... that is, you were careful, weren't you? I've heard he can be a bit of a shark and this is your family home as well as Cosplay's flagship."

"Thank you, Lauren, for caring." She patted her arm. "I didn't come down in the last shower. He tried but didn't succeed." A hardness came into her eyes. "He wanted my company for his daughter but she'll have to wait. I might prefer the sixteenth century but I'm not stupid." She flicked her fan. "I'd better go and circulate. You're welcome to join us any time, Lauren, for fun or information." She heaved her voluminous skirts around and said over her shoulder as she left, "And bring that yummy Robin Hood with you."

"Robert Carrig again," Trout murmured in Lauren's ear, causing her to jump,

She nodded. "And DeeDee doesn't sound like a fan of his."

They lingered in the courtyard, enjoying the ambience, and bit by bit returned to the conservatory to find a substantial buffet in place. The tables were laden with mouth-watering foodstuff: poached salmon, deviled eggs, bruschetta, a mix of savory bites and exotic salads. As they filled plates they got talking to The Penguin and Batman.

"Aren't you two supposed to be arch-enemies?" Lauren teased.

Batman smirked. "We've been together so long now it's hard to tell what we are to each other." The Penguin smacked his arm. "Hey, watch out! That's my Beef Wellington you're endangering!" He added conspiratorially, "I know these caterers. Their beef is to die for, you must taste it." He speared a morsel and added it to Lauren's plate.

"Come on, Bats, the girl might be vegetarian." The Penguin was busy piling his plate with everything in sight. "Although to be fair it wouldn't matter; this food is so good you'd eat it whatever your persuasion."

The four of them moved on together and commandeered a small table that became vacant as they approached. As the social chit-chat became more personal it turned out that Batman was a solicitor in everyday life and The Penguin was a well-known architect. They enjoyed Cosplay as a means of relaxation and were good friends of Alain's. They regularly attended DeeDee's house parties and were supportive of the expansion of the Clothes Locker. As a matter of fact, the design for the interlocking rooms and the formation of the quadrangle was the work of The Penguin. He was very pleased: the finished product had more than lived up to expectations. Lauren was fulsome in her praise of the development and adroitly introduced the topic of Robert Carrig and DeeDee's annoyance at his attempted take-over.

Batman scowled and commented that luckily DeeDee had enough business acumen to ask his advice before she signed anything. He had advised her to have nothing to do with the man.

"He was very persistent – only for the fact that DeeDee trusted us as old friends it could have been very different." The Penguin was talking directly to Batman. He turned to Lauren. "He wanted the whole shebang for that spoiled brat of a daughter." He turned back to Batman. "Only for you, DeeDee could have lost everything." He dabbed delicately at his lips. "As it was, I had a job persuading DeeDee to show Derek the contract. She won't admit it but in the beginning she was more than a bit in awe that a high-flier like Carrig might be interested. You nearly hit the roof, didn't you, Bats? When you saw what his people wanted her to sign."

Batman nodded. "It was very cleverly worded but in effect it would cede the company to Carrig Enterprises and gave control of its running to Caroline Carrig. I vetoed the whole thing asap and drafted a contract that allowed Caroline an executive title but no stake in the company and no access to the personal property of DeeDee and Alain." He speared a cherry tomato and popped it in his mouth. "We presented it to him as a done deal. If he wanted to invest money in the enterprise he could, on the condition that he or his daughter didn't attempt to take ownership of it. He was not impressed." He chewed thoughtfully. "Threatened to pull out he did but DeeDee, I'm glad to say, told him go ahead."

"The strap threw a tantrum when he went to pull out of the business." The Penguin screwed an eye around his monocle and gazed out at the lawn. "The daughter, that is. She was here *oohing* and *aahing* over the plans when he rang her. She made a complete spectacle of herself. A spoiled brat if ever there was one."

"Did he sign the contract?" Trout asked.

"He did." Batman snorted. "If he reckons he can manoeuvre his toehold to get something more substantial he's got another think coming. I'm well aware of Carrig's methods and I made sure that contract was airtight."

The three musketeers stopped to say hello at that point and the talk turned more general.

Trout caught Lauren's eye. She recognized his time-to-go look and stood. "Great meeting you guys – we may meet again."

The musketeers bumped fists and chanted, "*All for one and one for all!*"

Laughing, Lauren and Trout left.

Before starting the car Trout consulted the map on his phone. "As

I thought," he said. "We don't need to go back to the city." He studied the roads for a couple of minutes, "We can cut across here, take the R road there and we'll be on the motorway in no time."

"I'll take your word for it," Lauren murmured. She put her head back and closed her eyes.

"Tired?"

"A bit … I'm trying to get the day straight in my mind." Her eyes flew open. "Did you get a chance to look at what came out of Paddy's Locker?"

"Not yet. I figured time enough when we're home."

"It's such a shame when you see what a clever craftsman Freddy was … seems he must have put a secret compartment in the doll's house."

"Judging by what he was able to do with the game cabinet, I'd say it's most likely he did."

"And that Mrs Carrig gave him something to hide in it. Remember when she seemed to start to say something to that effect and cut herself off."

"Yes. We've a lot of information from today. Now we need to see how it all fits together, especially now that we've got whatever it is from the game console."

Chapter 34

They chatted over and back comparing notes and impressions on the different people they had met. By mutual consent they kept the tone light and the journey passed quickly. Sooner than expected they reached Knocknaclogga. The street was quiet and peaceful, no sign of anybody although it was only a little after ten o'clock.

"We'll stop at my place first and have a look – hey, look – is that smoke over the far end of the village? And sparks. Somebody has a chimney fire. *Jesus*. That's my place." Trout put his foot down, the car surged forward only to slam to a stop, in seconds, outside the gate.

"The front door is open." Lauren spoke through trembling lips.

Trout was out of the car and careering up the path before she had her seatbelt unclipped. He disappeared through the doorway. Lauren hurried in behind him. Intense heat was radiating from the small sitting room. The stove was glowing red and the room itself was in turmoil, chairs overturned, cushions scattered their innards pulled out, the smell of burning paper filled the air. Red embers glowed behind the glass stove-door but the intensity of the fire had died down although the whoosh and crackle in the chimney suggested that it was still on fire.

"Will I call the fire brigade?" Lauren could feel the heat but saw no sign of immediate danger.

"No, the chimney was cleaned recently – it's just the bits of paper burning off. Luckily no sparks reached the stuff on the floor." He kicked a pile of foam further away from the fireplace.

"Paper?" She looked around. "Oh no, our evidence!"

"I'm afraid so." Trout sounded grim.

"What –" Lauren stopped as Trout put a warning finger to his lips.

"I'm going to have a look around to check the rest of the rooms. Go out to the garden, Lauren. It's too hot in here for safety. I'll be out in a few minutes."

Lauren looked at him. He was still making the shushing gesture while his eyes searched the room for something. "OK."

She looked back from the door, Trout was picking up and examining any ornaments that were still upright, he moved to the pictures and pulled them out to look behind them. She went out to the garden, a perplexed frown on her face.

Trout joined her eventually. "The back door was also open. We must have disturbed them when we came back. I found this on the kitchen floor and there's another one behind one of the pictures in the sitting-room." He held out his hand to show her a small disk, like a round watch battery but with wires coming out of it.

"What is it?"

"A listening bug." At her start he added, "It's OK – this one is deactivated, we can talk freely – the one in sitting room is active though and I didn't touch it. Not yet anyway."

"Listening bugs? You're joking?" She shuddered at his headshake. "But who would be able to get listening bugs?"

"It's a lot easier than you think. Any google search will throw up numerous sites where someone with a credit card can buy half a dozen."

"But surely if they wanted to hear what we said, they shouldn't have drawn attention by burning our papers?"

"Throw us off the scent." Trout sounded grim.

"Are we getting too close to something?"

"Looks like it … Lauren …"

"Forget it. I'm not stopping now. Anyway, what difference would it make – everyone knows I'm helping you. I'd be more of a liability if I pull out because I won't know what's going on."

Trout sighed. "I know and I got you into it…"

"Now hold on a minute, I'm an adult. I went into this with my eyes wide open."

"This isn't one of your books, Lauren."

"One of my books?" Lauren was tired and shaken and before Trout could soften his comment, she had erupted into full-scale fury. "How dare you insult me like that! I've been a help to you all through this investigation. As a matter of fact, we wouldn't even have got this far without my input." She was shaking with temper and disappointment. "When have I hampered you in this? When? When?"

Trout saw the tears shimmer on the edge of her lashes.

"*Whoa, whoa, whoa!*" He held up his hands. "I'm not saying you hampered me. Only for you we wouldn't have got this far; I know that. Know it only too well. I'm just worried I've put you in danger. These people have no respect for life and if something happened to you –" Trout stopped. The sudden realization of what he was about to say dried the words in his mouth. Now was not the time to tell

Lauren of his feelings, not when he wasn't even sure himself what they were.

"You think that makes it OK to suggest I'm living in cloud cuckoo land?" She blinked away the tears, wrapped her arms around herself and shook her head. "It's been a long day. I need to get home, get out of this dress, rest."

"Lauren, I'm sorry. I didn't mean that the way it sounded." Trout drew a hand over his face. "Look, I'm only trying to say I don't want anything to happen to you. I … oh, now is not the time for –"

"No. Now is not the time." Lauren shook her head, pulled out a tissue and blew her nose decisively. "I'm going home. I can walk. It's not that far."

He caught her arm. "No way are you walking home. Give me a minute, I'll make sure everything is safe, grab my laptop and we'll go to your place." He sounded subdued. "We can have a quick look at what we found." He tried a smile. "We could both use a snack – if you're not too tired?"

Lauren gave him a long look. He saw the tension drain out of her. "No, I'm not too tired. I'll wait in the car." She walked slowly away and climbed into the car, weariness evident in every move.

He watched her slump onto the passenger seat, lean her head back and close her eyes. Nice one, Trout, he berated himself. You've just upset the best thing that's happened to you in a long time. He shook himself. She was still here – that must mean something. He hurried through the house; all was quiet. The fire was out and showed no sign of resurrecting, the chimney was quieter, the rooms were peaceful.

He retrieved his laptop from the locked drawer and secured the doors. They drove in silence to Lauren's house.

Chapter 35

While Trout set up his laptop on the kitchen table Lauren popped upstairs and returned in dark flowing yoga pants and a soft cashmere sweater. She looked composed and seemed to have recovered her good humour.

She rooted in the fridge. "I'm having toast," she announced. "I can make you a ham sandwich if you'd like."

"Toast with ham sounds good, brings me back to my youth."

"God, yeah. Lucy used to do that too. We'd come in from a night out. I'd get the toast and she'd get the ham and butter. Then we could have our," she laughed, "dissection and analysis, she used call it. It seems so long ago."

"Well, it was in the last century, you know."

She looked at him, indignant, then realized that he was right. "Imagine we've lived in two centuries. That feels awesome." She busied herself making toast and ham sandwiches. Her natural resilience was back in place. She carried two pints of water to the table.

"Water?"

"Channeling last century, home for the night."

He laughed and started on the sandwiches.

Trout examined the narrow egg-shaped tube; it was firm and light in his hand. As he chewed, he fiddled with it, pushing, pulling, twisting until it came asunder to reveal the square tip of a USB. "Now for it." He inserted it into the port of the laptop.

Lauren sat down beside him. She held her breath, watching him click through the process to configure the stick and open the data. The home page filled the screen, showing a list of stored files and folders, pictures and documents.

Trout clicked into one, then another and another. He skimmed a document, opened a random folder, read a line here and there.

He sat back. "Holy shite, this isn't just dynamite – it's gelignite primed to go off!" He closed out of the data. "I need to make a phone call." He looked at Lauren, "Please remember that we agreed I would give you a full explanation when this is all over."

She raised startled eyes, watched as he punched in a number, listened, put in another number and another. At last, he said, "Hello, Terence."

"It must be good, Trout, if you're ringing after midnight." There was no indication that Terence had been roused from sleep. "What news?"

Trout was conscious of Lauren hanging on every word he said. Nonetheless he recounted what had happened over the past week, without embellishment or speculation. He left nothing out and gave generous credit to Lauren for her assistance and input.

"You have the papers secure and you tell me this data-stick adds to and collaborates what's in them?"

"Yes. Actually . . ." He tilted back his chair and closed his eyes. "Terence, this stuff is way beyond dynamite. The information I've glanced at implicates people at the highest level. It gives us the leverage being used in a lot of our most trusted institutions. I've seen evidence of blackmail and coercion and I've barely scratched the surface of what's on it."

"Love a duck, Trout, you've hit pay-dirt. I knew if anyone could do it, you would." Terence came as near to getting excited as Trout had ever heard him. "We need to secure the data asap. Have you any ideas?"

"I've been thinking about that. How secure is your server?"

"Totally."

"I'll email you what's on it through the encryption zone – that way you can get to work on it in the morning and on top of that I'll post the USB to you. Once it's in the postbox nobody can touch it unless there's a problem at your end."

"We're good here. Nobody knows we exist – even if it's suspected they don't know where to look. The post's a thought – in this high-tech era it tends to be forgotten. Better still make a copy and post it but keep the original safe somewhere until I can organize a courier to collect it. Or you get a chance to deliver it personally. Get moving on it. You'll need a postal address – needless to say, it will be one that won't raise questions anywhere." There was a short silence. Trout waited. "Right. Use this," Terence gave him the name and address of a well-known fashion boutique, then added "the sooner it's dealt with, the safer you'll be. Once I have reviewed the contents, we can decide what way to go with it."

"Will do. Expect an email in the next few minutes."

"Well done, Trout. My compliments to your girl. We'll be in contact soon."

The call disconnected.

Trout looked at Lauren. "Terence sends his compliments and, no, I can't tell you anything yet." He sighed heavily. "Suffice it to say it's a state security issue that hopefully will be resolved soon."

"OK. I gave my word and I'll take yours. Is there anything I can do?"

"Coffee?" Trout said hopefully. "Water's fine but I need to get this organized and that will take coffee."

Trout opened a new window and called up an email account that was buried deep in cyber-space and didn't appear anywhere on his server. He copied the contents of the USB into a folder, checked that it had scrambled successfully and was technically unreadable without the appropriate key and pressed send. He waited for the sent message to appear then removed the data-stick, closed the account and deleted the history.

Lauren returned with two mugs of coffee. He took one with a heartfelt "Thanks", swallowed a mouthful and said, "Any chance you'd have an unused data-stick lying around?"

"Of course. I always have a few for work." She opened the cupboard under the record-player and extracted a data-stick, sealed in a card, and a small stamped padded envelope. She left them on the table beside him, turned back to the press and produced a bottle of Bailey's. She held up the bottle, "I don't know about you but I'm going for a bit of sweetness."

She added a good dollop of the liqueur to her cup and held it poised over Trout's. He was busy addressing the envelope.

He held up a hand. "Better not. Don't want to chance meeting the local patrol car. I'll pop down the village and drop it in the postbox." He ejected the device, popped it in the envelope and sealed it. "A strip of sellotape, to be sure to be sure."

Lauren handed him a large roll. "Will it be safe? It sounds like it's really important . . ."

"As safe as anywhere else. I have great faith in the post and if anything happens to it it's encrypted and we still have the original. Speaking of which, have you anywhere I can put that for the moment?"

"Here in the press. It will be one among many." She took the stick and dropped it into a small basket where it mingled with many others of every shape and size. "I presume you'll recognize it when you want it?"

"Hopefully. Now, I suppose I'd better make tracks. I'll see. . ."

The jangle of his phone interrupted. He made a small grimace. "Nothing good at this hour of the night. He flicked it open, swore, swiped the screen. "What's up, Miko?"

"Mr Tegan, a car just pulled into my yard and Maestro is going ballistic. Maestro is never wrong in his assessment of a car so I guess it's not good news."

"Are you safe, is your door locked?" Trout was on his feet.

"Well, now I only lock it when I'm not at home so I'll say it isn't."

"Jesus, Miko, have you never heard of security?" He grabbed his keys, indicated to Lauren they needed to go.

"Be japers, we have visitors," Trout heard in his ear. "Shush now, Maestro, until we see what these people want." The dog was barking furiously.

A voice, harsh and loud, was added to the mix. "*Hang up the phone, old man, and shut the fucking dog up or I'll do it for you.*"

Trout felt a cold shiver down his spine. He had heard that voice before, over the phone on the night Freddy was shot. He ran.

Lauren grabbed the envelope and followed him. He barely

waited for her to close the door before he peeled out the gate and turned for Killanee.

He tossed her his phone. "Get Mac on the line, tell him Miko Downes phoned to say some people arrived at the house who intend him harm, that we're on the way and will need back-up pronto."

She slipped the envelope under the seat, scrolled through the contacts and found the number. Mac's cheerful Cork accent filled her ear.

"How's the boyo? Who have you for me tonight?"

"Mac, this is Lauren. We have a situation. Miko Downes rang to say some people just arrived at his house who must intend him harm. Tegan and I are on the way there and will need back-up pronto."

"Bloody hell, the wasp's nest is bust! Get on with ye, I'll get the show on the road. Tell the gossoon to take no needless risks." The phone went silent.

In a heartbeat it chirruped again, the vibration sending a tickle along her arm. She stared at it.

"That might be Miko's visitors trying to see who he was ringing. Act pissed off as if you were trying to ring him back."

"Attack first," Lauren murmured, swiping the screen and simultaneously pressing the speaker icon. "What the hell you playing at, Miko? I've been trying to ring you back and getting a shagging machine. I'll remind you 'twas you rang me at this ungodly hour of the morning!"

A harsh voice demanded, "Who are you?"

"What d'you mean who am I? I'm your sister Winnie, the one you woke up to have a chat with in the middle of the night. Wait a minute, are you sure that's you, Miko? You sound different …"

A muttered "*Get rid of her*" echoed in her ear. "What's that? I can't hear you. Don't you know I'm a bit deaf?"

"I'm sorry for disturbing you, Winnie, go back to sleep." Miko's voice was calm. He gave no indication that anything was amiss either at home or with the phone call.

"Go back to sleep? Fat chance of that now. I'm awake so you might as well tell me what you wanted." Lauren made herself sound as if she was settling in for a chat. "Otherwise, I'll be awake worrying for the rest of the night."

"*Get her off the fucking line, old man!*" a voice hissed in the background.

"Just wanted to hear your voice and now I have. I'm thankful to you for answering. Good night, Winnie. God bless you."

Silence thrummed in the car. Lauren made sure the phone was off. The hedges flashed by in a blur of light and dark as the headlights flashed on them and sped past.

"Good thinking," Tegan said.

Lauren shivered. "Will he be all right?"

"I don't know." Trout sounded grim. He increased speed on a straight stretch. "They'll be looking for information, that should buy us time." Then, "*Shit!* My gun's at home and we've no time to get it."

"Do you think you'll need it?" Lauren asked on a gasp.

"I recognized that voice. He was on the mountain, he's the guy who ordered the search for the phone the night Freddy was shot."

"Oh my God!" Lauren clapped a hand over her mouth. "What will we do?"

"We'll decide that when we get there." He dipped the lights but barely paused at the junction. On the main road he pushed the car to the max. It seemed to take forever but in reality it was little enough time before they turned onto the narrow twisty road to Miko's place.

Chapter 36

Trout stopped and pulled the car into a gateway just before the turn onto the boreen that led to Miko's house. He jumped out but paused to close the door quietly, motioning Lauren to do the same. "Sound carries at night," he breathed into her ear as she came alongside him. Keeping in the shadow of the bushes, they flitted silently as far as the entrance to the yard. He indicated to Lauren to stop, flattened himself against the gatepost and peered around the corner. The yard was silent, grey and shadowed against the blackness of the night. He could make out Miko's jeep parked at the far end and, nearer, the silhouette of a long black vehicle was discernible in the pale light from the kitchen window. The yard otherwise looked to be empty but Trout was sure a look-out would have been posted somewhere out of sight. He felt around on the road and found a smooth stone. Taking careful aim he pitched it towards the far end of the outhouses. It made a satisfying clatter in the stillness. They waited. A shadow, deeper grey than the surrounding night, detached itself from the car and moving stealthily to the outhouses, slithered along the wall and pounced around the corner, turning on a beam of a powerful torch as he jumped. The indignant eyes of a hunting cat gleamed in response and melded into the dark with a haughty swish of its tail.

Trout watched the shadow saunter back to once again lean on the far side of the car. Now that he had identified where he was, he could see where the darkness deepened into the shape of a man. He jerked a thumb back down the boreen. About halfway down, he stilled Lauren with a hand on her arm and murmured into her ear, "The lookout is on the far side of the car. We need to deactivate him. I'm going to circle around from this side. Here's what I want you to do …"

Together they crept back to the gatepost. Trout nodded and melted into the shade of the hedge. Lauren counted ten, straightened herself and moved quietly to the far side of the opening. She bent down and picked up the biggest rock she could easily handle and threw it with all her might towards the outhouses. It made a startling loud thump when it hit the wall. The shadow at the far side of the car twirled into action. He switched on the torch and shone it across the houses. He moved away from the car, spotted the rock, surveyed it cautiously and reached out to touch it.

Silently and efficiently, Trout snaked an arm around his neck and the pressure on his carotid caused him to sink silently to the ground. Trout guided his fall and laid him out flat. He looked around and pointed to where a makeshift clothesline sagged between two poles, a lone dishcloth hanging on it damp and limp in the night air. He handed Lauren a heavy Swiss Army penknife, miming a cutting motion. She made short work of the line and soon the semi-conscious man was trussed and secure, the dishcloth stuffed loosely into his mouth. Trout plunged the knife into the two back tyres as a further precaution against an easy escape. He guided Lauren to the shadow of the house and, gesturing to her to stay, glided along the wall to the kitchen window.

Trout stood absolutely still, then leaned sideways and carefully turned his head. The light in the kitchen was low wattage but was more than adequate to illuminate the tableau inside. That single glance told him all he needed to know and he drew back to stillness. Miko was slumped in his usual chair beside the range, his head was thrown back as if he'd been slapped, a trickle of blood oozed from the corner of his mouth, one of his eyes looked to be closed. Two men stood either side, facing him, their backs to the window. One was holding a gun inches from his knee, finger poised on the trigger. The other was talking, the words indistinguishable. The dog growled and whined helplessly in another room. Trout took a deep breath. The man doing the talking was Marty Lambert.

He moved back to Lauren. "Looks like they're working him over and he's saying nothing," he whispered, anger coming off him in waves. "We need to get into the house. Maestro seems to be in another room." He thought for a moment, "We'll try round the front. There must be another way in. I need to access the kitchen. Maybe let the dog free – if he was loose, he'd be a distraction." He put a hand out and, using the wall as a guide, edged along the side of the house and around to the front. Lauren followed closely and together, silently, they mounted the footpath at the front.

Three windows crossed the front of the house with a door between the second and third. The windows were set at waist height and stared blackly out on a recently dug garden. The door looked like it hadn't been opened for years. From where they stood, the rumble of the dog's growls seemed very close at hand. Trout examined the first window. It appeared to be sealed by layers of paint. He moved to the next one and immediately Maestro let fly with a volley of barking. The window was an old-fashioned sash affair, the top half propped open and supported by a length of timber plainly visible. Trout climbed onto the sill and reached to dislodge the stick. It jerked out and he barely managed to stop the frame from crashing down. The dog again set up a cacophony of barking and ran at the window. A shout from the kitchen told him shut up but it was only when Trout called softly "Maestro!" that he quietened. He looked up at the window, wagging his tail. Trout levered himself into the room and perched on the inside sill. He leaned down, patted the dog and softly warned him to be quiet. He turned back and handed Lauren his phone. "I'm in. You go back down the lane, call Mac and tell him what's happening." He hung across the sash and spoke into her ear. "Tell him Marty Lambert is here and while you're at it you'd better send for an ambulance ..."

Lauren stifled a gasp and nodded.

Trout climbed carefully down onto the ground. An iron bedstead was directly in front of him. He maneouvred around it, put a hand on the dog's head and spoke quietly. "We need to rescue your master."

Maestro growled and ran to the door. Trout followed. Slowly and gently, he turned the knob. He had the door barely open when Maestro tore through and launched himself at the gunman. His front leg took the bullet meant for Miko's knee and the gunman ended up sprawled on the floor with the heavy dog bleeding on top of him. His gun was trapped between them.

"*What the fuck!*" Marty Lambert turned as Trout barrelled into him, and the two of them went flying across the room.

"*Maestro!*" Miko struggled to get to his dog but was unable to raise himself from the chair.

The gunman tried to push the dog off. Maestro growled under his chin and the dog's hot breath fanned the thug's neck. He lay still.

Tegan and Marty grappled wildly, each trying to get a grip on the other. Trout had Marty in a bear-hug. Marty landed a punch low in Trout's gut, knocking the wind out of him. Trout's hold slackened and Marty slipped from his grasp, swerved and collided with the door. He righted himself with an oath and turned, his lips bared in a snarl. "*You!*" A flash of silver and a knife flicked open in his hand. "*You've been the bane of my life for long enough!*" He lunged at Trout, the wicked blade slashing left and right. Trout jumped back, steadied himself, widened his stance and allowed his body soften. He swayed, over and back, staying just out of reach, moving backwards, gradually drawing Marty away from the door and back into the room. Marty swung the knife in an arc to the right and thrust forward, Trout swayed left, pivoted and chopped down on the extended arm. The knife went flying, Marty roared and kicked viciously at Trout's knee. The knee gave, Trout grabbed Marty's arm only to reel from a sharp blow to his jaw. His head snapped sideways hitting the wall and he saw stars.

The wail of sirens shattered the silence and speeding vehicles turned onto the boreen.

"*Fuck! Fuck! fuck!*" Marty jerked back. "*We'll finish this another day,*" he growled, turned and ran.

Trout heaved himself to his feet and staggered after him. Flashing blue lights were coming up the boreen. Marty bypassed the car and made for Miko's jeep. He hauled himself into the driver's seat and the vehicle shuddered to life then with a lurch trundled through the gate and into the fields, gathering speed as it went.

"Bloody hell, how did he start it?" Trout was livid.

"I might have left the keys in it," a tired voice said behind him.

Chapter 37

Two Garda cars and an ambulance screeched into the yard. A garda lurched from one of the cars and sprinted to the gate of the field only to skid to a stop when he realized he was too far away to do anything about the escaping vehicle. He watched the jeep navigate the bumpy field without slackening speed and disappear through the hedge at the bottom. He turned, hurried forward as a third squad car arrived and directed it back to the road, pointing out the direction the jeep went and where it would have exited. The car turned full circle and sped back the way it came in an effort to intercept the jeep.

Meanwhile the two thugs were officially secured. Both were handcuffed and transferred, in surly silence, one to each of the police cars. The one Trout had trussed up was found where he'd been left and was glad to get off the cold cobblestone. He huddled in the back seat and glared all around him. Maestro had kept the one in the kitchen immobilized until two of the gardaí had taken charge of him, after Miko had called the dog off. The thug was well soaked with the dog's blood and now sat looking thoroughly pissed off in the back of the second police car, his clothes slowly stiffening around him.

Miko was resisting the advice that he go to the hospital for a full check-up. He had insisted the paramedic attend to Maestro before he would allow them near him. The dog was sitting as close beside him as he could get. His leg was broken but the bullet had gone cleanly through and the break seemed stable. The paramedics had disinfected the wound and splinted the break although they did advise taking him to a vet in the morning. Maestro seemed quite content now that his master was safe. Miko himself had a nasty wound to the side of his head where the thug had hit him with the handle of the gun. It would require stitches or glue or both. One of his eyes was closed and swollen and the current negotiations were to persuade him to travel to the hospital for a thorough check-up and have his wounds attended to.

So far Miko was having none of it.

Two of the guards prowled around the kitchen, examining the scene. The knife was retrieved from the kitchen floor and the gun recovered from between Maestro and his captive. Both were safely contained in evidence bags and the general consensus was that all that could be done was being done and, as soon as forensics arrived, it would be time to move on.

Trout, eventually, gave in to Lauren's insistence and allowed himself be checked over. He was sitting on the step of the ambulance, staring straight ahead lost in thought. His wounds were superficial and after they were cleaned and dressed he was pronounced good to go. He sat now, a gleaming white wound-pad taped to his forehead, and nursed a bruised ego, aching muscles and a simmering anger at having let Lambert escape. Eventually he shook himself and focused on Lauren, thankful she had remained silent.

He made to rise, staggered and felt Lauren gently but firmly push him back onto the step.

"Sit down and be quiet for a few minutes," she said.

"We need to look in the workshop, examine the doll's house, make sure nothing has been tampered with …"

"They're all OK. I've checked. The padlocks are in place and the doors are locked."

Still Trout fretted. Something had brought Marty Lambert and his thugs to Miko and he would give a lot to know what that was. He beckoned Lauren closer and whispered they needed to be careful not to draw any attention to the workshop or its contents.

She simply nodded.

The squeal of a car taking the turn onto the boreen on two wheels caused heads to swivel in that direction. A high-powered BMW screeched to a halt on the far side of the yard entrance, leaving a clear run for exiting vehicles. Inspector Cooper erupted from the driver's seat and stormed into the relative calm. He stopped at the first police car and spoke a few words with the garda standing beside it. The garda spoke urgently, gesturing around him as if filling him in on what was happening, waited while the Inspector relayed instructions, nodded and with his colleague in the back with their prisoner, left. Cooper jerked a thumb indicating to the officers of the other squad car to do the same.

He marched to where Trout and Lauren waited. "I should have known you'd be stuck in it someplace." Cooper didn't look well. The night's stubble stood out starkly against the white of his face. The bags under his eyes suggested he hadn't slept well for days. He sounded tired and peevish.

"Morning, Coop." Trout straightened himself.

Lauren discreetly moved away and leaned against the side of the ambulance, watching and listening as the two men faced each other.

"What are you trying to prove, Tegan?" The question sounded more weary than belligerent.

Trout stared at him. "What am I trying to prove? That's rich, Cooper. You want the facts? Miko Downes rang me to say he was worried about a car that had turned into the yard. It was one o'clock in the morning so I came to check it out. I certainly didn't expect to find Marty Lambert torturing him when I arrived."

The Inspector started. "Marty Lambert? Are you sure?"

"Of course I'm bloody sure. In case you've forgotten we pulled him in often enough in the past for me to remember what he looks like." He tapped the bandage on his head. "Not to mention the close encounter we had before he skedaddled."

Inspector Cooper frowned at the toes of his boots. "Why was he torturing Miko Downes?"

"The sooner you catch him and ask him the better. Jesus, Cooper, talk about a new form of low. What could Miko know that brought Marty and his thugs to his door in the middle of the night?"

"Miko could know a lot of things." Cooper assessed Trout. "So, he got away from you, did he?"

"He got away." Trout couldn't keep the disgust out of his voice. "He took off in Miko's jeep and was last seen driving through the hedge there below. It borders the road so he had a good start but with a bit of luck the lads will catch him."

"Luck's overrated," Cooper muttered.

"Try telling that to Miko Downes after tonight's fiasco."

"*Shit on a brick!*" Cooper pushed rigid fingers through his hair. "*You've been nothing but trouble since you retired!*"

Trout felt a flash of anger sear him. "Hang on a minute. This elderly gentleman was being beaten by two thugs when I came on the scene." He pointed a finger at Cooper. "And you're accusing me of being trouble. You want to know who's causing trouble? Ask your pal Carrig what's going on!"

"Robert Carrig is no friend of mine," Cooper said stiffly. "What are you getting at anyway?" He frowned. "What's Carrig got to do with it? Do you know something? If you do, you'd want to produce it and it would want to be watertight. We've never been able to make anything stick to that fella. You know that better than anyone."

"His right-hand man was personally onsite, Coop – what does that tell you?"

"His presumed right-hand man ..."

"Bullshit. You're well aware how far back those two go – you were there. Remember?"

"Are you accusing me of something?"

"You told me yourself that it was either their gang or the get-out ..." Trout's gaze sharpened. He sat back. "Or was the get-out just for show? Jesus, Coop, are you their man on the inside?"

The Inspector attempted a laugh. It sounded hollow. "You're gone delusional altogether now, Tegan. I'm a cop as long as you. I've done my bit to clean up the garbage. Anyone can look at my record and see I've more than brought in my share of the gangs."

Trout was staring at him as if a gear had clicked into place in his brain. "So you did," he said slowly. "You routed the Talbots and fairly decimated the Cats but I'm thinking now that getting them out of the way left the field clear for Marty Lambert and his crew to balloon. Your biggest arrests were all rival gangs to Marty's. Jesus, Cooper, you opened up the way for Marty and Carrig to expand operations!"

Cooper pulled a crumpled pack of cigarettes from his pocket and selected one with fingers that trembled slightly. "That knock on the head must have scrambled your brains. You seemed to have forgotten that you were part of most of those arrests."

"Sure I was, with intelligence that you gathered from sources you wouldn't share."

"That's rich coming from you," Cooper scoffed. "Your boys were sacred to you alone, that's the way we worked. It was the only way to keep our informers safe." He flicked a Bic lighter and held the flame to his cigarette. His face was drawn and tense in the flare.

"You gave up smoking years ago." Trout cocked his head and studied his one-time friend.

"An illusion." Cooper dragged deep and allowed the smoke to trickle out slowly. "I gave up smoking in public. Not that it's any of your business."

Trout snorted. "That's what it was all the time! An illusion, a smokescreen! You fooled us all. How come nobody twigged?"

"*There was nothing to twig,*" Cooper growled. "*Get that into your thick skull!*"

"Hell, you even fooled me." Trout went on as if he hadn't spoken. "You were probably the only one of them who could have carried it off. Carrig was too arrogant and Lambert was an out-and-out hoodlum. You were the 'run with the hare, hunt with the hounds' guy ..."

"You're barking up the wrong tree, Tegan."

"Am I?" Trout stared at him. "Or am I so close that you've got a big decision to make?"

Cooper watched him through the smoke. "I'm all ears. What sort of a decision would that be?"

"To eliminate me now and to hell with the consequences or to wait until you can arrange a less noticeable hit?"

Trout heard Lauren gasp. They both ignored her.

Cooper laughed. "That screw is getting looser the more you talk." He finished the cigarette in one long draw and tossed the butt across the cobbles. It glowed for a second, fiery red against the grey until it fizzled out. "Move over in the bed." He squeezed in beside Trout on the step.

The two of them sat in silence for a few minutes.

"How long is it, Trout? How long have we known each other? Thirty, thirty-five years? Bloody hell, that's nearly half a century. You get to know a lot about a person in that many years. Yet here you are making wild accusations about me, my commitment to the force and that I'm about to kill you." Cooper leaned forward elbows on his knees, cupped a hand under his chin. "How did we end up like this?"

Trout felt a sense of deja vu creep over him. How often had they sat just like this? Himself and Coop, discussing a project, a case, a strategy or simply sitting in silence. "I don't know," he said eventually. "We were mates, friends ... and then we weren't."

"I looked for that transfer up north, you know," Coop said out of the blue.

"Was that when it started?" Trout looked straight ahead. The sky was beginning to lighten even though dawn was still two hours away.

"I could say when what started but knowing you that would be facetious." Coop was silent for a heartbeat. "I could also say I'll tell you if you tell me."

"What do you want to know that I could possibly tell you?" Trout turned to look at him.

Coop sat back. "What did Freddy Loftus take from Robert Carrig's house?" They locked eyes. "And do you have it?"

Trout held Cooper's gaze, allowed his eyes study him with deliberate calculation. A heaviness settled itself in his gut. Two questions. One of them alone consolidated his doubts and removed his last shred of hope as to where Cooper's affiliation lay. He thought about and discarded numerous comments and questions.

Finally he asked, "What hold has he got on you?"

"Always so black and white, Trout. 'This' happens so it must mean 'that'," Cooper mocked him but his eyes were bleak. "What's between me and Carrig is none of your bleedin' business."

"Then the question is irrelevant."

"Have you a fucking death-wish or something? Whatever was taken from Carrig's house got Freddy shot. You've seen what he's willing to do to recover it. And if the thing plays out differently it's part of the case and you're withholding evidence."

Trout said dryly, "Presuming I've evidence to withhold. You're the one investigating – surely you have whatever has turned up?"

"What's turned up points to Freddy taking something belonging to Carrig. He was your boy. Ergo he gave it to you or," Cooper frowned, "was he meeting you that night to hand it over? Was that the way it was?" He was half talking to himself. His gaze sharpened. "Were you on the mountain that night, Trout? Was the phone call all baloney to give you an excuse to go looking for Freddy when he failed to turn up with the goods? Or … no. He was your boy – you wouldn't have done him in yourself. Would you?"

"Jesus, Cooper, I don't go around killing off my informants. I didn't even know Freddy had anything to do with Carrig. If I did, I'd have told him to keep well away from him."

"You would, too." Cooper sighed. "Anyway, it was Carrig's missus did the mischief. She found Freddy, saw some fancy carpentry he'd done and nothing would do her but to have him make a replica of their house. She has a thing about doll's houses." His tone became vicious. "Stupid bitch must have been refused one when she was a girl."

"I've seen her doll's houses and not one of them is suitable for a child. They're positively macabre and that's saying something."

"Where did you see them?" Cooper asked sharply.

"In that mansion they call home – she invited me to see them."

"Does Carrig know you visited his missus?"

Trout shrugged. "No idea. I didn't see any sign of him, so unless Isolde told him, which I doubt, he doesn't know."

"You get around. Who else have you talked to?"

"Client privilege." Trout grinned. "You forget I'm a private investigator on this one. Can't share information unless it's in my client's best interest."

"You're really going ahead with this private dick business?"

"There's a lot to be said for it." Trout thought about it. "My hands aren't as tied as to where I can go and who I can talk to … It's funny, people talk more freely than they used to when I produced Garda ID."

"Human nature, never trust authority." Cooper sounded sour. "Always need to have that inside scoop to get ahead."

"Does that bring us round full circle?" Trout asked in an off-hand manner. "Are you Carrig's man inside the force?"

"Good try except you've forgotten my first rule for survival: don't implicate yourself."

"Seriously, Coop, if you're found out neither side will make a move to save you. At least if you turn state's evidence, you'll get some sort of protection."

"Trout, Trout, after all I taught you!" Cooper's pained expression said as much as his words. "You're still a bleeding innocent believing all they tell you as if it's gospel."

That stung. "I respect the law," Trout said sharply. "And I hate to see some scumbag profiteering at the expense of people who can't defend themselves."

"Most people aren't as helpless as you think. People make choices and if they have to live with them that's their look-out."

"Is that what happened with you? Are you living the consequences of a choice? You can always make a different one. I'll help you. Go bat for you, whatever it takes."

Cooper stared at him, a strange look on his face "You would too, wouldn't you? Tell me, Trout, how have you managed nearly forty years on the force and still believe that people are basically good?"

"Because they are."

"Bleeding culchie heart!" Cooper stood up. "If you've got what Carrig wants you might as well go top yourself before he does it for you. His method is likely to be more painful."

"I don't."

"I might believe you. He won't. As an old pal consider yourself warned." He stomped away without looking back.

Lauren levered herself from where she was leaning against the ambulance. She had her arms wrapped around herself and was shivering. "What on earth was that all about?"

"Here, you're frozen." Trout leaned into the ambulance and pulled a blanket from the stretcher. He wrapped it around her and held her to his warmth. "It sounded like . . . I don't know what to think. I wonder . . ."

They were interrupted by two paramedics who were supporting Miko out to the ambulance. "He's agreed to come with us if ye'll look after the dog."

"Of course we will." Lauren freed herself from Trout's arms but kept the blanket around her like a shawl. "We'll stay here, Miko, until you get back."

Miko handed her a bunch of keys. "You might need these. Work away with whatever you want. Only be careful."

"Thank you. We'll be careful."

"Maestro likes ye, that'll help." And on that cryptic statement he allowed the paramedic help him into the ambulance and settle him, sitting upright on the stretcher. He leaned sideways to squint at where Trout and Lauren were standing. "I'm right thankful for all ye've done this night. I'm thinking it would've been very different if ye hadn't turned up." He spoke gruffly. "Do whatever ye have to."

Chapter 38

The quietness in the yard after all the commotion was nearly unbearable. Trout felt his ears zing as he looked around. Streaks of red and yellow stained the horizon to the east. Himself and Lauren turned towards each other.

"I don't know about you but I could do with some food."

"I'd better check the dog."

They both spoke together. It broke the tension and they laughed. "Both valid, come on." Trout led the way into the house. "Christ." He stopped. Lauren bumped into him. "We left the package in the car. Anyone could have taken it."

"I pushed it under the seat so at least it was out of sight. You'd better go and get it."

"We'll need the car here anyway. Will you be OK here on your own while I'm gone?"

"Course I will. And I won't be on my own – I'll have Maestro. Hang on a tick and I'll check and see what provisions Miko has. You can pop over to the village, if need be – there's a twenty-four-seven petrol station and shop as you go in." Lauren was opening the door of an elderly fridge one side of the sink. "There's milk and butter, and what's this?" This was a plastic container with open packages of sausages and rashers. She squinted at the dates. "They're in date so we might as well use them."

"Is the village near?"

"Just over the ridge, about half a mile."

"I'm thinking I'll pop over and drop the envelope in the postbox. I presume there is one."

"You're in luck, there's two and one of them is at the petrol station so you won't even have to go into the village proper. I'll be cooking these while you're gone."

The car was as they left it. Trout felt relief sweep over him. Now for the package. A bit of groping under the passenger seat produced the padded envelope with the innocuous address. He sat for a moment and felt the tiredness wash through his muscles. Enough. There was still things to be done before he could rest.

He wasted no more time and in very few minutes he was pulling into the forecourt of a good-sized filling station. Two cars were at the pumps, a sleepy looking man, most likely heading out to work and a woman in a duffle coat with the starey eyes of someone coming off night duty, watched their respective cars guzzle fuel. A harassed-looking woman with a raincoat over pajamas was buying milk and ham at the shop window. Trout spied a sturdy iron post box bolted to the wall on the far side of the window. The surge of satisfaction as he dropped his package into it almost made him dizzy. The woman was leaving as he turned and he decided he'd get a few provisions to replace whatever of Miko's they would use.

As he drove back, the box of provisions on the passenger seat, he mulled over the events of the night. He was trying to figure out how he felt about Cooper's waffling – it wasn't an admission and you couldn't really say it was a denial so what was it? He had observed things through the years that suggested Cooper wasn't above taking a back-hander or turning a blind eye in certain situations but the level of perfidy implied by tonight's conversation was making him heart-sore. Basically, to his possibly jaundiced eye, Cooper had sold out his colleagues. That brought Trout back to the question of what hold the crime bosses had on him. Sure, he was with them from kindergarten and he used the law enforcement as an escape from the gangs but he refused to believe that Coop's whole career with the force was orchestrated by Robert Carrig. There must be something more. To his knowledge Jim Cooper wasn't a druggie, he'd no wife to cheat on, his sexual proclivities were straight up as far as he was aware, and he had never seen signs that he had a gambling habit. On the other hand, he'd hidden his smoking so what else could he be hiding?

Thinking about Cooper was giving Trout a headache. All he was doing was going round in circles. He hadn't actually seen his name mentioned anywhere in the data but then he'd only skimmed it. That it was gone out of his hands was another relief. Let those of a higher authority deal with the mess. The case was nearly wrapped up. Even if they didn't find out who had pulled the trigger on Freddy he would be exonerated. Nikki and Miko would have some sort of closure. Trout was quietly pleased at what himself and Lauren had achieved.

Lauren! He enjoyed working with her. She had a way of getting to the heart of a question that he found stimulating. She'd be disappointed when he explained to her that their little investigation agency was a once-off. A small voice in the corner of his mind muttered 'Does it have to be?' He wondered casually about the possibilities. He could see the potential of it, especially if they were selective in their investigations but . . .

Trout had got to this stage of his cognitions when he turned into Miko's yard. He turned off the car and silence settled over him like a wet woollen blanket, heavy and clinging. Somehow it felt too quiet. He frowned. His eyes scanned all around. His nose was itching. He rubbed it with the back of his hand. What was he picking up? He didn't believe in that psychic shit but his nose never failed to warn him that something was amiss and he had learned not to ignore it at his cost.

He got slowly out of the car. Nothing stirred. The house sat grey and squat in the morning light, the dull yellow from the window doing little to dispel the gloom that as yet remained untouched by the gleam of dawn. There was no sign of life in the yard itself nor any indication that anything was amiss. Yet Trout was acutely aware of something off. He studied the window. There was no reason to expect a sight of Lauren in the kitchen but somewhere deep in his thoughts he had imagined her there. He retraced his route with his mind's eye but could recall nothing that aroused suspicion, nor did he see any sign of a vehicle in the immediate vicinity. He briefly considered checking behind the sheds but the thought of Lauren inside waiting spurred him to make sure she was OK. He reached into the car, grabbed the box of groceries, closed the car door gently and trod softly to the kitchen door.

The scene that greeted Trout when he lifted the latch and shoved the door inwards would be etched in his memory forever. Lauren was sitting on Miko's chair by the range, a rope wrapped around her body tying her to the chair and effectively immobilizing her upper body and arms. Her head was extended, held in place by Marty Lambert's arm locked around her neck. Her eyes were very wide, very calm and trying to tell him something. One leg rested lightly on Maestro as if holding him in place. He was lying on an old blanket, his eyes fixed on the gangster's face. A low rumble coming from deep in his chest showed the dog was not happy with the situation. Marty looked wild and dishevelled and his right hand was pointing a pistol at the doorway.

Trout stilled, took a long slow breath and released it imperceptibly. "Morning, Marty. You joining us for breakfast?" He moved further into the kitchen, leaving the door open. "Are you OK, Lauren?"

She blinked her eyes twice. Trout took that as a yes.

Marty snarled at him, "Too much wise-cracking out of you and I'll soon make the lady OK."

"You do, Marty, and neither God nor man will save you from me." The softness of Trout's voice made the coldness of his words more chilling. He took a step closer. He still carried the box. He could see that Marty's arm was vibrating with tension.

"Big words, Tegan – just remember one jerk and this pretty neck will snap like a twig."

Trout shrugged. "Marty has a boast, Lauren, that he leaves no loose ends behind him. Haven't you, Marty?" He was now level with the dog's head. He noted Marty shift his stance – holding the gun extended and Lauren in an armlock was throwing his aim off. He bent his elbow and pressed the gun into Lauren's temple.

Trout stilled. His options had just become more limited. He could try a sideways sweep at Marty but with his finger on the trigger Marty would have fired before he got anywhere.

"One more step, Tegan, and it's curtains for your girlfriend."

"And then what, Marty? Your bargaining power will be gone."

"Thanks for reminding me. I guess I'll just have to try something else." He swung the gun back towards Trout. "Now, little lady, start talking or I will start to drill this here boyfriend of yours, one joint at the time. How about we start with that right knee?"

Lauren gave a strangled croak. Marty fractionally loosened his hold. "Don't shoot him," she said hoarsely.

Maestro stirred.

"Then answer my question." Marty jerked her head while never taking his eyes off Trout.

"*Aarrahh* ..." The choke hold was obstructing Lauren's windpipe and squeezing her larynx. Her leg fell heavily on the dog and he yelped.

"What are you saying? And it better be good!" Marty barely relaxed his hold.

Lauren coughed.

Marty went to tighten his hold.

"No. I can't talk ... when it's so tight,." she whispered. She swallowed hurriedly, trying to moisten her throat. "I've told you we don't have whatever you're looking for ..."

Marty jerked her head. "Not good enough."

Lauren gave a strangled croak. In the shadow of the chair Maestro struggled to his feet, his right foreleg dangling awkwardly. Lauren tried to keep him down but when he wouldn't stay used her leg to help him balance.

Trout's eyes were locked on Marty.

Lauren wheezed desperately, "Ask ... ask him, he'll tell you."

"What do you want to know?" Trout hefted the box.

Marty growled, "Don't even think about it." He turned the gun back on Lauren, took his arm from around her neck and thrust his hand towards Trout. "Hand over the data-stick that little shit Freddy Loftus stole from us."

"Us. Stole?" Trout narrowed his eyes. "Who exactly would us be?"

"Cut the bullshit, Tegan. You've got property that rightly belongs to Rob Carrig. He wants it back."

"So that's what you're after. A data-stick Robert Carrig has mislaid." Trout kept his voice conversational. "I wonder why he's using the likes of you to recover it?"

"None of your fucking business and, if you know what's good for your girlfriend, you'll hand it over pronto."

"Except we've agreed that you don't leave loose ends hanging around. So, the outcome will be the same no matter what I do."

"You think so? How about the difference between a slow painful death and one clean kill?" Marty's eyes gleamed in the dull light. "How would you like to hear your floozy scream? She might even beg – I like to hear them beg." Marty licked his lips. "Your call, Tegan."

Trout concentrated on keeping his breathing slow and quiet. He pushed his mind away from the fury burning in his gut, kept his voice neutral. "We have a bit of a problem here, Marty. I don't have a data-stick belonging to Carrig, or anyone else for that matter."

"The miserable little shit gave it you."

"And if I tell you Freddy gave me nothing, what then?"

"I'll know you're a fucking liar!" Marty snarled, spittle flying. He pulled himself back with some effort, gave a malicious parody of a smile. "Tell you what – I'll count to three and if your memory hasn't improved by then I'll give you a little hint. Like a bullet through this little titty here." Marty turned the gun and jammed it into Lauren's breast.

She jerked, grunted a strangled cry of pain.

"I can't give you what I haven't got."

"Two."

"But I can show you where it is."

"That's more like it. Well, where is it?" Marty jabbed viciously at Lauren. She moaned.

"I won't be saying another word while you're hurting her and, Marty ..." Trout lowered his voice, "if you shoot her all deals are off."

Marty eased the gun back but didn't remove it. "Where is it?"

"It's locked in Miko's workshop."

"Locked ..."

"I have the keys in my pocket."

"*Why the hell didn't say so and we could have got this farce over and done with a long time ago!*" Marty screeched. "*Hand them over!*"

"No offence, Marty, but I can't get at keys in my pocket without doing something with this box."

"Don't move." Marty's eyes darted around the kitchen.

Trout allowed his body to go fluid: the next move could be the difference between survival and an alternative he wouldn't allow himself think about.

Maestro leaned heavily against Lauren's knees and inched himself further around the chair.

"Okay. Here's how we'll do this." Marty's voice was tense. He swung the gun back against Lauren's temple. "One wrong move, Tegan." His body was rigid. "Put the box on the table, very slowly."

The table was to the right of Trout, almost but not quite within reach. He inched sideways, holding the box in front of him. Both hands were under it, although the bulk of the weight was on his left, leaving the right relatively free. His mind was calculating the odds and he'd have a better chance with the box gone. He slid it onto the table and made an exaggerated play of shaking the stiffness out of his hands.

Marty watched him, unblinking. "Quit the fucking stalling and get me the keys. No smart moves either – my finger is very itchy here."

"They're in my pocket." Trout spread his hands wide. "I'll need to get them out."

"Get on with it then."

Trout plunged his hand into his pocket and dragged out a large bunch of keys. In the dim light it was difficult to see what type of keys they were.

"Hold it." Marty's eyed the keys. "Put them on the ground and slide them along the floor towards me."

Suddenly things exploded in all directions.

A voice from the doorway demanded, "*What the fuck's going on here?*"

Marty swung the gun towards the door. Trout, who had crouched as if to put the keys on the floor, looked up and flung the keys upwards towards Marty's face. The dog buried his teeth in Marty's ankle. Marty shouted, jerked backwards, his finger squeezed on the trigger and a sharp crack echoed in the confined space.

There was an ominous *oomph* and a groan from the doorway.

Trout continued his momentum into a rugby tackle. Marty hit the ground with a thud, the gun skittered away. Marty lay still.

A heavy silence filled the kitchen.

Trout recovered his breath and bounced upright. In a flash he was beside Lauren. He grabbed the end of the rope and it pulled through. "Are you OK?"

Lauren was staring, her eyes wide with horror, at the door. Trout turned to follow her gaze. "Jesus!"

Jim Cooper lay in a crumpled heap on the threshold, his two hands clutching his belly, blood seeping through his fingers.

"*Fuck, fuck, fuck.*" Trout hurriedly unwound a couple of more rounds of the rope, loosening it enough for her to get an arm out. "Can you do the rest?"

"Yes." Lauren gulped. "See if you can help him."

Trout grabbed a couple of clean towels drying on the range rack and dropped onto his knees beside Cooper. He pried the fingers apart and stuffed the towels under them. "Hang on, Coop. I'm calling for help."

Inspector Cooper was mumbling something. Trout bent closer. He heard a faint "Sorry. I'm sorry …" The words faded.

Trout put one hand over Cooper's two, increasing the pressure on the wound and opened his phone with the other. He pressed one and swiped at a number and almost immediately was onto the precinct. "*Officer down. We need a couple of ambulances and gardaí at Miko Downes,*" he rattled off the address. "*Inspector Cooper has been shot – emergency services needed urgently.*"

Lauren came shakily to stand beside him. She had found a blanket somewhere and put it over Coop. "Marty's coming round – you'd better see to him. I'll keep the pressure on here."

He looked up at her. She was pale but had a determined set to her mouth. He nodded. "OK." He withdrew his hand and allowed her take his place beside Cooper. The blood continued to stain the towels and now could be seen staining the blanket. Trout feared the nature of the wound, the belly was a vulnerable area for major organs. He hoped the medics would arrive on time.

Trout stood looking down at Marty. He was beginning to groan but hadn't yet opened his eyes. An almost uncontrollable urge to pound him to a pulp shimmered on the periphery of Trout's consciousness. With an effort he shook it off, looked around for a suitable restraint. He eyed the rope Lauren had dropped on the chair, and reckoned it would have to do. He bound Marty's wrists together, looped the rope twice around the rung of Miko's chair and finished by tying Marty's ankles together. He saw the gun over near the dresser and decided to leave it where it was. No need to contaminate the fingerprints. In the distance a siren wailed, getting closer, louder, nearer.

Trout closed his eyes. He felt very tired but shook himself and went to direct the ambulance into Miko's yard.

Chapter 39

For the second time in the same twenty-four hours Miko's yard was full of flashing lights and official vehicles. Two paramedics worked quickly and efficiently on Inspector Cooper. They applied a pressure bandage, inserted a line and started replacing the fluid loss resulting from the bleeding. When they had stabilized him as much as they could, they transferred him to the ambulance and blue-lighted him to the hospital. He remained unconscious during it all and the controlled urgency with which the medics worked betrayed the gravity of the situation.

Marty Lambert was loaded into the other ambulance and handcuffed to a garda at one side and the trolley on the other side. He claimed that the knock to the head must have given him amnesia as he couldn't remember anything prior to waking up on the floor of Miko Downes' kitchen. He demanded loudly to know why he was trussed like a chicken and as an afterthought asked, "Where the heck am I anyway?" That his eyes looked more shrewder and calculating than glazed wasn't lost on anyone.

Sergeants Tony Driscoll and Moira Baker arrived in an

unmarked police car. Tony was driving at full speed, his face set and determined. Moira could be seen to say something sharply as the car skidded to a stop, inches from the remaining ambulance.

Tony lurched from the driver seat, went to the door of the ambulance, growled something unintelligible, cleared his throat and said, "Take him away, get him checked out and take him back to the station. We'll deal with him there." He locked eyes with Marty's. "Attempted murder of a garda is a capital offence," he said harshly.

Moira exited more slowly but with a sense of purpose that boded ill for anyone who got in her way. She had checked with the hospital as they hurried to the scene to be told that Inspector Cooper was in Accident and Emergency, that he remained unconscious and that he was being prepped for theatre as they spoke. The doctors were doing all they could for him and that was all they could say at the moment. Neither herself nor Driscoll had said much on the journey down. Both were occupied with their own thoughts. The possibility of a garda being injured in the line of duty was always in the background but one couldn't let it interfere with their work. It was one of those things that was easier to ignore when it didn't come too close to you. Tony and Moira were both on Cooper's team and had been working with the Inspector for long enough for a rapport to develop between them as colleagues if not friends. This shooting brought it home just how vulnerable they could be when on the job.

There was also the question of what Jim Cooper was doing in Killanee in the first place. He had driven there in his private vehicle. It was there in the upper side of the yard, driver door open, keys still in the ignition as if he'd left it in a hurry. A quick query to the precinct had elucidated that he hadn't been in to work that morning. Tony had taken hand-over from the night squad and was in the middle of briefing the team vis-à-vis the events of the night before when the call came. He had hastily allocated the day's tasks and himself and Moira had made tracks to see for themselves what the hell was happening. Driscoll was in nominal charge until someone else was appointed to take over the case. The responsibility felt onerous and at the same time made him determined to get answers, and get them fast.

The Garda Forensics van lumbered in soon afterwards and disgorged its white-suited occupants into the mix. They set to work gathering their evidence, more subdued than usual at the news percolating the ranks. The technicians grumbled automatically that the injured parties had been removed thus denying them the chance to see them in-situ. Nonetheless they worked with the utmost care and exactitude, photographed, dusted for prints and collected samples. They worked with concentrated efficiency, aware that the life of one of their own hung on a thread. It was, in many ways, a very straightforward crime scene and they took their measurements, calculated angles, secured the gun and the rope, recorded the blood-spatter and eventually, after what seemed a considerable length of time, left.

Lauren looked pale and shaken. The paramedics had pronounced her fine, suffering from shock and some bruising but to all intents and purposes well enough. They recommended fluids and suggested somebody make her a cup of hot tea. She pounced on the idea and busied herself with boiling water, finding cups and making tea. The everyday ritual gave her mind a focus and gradually calmed her. She was pleased to see her hands were no longer shaking and to feel her jelly-legs become more solid under her. She had to admit it was a relief to sit down with a steaming cup of tea, although she was careful to sit well away from Miko's big chair by the range.

Maestro had set his wound bleeding again and one of the paramedics had rebandaged it. He was curled up on his blanket in front of the range, opening an occasional eye to check all was under control.

Tony Driscoll and Moira Baker accompanied Trout into the kitchen. They gravitated to the table and sat, gratefully accepting a cup of the homely brew. The tea was warming and gave their hands something to do while they regrouped. The two sergeants had a lot of questions. Where to begin? Moira pulled out a notebook and waited, pen poised over the paper.

Tony began by asking Trout to fill them in on what had happened. "Just tell us in your own words to start with."

Trout did so, trying to keep the narrative in chronological order, beginning with the late-night call from Miko and the drama that unfolded at that stage. He told of Marty Lambert's escape in Miko's jeep and Cooper's arrival but carefully skirted over his own conversation with the Inspector.

The two sergeants were finding the bald facts unsatisfactory while Trout wasn't in a position to give them any clarity. Heck, he wasn't even sure himself if there was clarity to give. No, it didn't occur to him Marty would come back. If he had any inkling of it, he wouldn't have left Lauren alone in the house. Why did he leave her alone in the first place, they wanted to know. To get provisions. They had promised Miko they would stay with Maestro and they wanted breakfast. Surely Miko had something they could eat? Miko seemed to have very little food in the house so the best option seemed to be to get some in the all-night filling station. Did he see any sign of Marty or the jeep on his journey?

No. He'd like to know how Marty had evaded the police and doubled back to Miko's place. A quick search by the local boys had turned up Miko's jeep two fields over from where he'd driven it onto the road when he took off earlier.

"Why did he come back?" Tony Driscoll was frowning. "It must be something important."

"Actually, both of them came back." They all looked at Moira. She met their stares with one of her own. "Both Inspector Cooper and Marty Lambert came back here. What could be here that was so important?"

"Cooper knew Lauren and myself were staying on until Miko returned from the hospital," Trout said slowly. "But Marty was gone by that stage. Maybe Coop got some inkling that Lambert was doubling back and he came to warn us." He seemed to be thinking out loud.

"Then he'd have known what Marty was after ... or would he?" Tony Driscoll chewed over Trout's words. "What did he want?"

Trout told them that Marty had demanded a data-stick that he claimed Freddy Loftus had stolen from Robert Carrig, and that Marty was under the impression that Freddy had given the stick to him.

"Had he given it to you?"

Trout quite truthfully said no.

"Hang on a minute," Moira Baker interjected. "Does that mean Freddy was involved with Carrig?"

"No. Carrig's missus had commissioned him to make her a doll's house for her collection, a scale replica of their own house."

"Carrig's wife collects doll's houses?" Moira was openly sceptical.

"She does. And you can take it from me, Moira, they're not the type of doll's house you'd want your children playing with."

"They all have a history of murder and mayhem," Lauren chipped in from the end of the table.

"You've seen them?"

"Yes, and a more gruesome a collection would be hard to find." Lauren shuddered. "The very room they were in felt evil."

Moira frowned and turned back to Trout. "How did ye come to see Mrs Carrig's collection?" she asked in strange tone of voice.

"It was all above board, Moira," Trout reassured her. "We asked her and she offered to show them to us."

"You asked Robert Carrig's wife to show you her doll's houses."

"No, we asked her about commissioning Freddy to make her a doll's house and she offered to show us her collection."

"How did you know she commissioned him?" Tony Driscoll butted in. "We didn't hear anything about it."

"Actually, how did we come to hear about it?" Trout looked at Lauren. "I remember putting it in our notes early enough in the investigation."

"We'll need those notes, sir, asap."

"Sorry, chum, no can do. A private investigator has the right to guarantee his client confidentiality."

"Private investigator! So, the rumours are true." Tony sounded shocked.

"You can't have had time to get your licence yet, so we can subpoena them as all you really are is a nosy citizen," Moira challenged him.

"Well thought of, Moira, but as an affiliate of Danny Mortimer I share the privileges of his organization."

"You, Special Investigator Tegan, an associate of that sleazy –"

"Now, now, Moira, he runs the biggest and most successful PI agency in the country."

"By running with the hares and hunting with the hounds and not being caught by either!" Moira was getting heated.

"Back off, Moira," Tony was looking at Trout with the intensity of a laser beam. "Obviously you had your reasons, sir, for such a move. You were going to tell us where you heard about Freddy's commission."

Trout nodded, shot him a 'you'll-go-far' look and turned towards Lauren.

"It was Freddy's final year project," she said slowly. "I'm sure the college have it on file. They were very pleased to have secured the patronage of such eminent benefactors as the Carrigs."

"But you must have known all this – it's basic investigation stuff." Trout was pleased with Lauren's answer but wanted to keep the focus from Miko's workshop for as long as he could.

Tony Driscoll looked uncomfortable. "We talked to the college but haven't got as far as seeing their file yet," he mumbled, then rallying demanded, "How come you know all this?"

"We asked the relevant parties and they told us. Perks of a PI – we can follow up seemingly innocuous information without wondering if it's relevant."

"Well, is it relevant?" Moira was chewing the end of her biro. "I mean, even if Mrs Carrig commissioned Freddy to make a doll's house, does it actually mean anything in relation to this case?"

"It means Freddy had access to the Carrig home and could have acquired something he might have thought would be useful to me."

"And you know this because …?"

"Freddy made detailed drawings of the house and some of its rooms ... Carrig's wife told us she gave him a more or less free run of the place."

"And her husband allowed it?"

"He didn't know. When he found out, I take it there was a bit of a scene. It might even be what prompted Freddy to take whatever he took."

"Why would you say that?"

"Well ... he'd been around the house for a couple of weeks and there doesn't seem to have been any problem ..." Trout went into a reflective mode. "Freddy was very particular about giving his word ... on anything. To him it was sacrosanct. When Freddy made a pact, he stuck by it come hell or high water until it was done or he felt he had honoured whatever it was. Freddy's commission was from Isolde Carrig and I'd say he carried it out to the letter but when Robert interfered all bets were off – but only where Carrig himself was concerned."

"Have you any proof of this?" Driscoll asked sharply.

Trout smiled grimly. "No, but if I was a betting man I'd put money on it. Finding proof," Trout shrugged eloquently and spread his hands wide, "good luck with that."

"Maybe Marty Lambert will talk." Moira was looking hopefully at Trout.

"A lot will depend on who he's most afraid of, Robert Carrig or the prisoners he might meet who have old grudges to settle."

There was a loaded silence. The dog snored. Everyone jumped.

Moira looked at Tony. "Is there anything more we can do here?"

"I don't think so. Alright, Tegan, yourself and Ms O'Loughlin will have to come in to make –" Tony was interrupted by the *burr-*

burr of his phone. He frowned at the number and swiped the screen. "Sir!" He shot up ramrod straight only to quickly slump, the colour draining from his cheeks to leave him looking very young and lost. He listened intently, sighed and said "Yes, sir", closed the phone and looked at them miserably.

They waited.

"Inspector Cooper died on the operating table."

A heavy silence settled over them.

Tony Driscoll swallowed convulsively and managed to get himself under control. "The Super said we need to get back to headquarters for a debrief and regroup ..." He faltered. "He also says that Marty Lambert is being charged with first degree murder and ... and that new evidence has come to light that's likely to blow the Loftus case wide open."

Trout narrowed his eyes. "The Super said that?"

"Yes. He also said he'd like a word with you at your convenience."

"At my convenience?" Trout looked vaguely around the kitchen. "We told Miko we'd stay with Maestro until he came back from the hospital. Tell him I said we'll travel up as soon as we can."

Tony and Moira gathered their bits and pieces and left without another word.

Chapter 40

The tick-tock of the grandfather clock sounded loud in the quiet kitchen. Trout's head lolled onto his chest as he sank deep into his thoughts. He watched as Lauren carefully straightened her neck. "Are you OK?"

"A bit bruised and more than a little raw." She stared out the window.

Trout watched as her eyes tracked the play of light around what was visible of the yard. He followed her line of sight until it came to rest on the door of Miko's workshop.

"The doll's house!" he said.

"I was just thinking about it. Do you really think there's something hidden in it?"

"Isolde as good as admitted that there was."

"I suppose there is one way to find out . . ."

Trout smiled. "I agree. What became of Miko's keys?"

"The keys." Lauren half laughed, got stiffly to her feet and made her way to Maestro. The dog barely opened one eye as she slid a hand under him and fumbled around his blanket. At last, she withdrew her hand and raised it aloft to show a bunch of keys dangling from her forefinger. "I left them down while I was tending to Maestro and they got covered by his blanket. I figured they were as safe there as anywhere when Marty arrived and I sort of forgot about them since."

"Right." Trout took them from her. "Shall we go see what we might see?"

"Lead the way."

Trout opened the workshop door and flicked on the lights. The doll's house stood in pride of place on the workbench. Its storeys flowed gracefully up to its attic roof. The three dormer windows looked quaint and appeared to twinkle at them in the light. Together they studied it from the doorway before moving towards it.

"It's such a beautiful piece of work. I just can't imagine anything sinister about it," Lauren said softly

"Except the man who made it was murdered and if our hypothesizing is correct, it's most likely he hid something in it … and that something may have got him killed." Trout stood and took a careful visual inventory of the outside. "It looks to be completely in proportion."

"We know from the Paddy's Locker piece that Freddy was well capable of making an invisible hidden compartment." Lauren walked around the workbench. "Wouldn't it depend on the size of whatever he was hiding?"

"True … If you were Isolde Carrig and you wanted a secret stash, what would it be?"

Lauren thought about it, her head one side, staring at the house. "She had some array of jewelry on her the day we met her," she said thoughtfully. "Yes, jewellery or perhaps just jewels. Unmounted they would be easier to store and transport and possibly would be even more valuable than if set in some piece or other. Trading in precious stones can be very lucrative if you have the right contacts."

"Another book?" Trout teased lightly.

"Well, yes, actually," Lauren said defensively. "But what woman doesn't like a nice piece of jewellery?"

Trout nodded. He realized as he thought about it that Lauren always wore jewellery. Nothing ostentatious but usually with the gleam of a real gemstone. She'd notice and would understand the lure of jewels even if she didn't have the same penchant for them that Isolde Carrig seemed to have.

"Good idea," he said. "A very valuable amount of jewels could be hidden in quite a small space. So where did you put the secret compartment, Freddy?"

He walked around the bench, studying the house. It was constructed in a greyish wood with a straight grain, polished to enhance the silvery sheen. The side looked to be one complete board but on closer inspection was three separate units expertly dowelled together to give the impression of a single unit. It needed a discerning eye to pinpoint the area where the grain melded together rather than flowed continuously. The roof was speckled alder, a tree he knew well from the amount of it that grew locally and here was used with the bark intact. Trout had never before seen it used in woodwork. It made an ideal background for the perfectly proportioned dormer windows perched cheekily on the roof. Through them he could see into the empty attic space.

Lauren examined the inside, opening tiny doors, fiddling with ceiling lights, searching for switches that weren't immediately apparent. Nothing reacted, clicked or moved that wasn't supposed to.

"I wonder how one accesses the attic?" Trout ran his fingers over the end boards and was rewarded on the right side by the feel of a slight give. He pushed gently in and down as he had done in the Clothes Locker games room and the whole panel slid out like a long narrow drawer. It stopped on the edge where a slim lip acted as a stay. He wiggled the drawer and managed to unhook it off the edge. It was satin smooth and totally empty.

"Hand me that torch on the bench."

Lauren fetched the heavy-duty torch and Trout directed its broad beam into the attic space. The runner lay inset along the centre of the floor which was also the ceiling of the rooms below. There was nothing to indicate extra or unused space in the attic. He pushed the drawer back and it slotted neatly into place. He stood back. Lauren allowed the front to swing forward and they both watched as the magnetic strip drew it closed.

"It's there, somewhere, if only we knew where to look."

"We'll just have to ask Isolde," Lauren said with a laugh.

"Not a bad idea," Trout said seriously. "In fact, it might be just what we will do."

Chapter 41

A month later Trout and Lauren once again turned into Miko Downes' yard. It had been an exceptionally busy month for Trout. Most of it spent in Dublin, tying up loose ends in one of the biggest gangland routs in the history of the state. He had barely seen Lauren and admitted, albeit to himself, he'd missed her. The occasional phone call had served only to remind him of how he had come to enjoy her sharp observations and calm smile.

The yard looked much the same as the first time they had seen it. It even had two vehicles, only this time the one parked near Miko's jeep was a newer reg, bright-red Mondeo. Miko came to the door with a welcoming smile on his face and Maestro limped straight to Lauren and licked her hand. He looked as ecstatic as only a dog can when she hunkered down and gave him a good rub.

"Come in, come in! Ye're more than welcome." Miko beckoned them from the kitchen door. "Maestro, leave the girl alone! You see – he knows well we'll never be able to repay all you did for us …"

"Hush now, Miko, don't be talking nonsense." She reached forward and held his arm while she studied his face. "You've healed well. I'm glad. Are you OK otherwise?"

"Fine, glad to be alive and that's all thanks to you two, but come in, no point standing when you could be sitting comfortable." He stood aside and ushered them into the kitchen.

It was spotless. Miko saw Lauren looking around. He grinned. "You can see Nikki's here. Her heart's in the right place. Don't worry," he winked, "we'll be back to normal a few days after she goes back and I can find my books and things again!" He raised his voice. "Nikki, our visitors are here!"

Nikki hurried from one of the rooms. She wore a flowing dress cinched at the waist with a broad belt. She looked more substantial than the last time they saw her.

"Jenny's down for her nap so we'll have an hour or two uninterrupted. Tommy!" She darted to Trout and caught him in a fierce hug, then turned and did the same to Lauren, her eyes bright with the tears she was resisting.

"How are you, Nikki?" Trout asked gently.

"Sad. Glad it's over. Angry at the waste of Freddy's life, pleased you got the bastards who did it ..." She took a breath, "It's all mixed up inside me and jumbled in through it is the curiosity to know the full story." She looked at Trout. "You will tell us, won't you?"

"As best I can. It won't bring Freddy back but it might help to know that he was instrumental in taking some very bad people out of circulation."

She nodded. "It all helps a bit but it's hard ..."

"What's done can't be undone at this stage," Miko said gruffly. He looked at Trout. "You tell me there's a few more coming?"

"Yeah. Mrs Dillon and Brendan are coming together." He grinned at Lauren. "We reckoned we might get the story over in the one telling by having you all together."

"You've left young Sallins at the mercy of Martha Dillon? That was either a very brave or a very foolish move." Miko couldn't hide a chuckle as he pictured the young fellow ensconced in Mrs Dillon's ancient Toyota for the drive to Killanee. "We might as well wait until they arrive to make the tea."

"Oh, Miko, there's someone else may call later…" Trout drew Miko away from the women and spoke quietly to him.

Miko listened intently. "Like that, you reckon? OK, we'll say nothing. See how it plays out."

The table was set for six. Miko's big mug, Lauren's cup and saucer and Trout's Trinity mug were part of an assortment of ware on the table. That they had their recognized delf in Miko's home was a poignant reminder of all that had happened. This lunch-party was Miko's idea and he had outdone himself in preparing for it. Alongside his brown bread were doorstep sandwiches of pan loaf with thick slices of ham between them and a golden crusted apple pie. Nikki tut-tutted over the food but wisely said nothing.

They chit-chatted as they waited. Nikki's Eddie had hoped to be with them but an emergency at work meant he wouldn't reach Killanee until later that night. Not to worry – Nikki was looking forward to filling him in when the time came. They had decided to keep Freddy's car. Herself and Jenny had travelled down in the family car and Eddie would follow in Freddy's. It meant Nikki would be able to make more regular trips to see Miko in the future.

Maestro had made a full recovery. He had a limp but some times it looked worse than others. Miko reckoned that when he wanted a bit of petting he carried the leg and looked sorrowful until he got the sympathy he thought he deserved.

Lauren had finished the book she was editing and it was gone to the publishers. DeeDee Hirst had been in contact to sound her out about a follow-up Cosplay book. She had photographs and a detailed diary of the renovations carried out to turn her family home into a Cosplay world. Her plan was to turn them into a colourful, expensive and possibly lucrative coffee-table book. She had a good response when she pitched the idea to the publishers of the original book and wanted Lauren to edit the work for her. They were in negotiation but Lauren had as good as agreed to do it.

Finally, a *chug-chug-chug* could be heard and Mrs Dillon's Starlet trundled into the yard. Brendan was perched on the passenger seat, barely containing his excitement. Mrs Dillon smiled benevolently on him and everyone got the impression that the journey had been an enjoyable one.

Miko was an expansive host. He welcomed the newcomers with all the dignity of a king greeting a delegation from a foreign land, ushered them into the kitchen, settled them around the table and deemed that the talk stay general until everyone was fortified.

As it was there was plenty to talk about and talk they did. Current affairs, local gossip, the ways of the world, the wide-ranging topics of people who find themselves in convivial company and are feeling their way towards friendship. There was no particular rush and between them all they did justice to the prepared feast.

At last, Miko sat back with a contented sigh, reached for his pipe and began the ritual of filling it. Nikki went to check on Jenny and Lauren began to clear the table.

"Leave it there, girl," said Miko. "There'll be time enough for that when ye're gone."

"If you're sure, Miko?"

"I'm sure." He puffed his pipe to a glow and looked around at the expectant faces. "Now!" he said. "We're well prepared to hear the whole story."

"In some ways it's hard to know what the whole story is," Trout began, looking around at the assembled company. He took a deep breath, considered his commission from Terence and his former work in the Special Investigation Unit and decided to start in a more general way. Although he deemed it prudent to have Terence play a lesser role in the operation. He took a deep breath.

"Two years ago, an enquiry agency was set up to investigate rumours that corruption within the rank and file of the Force was a serious problem. Nobody knew who was appointed to carry out the appraisal but the word was everybody, from the top brass to the lowliest recruit, was going to be under scrutiny. The first task was to clear a number of people who could then be trusted to carry out any on-the-ground work that was needed. I was already part of the Special Investigation Unit and was lucky to be cleared almost from the beginning."

"Lucky!" Mrs Dillon sniffed. "You're not cut out for that underhand stuff. I could have told them that myself if anyone bothered to ask."

Trout grinned. "Thanks for the reassurance. Anyway, from that I went on to become an active liaison officer between the Force and the enquiry."

"Proper order is all I can say." Mrs Dillon's eyes flickered approvingly.

"That said, no more than anyone else did I know who the principal was. All I had was a name, a special phone number and an encrypted email."

"Cool!" Brendan was gazing at Trout with the rapt attention of a disciple at the feet of a guru.

Trout half smiled but carried on as if he hadn't heard him. "It became obvious fairly quickly that there was collusion at some level between the law, public representatives and certain gangs operating at strategic points around the country. One gang in particular seemed to have a charmed existence and that was the one run by Marty Lambert. He had known associations with Robert Carrig on one side and Jim Cooper on the other." He paused, chose his words carefully, "There was talk and innuendo, even well-respected names were being bandied about but no concrete evidence was found as to what exactly was going on. The morale within the Force was suffering... it was obvious that something drastic needed doing and fairly quickly at that." He took a deep breath. "That was when the principal conceived the idea of offering me a solo run." Trout stopped. They all waited expectantly. "I didn't agree lightly. He made it plain I would be on my own and that if it all went belly-up I'd have to take the consequences whatever they were ... In the end I had to chance it. I couldn't let the Force I'd given my life to go down the drain because of a few corrupt individuals and anyway I'd run out of extensions and would have to retire whether I liked it or not..." His voice hardened, "And I was convinced there was only one or two rotten apples in the barrel."

"You did what you had to do," Miko said matter-of-factly.

Trout smiled. "Something like that. Bits of it go back a long way, to when the Three Amigos were lads."

"The Three Amigos?" Mrs Dillon said sharply.

"Robert Bowser Corrigan, Jim Cooper and Marty Lambert all grew up together in the flats and by all accounts they survived because if you messed with one you brought the wrath of the three of them on you. They were street Arabs from a very young age and dabbled in everything from picking pockets to acting as look-outs for the gangs. By the time they were teens they were getting paid as runners and had their noses stuck in every bit of every nefarious business in the city." He paused to gather his thoughts. "The biggest difference between the Three Amigos and other street kids was Bowser Corrigan. He was ambitious and ruthless in pursuit of fulfilling that ambition. And he hated drugs. Don't get me wrong – he saw that, as a commodity, drugs had a sale value and he eventually had a finger in every drug deal in the city. But, his mother died of an overdose when he was ten, with the result he despised anyone who used them. Not to mention that any one of his gang caught using was cut adrift or eliminated depending on his hierarchy in the group."

"Bowser was a bit of a legend in the flats." Nikki was nodding. "We were only small but we heard the talk. We knew that that he gave no second chances. One hit and you were out with no hope of return."

"He set his marker early and has never deviated to the best of my knowledge," Trout agreed. "The other thing Bowser valued was education. He figured if you wanted to get anywhere you needed to have some book learning. So, he insisted his gang attend school and do enough to get an education. Of course, the Amigos saw the other benefits of school…"

"A captive population." Mrs Dillon sighed. "It was hard enough in a small school – it must have been a nightmare in big ones."

"Yep, you've called it. School showed the Amigos what could be achieved with a bit of focus. They ran every sort of scam they could get away with: blackmail, false identities, drug supply and a protection racket that still has reverberations to this day. Bowser also formulated his great plan. He wanted power..."

"To know what a man is, give him power," Miko muttered around the stem of his pipe. He took it out and tamped down the tobacco. "My old granny always said that."

"He figured out his best way to get it was to know something he could use for leverage or be one of the boys who made the rules."

"What I don't understand is," Lauren burst out then stopped. "Well, they all went their separate ways...are you suggesting that was all part of the plan?"

"That's the conclusion we're looking at. But," Trout shrugged, "nobody's talking. Ye know Bowser Corrigan became Robert Carrig through the good offices of his father-in-law?" There was a general nodding of heads around the table. "Carrig has surrounded himself with solicitors and barristers and won't say a word they haven't sanctioned. Lambert only opens his mouth to eat since his arrest and Cooper is dead. The burden of proof is on the Force and with all the entanglements it could take months, years even, before there's any sort of case to put together."

"Poor Inspector Cooper," Lauren murmured.

"Poor, my foot! He was a bad one." Mrs Dillon was having none of it.

"In all fairness," Trout said mildly, "it looks like Coop had somehow found out that Lambert was after myself and Lauren and had come back to warn us. He died in the line of duty and there was nothing to show otherwise."

Mrs Dillon snorted. "We know what we know."

"He died in the line of duty and will be remembered accordingly,"

Trout reiterated. "And what's more the bullet that killed him is a match for the one that the boys removed from Freddy. Marty Lambert is being charged with two counts of first-degree murder. That's well documented evidence. Marty is going down for a long time… If he doesn't bring Carrig with him at least it will make things mighty uncomfortable for him, for the foreseeable."

A heavy silence settled over the gathering. This was what they needed to hear, yet at some level they were all aware that it wasn't the full story. And they would never be privy to that.

Lauren stirred herself. "What about the USB?" She was careful not to mention the papers. Trout had already told her they were being kept in reserve until they could make the most impact in any upcoming case.

"Carrig is claiming that he knows nothing about it. The politicians and business people implicated on it are singing dumb. After all, they were being blackmailed by the contents so they see it's in their own best interests to stay quiet and hope it will all go away."

"But surely you can check if what's on it is true?" Nikki sounded breathless. "And then make them tell the truth."

"Except the gardaí have to be careful not to be seen in the same category as the blackmailer."

"He was looking for something he claimed Freddy had stolen from him," Lauren protested. "At least that's what Marty Lambert said."

"Ah, there's a crux. He's now claiming that he severed all contact with Marty when he left his old life and has no idea why Marty would implicate him in his crimes…"

"That's some cheek!" Lauren burst out. "When you think of what Marty did to Miko and us on his behalf!"

"To say nothing of Maestro!" said Miko.

"And now for the final piece of the puzzle: the doll's house," said

Trout. "According to Carrig, it's his wife's property and all he wants is to secure it for her, as per the agreement she had with Freddy. He's keeping it all a bit vague…"

"Bloody doll's house!" Miko spoke with vehemence, then, "Pardon me, ma'am" to Mrs Dillon.

Mrs Dillon inclined her head. "You're quite within your rights to swear. I'd do it myself if I indulged." She turned to Trout. "Are you suggesting the doll's house made by Freddy was the catalyst for the whole affair?"

Nikki gave a strangled sob and clapped her hand over her mouth.

"Yes, in so far as it brought Freddy into contact with the Carrigs. But there must be more to it than that. Isolde Carrig seems hellbent on getting her hands on it." Trout tapped restless fingers on the table. "We have to ask ourselves if there is something stashed in it. Lauren and myself have been over the house but we couldn't see anywhere a secret compartment could have been hidden. What did you think, Miko, when you looked at it?"

"Freddy was fascinated with the idea of secret hiding places in furniture." Miko cleared his throat. "He was clever at fitting in little extras spaces that couldn't be discerned…And he was getting better at it."

"It's like in a spy a book." Brendan could barely contain his excitement. "Did he really make secret hiding places?"

"He did indeed. The one in Paddy's Locker was disguised as a knot in the wood and only we were actively looking for it we'd never have found it."

There was a lull as everyone mulled over the possibilities.

Into the quiet the purr of a powerful car could be heard coming up the boreen. Maestro barked. Miko shushed him and looked at Trout. "You'd better see who that is."

Chapter 42

A current-year Mercedes S-class, its shining paintwork the glossy blue-black of a swallow's back, glided to a stop beside Mrs Dillon's Starlet. The passenger door opened and Isolde Carrig emerged, looking around like she had landed on another planet.

Trout suppressed a smile at her shudder even as he noted her country attire: black jeans, tooled cowboy boots and a fleece-lined denim jacket. The hand grasping the collar of her jacket blazed as the afternoon sun reflected the brilliance of her rings.

Her gaze turned towards Trout. He felt a moment of disquiet at how small and lost she looked – like a child or an alien in a strange land.

Then she shook herself and with a haughty arrogance moved towards him as briskly as the cobbled yard allowed.

"Mr Tegan. You have my doll's house. I wish to see it and ascertain that it is intact." No hint of the lost child remained in her features or her demeanor.

"Good afternoon, Mrs Carrig. Welcome to Killanee. Would you like a cup of tea after your journey?"

She made a moue of disdain. "I would like to get my business over and done with and get back to some semblance of civilization."

Trout openly grinned. "The relevant parties are all here. I trust you can substantiate your claim on Freddy's doll's house."

"I will pay the money I agreed to give Freddy for making the house and, if necessary, present the knowledge to show conclusively that the house is mine."

"I'll just ask my friends to step out then and we'll all repair to the workshop." Trout made his words formal and his tone dry.

He turned back to the door and grinned at the eager faces awaiting him. "Come on, everybody. It's showtime! Miko, have you the key to the workshop?"

"Right here." Miko patted his pocket.

One by one they trooped out, Miko leading the way.

"Morning, ma'am," Miko greeted Isolde.

"Hello again, Mrs Carrig," Lauren said with a smile.

Nikki had a sleepy Jenny cradled in her arms. She looked at Isolde with angry eyes and said nothing.

Brendan allowed Mrs Dillon link her arm through his and steadied her as she stepped onto the cobbles. His eyes were wide and observant. Mrs Dillon inclined her head and said, as haughty as Isolde herself, "You're welcome, I'm sure."

Isolde turned baffled eyes towards Trout. "Who are all these people?"

"These are the interested parties I mentioned. Allow to introduce them. Miko Downes owns the workshop where Freddy worked and he has agreed to give us access to it. Lauren you've met. Nikki Gill is Freddy's sister and as his heir has the right to claim the doll's house as it's part of his estate. That's her daughter Jenny, Freddy's niece, with her. Mrs Dillon and Brendan Sallins are our unbiased witnesses to whatever transpires."

"Witnesses?" Isolde's voice was harsh.

"Unbiased witnesses," Trout said mildly. "You understand this is all undocumented therefore we need people we can trust to speak for us if need be." He injected a warning note into the final words.

An ugly tide of red surged over her face and for a moment Isolde Carrig looked like she was going to explode. With an effort she controlled herself. "Let's get it over with."

They trooped into the workshop and gathered around the doll's house. It stood serene and elegant on its bench.

They all heard Isolde Carrig's indrawn breath and involuntary "*Oh!*"

"What a magnificent piece!" Mrs Dillon moved forward to peer in the windows. "Superb workmanship. What a waste!" The last was said with a sigh and a significant look at Isolde.

"Well, Mrs Carrig," Trout extended a hand towards the doll's house, "how do you intend to prove it is yours?"

Isolde Carrig was staring at the doll's house as if in a trance. Her face had lost all its haughty superciliousness. She looked like a child on Christmas morning. "It's perfect," she breathed. "Perfect, perfect, perfect. It will be an outstanding centerpiece for my collection."

Trout cleared his throat. "It isn't yours yet. Had you a written contract with Freddy or the college for the finished project?"

"No. We had an agreement, Freddy and I." She slanted a look at Trout. "I saw his work at an open evening in the college and was impressed with what he could do."

"And from that you commissioned him to make you a doll's house?" Trout made no effort to hide his skepticism.

"Well…" Isolde chewed her bottom lip. "I saw what he was making for the Clothes Locker. He showed me the secret drawer… He was showing off how clever he was really…"

Miko made a strangled sound at her condescending tone. Lauren laid a hand on his arm and shook her head. He contented himself with glaring at the back of Isolde's head.

She continued, oblivious. "We made a deal and shook hands on it. That was good enough for me."

"What sort of a deal?"

Her voice hardened. "I agreed to pay him twenty thousand euro for a doll's house replica of my home with some special features."

There were gasps and murmurs all around.

"I knew he was good but I didn't think he was that good," Miko muttered.

"Twenty thousand euro!" Nikki tightened her grip on Jenny as she whispered the number.

"Glory be to God!" Mrs Dillon blessed herself.

"Nice one!" Lauren was grinning all over her face.

"Cool!" Brendan paid more attention to the doll's house than he had up to this. He had been examining Isolde as if he was committing every nuance of her to memory. Now he turned his laser eye to the house and wondered what made it worth so much money.

Trout paid no attention to any of them. "Special features?" he said softly. "What special features?"

Isolde had gone back to staring at the house. At Trout's question, she again slanted him that sly sideways look. "A hidden space for some valuables I wanted to keep securely."

"And did he make it for you?"

She laughed, a strange strangled sound. "Oh yes. He made it and he hid my valuables in it."

A chorus of exclamations greeted her words: "*Japers! Holy cow! Mother of God!*" And Lauren and Brendan together, "*Cool!*"

"Do you know where he put it?" Trout persisted with his calm questioning.

"Oh yes," Isolde Carrig said smugly. "Freddy told me exactly how I would be able to access my valuables once I had possession of the house."

"You still haven't told us how you are going to prove the house is yours."

"It is mine." She turned on him, her eyes glittering with fury. "I made a deal with Freddy. I intend to honour my end of the bargain. I expect his people to honour his side of it accordingly." She pulled a slim-line smart phone from a pocket inside her jacket and waved it in the air. "I will transfer the full amount that Freddy and I agreed on to any account you nominate." She pulled a folded piece of paper from the pocket of her jacket and waved it in the air. "I will transfer the full amount that Freddy and I agreed on to any account you nominate."

"Tommy!" Nikki turned anguished eyes towards him.

"It's all right, Nikki. Mrs Carrig will need to prove what she says is true before there will be any deal in the matter."

"What more proof do you want? I am offering the money agreed on to claim my property."

"That's the thing, isn't it? There's nothing any of us can see that would establish your claim to the doll's house. Covetousness doesn't automatically guarantee title."

"How dare you talk to me like that! Have you forgotten who I am?"

"I know exactly who you are, just as I know your name gives you no rights to demand Freddy's work from his family; without some verification." He held up a hand as she went to speak. "Whether you're paying for it or not ... after all," his voice went silky smooth, "a doll's house would make a very nice memento for Jenny, of her Uncle Freddy."

If looks could kill, Isolde Carrig would have struck Trout down with a lightning bolt from her eyes. "What exactly do you expect me to do?" she spat.

"Well, since you ask, it occurred to me that Lauren, Miko and myself have all examined this house and can find no sign of this secret compartment you claim it holds." He spread his hands wide. "If you can find it and show us the compartment and its contents it will go a long way to upholding your claim."

"You expect me to expose the secret of the doll's house and my valuables to these?" She gestured at the avid faces around her. "These people who – who could go and tell anyone?"

"Nobody here will be telling anyone anything. That I can guarantee you." Trout spoke with conviction. "It's in nobody's interest to do so."

Isolde was chewing on her lip, her eyes darting between the house and Trout. "And you expect me to leave the house here with you all knowing what it contains?"

"I'll tell you what, ma'am, when you leave here I'll follow you in the old van and deliver the house wherever you go to," Miko offered behind her. "If it's yours by then."

She turned doubtful eyes towards him. And, still, she hesitated.

"Look around you," said Trout. "You have the family, a couple of impartial witnesses and myself and Lauren. The contents of the house are indifferent to us – it's the ownership of the house itself we're querying." Trout was at his persuasive best.

A heavy silence fell over the group. They all watched Isolde Carrig. She was staring at the doll's house as if she could commune with it. Jenny sucked her thumb and snuggled her head into the crook of Nikki's neck. Mrs Dillon's eyes flickered alarmingly. Brendan seemed to hold his breath.

"OK." Isolde stirred herself. She looked directly at Miko. "You will take it home for me. I'll accompany you."

"In the van?"

She shrugged. "Why not? It will be easier to direct you than have you trying to keep up with the car."

"Fair game to you, girl! I've no problem with that."

Once she had made her decision, Isolde ignored the group around her. She moved confidently to the house, manoeuvred the attic panel as Trout had done and gently removed the whole piece. She laid it reverently on the bench. You could have heard a pin drop. All eyes were fixed on her. She peered into the attic space for a moment then reached in and manipulated the back wall. It seemed to release some sort of a catch because a thin panel of wood detached itself from the interior and Isolde Carrig carefully drew it out. The end of it was shaped like an L. She handled the piece with the utmost delicacy and laid it gently on the bench. She cast a glance at her audience, went to say something, stopped and took a deep breath before reaching her arm, full length into the space and withdrawing a black velvet pouch. She clasped it tightly in her fist and turned triumphant eyes on the group.

Trout held out his hand. She stared at it for a long moment, sighed and placed the pouch on his palm.

"They are all mine. If necessary, I can produce the invoices to show they were bought legally and ethically."

Trout looked at it. Flat on his hand, it was slim and he realized once it was positioned upright would take up very little space. He hefted the pouch – it seemed fairly full but felt light enough. He rolled it between his fingers and was aware of the pebble-like movement within. Without further ado he pulled the drawstring and opened out the top the pouch. A rainbow of glittering colours caught the light and dared them not to be impressed.

A sprinkling of oh's and ah's rippled through the group. Even Mrs Dillon wasn't immune to the treasure revealed. Trout tipped some of the stones onto his palm: diamonds, rubies, sapphires and a magnificent square-cut emerald winked up at them.

"My running-away fund." Isolde Carrig's voice cut through the dazed silence in the workshop.

Startled eyes turned towards her.

"Should I ever need it." She looked between Lauren and Nikki, shrugged. "Every girl should have one."

"Right. Well …" Trout cleared his throat. "It appears you've established your claim by the criteria we suggested. What do you think, Nikki?"

He poured the gems back into the pouch, drew the string tight and handed it back to Isolde.

She grasped it with such fierce intensity her knuckles bleached white.

Nikki turned big eyes towards Trout. She rubbed Jenny's back. "Freddy always kept his word," she said. "It was very important to him."

"Well, so do I." Isolde again brandished the phone. "All I need is your account details and the money is yours, if the house is mine." She locked eyes with Nikki.

"I don't know our account details." Nikki was on the verge of tears.

Miko, seeing Nikki's distress, pulled a battered chequebook from his pocket. "We can run it through the company account and you can draw it as you need," he said.

"I'd want a proper receipt," Isolde said abruptly. "And all of you to promise to keep the hidden compartment a secret."

"We've already guaranteed you that," Trout said. "It's your call, Nikki."

Nikki took a deep breath. "Yes … I'll … I'll honour Freddy's deal. The house is yours, Ms Carrig."

Isolde sagged as if a pressure valve had been released. "Thank you." She turned back to the house and set about reassembling the attic, replacing the precious pouch back into its hiding place.

When she was done, she turned to Miko. He showed her the bank details on his chequebook, she accessed a bank app, input the data, turned the phone to show him and Trout what she'd written and pressed enter. "It's gone straight into your account," she said.

Miko moved to the further bench and opening a drawer removed an old-fashioned receipt book with a biro stuck in the middle of it. Slowly and carefully, he wrote: *One Doll's House, designed and made by Freddy Loftus sold to Mrs Robert Carrig*. He signed and dated it and wrote across it with a flourish *Paid in full*.

He tore it carefully from the book, leaving the copy intact and handed the script to Isolde who read it over, nodded, folded it and put it in her pocket.

"I'll get the van," he said.

"I'll tell James to take the car home." Isolde had the house settled to her satisfaction. "I'm really looking forward to seeing it in my collection." She stood back to admire it. "It's just so perfect."

Mrs Dillon harrumphed and jerked her head towards the door.

Lauren, Nikki and herself slipped out into the late afternoon sunshine.

"That girl has serious problems," Mrs Dillon muttered, then raised her voice to say, "I don't know about ye but I'm parched for a cup of tea."

Brendan hesitated, caught Trout's beckon to him to come forward, "We'll need you to help lift the house into the van."

"Cool." He was pleased to be staying with the men.

Miko's Ford Transit was ten years old and had seen a lot of service. The back was laid out for transporting furniture as well as tools and had restrainer straps fitted to make sure nothing moved inappropriately. He produced an industrial handcart and after lowering the bench level with it, between them, the three of them gently maneuvered the house on to it. He had already clipped two iron ramps to the back of the van and the cart moved easily along them. Miko attached the straps to the house while Brendan secured the trolley. The whole lot fitted neatly into the space and having it on the cart already lessened the work at the other end.

"Do you think I should come with you for the unloading?" Brendan asked diffidently.

Miko scratched his chin. "'Twould be mighty handy. Could they spare you from home for the evening? I can drop you back after."

"I'll tell them I'm helping you." Brendan was delighted. He pulled out a phone. "I'm sure Dad will say OK but I'll just check."

"Miko? Have you forgotten Lady Muck?" Trout asked sotto voce.

"Naw." Miko's eyes were twinkling mischievously. "Sure, there's room for the three of us up front."

Trout laughed. "On your head be it."

Miko winked.

Brendan hurried over. "He says no problem."

"Great. Climb in there and belt up." Miko slammed the back doors and locked them.

Isolde Carrig stomped over to them. "James is insisting he stays with us," she said crossly. "He says Robert would eliminate him if he leaves me to my own devices. As if!"

Trout and Miko exchanged glances.

Isolde made to climb into the van. "I told him I'm travelling with you. He can follow along behind or whatever ... Oh hello! ... Are you coming too?"

"The young lad will help me unload when we get there."

"Good idea." Isolde clicked her seatbelt into place. "Let's get this show on the road."

Trout watched Miko's van trundle down the boreen. The sleek black car pulled out after it. He shook his head and gave way to the laughter building in his chest.

Epilogue

Trout and Lauren stayed with Nikki and Jenny until Eddie arrived. After numerous cups of tea, Mrs Dillon reluctantly left. She had plied Trout with questions and eventually seemed satisfied that she had learned all she could. For the moment anyway.

Nikki seemed a bit dazed by all the happenings. She sat completely still and stared for a long time at the cheque before saying, "Is this the price of Freddy's life, Tommy?"

"No, Nikki." Trout sat beside her and put an arm around her shoulders. "It's payment for a magnificent piece of furniture that Freddy made. He'd have wanted to leave something to help yourself and Jenny out and this is it."

"I suppose." She sounded infinitely sad.

"In reality the doll's house would have been a hindrance to you," Trout said softly. "You'd have no place to put it and eventually you might have had to sell it without getting anything like what it was worth to Isolde Carrig."

"He was such a clever boy. Why did he have to die?"

"I don't know, Nikki, but remember this: the people who did it to him underestimated him and are going to pay the price whatever way they may try to wriggle out of it."

Nikki sighed. "I know... but I miss him, Tommy. He always

came back to me. He was always mine more than Mama's." She gazed at Jenny, who was chuckling as she allowed Lauren entertain her by playing this little piggy with her toes. "I have Jenny to think of now."

Trout said nothing, just sat quietly beside her.

In a moment Jenny looked over and realized her mammy was there. Her little lip started to tremble and she held up her arms appealingly. Nikki smiled. "The little madam will keep me on my toes anyway." She rose to get her daughter, steadied herself with a hand on Trout's shoulder. "Thank you, Tommy. Your friendship means more than I can say." She moved forward her eyes on Lauren and Jenny. "Keep in touch." Then she turned her head so only he could hear her: "This one's a keeper, Tommy, don't you forget it."

Lauren cast a lingering look at Miko Downes' house as Trout navigated away from it. "That's it, I suppose," she said softly.

They journeyed in silence for a few miles until Trout indicated and pulled into a look-out area that gave them a fine view of Slí Buí and the valley which curved to where Knocknaclogga lay out of sight. He stared at the view for a long minute, then turned to look at Lauren. Her eyes were glued to the scenery. Side-faced the creamy skin looked pale, the angle of her jaw tense. The jut of her chin suggested she was bracing herself for what was to come.

"Terence rang me last night," Trout said eventually. "He offered me a Special Investigation Department to be run as I saw fit that would be answerable directly to him. And my pick of the staff to work in it."

"That's awesome. I'm glad he got to see how good you are at what you do." Her tone was nonchalant but she kept her head averted.

"He knew how good I was." Trout was terse, "He also knew the chance he was taking when he asked me to retire. In theory it was so I'd have a free hand but there was always the chance I'd discover I liked retirement."

"How would you discover that? You've never stopped investigating so it's immaterial."

"Maybe I need to find out."

"You're a born investigator." Lauren started to smile. "Possibly from the nosy little boy Mrs Dillon talks about."

"I said no thanks."

She swivelled to stare at him. "What? You can't turn down a job like that. It's a brilliant opportunity, doing what you love to do."

"I told him I wouldn't have time ..."

"Come off it!"

"I had a Detective Agency to run."

Lauren stilled. Her eyes went very wide. She drew in a long slow breath.

Trout smiled at her, in the way that caused his eyes to crinkle and made him look like a delighted little boy.

"Actually, I said myself and my partner had a Detective Agency to run."

"Trout ... I ..." A faint tinge of pink washed over the pale cheeks.

"Don't say anything. Hear me out." He made to reach for her hand, reconsidered and leaned an elbow on the steering wheel, all the while holding her gaze.

"TLC Investigations were brilliant. Let's face it, your insights and my nose make a great combination. Between the two of us, we cracked the case in record time and you might as well know that it was noted by the powers that be."

Lauren made a movement to say something. Trout held up a hand.

"Wait! I thoroughly enjoyed working with you, your perception and astuteness is second to none and, I'll admit, you put me on my mettle more than once." He paused to appreciate the bloom of shy delight that surged into her face. "Make the most of it. I don't often admit to that … Anyway, I made a counter proposal. You'd apply for your PI licence as an associate of mine – in other words, I'd supervise the hours you need to become qualified – and Terence would retain TLCI on a contract and we'd make ourselves available whenever he had something extra sensitive he needed investigated." Again, Lauren made to talk. Again, he stopped her. "I told him that the answer was dependent on you. The way I see it is, you have your editing, I'm going ahead with the wine business but we could do our investigating on the side as it were. Or even vice versa if it got busy. The other thing …" He stopped, took a deep breath, gave a here-goes look and said quietly, "I'd like to explore the attraction between us, have it up-front, on the table so we'd both know where we stand. I want your friendship, Lauren O'Loughlin, and a lot more with it but if that isn't what you want, I'd like to keep the friendship."

Lauren was staring at him. The tide of colour in her cheeks had receded to leave a creamy softness that Trout had to hold himself back from tasting. Her eyes were smiling but she spoke very seriously. "I think, Trout, I'd like that."

"That?" he queried cautiously.

"All of the above," she said and smiled.

The End